GHOST IN THE FORGE

JONATHAN MOELLER

THE GHOSTS # 6

GHOST IN THE FORGE
Jonathan Moeller

LEGAL

1

A MASK OF JADE

"Then," said Caina Amalas, her voice hoarse, heart hammering against her ribs, "then I think you had better do that again."

Corvalis Aberon looked down at her, hands resting upon her arms. He was a tall man, handsome in an austere sort of way, with a hard face and eyes like cold emerald disks.

He put his arms around her, pulled her close, and kissed her long and hard upon the lips. She reached up and took his face in her hands, her fingers sliding along his jaw and neck. Her heartbeat sounded like a drum in her ears, a slow warmth spreading through her chest and into her arms as she leaned into him.

Corvalis stumbled, lost his balance, and fell against the wall of the sitting room with a thump. The breath exploded from his lungs and into Caina's mouth with a startled exhalation.

She laughed in surprise, and he did, too.

"Gods," said Corvalis. "I haven't done that in a while."

"Nor I," said Caina. "I wasn't...I wasn't expecting that."

It had been a long time since someone had touched her. Her head almost spun with the sensation.

"No," murmured Corvalis, one hand rising to brush her cheek.

"I thought," said Caina, "I thought you were going to leave with Claudia."

"So did I," said Corvalis. "But I found I could not. Caina...I have never known a woman like you." He shook his head, a brief expression of wonder flickering over his face. "I thought you a spy with veins of ice. Yet you put yourself at terrible risk to save Claudia and all of Cyrioch."

"And I thought you a Kindred assassin," said Caina. "A killer without a conscience. But I saw what you did to save your sister. You are a better man than I thought."

Corvalis barked a harsh laugh. "Perhaps, but I am not a very good man. I..."

"You do have one flaw," said Caina.

"Oh?" said Corvalis.

"You're talking too much," said Caina. "Kiss me."

He obliged.

After a long moment they broke apart, breathing hard, a tremor of excitement going through Caina's hands.

"Come with me," said Corvalis.

"Here?" said Caina. "Theodosia will be shocked when she returns."

"I have my own room at the Inn of the Defender," said Corvalis. "Away from the others. No one will disturb us."

Caina smiled, the warmth spreading through her...but the cold part of her mind, the part the Ghosts had trained, did not remain still.

It pointed out the many ways this was a terrible idea. She was a nightfighter of the Ghosts, a spy and an agent of the Emperor of Nighmar. He was a former assassin of the Kindred, and had only recently left them. And though she and Corvalis had gone through great danger together, had faced powerful foes side-by-side, she did not know him very well. Perhaps he had been planning to seduce her from the beginning, had been hoping to infiltrate the Ghosts...

No.

She had seen what kind of man he was, how he had risked himself again and again to save Claudia.

And Caina was so tired of death, of killing, of fighting.

She wanted this.

Corvalis's expression did not change, but the cold shield fell back over his green eyes. She had hesitated too long. He had trained in the brutal regimen of the Kindred families since childhood...and every one of his instincts must have screamed against making himself vulnerable to her.

He would step away, make a polite excuse, and then leave.

"Corvalis," said Caina, and she kissed him again. "Lead the way."

∾

HIS ROOM WAS nicer than she had expected.

It occupied the Inn of the Defender's second floor, its narrow windows overlooking the alley behind the Inn. Yet the carpet was thick beneath Caina's boots, and the room boasted a bed, a pair of chairs, and a gleaming wooden table. Corvalis's weapons and supplies rested in neat order upon the table, no doubt fetched from his rooms in Cyrioch's Seatown slums.

The bed was large enough for both of them.

∾

THE NEXT MORNING Caina blinked awake.

Only a faint glimmer of dawn sunlight came through the shutters. For a moment Caina could not remember where she was.

Then she heard Corvalis's slow, steady breathing, felt his warmth against her, and remembered.

For a moment she lay motionless, simply enjoying the sensation. She often woke up alone in the dark, the final threads of a nightmare dancing through her head. She had so many nightmares. Gods knew she had seen and experienced enough horrors to fuel them.

This was much nicer.

After a moment she stood up, her bare feet making no sound against the thick carpet, the blankets sliding over her skin.

She needed to clear her head, and working through the unarmed forms would do the trick.

Her arms and legs moved through the motions she had learned as a child in the Vineyard. Kicks and punches, blocks and holds. A high leg sweep, a middle block, and a low kick. She went through the forms over and over again, the motions imprinted upon her very muscles. Time and time again the knowledge and skill had saved her life. She practiced until her breath came hard and fast, a sheen of sweat beading her forehead.

She turned, balanced upon one leg, and saw Corvalis watching her from the bed.

Belatedly, Caina remembered she wore nothing but a golden signet ring on a leather cord around her neck.

"I didn't realize," said Caina, lowering her leg, "that I was putting on a show for you."

Corvalis smiled and stood. "I am not vain enough to think it was for my benefit...though I enjoyed it nonetheless." The swirling black lines of his tattoos marked the muscles of his arms and chest. Those tattoos, inked by an Ulkaari witchfinder, gave him a measure of resistance against sorcery. "A fighter needs to practice to remain sharp. That I happened to enjoy watching you practice...well, I shall not complain."

He put his hands upon her shoulders and kissed her.

They regarded in each other in silence.

"I thought," said Corvalis at last, "that I might awaken to find that you had slipped away."

"If that was my plan," said Caina, "then I made a botch of it by practicing the unarmed forms in front of your bed for an hour."

A brief smile went over his face. "True."

"But why did you think I would slip away?" said Caina.

"I don't know," said Corvalis. "You could win the eye of a wealthy lord or a noble easily enough..."

"No," murmured Caina. "I am not...I do not do things casually, Corvalis. At least not this."

"Nor I," said Corvalis.

"I thought you might," said Caina, her fingers wandering over his chest. "I know how the Kindred assassins live. How they are rewarded with gold and slaves to...use as they wish."

"Aye," said Corvalis. "When I was a new assassin of the Kindred." His eyes grew distant. "But I stopped. My father thought it made me weaker, you see, so...once he arranged for one of the slave women to kill me. As a test. After that, it became...difficult to lower my guard."

"Oh, Corvalis," said Caina, touching his cheek.

He blinked, once, and then shrugged. "That is in the past." His eyes strayed to the scars below her navel. "And I am not the only one to have known pain, am I?"

"No," said Caina.

"I do not know what the future holds," said Corvalis. "No man does. But...this is not an idle dalliance. Not for me."

"Or me," said Caina.

Again they fell silent, and then she laughed.

"What?"

"Did you really think I would want to lure a lord of the Empire to my bed?" said Caina. She grinned at him. "Have you seen most of the lords of the Empire?" She ran her hands over his chest and stomach. "I would much rather have you in my bed."

He grinned back. "Prove it."

She did.

~

AFTER, Caina stretched against the bed. She felt tired, but it was a pleasant sort of exhaustion.

"I," she said, "am ravenous."

"As am I," said Corvalis. He barked his short, harsh laugh. "You have a gift for wearing a man out."

"Good," said Caina. "We can get breakfast in the common room."

She sighed. "Though I suppose we'll have to explain things to Theodosia and your sister."

Corvalis shrugged. "Why? It's not as if they need to know."

"No," said Caina, "but neither one of them are idiots. They'll figure it out."

Corvalis nodded. "Or we could slip away for the morning."

"Wouldn't that be transparently obvious?" said Caina.

"Not if we tell the truth," said Corvalis. "We'll simply say we went to see the mood of the city after the earthquakes and the death of the Lord Governor." Caina remembered the golden light flaring at the heart of the Well, remembered the master magus Ranarius screaming as his enslaved earth elemental turned upon him. "It will be pure coincidence that we'll walk past the man who sells the best sausage rolls in the city."

Caina laughed. "Indeed."

"I'll leave a note for Claudia and Theodosia," said Corvalis. "After one of Lord Khosrau's dinners, they'll likely sleep until noon anyway."

He pulled on his clothes and left as Caina dressed herself. A mirror stood on the table, and she examined herself. Her black hair was a mess, and she needed a bath, but she looked like any other commoner walking the streets of Cyrioch. Dark circles ringed her blue eyes. The last few days had been exhausting...and she hadn't gotten very much sleep last night.

Her reflection smiled back at her.

She strapped throwing knives to her forearms beneath her sleeves, checked the daggers in her boots, and tied a blue headcloth over her hair, lest the Cyricans take offense. Corvalis returned, turned her from the mirror, and kissed her.

"They're both asleep," said Corvalis. "Shall we?"

Caina nodded and took a rope and grapnel from the tablet. "Out the window?"

"Why?" said Corvalis.

"So we can slip away unnoticed," said Caina. She lifted an eyebrow. "Unless you think you can't keep up?"

"Watch me."

∼

THEY WALKED through the Plaza of the Defender, Caina's arm resting in Corvalis's. The morning sun reflected off the whitewashed walls of the shops, and crowds hurried through the Plaza, men going about their business, women visiting the shops, slaves in orange attending to their masters. The sight of the slaves angered Caina. With Lord Governor Armizid Asurius's plot defeated, Cyrica would remain in the Empire, yet Cyrioch's slaves would remain in their chains.

Still, it was pleasant to walk arm-in-arm with Corvalis through the crowds.

"Fisherman," said Caina, looking at a man in salt-stained clothing.

Corvalis snorted. "A guess. He could be a porter or a shipwright." He wore chain mail and leather, and looked like a caravan guard or perhaps a mercenary soldier.

"Neither," said Caina. "He walks like a sailor. A porter or a ship-wright would be at work this time of day."

"So would a fisherman at this hour," said Corvalis. "They wouldn't have yet come in with the catch."

"They wouldn't have," said Caina, "because the tides are wrong for fishing at this time of the month. The fishermen won't put out for another day. That fellow has the day off, and he's on his way to the Ring of Valor or the hippodrome to enjoy the games."

Corvalis opened his mouth to argue...and then the man in the salt-stained clothing turned in the direction of the Ring of Valor, revealing the sheathed scaling knife at his belt.

"Very clever," said Corvalis with a laugh. "How about that slave?" He looked at a stout middle-aged man in a slave's orange robe hurrying across the plaza.

"A seneschal," said Caina. "Probably for a wealthy merchant. He doesn't belong to a noble house, since his robe has no sigil. And he's a seneschal, since he's too fat to have done manual labor for years. He's going to one of the shops to...yes, complain about a late order. You see that paper under his arm? That's the invoice. His master made an order and it hasn't been fulfilled. So his master sent the seneschal to sort it out."

"Perhaps he's simply going to pick up his master's order," said Corvalis.

"No," said Caina. "See how he gets angrier the closer he gets to that jewelers' shop? He's going to throw a fit. Slaves don't get to show anger often, and I think the poor man is going to enjoy having a fit of righteous indignation on his master's behalf."

Corvalis shook his head. "You have a mind like a razor. To think I once thought to keep my business in Cyrioch secret from you." He squeezed her hand. "Just as well that I failed."

Caina smiled, and they kept walking.

He led them to a deserted side street lined with less prosperous shops, and stopped at a wooden cart. A brazier topped with a metal grill stood atop the cart, its interior filled with smoldering coals. An old man puttered at the grill, humming to himself as he arranged sausages. Corvalis cleared his throat, and the old man looked up with a smile.

"Ah, young master!" said the old man in Cyrican. "It is good to see you again!" He lowered his voice. "Have you heard the news?"

"What news is that, Barimaz?" said Corvalis.

"Both Lord Governor Armizid and the preceptor Ranarius plotted to murder old Lord Khosrau," said Barimaz, "and claim Cyrica for themselves."

"Truly?" said Corvalis, feigning astonishment. "Alas for Lord Khosrau!"

Barimaz shook his head. "Aye! Lord Khosrau kept the Cyrican provinces in order for thirty years, and his ungrateful son tries to murder him. Alas for the ingratitude of children!"

"I had heard," said Caina in Cyrican, giving her voice a singsong lilt, "that the Balarigar descended upon the Palace of Splendors and slew Lord Armizid with his own hands."

"The Balarigar!" said Barimaz with a wheezing laugh. "Just a legend of those Szaldic barbarians, my dear."

"I heard," said Corvalis, "that the Ghosts assassinated Armizid."

"The Ghosts!" said Barimaz with another laugh. "You young folk and your fanciful tales. The Ghosts are a story."

Corvalis kept his face calm, but she felt the twitch in his arm as he stifled a laugh.

"Two rolls," he said, handing over some coins, "if you have them."

"I do, young master, I do," said Barimaz, making the coins disappear. He worked for a moment, and then handed Corvalis two rolls of flaky brown bread. Corvalis kept one and handed the other to Caina.

She gave it a dubious look.

"Fear not, dear lady," said Barimaz. "Barimaz uses only the finest ingredients, and if I lie, may the gods of the desert send their vultures to feast upon my entrails."

"Charming thought," said Caina, and she took a bite. "That's...a lot better than I thought it would be!"

"Aye," said Corvalis. He was already halfway through his roll. "When I went about my business in the city, I needed food to carry with me." He finished the roll and brushed the crumbs from his fingers. "Certainly better than jerky and hard biscuits."

Caina swallowed another bite, opened her mouth to answer...and saw the man staring at her from across the street.

He was about fifty, gaunt and lean, his face unshaven, his brown hair streaked with gray. His clothes looked as if they had once been expensive, but were dusty and tattered. He leaned heavily upon a cane in his right hand.

Caina glanced at him, but his eyes never wavered.

She turned, looked at Corvalis, and saw his faint nod.

The man with the cane limped across the street, his cane tapping against the cobblestones. He stopped at Barimaz's cart, and Caina stepped to Corvalis's side, reaching for the knives hidden in her sleeve. For a moment she wondered if the man would simply buy a sausage roll.

But his blue eyes focused upon her.

"You were speaking," he said in flawless Cyrican, "of the Balarigar?"

Caina smiled at him. "But, sir, I don't know what to say. It's just a story I heard. They say there are djinni in the Sarbian desert and serpents in the deeps of Cyrican Sea. But I don't know if that's true or not."

The man frowned. "That word. Balarigar. Do you know it? It is from the Szaldic tongue. It means...the slayer of demons, the hunter of darkness."

"I am sorry, sir," said Caina, "but I was born in Malarae, and came to Cyrica Urbana with my father as a child. The only Szalds I've ever seen have been a few slaves. I don't know anything about Szaldic legends."

Perhaps he was just a lonely scholar, eager to lecture an unwilling audience. But his eyes did not waver, and Caina had the sudden feeling that the man was much older than he appeared.

Suddenly he reminded her of Jadriga, and she felt a tingle of alarm.

"They're real, you know," said the man. "All the Szaldic legends. All their tales of blood and horror. They're all real."

Caina knew that very well. She had seen the black pit below Marsis. She had seen Jadriga's mighty sorcery.

And she knew what had become of Jadriga's spirit.

"Be off with you," said Corvalis. "There's no need to frighten her with Szaldic ghost stories."

"They're not," whispered the man with the cane, "stories."

Corvalis's smile showed teeth. "Come now, fellow. No need for this to get unpleasant." His hand dropped to his sword hilt. "Be. Off."

Barimaz looked back and forth, blinking.

"Very well," said the man with the cane.

He limped away.

"Peculiar," murmured Corvalis. "Do you recognize him?"

"No," said Caina, "I've never seen him before."

"Forgive me, young sir," said Barimaz, "but if this man is an enemy of yours, I ask that you kill him away from my cart. Killing draws the attention of the militia, which would be most unwelcome."

"No fear, Barimaz," said Corvalis. "We'll..."

The man with the cane reached into his coat, drew something out, and lifted it to his face.

"Look," hissed Caina.

A jade mask covered the features of the man with the cane. The mask had been carved with a face of inhuman beauty, its features serene. A ring of peculiar glyphs encircled the mask, stylized images of animals and birds and men, symbols that tugged at Caina's memory.

She had seen those symbols somewhere before.

"What the devil?" said Corvalis.

The man in the jade mask lifted his cane, and it broke in half, the wood clattering on the street. He was left holding a rod of a peculiar silvery metal, about two feet long, its length carved with more of those odd symbols.

"Yes," said the masked man, his voice distorted behind the jade lips. "You are her. I should have known."

"Enough," said Corvalis, starting to draw his sword. "Identify..."

The man flicked his wrist, and Caina felt the crawling tingle of sorcery. She had been scarred by a necromancer of terrible power in her youth, and ever since she had been able to sense the presence of arcane force. The sensitivity had sharpened as she grew older, and now she could distinguish between the kind and magnitude of spells.

The silver rod in the masked man's hand radiated tremendous power.

White light flared around the rod, and both Barimaz and Corvalis fell limp to the ground. Caina shot a look at them, keeping her eyes on the masked man. Both Corvalis and Barimaz were both still alive, but unconscious. Yet in Corvalis's sleeve she glimpsed a glimmer of white light.

His tattoos. Would they have resisted the masked man's spell?

"You killed them!" shouted Caina, hoping to distract his attention from Corvalis.

"I did not," said the masked man, stepping towards her. His right leg twitched and trembled. Apparently he had needed that cane. "I don't know what vile use you had in mind for that Kindred assassin, but it matters not. Whatever design you planned for Cyrioch will not come to pass."

"Design?" said Caina. "What are you talking about?"

She snatched a frying pan from Barimaz's cart and stepped to the side.

"Enough," said the masked man, pivoting to follow her. "We have played this game too many times before, but this time, I have the better of you."

"I've never seen you before in my life," said Caina, talking another step to the side.

The masked man turned to follow her, keeping the rod pointed at her chest...and turned his back on Corvalis.

She saw his eyes open.

"Your latest death will not undo the harm you have caused," said the masked man, "but it least it will stop you from wreaking future harm. For a time."

Corvalis rolled to a crouch and drew his sword.

"For the gods' sake," said Caina. "I have no idea what you're talking about. Could you at least tell me what this is all about before you kill me?"

"A likely trick," said the man. His rod flared with white light, and Caina felt the surge of sorcerous power.

Corvalis jumped to his feet, and the masked man turned to face him, leveling the silver rod at his chest.

Caina gripped the frying pan like a discus and flung it with all her strength. It slammed into the masked man's bad leg. The masked man dropped him to one knee, a pale pulse of white light spitting from his rod, but the blast missed Corvalis to splash against the side of Barimaz's wagon.

Corvalis lunged forward and buried his sword in the masked man's chest. The man toppled backwards without a sound, the rod and mask falling away. Corvalis released his sword and stepped back, and Caina hurried to his side, shooting a quick look around the street.

No one had noticed the fight.

"Damn it," said Corvalis, looking at the dying man. "I should have taken him alive." He reached for the silvery rod.

"No!" said Caina. "Don't touch it! There's a spell on it. I don't know what it will do to you."

Corvalis stepped away from the rod. All at once Caina remembered where she had seen the symbols before. They were Maatish hieroglyphs, the same kind that adorned the ancient scroll her father had found.

The ancient scroll that had led to his death, that Maglarion had almost used to destroy Malarae.

Caina looked at the dying man. Blood bubbled at his lips, and his skin had turned gray.

"Who are you?" she said.

The man glared at her, his blue eyes full of pain and fear.

"Moroaica!" he spat, and then died.

2

TO THE HIGHEST BIDDER

T he next morning Caina sat next to Corvalis at the table in Theodosia's sitting room as he cleaned his weapons.

He cleaned, sharpened, and oiled his swords and daggers every day, whether they needed cleaning or not. He had told her that the Kindred had drilled the habit into him as a child. From went Caina knew of the Kindred, it meant that if his weapons and armor had shown a single spot of rust, his trainers would beat him black and blue.

So he cleaned his weapons.

Caina understood. Her own experiences had taught her the value of keeping her blades sharp.

"Nothing," said Caina, keeping the annoyed frustration out of her voice. She rolled a throwing knife across her fingers over and over again. The motion helped her to concentrate. "We checked every inn and tavern for a mile in every direction. No one remembered him or had ever seen him."

Across the table, a blond woman in her middle forties frowned. She was a bit plump, but tall enough to bear the excess weight. She was the leading lady of the Grand Imperial Opera company, and looked the part of a temperamental and demanding singer. Caina knew better. Theodosia of Malarae was as dangerous as any assassin of the Kindred.

"Nothing in his pockets?" Theodosia said.

"Nothing," said Caina. "No coins, no notes, no weapons." She gazed at the balcony doors. "Some sand inside his boots and in the folds of his coat. He probably traveled through the Sarbian desert to get here. But beyond that, we know nothing."

Theodosia grunted. "A man of mystery. What about those enspelled toys of his?"

Both Caina and Theodosia looked at the woman sitting at the end of the table. She was twenty-seven, three years younger than Corvalis, with bright green eyes and long blond hair. She wore a green gown that matched her eyes, its sleeves and bodice adorned with black embroidery. Caina thought it suited her.

Certainly it suited her better than the black robe of a magus of the Imperial Magisterium.

"They're dangerous, whatever they are," said Claudia Aberon, brushing a bit of dust from her sleeves. "The spells upon them are... complex. Certainly beyond my skill, and far beyond the skill of all but the most powerful magi of the Magisterium."

"Did you have Nicasia look at them?" said Theodosia.

"Yes," said Claudia. "But the Defender was...less than forthcoming." An earth elemental had been bound within Nicasia's flesh, and would inhabit the girl until the day she died. "Or, rather, it was candid, but I could not understand it. The Defender only said that the spells upon the objects were potent, more potent than anything mortals should use. That was all."

Caina found herself agreeing with the Defender. She had seen firsthand the horror sorcery wreaked. If she could kill every last magus, every last wielder of arcane forces, she would do it.

But Claudia was a magus. Corvalis swore his sister had a kindly heart, had risked everything to save her.

But she was still a sorceress.

Caina kept a close eye upon her.

"Then it seems," said Theodosia, "there is nothing more to be done. I've arranged for Marzhod to dump the corpse in the harbor, and we'll keep that mask and rod under lock and key. We'll take it back to Malarae. Meanwhile, we'll see if any of this mysterious sorcerer's associates reveal themselves."

Claudia nodded, but Caina said nothing.

She had her own theory, one she did not want to share with Claudia.

"Moroaica," the masked man had said.

Somehow, he had known the Moroaica's spirit was trapped within Caina. Had he been one of her students, like Maglarion or Ranarius? Or had he been one of her enemies come to hunt her down? If so, he had been a fool. Killing Caina would only release the Moroaica to claim another host.

Again Caina wished they had captured the masked man alive.

Still, she and Corvalis were unharmed, so it could have been worse.

"So," said Corvalis, "we will wait here until we receive instructions from your superiors?"

"Does that trouble you?" said Theodosia.

"Not at all," said Corvalis. "In deference to your venerable majesty, I will gladly wait."

Claudia laughed.

"Venerable?" said Theodosia. "I may yet have you killed, but not today. We'll leave for Malarae in a few days, when Lord Corbould Maraeus departs for the capital. And since I have a former assassin, a former magus, and a girl with an earth elemental in her head who want to join the Ghosts, I imagine my superiors will want to meet with you in..."

Someone knocked at the door.

Caina slipped her throwing knife against her palm, while Corvalis sat up straighter, hand tightening around his sword hilt. Claudia looked at the door, and Caina felt the low thrum of arcane power as she gathered force for a spell.

"Enter," said Theodosia, her voice calm.

A middle-aged man wearing the fine fur-trimmed robe of a prosperous merchant stepped into the room. He wore a cap with a gleaming silver badge over iron-gray hair, and carried a short sword and dagger at his belt.

Caina grinned, and Theodosia blinked in surprise.

"Well, well, this is certainly a surprise," said Theodosia.

"I doubt," said Halfdan, looking at Claudia and Corvalis, "that you expected to see me quite so soon."

His tone was light, but Caina saw the tension around his eyes. Halfdan was one of the high circlemasters, one of the Ghosts' leaders, and he was one of the most dangerous and knowledgeable men in the Empire.

Lord Armizid and Ranarius had been slain a few days ago, and it was a week's journey from the Imperial capital. Which meant Halfdan had left before Armizid's plot had been foiled and Ranarius had been stopped.

And that meant something was wrong.

"I admit that I did not," said Theodosia. "Has something happened? You couldn't have received any of the news from Cyrioch yet."

Halfdan looked at Caina, and Corvalis, and then back at Caina, and his eyes widened, just a little bit.

"Yes," he said. "It seems you have a tale of your own to tell me."

"Well," said Theodosia. She stood, as if preparing to deliver an aria. "Wherever shall I begin?"

She told Halfdan what had happened, albeit with plenty of dramatic flair. Halfdan listened in silence. Once or twice he scowled, and he laughed aloud when Theodosia described how Caina had infiltrated the Haven of the Kindred assassins.

"And that," said Theodosia, after she described the strange man in the jade mask, "is everything."

"Well," said Halfdan. "You have been busy, haven't you?" He rubbed at his jaw, thinking.

"What is," said Caina, "this grim news of yours?"

"In a moment," said Halfdan. "Some of what you've done here changes things. Especially that fellow in the mask." He nodded to himself. "But let us deal with business before news. First, Corvalis Aberon, Claudia Aberon, if you wish to join the Ghosts, you will be welcome among us. I cannot tell you my true name for obvious reasons. But you may call me Basil Callenius, a master merchant of the Imperial Collegium of jewelers."

"Master Basil," said Claudia, rising and offering a bow to him. "If you will have us, we shall be glad to join." Caina noted that she spoke for Corvalis, rather than the other way around. "We have seen the corruption within the Magisterium, and the harm my father would do if he gained control of the Empire. We shall gladly to lend our talents to your cause."

"The Ghosts always have need of men and women of skill," said Halfdan. "Even sorcerous talent, if they are willing to serve." Caina ignored the cutting remark that came to mind. Claudia was a magus...but she was Corvalis's sister. "Magi have joined the Magisterium before. Your father rules the Magisterium with an iron fist...but he has a knack for making enemies."

"Indeed," said Corvalis, voice quiet. "Even his own children."

"Indeed. And Nicasia's particular...gifts would be welcome," said Halfdan. "But it seems we owe you a great deal. Without your aid Ranarius would have destroyed Cyrica Urbana."

"Give the credit to her," said Corvalis, and Caina felt his hand touch hers beneath the table. "She unraveled the mystery, and her wits defeated Ranarius. Had I turned away her aid as I thought to do, Ranarius would have destroyed Cyrioch and left my sister imprisoned within the stone forever."

Halfdan smiled at Caina. "Child. Again you have done it. Malarae, Rasadda, Marsis, and now Cyrioch. The Empire would lie in ruins, if not for your valor."

Caina shrugged. "It was...a very close thing." If Sicarion had managed to kill her. If the Kindred Elder had foreseen the trap. If Caina hadn't unraveled the nature of the Defender's imprisonment. If she had been a heartbeat slower, she would have been slain...and Ranarius would have released the great elemental below the Stone.

Hundreds of thousands of people, dead in an instant.

She shivered.

"But you all have done well," said Halfdan. "This news is far better than I hoped. I expected Cyrica to revolt against the Empire and join Istarinmul. Instead Lord Khosrau will keep the Cyrican provinces within the Empire."

Theodosia smiled. "Lord Khosrau has fine taste in opera. But come! What is this grim news of yours?"

"That mask and rod," said Halfdan. "Show them to me."

Claudia rose, retrieved the jade mask and the metallic rod from a locked chest, and brought them to the table. She carried them wrapped in cloth. "I suggest, Master Basil, that you do not touch them. I don't know what effect they might have."

"Sound counsel, my dear," said Halfdan as Claudia tugged away the cloth. The empty eyes of the jade mask gazed at Caina, and she felt the crawling tingle of sorcery from the aura of power surrounding both the mask and the rod.

"Those hieroglyphics are Maatish," said Caina. "I'm sure of it."

She remembered the Maatish scroll upon the podium atop Haeron Icaraeus's mansion, the storm screaming overhead, Maglarion laughing as he worked the spell that would have killed every living thing in Malarae...

"You're right," said Halfdan. "Those are Maatish symbols. But this mask and rod aren't Maatish. They're Catekhari."

"Catekhari?" exclaimed Claudia. "But that is impossible. The Catekhari are reclusive."

"You know of them?" said Halfdan.

Claudia straightened up, hands behind her back, and she reminded Caina of a student about to recite a lesson for her tutor. "Catekharon is one of the free cities, west of Anshan and southeast of New Kyre. A reclusive society of sorcerers who call themselves the Scholae rule the city, though outsiders refer to them as the Masked Ones..." She blinked. "You mean Marina was attacked by a Masked One?"

Corvalis glanced at Caina. She had told him her true name, but she had not given it to Claudia. Caina could not bring herself to do it.

Her true name was a measure of trust...and she could not bring herself to trust a magus that much.

Not even Corvalis's sister.

"That seems likely," said Halfdan.

"But that is impossible," said Claudia. "Everything I read about the Masked Ones said they were reclusive, and loathed leaving their city for any reason. And by all accounts the Masked Ones are sorcerers of great puissance. How are Marina and my brother still alive?"

Halfdan shrugged. "Perhaps the Masked One was overconfident. Or unused to physical fights. Or Marina simply outwitted him. She's rather good at outwitting sorcerers."

"If those are Maatish symbols," said Caina, "then are the Masked Ones necromancers?"

"No," said Halfdan. "From what I understand, it seems the Masked Ones were once a society of some sort in ancient Maat. The necromancer-priests and the pharaohs ruled Maat, while the Masked Ones were a lesser order of sorcerers charged with making enspelled artifacts for the necromancer-priests. When the Kingdom of the Rising Sun collapsed two thousand years ago, the Masked Ones fled north and settled in Catekharon."

"The Masked Ones are rumored to be artificers of unequalled skill," said Claudia.

"They are," said Halfdan. "What I am about to tell you is a secret known to few outside of the Ghosts. Even I did not know it until two weeks ago. The Masked Ones are perhaps the most powerful sorcerers in the world. The Magisterium, Istarinmul's College of Alchemists, the stormsingers of New Kyre, the occultists of Anshan... none of them dare challenge the Masked Ones and their enspelled artifacts."

"If they have such power," said Caina, "why do they not rule the world?"

"Apparently they have no interest in it," said Halfdan. "The Masked Ones study the arcane sciences and little else. They ignore the outside world, but if threatened, they respond with deadly force.

Both Old Kyrace and Anshan tried to conquer Catekharon. Both were utterly defeated. The Anshani were defeated so badly that they suffered seventy years of civil war afterward."

Something clicked in Caina's head.

"That's why you're here, isn't it?" said Caina.

Claudia frowned. "How could you possibly know that? He hasn't said anything yet!"

Halfdan lifted a hand. "Go on."

"You're here," said Caina, "because the Masked Ones have done something to the outside world, something that threatens the Empire. You have too many duties to come this far south otherwise."

"You're right," said Halfdan. "A few days after you left Malarae, an embassy from Catekharon arrived before the Emperor. We also know the Masked Ones sent embassies to the Shahenshah of Anshan, the Padishah of Istarinmul, the Assembly of New Kyre, and numerous others."

"What did the embassies say?" said Theodosia.

"They said," said Halfdan, "that the Scholae of Catekharon had created a weapon of sorcery. A weapon so powerful, so potent, that it would grant its bearer dominion over the entire world."

"And they demanded that the Empire submit to Catekharon, I suppose?" said Corvalis.

"Not at all," said Halfdan. "The embassy said the Masked Ones would sell the weapon to the highest bidder."

Silence answered him.

"That," said Caina at last, "is the most ridiculous thing I have ever heard. If they had such a weapon, why would they sell it? Why not use it themselves? Or if they want to be left alone to study sorcery, why not keep the weapon a secret and use it if they are attacked? No one in their right mind would sell it." She shook her head. "This has to be a trick of some sort."

"I agree," said Halfdan. "But I do not know the nature of the game. And there is the remote possibility that they are telling the truth. That they do indeed possess such a weapon, and are unworldly and foolish enough to sell it." He drummed his fingers on the table. "All this...and then you are attacked by a Masked One on the street."

"A coincidence, perhaps," said Claudia.

Caina laughed. "A coincidence means only there is an underlying pattern that we cannot yet see."

"Precisely," said Halfdan. "The Emperor has sent Lord Titus Iconias to act as his ambassador to the Catekhari. Our ships came into the harbor this morning. Tomorrow he will take the Great Western Caravan Road to Catekharon, and we will accompany him."

"We?" said Theodosia. "Basil, you know that desert air is dreadful to my skin."

"You're going back to Malarae with Lord Corbould," said Halfdan. "And you'll take Nicasia with you. Bringing a girl possessed by an earth elemental into a city full of sorcerers is a poor idea." He looked at Caina. "You, Corvalis, and Claudia will accompany me to Catekharon, and together we will get to the bottom of this."

"Why take me?" said Caina. "I've never been to Catekharon, and I don't know the language."

"That hardly matters," said Halfdan. "Catekhari is a form of Maatish, and the Masked Ones use it as a formal language. Most of the Catekhari speak either Anshani or Kyracian, and you know both of those. But you have a more important skill. You can sense the presence of sorcery, and that will prove invaluable." He looked at Claudia. "You are a trained magus, and your expertise will be useful." Claudia nodded, and Halfdan's gaze shifted to Corvalis. "And if we need someone killed...I suspect you shall be capable."

Corvalis nodded.

"Though if I might ask, Basil," said Theodosia, "why bother at all? Marina is right. The entire business sounds preposterous."

"Because," said Halfdan, "the Emperor does not want the weapon, if it exists, to fall into the hands of the Kyracians or the Istarish. The war is a stalemate. Right now, the Kyracians cannot defeat the Legions upon land. But neither can we defeat the Kyracians at sea." He shook his head. "Kylon Shipbreaker has made quite a name for himself."

"Kylon?" said Caina. "You mean Kylon of House Kardamnos?"

"Aye," said Halfdan. "You've met, I recall? The Assembly and Archons of New Kyre named him thalarchon of their western fleet. He's won victory over victory over the Emperor's warships."

Caina remembered Kylon well. He had come within a hairs-breadth of killing her, and she had almost slain him. When she had last seen him, he had been crushed by the knowledge that his sister Andromache had been a disciple of the Moroaica, that she had engineered New Kyre's war with the Empire to seize the power in the Tomb of Scorikhon. She had wondered how Kylon would respond to that betrayal.

Apparently, he would deal with the guilt by winning the war his sister had started.

"That is our task," said Halfdan. "We will leave tomorrow."

Caina saw Halfdan's plan well enough. They would go south to discover whatever the Masked Ones had in mind...and the journey would also give him an opportunity to test Corvalis and Claudia.

To see if they truly intended to join the Ghosts.

She was sure about Corvalis. But she was not so certain about Claudia. She knew how much the Magisterium hated the Ghosts. Of course, Claudia had spent the last year trapped as a living statue, and claimed that her father had turned against her. But if it was a trick, if Corvalis had only seduced her to get a spy into the Ghosts...

The thought hurt more than she had expected.

No, she could not think like that.

"Very well," said Corvalis. "If I am to work for the Ghosts, I suppose you shall be my Elder."

"Gods!" said Halfdan. "Don't compare me to a Kindred Elder." He laughed. "Especially after what you did to the Elder of Cyrioch."

Corvalis grinned. "I mean only that I shall follow your commands."

"Smart lad," said Halfdan.

"And I, too, shall obey you, Master Basil," said Claudia.

"As wise as you are lovely, my dear," said Halfdan. "Marina, Theodosia. Join me for a moment, please."

He walked to the balcony, and Caina and Theodosia followed him. Below them the Plaza of the Defender bustled with activity, the Cyricans in their bright robes moving from shop to shop. Crowds went past the white stone statue of the armored warrior in the center of the square, the statue that gave the Plaza its name. Caina wondered how the Cyricans would react if they knew the elemental spirit that had once inhabited the statue now resided in the flesh of a former slave girl.

Halfdan closed the doors behind them.

"They'll know," said Theodosia, "that we're talking about them."

"I hope so," said Halfdan. "I prefer not to recruit idiots. What do you think?"

"Corvalis is telling the truth," said Theodosia. "He put himself through hell to save his sister from Ranarius." She glanced at Caina. "And he has...other reasons to remain loyal to the Ghosts."

"Ranarius," said Halfdan. "You did well, killing him."

"The Defender killed him," said Caina, "not me."

"Regardless," said Halfdan, "he has been a foe of the Ghosts for years. We are well rid of him. What do you think of the woman?"

"Claudia?" said Caina. "Corvalis...says she has a good heart."

"He would say that," said Theodosia. "Frankly, I'm not certain what to make of her. She's kindly, true...but it is a patronizing sort of kindness. She's arrogant. Her experience with her father has shaken her, but she truly believes that those with arcane talent are a higher order of men, that they have the duty to shepherd and guide the commoners."

"And many of the most tyrannical magi," said Halfdan, "have said the exact same thing. The First Magus would claim as much."

"Aye," said Theodosia. "And Corvalis loves her. He'll do whatever she asks of him. Including, if necessary, betraying the Ghosts."

"What do you think?" said Halfdan to Caina. "As we've often noticed, you have a knack for observing things."

"I think that Theodosia is right," said Caina. She took a deep breath. "And there is something else you should know." She would not keep it secret from Halfdan and Theodosia. She trusted them more than she trusted anyone. "I took Corvalis into my bed."

Theodosia grinned and gave a little exclamation of delight.

"Oh, my dear child," she said. "It is well past time. And he is very handsome, is he not? A bit more ruthless than I would have preferred for you, but a soft man is no use to anyone..."

"It is," said Halfdan, "certainly a point in his favor. You are not a fool, Caina. I trust your judgment." A sad smile flickered over his face. "You have made yourself into a weapon in the service of the Ghosts. But that doesn't mean you should deny yourself what joy you can find."

"But do be careful," said Theodosia. "The heart has a way of running away with the head."

"I remember," said Caina, thinking of Alastair Corus.

Of how her father had given her mother one last chance...and that last chance had led to his death.

"Well," said Theodosia, "if I am to leave for Malarae on the morrow, I have preparations to make."

"As do I," said Caina.

"Go and make them," said Halfdan. "I am traveling as Basil Callenius, and you will masquerade as my daughter Anna." He looked at the Plaza. "Oh, and send Corvalis out, will you? I would like a word with him."

3

A GHOST NIGHTFIGHTER

C orvalis Aberon stepped onto the balcony, closing the doors behind him.

His mind noted took in the details. He saw the crowds going about their business below. Basil Callenius stood with one hand on the railing, his face betraying nothing of his thoughts. He wore a short sword and a dagger at his belt, but Corvalis was certain the Ghost circlemaster had other weapons hidden.

His instincts worked out different ways to kill Basil. Best to wait until the conversation had begun, stun him with a blow to the neck, and heave him over the railing...

With an effort, Corvalis forced aside the thoughts.

The Kindred had trained him to be an assassin, and even though he had left their brotherhood behind, the skills and mindset they had forced upon him remained.

Basil smiled. "I am pleased you decided not to kill me."

He was perceptive. Of course, he was a Ghost circlemaster.

Corvalis shrugged. "Caina would have taken it amiss."

She loved Basil, Corvalis was sure of that. Since the magi had murdered her father, Basil seemed to have become a surrogate father of sorts for her.

"Yes, Caina," said Basil. "Theodosia told an interesting story of how you came to join the Ghosts. How much of it was true?"

"All of it," said Corvalis.

Basil raised an eyebrow.

"You've caught me," said Corvalis. "My father had Claudia turned to stone and sent me to save her so I could infiltrate the Ghosts. But you have unraveled our brilliant scheme."

"That," said Basil, "is not as farfetched as you might think. The Magisterium tried some bold plots in the past. The First Magus would kill every last one of us if he could."

Corvalis offered a bleak smile. "He tried to kill me, and I am still here."

Basil said nothing.

"What do you want me to say?" said Corvalis. "I am what I am. My father sold me to the Kindred, and they turned me into a killer. I'm good at it."

"What changed?" said Basil. "Why join the Ghosts?"

"Claudia," said Corvalis.

"She asked you to leave the Kindred?" said Basil.

"Not like that," said Corvalis. He still remembered it, years later. "We were close as children. We had the same mother, one of the First Magus's favorite mistresses. When I met Claudia again, I thought our father would have twisted her into a monster. Like he did with me." He shook his head. "Instead...she had not changed. She wanted to use her powers to help people, to make their lives easier, not to rule over them. Talking to her, telling her about the things I had done, I..."

"She awoke your conscience," said Basil.

"Yes," said Corvalis. "She saw what the Magisterium really was. What kind of man our father really is. She decided to abandon the Magisterium and leave the Empire, and convinced me to go with her."

"And to punish you," said Basil, "your father had Ranarius turn your sister to stone."

"Aye," said Corvalis. "Then he tried to have me killed. I had to go into hiding for a year."

"Where, I assume," said Basil, "you acquired those useful tattoos. How did you get them, by the way? The Ulkaari witchfinders are notoriously secretive."

"I helped them track down a demon," said Corvalis. "Once I had the tattoos, I stole Claudia from the Magisterium's motherhouse in Artifel, pursued Ranarius to Cyrioch...and you know the rest."

"Indeed," said Basil.

He fell silent, his fingers tapping on the railing.

"As much as I enjoy suspense," said Corvalis, "are you going to kill me?"

"What? No." Basil laughed. "You're twenty years my junior and a trained Kindred assassin. I doubt I could kill you."

"Nevertheless," said Corvalis, "if you want me dead, I suspect it will happen."

"True," said Basil without rancor. "But that may not be necessary."

"May?" said Corvalis.

"You will make an excellent Ghost nightfighter," said Basil. "The Ghosts always have need of talent, and finding a man of your skills is a boon. We have no end of work for you, and we can keep you near Caina. Which, I think, you will prefer."

Corvalis gave a cautious nod. "But I suspect there is a caveat."

"Indeed," said Basil. "What do you want?"

Corvalis blinked. "I don't understand."

"You were content to be a killer," said Basil. "Then Claudia awoke your conscience, and you devoted yourself to saving her. A remarkable feat – not many cross the First Magus and live to tell of it. But you saved her. So what now? What do you want?"

Corvalis opened his mouth to answer...and found that he did not really know.

Revenge, perhaps? He had dreamed of killing his father for years. But while he would not pass up the chance to kill Decius Aberon, he knew he could not live on revenge alone. Not forever.

So what then? He could hardly open up a tavern or go into trade. Did he want wealth and power? He could win them easily enough, but the thought bored him. But he did like fighting. The Kindred had given him skills, and as much as he loathed the Kindred, he enjoyed using those skills, enjoyed the challenge. Before he had used his skills to kill the enemies of the Magisterium. Then he had seen how Caina used her wits and skills to save Cyrioch from destruction.

The thought of using his skills for a good end...yes, he wanted that very much.

And he wanted Caina.

Perhaps he could have both.

"I want," said Corvalis at last, "to make the Magisterium howl."

"Ah," said Basil. "Revenge, then."

"But only a little," said Corvalis. "This is a peculiar thing to admit, but Caina has shown me the work the Ghosts do. I find I can support it with an enthusiasm I never had for the Kindred."

"Not so strange," said Basil. "I have seen it before. You are a fighter, Corvalis, and a man can be a fighter for a bad cause or a good cause. And a man who has fought in a bad cause can be pleasantly surprised how much he enjoys fighting for a good cause."

"I suppose you are right," said Corvalis.

"I am," said Basil. "Will your sister accept that?"

"Claudia?" said Corvalis. "She sees her sorcery as a gift, not a right. She wants to use it to help people. She convinced me to turn my back on the Magisterium, once she understood the sort of man my father was."

"Will she do what is necessary?" said Basil. "Will she use her power to protect and defend, whatever the cost?"

"I think so," said Corvalis. "Though I hope it will not come to that. I am a killer, Basil Callenius, but she is not. I have never seen her use her spells in anger." He shrugged. "I think she would be hard-pressed to harm a mouse. If not, Ranarius and the Defender would not have overpowered her so easily."

"As I thought. Thank you, Corvalis," said Basil. "Lord Titus Iconias is traveling south in a caravan tomorrow, and we shall leave with him. I think we will disguise you as Cormark, a Caerish mercenary working for me as a guard."

"A master merchant of the jewelers' collegium requires guards," said Corvalis. "I can pull off the masquerade easily enough."

"Good," said Basil. "Equip yourself with whatever you shall need. If you need any coin, Theodosia will provide it."

He gazed into the Plaza, towards the Palace of Splendors atop the white bulk of the Stone.

"That's all?" said Corvalis.

"Did you expect something else?" said Basil, raising an eyebrow.

"In all candor, yes," said Corvalis. "Caina trusts you as much as anyone...and I cannot image you would be pleased that she took a former Kindred assassin into her bed."

Basil shrugged. "Caina is no fool. Young women can be swept away in a tide of emotion, true...but I do not think she is one of them. Frankly, I am more relieved than anything else. There has been great pain in her life, and her mood has been...grim since the attack on Marsis. And it is a point in your favor that she would choose you."

"Thank you," said Corvalis. "So this isn't the conversation where you promise to cut off my head if I hurt her in any way?"

Basil snorted. "Don't be absurd, boy. Sometimes it is necessary to hurt people. Even people you love." He shrugged. "And I am not her father. Her father was murdered. I am...merely the man who turned her into what she is."

They lapsed into silence. Corvalis realized that he saw Caina reflected in some of Basil's movements, his patterns of speech, his methods of thought. Basil Callenius might not have been Caina's father, but he had left a greater impact on her than anyone else.

Save, perhaps, the man who had murdered her father.

"She is not my daughter," said Basil at last, "but she is the best decision I have ever made."

"What do you mean?" said Corvalis.

"I didn't know what to do with her at first," said Basil, "when I found her. I thought to send her to the temple of Minaerys to become a scholar-priestess, or to have one of the Ghosts' friends among the noble houses adopt her. Instead, I made her into a Ghost nightfighter. I had my doubts, but if not for her...well, I would be dead."

"She saved your life," said Corvalis.

"The Empire would be dust upon the wind," said Basil, "if not for Caina Amalas." He looked at Corvalis, his eyes hard, all trace of the friendly jewel merchant gone. "If not for her, every man, woman, and child in Malarae would have perished. Rasadda would have burned to ashes. Demons would have risen from the pit to devour Marsis, and you know what happened in Cyrioch. Two million people live in those four cities, Corvalis. All those people, all their lives, all their children, all the children they would have ever had...dead, if not for Caina Amalas. And gods know how many more dead in the civil war that would have followed the destruction of Malarae. All those people live and breathe because of her...and they will never know it. So hear me well, boy." His voice remained calm, the tone of a man discussing a pleasant dinner. "If you hurt her in a way that is not necessary, I swear upon every god that ever was that I will give you such a death that even the First Magus will blanch when he hears of it. Is that what you were expecting?"

"I think," said Corvalis, "that I believe you. And I will not hurt her, not if I can help it. If not for her, Claudia would be a statue and I would be a corpse."

"I'm glad we understand each other," said Basil, turning from the railing. "Come! Let us have some wine. Death threats are such thirsty work."

"Killing is thirstier," said Corvalis, reaching for the door.

"Mmm. Well, threatening sometimes..."

A flash of white light came through the doors, and Corvalis heard Claudia shout in alarm.

Corvalis drew his sword and dagger and dashed into the sitting room, Basil a half-step behind.

Caina, Claudia, and Theodosia stood around the table. Caina had her curved ghostsilver dagger in hand, her blue eyes narrowed, while Theodosia held a throwing knife. All three women stared at the table.

At the empty table.

"What is it?" said Basil.

"The mask and rod," said Caina, her voice calm, though her eyes roved everywhere, seeking for foes. "They're gone."

"They just...vanished," said Theodosia. "Marina said she felt a spell, the rod and the mask started to glow, and then they simply...disappeared."

"Did they turn invisible?" said Corvalis.

Claudia cast a spell to sense the presence of arcane force. "No. Corvalis, they're just...gone. I don't understand."

"Could the Masked Ones have been spying on us?" said Caina. "Through the rod and the mask? If the Masked Ones plan to sell this weapon of sorcery, they must have known the Ghosts would get involved. Perhaps that Masked One attacked me to plant the rod and the mask."

"But how would they have known you were a Ghost?" said Theodosia.

Claudia shook her head. "The spells upon the rod and the mask were not divinatory, I am certain of it. Spells of defense and attack, yes. But not of far-seeing or far-hearing." She again cast the spell to sense the presence of arcane force, and Corvalis saw the faintest twitch go across Caina's face.

She hated sorcery, hated it the way Corvalis hated his father.

"Perhaps they destroyed themselves," said Theodosia, "now that their master is slain."

"I think," said Claudia, "I think they returned to their master."

"Their master is dead," said Caina. "Marzhod dumped his body in the harbor."

"Then to their master's superior, then?" said Claudia. "The other Masked Ones? I fear without examining the objects closer, I can only offer theories."

"And the objects," said Caina, "are gone."

"This changes nothing," said Basil. "Most likely Claudia is correct, and the mask and the rod were created return to the Masked Ones if their bearer was slain. And if they could spy on us, well, we are leaving tomorrow. Any information they have will soon be out of date. Meanwhile, I suggest we get to work."

Basil left, followed by Theodosia and Claudia, leaving Corvalis alone with Caina. She gazed at the empty spot on the table, rolling her throwing knife over her fingers.

"Basil is most likely right," said Corvalis. "The Masked Ones likely enspelled the mask and the rod to return to Catekharon."

"I know," murmured Caina, her eyes distant. "Yet if they would go to such trouble to secure two relatively minor artifacts...then why offer a potent weapon of sorcery for sale to the highest bidder?"

Corvalis did not know.

"It must be a trick of some sort," said Caina. Her eyes met his. "But if such a weapon exists...I am going to destroy it."

Corvalis frowned. "Wouldn't Basil like to bring it back to the Emperor?"

"I doubt it," said Caina. "The task of the Ghosts is to serve the Emperor and to defend the people of the Empire. Even if it means protecting the Emperor from himself. Corvalis...I've seen spells that have that kind of power. Sorcery strong enough to destroy cities." He remembered what Basil had said about the people Caina had saved. "No one should have that kind of power. If that weapon exists, I'm going to destroy it."

Corvalis nodded. "You shall have my help."

She smiled at him and took his hand. Yes, Basil had been right. Corvalis needed a challenge, a fight in a worthy cause.

And helping Caina Amalas to destroy a weapon of fell sorcery... well, Corvalis could think of none better.

4

STORMDANCER

Kylon, the High Seat of House Kardamnos and thalarchon of New Kyre's seventh fleet, stood upon the trireme's prow, his sword of storm-forged steel in his right hand, the wind blowing salt spray across his face. Part of his mind noted the lines of the Imperial fleet across the expanse of blue-gray waves, counted the number of ships, a number that exceeded those under his command.

But another part of his mind considered his memories of Marsis.

Some part of his mind always remembered Marsis.

Andromache's lightning ripping from the sky, scattering Legionaries like toys.

The mocking sneer on Sicarion's face as he plotted his betrayal.

Andromache's face distorting as Scorikhon's spirit donned her flesh, the pain on her face as Kylon's sword sank into her chest.

And the Ghost most of all. The Ghost with eyes like blue ice, her mind like a weapon. She had warned Kylon and Andromache both, and Andromache had ignored her warnings.

And now Kylon would continue to pay the price for that failure.

"Thalarchon?" said a man's voice.

"I see them," said Kylon without turning.

How things had changed in the months since Andromache had

been slain. Once she had been the High Seat of House Kardamnos, one of the nine Archons of New Kyre, and in all things Kylon obeyed her without question. He left strategy and tactics up to her, and he had merely carried out her designs.

But now he was the High Seat of House Kardamnos and the thalarchon of the seventh fleet...and the burden of command fell to him.

He turned and looked at the two men standing on the trireme's bow. The first, like Kylon, wore the gray leather of a stormdancer of New Kyre, sword ready at his waist. His expression was grim, but it always was. Cimon of House Siltarides was Kylon's senior by ten years, but he obeyed without question.

The second man did not. Alcios was the High Seat of House Kallias, a vigorous gray-haired man in his fifties. He wore the armor and plumed helm of the ashtairoi, an ashtair, the sword of the Kyracian foot soldiers, hanging at his belt. Alcios thought he should have been made the thalarchon of the seventh fleet, and he made no secret of that fact.

But he had not been disobedient. Which was just as well. Kylon would have regretted executing him.

"Yes, lord thalarchon," said Alcios. "I am pleased you see the foe. It would be beneath the dignity of a thalarchon for his underlings to point out the obvious to him."

"Indeed it would, my lord High Seat," said Kylon.

"The enemy has twice our ships," said Alcios. "And their vessels are quinqueremes, heavier and better armed than ours."

"You are stating facts," said Kylon. "I assume you intend to draw a conclusion from them."

"Aye," said Alcios. "I suggest, my lord thalarchon," he said with the faintest hint of condescension, "that we break formation and sail north. With the stormsingers to command the winds, we can strike the villages south of Marsis and bring chaos to the Empire."

"We've already picked clean the villages south of Marsis," said Cimon with a frown. "The only target left of any value along the Empire's western shore is Marsis itself. And we cannot take the city."

"No," said Kylon. "We already tried."

"And your sister failed," said Alcios.

Kylon looked at him.

"Though I do not mean to speak ill of the dead," said Alcios.

Kylon shrugged. "Why not? She did fail, did she not? She started this war." He wondered how the Assembly would react if they knew Andromache had started the war with the Empire at the behest of the Moroaica, the ancient sorceress of legend and terror. "But she started it, and we must finish it."

"Indeed," said Alcios. "Which we will not do if the Empire's fleet destroys us here."

"Or," said Kylon, "we will destroy the Imperial fleet."

"Why would we take such a foolish risk?" said Alcios.

"Because," said Kylon, "this is all that remains of the Empire's western fleet. We've hit them too hard, my lord High Seat, and destroyed too many of their warships. We cannot overcome them on land...but they cannot overcome us on the open sea. So they have gathered their remaining ships to crush us in one solid blow." He pointed with his sword. "Instead, we shall reverse their trap and crush them in turn."

"It would be better," said Alcios, "to withdraw to New Kyre. The fleets are the city's only line of defense against the Empire. If we are slain and the ships destroyed, we will leave New Kyre defenseless. My lord thalarchon, if I may be blunt?"

Kylon nodded.

"You are young," said Alcios, "and eager for fame and renown. This is understandable. Laudable, even. But do not let your pride lead you astray. For the loss of our fleet would be a crippling blow to New Kyre."

For a moment Kylon wavered. Perhaps Alcios was right. Andromache been defeated at Marsis, and it now fell to Kylon to succeed where she had failed. Perhaps Kylon's grief had led him astray. Perhaps he was driving his fleet to destruction.

He closed his eyes, took a deep breath, and drew upon his sorcery, the power to command wind and wave, water and storm. He was a stormdancer, and while he lacked the raw power of a stormsinger, he could use his sorcery to move with the speed of a hurricane and strike with the force of a tidal wave. Kylon's talents gave him an affinity for the element of water, and this gift let him sense things hidden to other men.

For men, after all, were fashioned of water.

A storm of emotion washed over him. He felt the fears and grim determination of the men in his fleet. Across the water, he sensed the emotions of the men crewing the ships of the Empire of Nighmar. He felt their fear, far more fear than his own men. And he sensed loci of sorcerous power aboard one of the other ships. Magi, sorcerers in service to the Imperial Magisterium, come to counter the powers of the stormsingers and the stormdancers.

And Kylon knew his pride had not let him astray.

He could crush this fleet and inflict a staggering defeat upon the Empire.

He opened his eyes and faced Cimon and Alcios.

"We attack," said Kylon. Cimon nodded, and Alcios sighed...but both men drew themselves up. "Issue the following commands."

The signal drums boomed out from the flagship, and the Kyracian fleet arranged itself for battle.

"Row, you bastards!" roared the hortator, thundering upon his drums. "Row, damn you! Show these weak-livered dogs of the Empire how the men of New Kyre fight!"

Kylon braced himself on the bow as the trireme spun about, the oarsmen working in perfect harmony. The navies of Anshan and Istarinmul used slaves to man their oars. In New Kyre, only free men wielded the oars of a warship, and they achieved a degree of skill and prowess that slaves lacked.

Of course, the Nighmarian Empire used free men to crew its ships as well.

"I hope, my lord thalarchon," murmured Alcios, "that you know what you are doing."

"As do I, my lord High Seat," said Kylon, gazing at the enemy ships.

The Kyracian fleet split into three squadrons, two attempting to flank the line of Imperial ships, while the third squadron, gathered around Kylon's flagship, drove at the heart of the Nighmarian fleet. Kylon's arcane senses told him that the enemy magi waited upon the flagship, a huge quinquereme bristling with catapults and ballistae.

His plan banked upon killing those magi. The stormsingers could use their spells to drive their ships far faster than the bulky Imperial warships...but only if the magi did not interfere.

And to keep them from interfering, Kylon would simply have to kill them all.

"High Seat," said Kylon. "Now."

Alcios turned to the polemarch in command of the ship. "Ramming speed!"

The polemarch relayed the order to the hortator, who howled imprecations at the oarsmen. The oarsmen grunted, faces red with strain, sweat pouring down their chests. Yet the trireme picked up speed and made for the port side of the Imperial flagship, the waters foaming white around them.

The Imperial flagship tried to turn, its five banks of oars lashing at the waters, but the vessel was too heavy, its oarsmen too unskilled. The Legions of the Nighmarian Empire were the finest infantry in the world, but the Kyracians were masters of the sea. The men of Old Kyrace had ruled a maritime empire, and their descendants of New Kyre were the best sailors in the world. The catapults on the quinqueremes spat balls of burning pitch, but the trireme came too fast, the shots missing to splash in the waves.

"Brace yourselves!" shouted Alcios, hand on the hilt of his ashtair. "Prepare to board the foe!"

"Cimon," said Kylon, and the second stormdancer stepped to his side.

"I am with you, my lord thalarchon," said the older man.

"Good," said Kylon, lifting his sword. "Follow my lead. Remember, slay the magi first."

Cimon nodded, and the trireme hurtled towards the Imperial flagship. Kylon saw soldiers scrambling across the deck, clad in chain mail, shields on their arms and spears in their hands. Auxiliaries, then - the Legions themselves rarely fought aboard ships.

And in their midst Kylon saw the black armor of battle magi.

A heartbeat later the massive steel spike of the trireme's prow plunged into the side of the quinquereme. The shock of the impact traveled through both ships, accompanied by the sound of shattering wood, and Kylon saw men stagger as the decks trembled beneath their boots and sandals.

And in that instant, Kylon moved.

He drew upon his power and leaped into the air, the sorcery of water lending his muscles the power of a roaring river. He soared over the trireme's prow, over the railing of the Imperial flagship, and hurtled towards the startled auxiliaries.

"Stormdancer!" a man screamed, but it was too late.

Kylon landed among them like a thunderbolt, and the killing began.

He struck left and right, the sorcery of air giving his arms the speed of a hurricane wind. White mist swirled around his blade, a rime of frost spreading over the steel. Kylon's storm-driven strength drove the blade through armor and flesh alike. Men fell dead from his blows, his frost-wreathed sword turning their blood to ice. Cimon fought behind him, driving into the auxiliaries. He moved slower than Kylon, but blue-white lightning snarled up and down his sword, and crackling daggers of lightning leapt from his blows to encircle his foes.

Behind them the ashtairoi scrambled aboard, Alcios at their head. For all his bluster, the High Seat of House Kallias was no craven, and wielded his ashtair and shield with vigor, shouting exhortations to his men. The auxiliaries, already scattered by the stormdancers, crumbled beneath the assault of the ashtairoi.

Kylon whirled, cut down another soldier, and found himself face to face with the magi.

There were four of them, all wearing the black plate armor of the battle magi, black maces and swords in their hands. A black cloak with a purple fringe hung from their leader's shoulders. A master magus, then, no doubt skilled in both arms and battle sorcery.

Even as the thought crossed Kylon's mind, all four men lifted their hands and released arcane power.

A fist of invisible force slammed into Kylon and threw him backwards towards one of the masts. But Kylon drew on his own sorcery, filling his limbs with the power of a surging torrent. His boots slammed into the mast, but his enhanced strength absorbed the impact, and he shoved off the mast, hurtling at the magi.

The eyes of the magi widened in astonishment, and Kylon's sword shot forward in a white blur. One of the magi fell dead, his face covered in frost, and the others backed away and raised their weapons.

"Kill them, you fools!" shouted the master magus, raising an enormous mace. "Kill the stormdancers and the day is ours!"

The three magi attacked, psychokinetic force driving them forward with terrific speed. Cimon raced to Kylon's side, and the furious duel began. Kylon's sorcery gave him the speed of the wind and the strength of a waterfall, but the magi used bursts of psychokinetic force to drive their blows. Sword rang against sword, and Kylon dodged the shattering blows of the master magus's mace. Cimon slapped his sword against the black armor of the magi, but the magi had warded themselves against his lightning.

But they had not warded themselves against the cold.

So many stormdancers and stormsingers made the same error. They trusted too much in the power of lightning and ignored the sorcery of frost and ice.

Kylon knew better.

He faced off against one of the magi, his storm-forged steel meeting the magus's black blade. Time and time again Kylon's sword struck the magus's sword arm, rebounding from the plates of black steel.

"Pitiful, Kyracian dog," growled the magus, driving a spell-enhanced blow at Kylon's face. "Pitiful! Lie down and die."

But a layer of frost covered the magus's sword arm.

Kylon forced his will and power into his sword, a vortex of freezing white mist swirling around his blade, and struck once more at the magus's sword arm.

The battle magus sneered and drew back his blade for a killing blow.

And as he did, the armor plates covering his arm stuck together, bound by the frost.

It did not slow him for long. Not for more than a half-second. But that was more than enough for Kylon to plunge his frost-wreathed sword home. The battle magus stiffened and collapsed to the deck with a clatter of black armor.

Kylon saw that Cimon had dispatched the other remaining magus, and now faced off against the master magus in the purple-trimmed black cloak. Cimon was getting the worst of the fight, and his leather armor had been torn by a glancing blow from the master magus's mace. Cimon had slowed, and the master magus drove him back step by step.

Kylon charged forward, darting through the struggling ashtairoi and auxiliaries, his legs moving with the speed of the storm.

The master magus was faster. The older man spun, the mace a black blur. Kylon jerked back, the steel head whipping past his face, and drove his blade for the magus's neck, but the mace came back and blocked his thrust. Cimon drew back his lightning-sheathed blade for a strike, and the master magus thrust out his hand.

Psychokinetic force blasted in all directions, the deck creaking, the sorcery flinging both auxiliaries and ashtairoi to the planks. Kylon drew on the power of water and held his ground, but the blast flung Cimon to the deck. The magus loomed over him, mace raised for the killing blow.

Kylon sprang forward, but once again the master magus reacted with greater speed. The huge mace snapped up and deflected his swing, and the black-armored figure pursued him. Kylon dodged and ducked under the magus's swings. He did not dare to block the blows. The mace would snap his sword in two like a twig.

His mind flashed back to the fighting in Marsis, to pursuing the blue-eyed Ghost through the dockside district's alleys. She had outwitted him, and almost killed him. One spy, one woman without sorcery, had almost killed a stormdancer of New Kyre.

She had turned his strength against him.

Perhaps Kylon could do the same to the master magus.

The mace came around in a sideways blow, and Kylon dodged, letting the edge of his blade tap the mace. The sheer force of the blow knocked him off balance, almost ripping the sword from his fingers, and Kylon let himself fall. The magus sneered and stepped forward, his cloak billowing as he raised the mace for a massive overhand blow.

Kylon drew on his power, and the mace's black head shot towards him like a falling mountain.

At the last moment he threw himself to the side. The mace missed him by a few inches and slammed into the deck. The planks shattered...including the plank resting beneath the magus's armored left boot.

The master magus fell to one knee with a grunt of surprise. He raised his mace, but it was too late. Kylon surged to his feet, all his strength and sorcery driving his blade in a two-handed swing.

The master magus's head jumped off his head and rolled across the deck, black icicles of frozen blood jutting from the stump of his neck. The armored body fell to the splintered deck with a clang. Kylon stepped back, breathing hard, seeking for additional foes.

But the fighting was over.

Most of the auxiliaries had been killed, and the survivors had shed their armor and jumped into the water, hoping to escape to the other Nighmarian ships. The Imperial flagship belonged to the Kyracians.

But the rest of the quinqueremes had turned to face them.

Cimon got to his feet with groan. "I thank you, lord thalarchon. That magus had the better of me."

"New Kyre has too few stormdancers to lose even one," said Kylon. "Lord High Seat?"

"The ship is ours," said Alcios, blood dripping from his ashtair, his round shield dented. "But little good it will do us." He pointed his blade over the railing. "The enemy moves to meet us. I suggest we withdraw to the trireme and sink this vessel. Otherwise we shall be overrun."

Kylon looked up, felt the stirring power in the air. "We will withdraw to the trireme and sink this ship. But there's no need to flee."

"Why?" said Alcios.

"Because," said Kylon. "The day is ours."

Even as he spoke, the remaining squadrons of the seventh fleet crashed into the line of Imperial ships. Without the magi to disrupt their spells, the stormsingers summoned wind to fill the triremes' sails, driving them faster than the oarsmen could row unaided. The smaller, faster Kyracian ships avoided the catapults and ballistae of the quinqueremes and rammed into them, their prows tearing gaping holes in the Nighmarian ships.

One by one, the Imperial warships sank or burned.

THE BATTLE WAS over by afternoon.

Kylon stood at the bow, watching his ships maneuver back into formation. Here and there one of the quinqueremes still burned, the hulks slipping below the waves. Other triremes circled through the floating wreckage, looking for loot and picking up survivors. The Imperial sailors and auxiliaries who survived the hundreds of frenzied sharks swimming through the waters would be sold as slaves in New Kyre.

Kylon remembered how the blue-eyed Ghost burned with rage against slavers. Would she try to kill him now, if she saw what his men did?

Of course she would. She was a servant of the Emperor...and he had just destroyed the Emperor's fleet.

"A great victory, my lord thalarchon," said Alcios. There was more respect in his voice now. "An utterly crushing victory. The Empire of Nighmar has a handful of warships left in the western sea. We can launch raids into the Cyrican Sea with impunity, perhaps even to the harbor of Malarae itself."

"Yes," said Kylon. "A great victory."

Thousands of men dead, and all because Andromache had launched a useless war at the Moroaica's bidding.

"A great victory," said Kylon, "but futile."

Both Cimon and Alcios frowned. "Lord thalarchon?"

"We have destroyed the fleet, aye," said Kylon, "but we cannot conquer the Empire. The Nighmarian Empire is vast, and New Kyre is but one city and a dozen colonies. We could destroy a dozen fleets and it would not matter. Commerce is New Kyre's lifeblood...and the Empire will slowly strangle us."

"They cannot stop our ships," said Alcios.

"No," said Kylon. "But they can deny our merchants entrance to their harbors, and they can persuade others to do the same. The Assembly of New Kyre cannot wage war if there are no funds to pay the oarsmen and the ashtairoi."

New Kyre needed peace. The Istarish had proven to be useless allies, and now the Empire and New Kyre were stalemated, like two men with death grips on each other. This war was a waste.

But for the defense of his city and the honor of House Kardamnos, Kylon would wage it.

"We will return to New Kyre," said Kylon. "The fleet must be resupplied, the prisoners sold, and the men have earned some rest. We shall see what new commands the Archons and the Assembly have for us."

～

SIX DAYS later the seventh fleet returned to New Kyre.

Kylon stood upon the prow and gazed at his home. The city rose at the edge of the water, its fortified walls guarding one of the best natural harbors in the world. Twin colossal statues of armored ashtairoi stood atop towers at either side of the entrance to the harbor, catapults and ballistae waiting at their feet. Past the harbor rose great ziggurats of gleaming stone, home to the noble Kyracian Houses, and beyond them the stone slopes of the Pyramid of the Storm, where the Assembly and the Archons met to govern the Kyracian people. At the feet of the ziggurats and the Pyramid stood the dwellings of low-born Kyracians, of merchants and tradesmen and foreigners.

New Kyre housed half a million people within its walls, and was the richest city in the world, its vessels trading in every port and nation, its navy the most powerful upon the seas. Yet that wealth and strength were fragile. The city did not control enough farmland to feed itself, and if the Empire convinced the Anshani and the petty lords of the free cities not to sell their grain to the Kyracians, the Empire could strangle New Kyre within a year.

He wished Andromache were here. She had led House Kardamnos for years, and she would have the foresight and wisdom to find a way out of this trap.

But her folly had created the trap in the first place.

"Put us into the harbor," said Kylon. "The men have liberty for three days. The Assembly will have new commands for us by then."

"My lord thalarchon," said Alcios, and relayed the commands.

The trireme pulled alongside one of the great stone quays in the harbor, and Kylon strode ashore. A young slave in the livery of the Assembly itself waited for him on one knee.

"Lord Kylon," said the slave, "High Seat of House Kardamnos and thalarchon of the seventh fleet?"

"I am," said Kylon.

"The Assembly commands your presence at once," said the slave.

"Good," said Alcios. "They will congratulate you on your triumph."

Or the Assembly would execute him. Throughout the history of the city the Assembly had sometimes executed successful generals, lest they try to make themselves tyrants. But Kylon lacked Andromache's political skill, and he had neither the ability nor the desire to overthrow the Assembly. Most likely the Assembly intended him to return to battle with the seventh fleet.

"Lead the way," said Kylon.

As the sun set, Kylon left the Pyramid of the Storm and strode into the Agora of the Archons. The temples to the gods of Old Kyrace, the gods of storm and sea, lined the Plaza. Few people came here, save during the ceremonies of the nobles and Archons. Most of the city's population conducted business in the sprawling Agora of Merchants, or amused themselves watching the trials of combat in the gladiatorial rings, a barbarous custom imported from the Fourth Empire.

Cimon and Alcios waited him at the foot of the Pyramid.

"It seems," said Kylon, "the Assembly has chosen us for a new task."

"Battle against the Empire?" said Alcios.

"No," said Kylon. "I am now New Kyre's Lord Ambassador to the city of Catekharon. And you, my lord High Seat, will accompany me as the High Seat of one of the oldest Kyracian noble houses."

Alcios scowled. "A Lord Ambassador? Why? We crushed the Imperial fleet! What have we done to merit such a...a useless sinecure?"

"It seems," said Kylon, voice quiet, "that it is not so useless. The Masked Ones of Catekharon claim to have created a weapon of sorcery so potent that its bearer will have dominion over the entire world."

Alcios's scowl deepened. "And the Masked Ones expect us to grovel?"

"No," said Kylon. "They expect us to bid. Apparently they are offering this weapon for sale to the highest bidder...and they have sent emissaries making the same offer to every kingdom and realm upon the earth. Including the Empire of Nighmar."

"This is madness," said Cimon. "If the Masked Ones have such a weapon, why sell it? Why not use it to rule the world themselves?"

"I don't know," said Kylon. "But if the Empire claims the weapon, they will use it to destroy us at once. The Assembly has charged us to keep that weapon from the Empire, regardless of what we must do. Even if it means war with Catekharon."

Alcios shook his head. "That would be folly. Old Kyrace tried to conquer Catekharon, and our ancestors were utterly defeated."

"I know," said Kylon. "But the Empire cannot have that weapon."

And Kylon would make sure of that. Andromache had started this war...and unless Kylon took action, the war would destroy New Kyre. If the Empire gained the Masked Ones' weapon of sorcery, if it really existed, the Emperor would certainly destroy New Kyre.

But what would happen if Kylon brought that weapon back to New Kyre?

He remembered how Andromache had sought the power in the Tomb of Scorikhon, power that had destroyed her. Would the Masked Ones' weapon destroy whoever wielded it?

"Come," said Kylon. "The embassy leaves tomorrow."

5

CARAVAN

The embassy of Lord Titus Iconias left Cyrioch and traveled southwest.

Caina had not expected the embassy to include so many men.

Titus Iconias, a stout, scowling man in his forties, rode an impressive-looking stallion at the head of the column. A steady stream of pages followed him, leading remounts for Titus and his entourage. Lord Titus's personal guards, hard-eyed men in chain mail, surrounded him. Behind them rode Titus's scribes, seneschals, and a petulant noblewoman Caina suspected served as Lord Titus's mistress.

After them marched an entire cohort of the Imperial Guard, men clad in black plate armor and purple cloaks. As an ambassador of the Emperor, Lord Titus was entitled to protection from the Emperor's own Guard. So the six hundred black-armored soldiers marched in orderly precision around Lord Titus's men, and the tribune in command sent mounted patrols ranging seeking for any bandits foolish enough to assault the Emperor's ambassador.

Hangers-on followed the Imperial Guard. Merchants on their way to Anshan, New Kyre, or the free cities. Other merchants who hoped to sell their goods to the men of the Imperial Guard. And Halfdan, disguised as the master merchant Basil Callenius of the Imperial Collegium of Jewelers. Caina traveled with him as his daughter Anna Callenius, while Corvalis took the name of Cormark, acting as a mercenary Basil hired to protect his merchandise and his daughters.

That Caina fully intended to share a blanket with Corvalis during the journey only added verisimilitude to the disguise. It was not uncommon for a master merchant's guard to seduce the master merchant's daughter.

She smiled at the thought.

Claudia took the name of Irene Callenius, Basil's older daughter. She played the part of the spoiled merchant's daughter very well, clad in a rich green gown chosen to match her eyes and ordering anyone in her path with arrogant hauteur.

"She is better," murmured Corvalis to Caina, "at playing a part than I thought she would be."

"Aye," said Caina, though she wondered how much of it was a masquerade. Claudia had been a magus. Surely she was accustomed to giving orders. Sometimes Caina wondered if Corvalis's opinion of Claudia was correct, or if the years of pain spent trying to rescue her had caused him to idealize her.

But that was Halfdan's concern, not hers.

Halfdan himself drove a wagon laden with goods and supplies, surrounded by a ring of thirty grim Sarbian mercenaries in their sand-colored robes. Their leader, a towering man named Saddiq, was a Ghost. He was one of Marzhod's lieutenants, and Caina admired his level head.

Of course, Caina had rescued him after Nicasia and the Defender had turned him to stone, so Saddiq admired her, too.

In the end, over a thousand men marched south towards the low mountains dividing the fertile coastlands of Cyrica from the harsh land of the Sarbian desert. They passed hundreds of plantations growing wheat and tea and rice on land owned by Lord Khosrau Asurius or another powerful Cyrican noble. Caina saw countless slaves toiling among the crops, men from Caeria and the Szaldic provinces and Istarinmul and Anshan and Alqaarin, men kidnapped from every nation under the sun.

Gods, but Caina hated slavers.

"So many of them," said Claudia. They sat in Halfdan's wagon, Corvalis striding alongside them. Caina would have preferred to walk, but the haughty daughter of a wealthy merchant would not walk. Later, she could find an excuse to stretch her legs.

"Aye," said Caina. "It was part of the treaty that ended the War of the Fourth Empire. The Cyricans wanted to keep their slaves in exchange for rejoining the Empire. The Emperor was in no position to refuse, so he accepted. And this was allowed to continue."

"I see why you oppose it so strongly," said Claudia, staring at a Szaldic man naked but for an orange kilt wrapped around his waist. The layers of whip scars covering his back flexed as he walked. "This is vile. Men should not be chained and driven as beasts."

"It is the way of the world," said Corvalis. "The strong do as they like, and the weak suffer as they must. Or are turned into weapons to serve the strong." He looked utterly weary as he said it, and Caina wanted to take his hands. But it would not do for Master Basil's daughter to show affection to Master Basil's guards.

"Nevertheless, it is still wrong," said Claudia. "It ought to be stopped."

Caina felt her opinion of Claudia rise a notch.

Claudia sighed. "I only wish the high magi of the Magisterium could be made to see reason. They could take the nobles in hand and force them to end these corrupt practices. The magi could do so much good for the Empire."

"Then," said Caina, keeping her voice mild, "you think the magi should rule the Empire?"

Corvalis shot her a look.

"No, of course not," said Claudia. "Certainly not with men like my..."

Halfdan cleared his throat.

"With men like the First Magus ruling the Magisterium," said Claudia. "But if better men governed the magi, the Magisterium could shepherd the Empire, could guide the nobles and the commoners to be better than they are."

"To force others," said Caina, "to do as the magi will?"

She had heard similar speeches from the magi before.

"Yes," said Claudia. "But only in the name of the greater good."

"Pardon," said Caina. "I need to stretch my legs."

She dropped from the wagon seat and walked away without another word.

THANKFULLY, Caina and Claudia had separate tents, so that night Corvalis was able to sneak into Caina's.

After they finished, Caina rolled off him and flopped against the blanket, her skin beaded with sweat. She rested her head against Corvalis's chest as he caught his breath.

"I have taken," he said at last, wiping sweat from his forehead, "many journeys across the eastern Empire. Never have I had something so pleasant to look forward to at the end of the day's traveling."

Caina laughed. "Nor I. I have been to Marsis in the west, Rasadda in the east, and Cyrioch in the south...and you are right. This is more pleasant by far than a cold blanket at the end of the day."

"Then you are better traveled than I," said Corvalis. "I have never been farther west than Malarae."

"I've never been to Artifel," said Caina, "nor to the northern provinces."

Corvalis snorted. "You haven't missed much. The Magisterium's Motherhouse dominates Artifel, and the magi rule the city in all but name. The northern provinces are nothing but cold forests and mountains. Not many towns. The Ulkaari and the Iazns keep to their villages and don't go out at night for fear of the things that haunt the forests."

She traced one of the tattoos spiraling over the muscles of his chest. "Where you got these from an Ulkaari witchfinder."

"Aye," said Corvalis. "The Ulkaari hate sorcery. Too many creatures in the forest. Sometimes Iazn shamans call up beast-demons and invite them into their bodies to transform themselves into monsters. And the Magisterium has hardly endeared itself to the people of the northern provinces."

"Too many magi eager to do things to them for their own good, I suppose," said Caina, "much like Claudia."

She felt Corvalis tense, and regretted the words.

"She means well," said Corvalis at last. "They are not just empty words for her. She used her powers to aid people in Artifel. Warding grain warehouses against rats, using her spells to help heal."

"They all say that," said Caina. "Every magus that goes bad says..." She made herself stop. "No. Let's not argue about this. Not now."

"Very well," said Corvalis.

They lay in silence.

"That ring," said Corvalis at last. His hand slid down her shoulders to where the gold signet ring rested on its cord against her chest. "You never take it off. Who did it belong to?"

"Jealous?" said Caina.

Corvalis smirked. "If you are not as satisfied as you look right now...well, then you are a better actress than any I have ever met."

Caina laughed. "A fine argument." Her laughter faded away. "It belonged to my father."

"Ah," said Corvalis. "Then you wear it to remember."

"Yes," said Caina. "My mother murdered him." She sighed. "She was an initiate of the Magisterium, but they expelled her because she wasn't strong enough to become a full magus. So she made a pact with a renegade necromancer named Maglarion. My father found an old Maatish scroll, and my mother sold it, and me, to Maglarion in exchange for his teachings. When he found out, my father tried to stop her. So she wiped his mind, and Maglarion killed him and used his blood for his spells."

"Maglarion?" said Corvalis.

"You knew him?" said Caina.

"I knew of him," said Corvalis. "He was a legend among the high magi. He had some sort of pact with the magi, teaching them in exchange for service."

"It was a trick," said Caina, remembering that dark day when Maglarion had almost killed everyone in Malarae. "He would have killed them along with everyone else."

Again Corvalis paused.

"Then...you killed Maglarion?" he said.

Caina nodded, her hair sliding over his chest.

He laughed.

Caina looked at him. "It wasn't funny."

"No," said Corvalis. "But, gods...that was three years ago?" Caina nodded. "That was right before Claudia convinced me to leave the Kindred. My father was furious when someone killed Maglarion. I'd never seen him so angry." He laughed again. "And all the time it was you."

"Well," said Caina, pushing aside the memories. "I am pleased I could discomfort him on your behalf."

"Basil praised you," said Corvalis, "but if you killed a man like Maglarion, then he was too modest by far."

"I was lucky," murmured Caina, resting her head back on his chest. She had defeated powerful foes...but had she been lucky. If she had been a half-second slower, if she had been a touch less clever, then she would have been killed.

Along with millions of others.

Someday, she knew, she would be killed. Someday she would be too slow, someday she would face a foe she could not outwit.

But not today.

"Let's not talk about the magi," said Caina, "or about killing. I am weary of them both."

"I'll have to go," said Corvalis, "before dawn. Else there will be talk."

"Let them talk," said Caina, smiling. "A mercenary seducing his employer's daughter? What better disguise do we have?"

They drifted to sleep.

~

DREAMS FILLED Caina's mind as she slept.

She often had nightmares. She had seen too many terrible things not to have nightmares. Sometimes she saw them over and over again, or her memories blurred together in a scattered haze of twisted images.

And occasionally she dreamed of the Moroaica.

Caina stood in a field of gloomy gray mist, wearing a blue gown with black trim. Six paces away stood a Szaldic woman of about twenty, clad in a crimson gown, her hair and eyes black. She looked young, younger even than Caina, but her eyes were heavy with age and power.

She called herself Jadriga, but the Szaldic legends named her the Moroaica, the ancient sorceress of terror and might.

And her spirit was trapped within Caina.

"You," said Caina.

"So I am," said Jadriga.

"What is it now?" said Caina. "Trying to convince me to join your great work, whatever it is? Or to warn me about another of your disciples?" She frowned. "The Masked One that attacked me in Cyrioch. He was one of your disciples."

"No," said Jadriga. "He is an old, old enemy of mine. I'm surprised he found you. Still, I should not have underestimated him."

"Then what is it?" said Caina.

The Moroaica stared at her for a long time, and to Caina's astonishment, sadness flickered over the pale face.

"Child of the Ghosts," murmured Jadriga. "You should beware love. Betrayal is a blade that cuts deeper than any other."

She gestured, and the dream dissolved into mist.

~

TWO DAYS SOUTH OF CYRIOCH, Lord Titus's column crossed Cyrica's low mountains and entered the Sarbian desert.

And for the first time in her twenty-one years, Caina left the Empire of Nighmar.

Cyrica had been hot but wet. The desert was dry as a centuries-old bone. The road led southwest, the arid wastes stretching in all directions, bleak and empty.

"If this is your homeland," said Caina to Saddiq, "I understand why your people seek employment elsewhere."

Saddiq chuckled, his voice a basso rumble. "The desert is a harsh mother, mistress, and she raises harsh sons. There are only two things to do in the desert. We can fight each other, or we fight outlanders in exchange for pay. One is more profitable than the other. But when we are bored, we fight each other."

"I wonder if the Catekhari sent an ambassador to the Sarbian tribes," said Caina, "and offered to sell them the weapon."

Saddiq's white teeth flashed in his dark face. "More likely that my kinsmen would agree to purchase the weapon...only to ambush the Masked Ones, steal the weapon, and use it to extort tribute from the Empire, Anshan, and Istarinmul."

"Do you think the tribesmen will attack us?" said Caina.

"I doubt it," said Saddiq. "There are too many of us, and the tribes prefer easier prey. But if they choose the path of folly, we shall simply have to teach them wisdom."

Saddiq proved correct. From time to time to the scouts saw Sarbian horsemen in the distance, but the tribesmen always moved one.

Four days later the caravan crossed the desert and entered the borders of Anshan.

≈

"THIS IS EGREGIOUS," grumbled Lord Titus.

"Think of it, my lord," said Halfdan, "not as an escort, but as an honor guard to see you safely through the Shahenshah's lands."

Caina watched the exchange. Halfdan stood alongside Titus's horse, and Lord Titus seemed to know that Halfdan was a Ghost.

Certainly he seemed more willing to accept a jewel merchant's advice than Caina would have expected from a lord of high Nighmarian birth. Corvalis stood a discreet distance behind Halfdan, hands near his weapons.

The objects of Lord Titus's ire waited twenty paces away. Four hundred Anshani cavalrymen, armored in scale mail and spiked helmets, spears resting in their hands, long oval shields upon their arms, and bows and quivers hanging from their saddles. Their leader, an Anshani khadjar, wore a cloak of brilliant crimson silk. The other horsemen were anjars, lesser nobles who owned enough land to equip themselves with horse and armor. The Imperial Legions produced the finest infantry in the world, but the Anshani nobles fielded the best horsemen.

If it came to a fight, Caina was not sure who would win.

"It is still egregious," said Titus. "Are we brigands, that the Shahenshah should send soldiers to dog our path?"

"It is part of the Emperor's agreement with the Shahenshah," said Halfdan. He sounded as if he were soothing a truculent child. "The Shahenshah agreed to allow the Emperor's Lord Ambassador to cross his lands with a cohort of the Imperial Guard. But until we leave the boundaries of Anshan, a guard of the Shahenshah's soldiers will escort us."

"To make sure we stay out of trouble," said Titus.

"In essence, yes," said Halfdan. "But it would be impolite to say so."

"No one," said Titus, "will match a Lord of the Empire for courtesy. Very well. Let us greet our...escort."

He spurred his horse forward, accompanied by his bodyguards and a squad of the Imperial Guard.

~

THE COLUMN TRAVELED south across the grasslands, and then came to the Great Western Caravan Road.

Caina had read about it in her father's books as a child. The road began in Anshan and traveled through the hills and mountains at the heart of the Shahenshah's domain. It cut through the western grass-lands, the Red Forest and the petty domains of the free cities, and reached the gates of New Kyre. There were many romantic tales about dashing highwaymen preying upon the merchants of the Road, highwaymen who sometimes abducted the merchants' petulant daughters and won their hearts with roguish charm.

Caina suspected the reality was rather more prosaic.

"All those grain wagons," said Corvalis. A constant line of grain wagons traveled west along the Road. "Where are they going?"

"New Kyre," said Caina, walking at his side. She had given up riding in the wagon. Claudia rode in the wagon, and she constantly offered suggestions on how the teamsters could handle their animals, how the Imperial Guards could clean their weapons, and how the merchants could store their cargoes. If she was masquerading as a merchant's spoiled daughter, Claudia was doing a fine job.

Caina suspected she was not masquerading.

"Why New Kyre?" said Corvalis.

Halfdan spoke up from the wagon. "New Kyre controls only a few hundred square miles outside of its city walls. Half a million people live in New Kyre, and the city cannot possibly feed itself. So they must import grain. Their fleets carry grain to their harbors, and they buy the rest from Anshan. Anshani khadjars have made vast fortunes selling grain to the Kyracians. Cyrican lords, too, before the war started."

"A pity," said Claudia, "that the Legions cannot strike these grain caravans. The Empire could strangle New Kyre and end the war."

"If we did that, my daughter," said Halfdan, "that would mean war with Anshan. The Shahenshah allows those caravans to pass through his lands, and his khadjars reap great profits selling grain to the Kyracians. Were the Empire to attack a single Anshani caravan, the Shahenshah would declare war upon the Empire...and the Emperor would lose any chance of forcing the war to a truce." He wiped some sweat from his brow. "Though such concerns are far above a simple merchant of jewels."

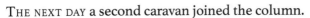

THE NEXT DAY a second caravan joined the column.

And unlike the others, it was not carrying grain.

The caravan had a dozen wagons, and though none of the wagons were particularly full, the oxen nonetheless appeared burdened. A quick look at the wagons told Caina why. They carried stacked ingots of crimson steel.

"That's red steel from the mines of Nhabatan," murmured Caina to Corvalis.

Corvalis frowned. "If I remember rightly, that's the only place where red iron can be found."

"Aye," said Caina. "It's incredibly valuable. Which explains the guards."

A score of men in elaborate gray plate armor surrounded the wagons. Their breastplates were adorned with elaborate, stylized reliefs that looked almost Maatish. Despite the bulky armor, the men seemed to move without encumbrance. Each man also wore an elaborate helmet fashioned from red steel. Caina took a step closer, hoping to get a better look...

And then stepped right back, bumping into Corvalis.

"What is it?" said Corvalis as Claudia joined them.

"I think," said Caina, voice low, "I think their armor is enspelled."

"You're right," said Claudia. "I suspect that armor is Catekhari."

Caina blinked. "So Catekhari soldiers are escorting this caravan?" That warranted further investigation. "Come with me."

She walked to the front of the long column, Corvalis and Claudia following her. Lord Titus sat on his horse, flanked by his bodyguards. Halfdan stood nearby, ready to advise Titus. A middle-aged man wearing a fine tunic of white linen and sturdy sandals stood before the lord's horse. A leather belt wrapped around his waist, holding a sheathed short sword and dagger, and he had a hawkish, weather-beaten face.

"Khaltep Irzaris at your service, my lord Titus of House Iconias," said the man with an elaborate bow, "a humble merchant of Catekharon."

"A curious coincidence," said Titus. "My party and I are traveling to Catekharon at the invitation of the Scholae."

"Perhaps we can travel together, my lord," said Irzaris. "The Red Forest is only a few days ahead, and bold bandits sometimes prowl beneath its branches. There is safety in numbers."

"Indeed," said Titus. "Though I am curious about what sort of wares the Masked Ones might purchase. One would assume they simply conjure up spirits to provide whatever they need."

"Perhaps, my lord," said Irzaris, "but for all their power, the Scholae are still men of flesh and blood, and enjoy meat and wine and comely slaves. And the Sages of the Scholae are artificers without peer, but still require raw materials to create their enspelled artifacts." He gestured at his wagons. "The red iron of Nhabatan is rare, but the Scholae prefers to use it for their work. So if a daring man makes the long journey from Catekharon to Nhabatan and back, the risk is great, but the profits are greater."

"Very well," said Titus. "You would be welcome to travel with us." He glanced at Halfdan. "This is Basil Callenius, a master merchant of the Imperial collegium of jewelers. He will find a place for you in the line of march."

Irzaris bowed again. "Thank you, my lord." He strode to Halfdan. "May you find profit and shelter, Master Basil."

"And you as well, Master Khaltep," said Halfdan. "These are my daughters, Irene and Anna."

Irzaris's smile widened a bit when he saw Claudia. "Master Basil, you are indeed a bold man to take your treasures with you upon the road." He bowed over Claudia's hand, kissing her knuckles, and did not release her fingers right away. "Though I am sure you have chosen strong husbands for your daughters."

"Alas," said Halfdan, "my daughters are yet unwed."

Claudia looked appalled. She had been a magus and the bastard daughter of the First Magus, and only a bold or suicidal man would attempt to seduce such a woman. But a rich merchant's pretty daughter made for a tempting prize.

"Indeed?" said Irzaris. "I grieve to hear it. It is a cold and cruel world. Perhaps, Master Basil, you would allow me to keep your daughters company during our journey to Catekharon?"

"Please, Father?" said Caina, putting just the right note of petulant pleading into her voice. "The countryside is ever so dull, and some conversation would be welcome." And it would give her the opportunity to learn more about Catekharon and the Masked Ones.

Claudia's lip crinkled in disgust.

"Oh, very well," said Halfdan, playing along. "Though I certainly do not have the time to chaperone the two of you."

"That shouldn't be a problem," said Caina, looking at Corvalis. "Cormark will chaperone us. Won't you, Cormark?"

Corvalis bowed, his expression grave. "It would be my solemn honor, mistress."

THREE DAYS later the column left the grasslands and entered the Red Forest, while the Anshani horsemen rode away to the east.

"This is the boundary of the Shahenshah's domain, you see," said Irzaris, walking alongside his wagons. "The lands east of the Red Forest swear to the Shahenshah. The various petty princelings of the free cities rule the lands west of the Red Forest."

Caina nodded, keeping her eyes wide. Irzaris, she suspected, was more attracted to Claudia, but Claudia's icy disdain for the man never wavered. Caina had found that men of wealth and power enjoyed a woman who hung on their every word...and so she hung on Irzaris's every word.

And learned a number of useful things.

"So we are in danger," said Caina, "of being attacked?"

She looked around the forest and made a show of shivering. Huge redwood trees, larger than any Caina had ever seen, rose around the road. Some of them stood at least three hundred feet tall. Their roots transformed the ground into a wrinkled mossy sheet, and their vast branches cast patterns of light and shadow across the road.

Irzaris laughed. "Not particularly, my dear. The free cities ignore caravans. If they attack too many they will earn the ire of the Emperor or the Shahenshah. Or, worse, of the Assembly of New Kyre. The Emperor and the Shahenshah can only make war upon the princes of the free cities. New Kyre can do far worse to them."

"What's that?" said Caina.

"Drive them bankrupt," said Corvalis.

Irzaris laughed. "Well spoken, Cormark. Master Basil is fortunate to have such a wise man in his service. Perhaps you should check on your master? The women will be safe enough with me."

Corvalis shrugged. "I am sorry, Master Khaltep, but Master Basil bade me to guard his daughters until we stopped for the night."

"Your vigilance does you credit," said Irzaris, with only the faintest hint of irritation in his black eyes. He had never stopped trying to get Caina and Claudia alone. He turned to Claudia. "What do you think of the forest?"

Claudia looked away. "I suppose the trees are large."

"Truly," said Irzaris. "Men come from all nations to marvel at the great redwoods."

"Why haven't they been cut down?" said Caina. "Surely such fine wood would fetch a high price."

Irzaris shrugged. "A dozen different cities claim this forest for their own, but I fear the real reason is mere superstition. Men say that spirits guard the forest, and will rise in wrath should any man assail the trees."

"I've heard Ulkaari men say that demons haunt their forests," said Corvalis.

"And I had have heard the most dreadful tales from Szaldic slaves," said Caina, "of a terrible sorceress called the Moroaica."

Irzaris laughed. "Simple superstition, my dear. You mustn't let the idle words of illiterate slaves trouble you. There's no such thing as the Moroaica or demons."

Caina caught Corvalis's eyes and saw the amusement there. Baiting Irzaris had become something of a game between them.

"I am glad, sir," said Caina, "that you travel with us. It indeed makes me feel better."

"Good," said Irzaris, looking at Claudia. "Would you like to take a ride into the trees, my dear? Some of them are truly magnificent."

Claudia frowned. "I would fear robbers."

"Did not your sister say she feels safer at my side?" said Irzaris. "There would be no danger." He kissed her hand and lowered his voice. "I would please me greatly to show you a...most magnificent tree."

Claudia's face crinkled in disgust.

"Sister," said Caina. "We must have lunch with Father. Do you not remember? He is taking his midday meal with Lord Titus, and Father bade us to join him." She paused. "And I hear Lord Titus has unwed sons."

Claudia shot her a grateful look.

"Ah. Perhaps later, then," said Irzaris.

"It is a pity," said Caina. "My sister said she was so looking forward to seeing the trees."

Claudia's grateful look turned just short of murderous.

"Mistress," said Corvalis, "your father will be wroth if you are late."

"Yes. Good day, Master Khaltep," said Claudia, striding away. Caina and Corvalis followed them, and Irzaris turned his attention to his wagons.

Once they were out of earshot, both Caina and Corvalis started laughing.

Claudia whirled to face them. "What the devil do you find so amusing?"

"Irzaris," said Caina.

"The man is a fool," said Corvalis.

"Actually, I think he's clever," said Caina. "He's been trying to worm his way into Claudia's blankets for three days...and he's never once mentioned the weapon of the Masked Ones."

"And," said Corvalis, "he's never said who is buying that red steel of his."

Claudia's frown deepened. "Then he knows what the weapon is?"

"Probably," said Caina. "But he won't tell us. It wouldn't surprise me if those Catekhari soldiers report to the Masked Ones, not to him. He won't boast of his secrets, not even to impress a merchant's daughter he wishes to bed."

Claudia's scowl returned. "The temerity of the man! I was a magus, a daughter of the First Magus himself, and of noble birth. And he thinks to seduce me like some common tavern wench!"

"But he doesn't know any of that, does he?" said Caina. "To him, you're simply Irene Callenius, the daughter of a particularly successful merchant. Preferably a daughter with a large dowry...but if he can lure you into his tent for a night, well, that would also be to his liking."

"I know that," snapped Claudia. "I am not a complete fool! Do you and Master Basil expect me to seduce him and discover his secrets?"

Caina shrugged. "Only if you wish. And I doubt he's that foolish." She thought of Alastair Corus. "That can have...consequences."

"I suppose you would know, wouldn't you?" said Claudia. "Given how you lured Corvalis into your blankets. And gods knows how many others over the years."

Caina felt her face go blank.

"Sister," said Corvalis at last.

"I'm sorry," said Claudia, blinking. "That was...that was rude, Marina. You saved me from the stone, and...and forgive me. I am overwrought. It's...this place, the stink of all these unwashed men, and that toad Irzaris drooling over me..." She shook her head. "When I was part of the Magisterium, I wanted to use my powers to help people. I joined the Ghosts to do as you did, to save people like you saved us." She scowled. "Instead we have been walking for days, and I have to endure the odious attentions of that money-grubbing lecher."

Caina shrugged. "We're spies. This is what we do. You want to help people? Sometimes the right secret taken from the right man can save thousands of lives."

"Yes," said Claudia. "Excuse me. I think I shall ride in the wagon for a while."

She walked off, rejoining the rest of the column, and for a moment Caina stood alone with Corvalis in the patches of light and shadow below the vast branches.

"Do not mind her," said Corvalis. "Before Ranarius, she had never left Artifel. She's not like us. She hasn't had training in disguise or stealth..."

"I know," said Caina, not looking at him. "Do you think she's right?"

"About what?"

"That," said Caina, "I seduced you for the Ghosts?"

Corvalis barked his harsh laugh.

"What?" said Caina.

"I am a penniless former Kindred assassin," said Corvalis, "and the Kindred want me dead. My father is one of the most powerful men in the Empire, and he also wants me dead." He smiled. "If you are trying to seduce me for personal gain, you're doing it wrong."

Despite herself, Caina laughed.

"Come," said Corvalis. "Let us rejoin the others. If we disappear for too long, there will be talk."

Caina grinned. "That would only strengthen our disguise."

"Did I say it would be a bad thing?"

They rejoined the column.

Two days later they left the Red Forest and entered hilly country dotted by pine trees, and Caina developed a headache.

Her skin crawled, and she felt the tingling of arcane force. For an instant she wondered if Claudia had cast a spell over her. But it was too faint for that. It reminded Caina of the mighty spell Kalastus had cast over Rasadda, of the awesome forces the magus had wielded.

She was sensing distant sorcery.

Powerful, distant sorcery.

"We have almost reached Catekharon," announced Irzaris. The Catekhari merchant walked at the head of the column with Lord Titus and Halfdan. The merchant's easy manner had ingratiated him to Lord Titus, and the two had become friends.

It was just as well. Caina doubted Claudia could have handled Irzaris's attentions with good grace for much longer.

"Splendid," said Titus. "A good bed would be welcome. And I must present the Emperor's message to the Masked Ones."

Irzaris smiled. "My lord, have you never been to Catekharon before?"

"I fear not, master merchant," said Titus. "To my knowledge, no lord of the Empire has ever crossed its gates. You Catekhari are not sociable folk. But I have visited the other free cities, and so the Emperor chose me as his Lord Ambassador."

Irzaris grinned. "Then you are in for a splendid sight."

Caina took a step forward, blinked, and shook her head.

"Are you all right, mistress?" said Corvalis, stepping closer.

"I'm...fine," said Caina, shaking her head again. The tingling had gotten worse, and her temples throbbed. "Just...I could use some water, that's all."

The road rounded a curve of the hill, and the city of Catekharon came into sight below.

Caina's eyes widened, and exclamations went up from Lord Titus and his men.

"Gods," breathed Corvalis. "That lake..."

"It's called a caldera," said Claudia, voice soft. "In ancient times, a volcanic mountain stood there. It exploded with enough force to destroy the mountain entirely...and the resultant crater became the lake."

"Just," muttered Caina, "as Old Kyrace was destroyed."

A brilliant blue lake, perhaps four miles across, stretched below. An island filled the center of the lake, an enormous white tower rising from its heart. Stone terraces adorned the rest of the island, supporting elaborate palaces built of wood with peaked roofs, their walls carved with intricate figures. A dozen different bridges connected the island to the ring-shaped shore. A wall of white stone, its face adorned with sigils of gleaming silver, encircled the lake, and between the wall and the shore stood a city, a hodgepodge of houses and temples and warehouses and tenements built in the architectural styles of every nation upon earth.

"Behold Catekharon," said Irzaris, "the City of the Artificers."

A strange cherry-red glow rose from the ring of the city and the bridges connecting it to the island in the crater lake.

Halfdan frowned. "Is the city on fire?"

"Only in a sense," said Irzaris. "Look closer."

Caina felt her eyes grow wider.

The bridges were actually aqueducts connecting to the central island, joining in a series of concentric rings running through the outer city. But water did not flow through those aqueducts and canals.

Molten steel, glowing white-hot, filled the channels.

Rivers of liquid steel encircled the City of the Artificers.

6

THE CITY OF THE ARTIFICERS

Caina gazed at the molten steel flowing through the canals.

If the Masked Ones possessed the power to do that... then perhaps their claim of a mighty weapon was no bluff.

"How is that even possible?" said Lord Titus, wonder in his voice. "Surely all the coal in the world, burned at once, could not melt that much steel. And keep it liquid, for that matter."

Irzaris shrugged. "I am no sorcerer, my lord. But from what I understand, a great spirit of fire was once imprisoned below the volcano. Its rage destroyed the mountain, and when the Scholae fled here after the fall of the Kingdom of the Rising Sun, they discovered the spirit sleeping below the lake. They bound it to fuel their sorceries."

Caina shared a dismayed look with Corvalis and Claudia.

If Irzaris was right, that meant the Masked Ones had bound a greater fire elemental. Ranarius had tried to awaken the greater earth elemental within the Stone of Cyrioch, and if he had been successful, he would have destroyed the city and killed countless thousands. And centuries ago, the stormsingers of Old Kyrace had bound a greater fire elemental beneath their island.

The breaking of that binding had been the destruction of Old Kyrace.

"I fear this is where we part ways, my lord," said Irzaris. "My warehouse is on the western end of the city, and it is easier to steer wagons outside the walls than within."

Titus offered a gracious nod. "Farewell, Master Khaltep. If you ever travel to the Empire, seek me out. I may have a use for a man of your talents."

Irzaris bowed again, and his wagons and Catekhari guards broke off from Lord Titus's column and circled around the city. The Imperial Guards continued towards the eastern gates of Catekharon, the golden eagle of the Emperor flying on its purple banner overhead.

A wave of dizziness went through Caina, the prickling getting worse with every step.

"Are you all right?" said Corvalis.

"Probably not," said Caina, and pulled herself into the seat of Halfdan's wagon. Saddiq and his tribesmen followed the wagon, staring at the city and the huge white tower with wide eyes. Caina could not blame them. The tower rising from the island dwarfed even the Palace of Splendors in Cyrioch.

"Well?" said Halfdan, voice low.

"There's power inside the city," said Caina. "Unlike anything I've ever felt. Stronger than Maglarion, stronger than Kalastus." She swallowed. "Even stronger than Jadriga, I think."

"You heard," said Halfdan, "Irzaris's story about the fire spirit?"

"Aye," said Caina. "Ranarius thought he could harness the earth elemental, but I think the Masked Ones actually did it. And if they have the power to do that...then they truly could create a weapon to conquer the world."

Halfdan nodded. "Can you cope? I know the presence of sorcery...affects you, for want of a better word."

"I'll manage," said Caina.

"Good," said Halfdan. "Walk with Claudia. I'd like the two of you to watch the city and tell me what you learn. Try not to kill her if you can avoid it."

"Do accidents count?" said Caina.

Halfdan raised an eyebrow.

Caina nodded. "As you wish." She pushed off the seat, caught her balance, and circled past Saddiq and his mercenaries. Claudia walked at the side of the road, gazing at the city's white walls with Corvalis.

"What do you think?" said Caina.

"Defensible," said Corvalis. "Those walls are solid, and with that lake in the crater they'll have all the water they'll ever need."

Claudia laughed, her voice a little wild. "Those walls are an affectation. The Scholae doesn't need them." She waved her hand, and Caina felt the faint prickle as Claudia worked the spell to sense sorcery. "They have the kind of power that could sweep an army from the field like dust. Those sigils upon the walls? Warding spells. When activated, those walls would be impervious to any physical or sorcerous attack." She shivered. "And that is only a defensive spell. I cannot imagine...I cannot image what their sorcery would do if they wielded it for attack." Again she shivered. "I thought...I thought I knew what power was. Our father had it. The high magi of the Magisterium had it. But this...this is power."

Her tone was horrified, but Caina saw an intrigued light in her eyes. Like a child enraptured by a fire, right before he burned his hand.

"Think of all the good the Masked Ones could do with that power," said Claudia.

"Yes," said Caina. "Like creating a terrible weapon to sell to the highest bidder."

Claudia blinked, and the strange look faded from her eyes.

"Come on," said Caina. "Let's see what kind of men would create such a weapon."

Lord Titus rode through the great gate of white stone, flanked by his Imperial Guards. A large open square stood on the other side of the gate, ringed by a curious mixture of buildings. Caina saw an inn built in the Nighmarian style, a whitewashed Cyrican townhouse, a Kyracian ziggurat, and a score of other buildings. Yet many of them looked dilapidated or abandoned.

Caina guessed that many people came to Catekharon in hopes of learning or profiting from the Masked Ones only to be disappointed.

Lord Titus reined up his horse, and his bodyguard and Imperial Guards spread around him, an array of pomp and splendor and power.

A single man in a robe of white linen awaited them.

For an alarmed instant Caina thought the Masked One she and Corvalis had killed in Cyrioch had returned. The robed man wore the same jade mask and carried the same silvery rod. Yet this man was fatter and taller. And Caina saw the pattern of hieroglyphics upon the mask was different.

"Titus, Lord of House Iconias!" boomed Titus's herald in High Nighmarian. "As the Lord Ambassador of the Emperor Alexius of House Naerius, he comes to treat in the Emperor's name with the Scholae of Catekharon!"

The masked figure in the linen robe stepped forward, and Caina felt the power in his mask and rod.

"I greet you, Lord Titus," said the masked man in High Nighmarian, "in the name of the Scholae of Catekharon. I am Amendris, a Sage of the Scholae." He gestured at the pale tower rising from the island. "Please, follow me. Lodgings have been prepared for both you and your men in the Tower of Study."

"Lead the way, ah...my lord Sage," said Titus.

Amendris bowed and led Titus deeper into the city, walking alongside the lord's horse. The Imperial Guards marched after them, and Halfdan started the wagon forward.

"Daughter?" he called.

Caina looked up at him.

"Go with Cormark and purchase some wine while Irene and I see to our lodgings," said Halfdan, handing her a money pouch. "There's profit in wine, and I wish to assess the market here." He lowered his voice. "And we have a...contact in Catekharon."

Caina looked around to make sure they were not overhead. "A Ghost?"

"Aye, a nightkeeper," said Halfdan. "There's no proper circle in Catekharon, but we do have a contact. A woman named Annika. She owns a pawn shop on the Street of the Crater. Find Annika and talk to her. She'll have news for us. Once you're done, rejoin me at the Tower of Study. We'll decide what to do then. The Masked Ones will reveal their weapon tomorrow, but I'd like to have more information first."

Caina nodded and went to find Corvalis.

"THIS IS," said Corvalis a short time later, "the strangest city I have ever seen."

"Most cities," said Caina, "don't have canals of molten steel flowing through them."

One of the canals flowed alongside the street. It was thirty feet deep, its stone walls carved with warding sigils, a sheet of white-hot metal flowing along its bottom. The air over the canal rippled with heat, and Caina felt a sheen of sweat upon her forehead. She supposed murder would be an easy crime to commit in Catekharon. Dump a corpse into a canal, and the evidence would burn to ashes within moments.

On the other hand, she saw Catekhari soldiers patrolling in their elaborate gray armor and red helms. And the streets seemed safe enough, lacking the air of menace in places like Cyrioch's Seatown or Marsis's dockside district.

"True," said Corvalis. "But half the buildings are abandoned. For all the size of the city, there cannot be more than fifteen or twenty thousand people living here."

"It's not surprising," said Caina. "The only reason for a city to be here is to support the Masked Ones. And it would take a daring man to traffic with sorcerers of such power." She shook her head. "I suppose some sorcerers come here to study under the Masked Ones, and build their own households."

They crossed a stone bridge over the canal of metal and came to a street curving along the edge of the lake. The massive Tower of Study rose from the island's heart, at least as tall as Black Angel Tower in Marsis. Despite all the aqueducts of molten metal, Caina saw only one causeway going to the island. Even without their sorcery, the Masked Ones possessed a defensible stronghold.

"Here we are," said Corvalis. "Perhaps Annika will be able to explain why someone would want to live here."

A row of dingy shops and taverns faced the lake. A sign painted with three golden balls hung over one of the shops, its windows shuttered. Corvalis strode to the door and pushed it open, a bell ringing overhead. The shop's interior was gloomy, lit only by a few streamers of sunlight leaking through the shutters. Shelves heavy with clothes, pots, knives, and tools lined the walls. A counter divided the shop in half, and on the other side Caina saw more valuable goods. No doubt Annika kept her most valuable wares locked in a strongbox in the cellar.

A door behind the counter opened, and a gaunt woman in an Anshani-style robe and headcloth limped into sight. She was Szaldic, and was about forty, with long gray-streaked black hair and pale blue eyes. The left side of her face drooped in a livid red scar, and she leaned upon a cane in her right hand.

"Welcome, welcome," said the woman in Anshani with a strong Szaldic accent. "You speak Anshani, yes? Good, good. If you wish for cheap goods of excellent quality, you have come to the right place." Her pale eyes took in Caina at a glance, examining her blue gown and silver earrings. "And if you wish to raise money...ah, Annika will help you. Your jewelry will fetch a fine price, and you need not turn to... disreputable methods to pay your bills."

Corvalis snorted in amusement.

"I do speak Anshani," said Caina in High Nighmarian, "but I prefer this tongue."

Annika blinked. Caina suspected very few people in Catekharon spoke High Nighmarian.

"And I do not wish to purchase goods," said Caina, "but I am curious about the shadows."

"The shadows?" said Annika in High Nighmarian.

"Does anything hide in the shadows?" said Caina.

"The Ghosts hide in the shadows," said Annika. Her hand dipped behind the counter, no doubt reaching for a weapon.

"And let the tyrants beware," said Caina.

Annika relaxed. "For the Ghosts hide in the shadows," she said, completing the countersign. Her fingers, thin and bony, drummed against the handle of her cane for a moment. "So it seems the Scholae and their weapon have drawn the attention of the Emperor himself."

"They have," said Caina. "Which is why we are here."

"Might I know your names?" said Annika.

"Of course not," said Caina, and the older woman smiled. "But you can call me Anna Callenius, and this is Cormark, a guard in my father's service. My father is a master merchant of the Imperial Collegium of jewelers, and traveled south with Lord Titus's embassy in search of trading opportunities."

"Yes," said Annika. "A fine story. And Anna is a pretty name. Though I am partial to it." She limped around the counter. "I assume you have come for information?"

"Aye," said Caina. "Anything you know about the weapon will be helpful."

Annika laughed, a harsh, rasping sound. "Very little. Still, I will tell you what I know."

"Do you know what the weapon is?" said Caina. "What it does?"

"I fear not," said Annika. "The Sages are most secretive." She waved her cane at her shelves. "I have many friends among the slaves and the poorer laborers of Catekharon. For sometimes information about their masters is far more valuable than any coin. But the Sages of the Scholae do not speak with lesser men." She frowned. "Though I can tell you who created the weapon."

"Who?"

"Zalandris will take the credit," said Annika.

"A Masked One?" said Caina. "One of these...Sages?"

"He is," said Annika. "You must understand. The Scholae, those you call the Masked Ones, are not like the Magisterium of the Empire. The Magisterium is...hierarchical, rigid, and the First Magus's word is law."

"Believe me," muttered Corvalis, "I know it well."

Annika favored him with a smile. "You do, my handsome fellow? Well, Zalandris is the Speaker of the Scholae, the chief of the Sages... but the Scholae is an assembly of equals. He holds little authority over them, and his chief responsibility is dealing with outsiders so the Sages can study without the burden of temporal affairs."

"So this Zalandris," said Caina, "created the weapon, and offered it for sale to the various nations entirely under his own authority?"

"He did," said Annika. "Most of the Sages would not have approved. But I doubt Zalandris did it of his own volition. Mihaela likely drove it to him."

"Mihaela," said Caina. There had been a hint of bitterness in Annika's voice. Mihaela was a Szaldic name, like Annika. Ark and Tanya had been planning to name their next child Mihaela, if it was a girl. "Another Sage?"

"No," said Annika. "She is one of Zalandris's Seekers."

"Seekers?" said Corvalis. "Is that...like an initiate of the Magisterium? A student?"

"You see keenly," said Annika. "The Scholae has two levels. The Sages are the masters, the ones who have passed the trials and earned the right to wear the mask and carry the rod. There are no more than three hundred Sages, to my knowledge, and by some secret science they live for centuries."

"Necromancy," said Caina.

"No," said Annika. "The Sages forbid necromancy. From what I understand they fled from the Maatish necromancers long ago, so necromancy is the one arcane science forbidden in Catekharon." She rubbed at her hip for a moment. "The Seekers are the sorcerers the Sages deign to accept as students. Some come for only a few years, learn what they need, and depart. Others aspire to become Sages themselves. Very few ever do. The Sages are selective, and set rigorous trials." She grunted. "I urge you to beware the Seekers. The Sages themselves are not very dangerous unless provoked."

"You are certain of this?" said Caina, remembering the Masked One who had attacked her in Cyrioch. Had he been a full Sage? Or a renegade Seeker who had stolen a mask and a rod?

"I am," said Annika. "The Sages ignore lesser men unless threatened...but the Seekers do not. Many of them have burning ambition, and hope to master the secrets of the Sages, return to their homelands, and exact vengeance upon their foes. A few even think to transform themselves into gods through sorcery."

Caina thought of Maglarion. She knew he had spent decades traveling outside the Empire. Had he studied as a Seeker at one time?

"So," she said, pushing aside the memories of Maglarion. "You think the Seeker Mihaela is the one who convinced Zalandris to announce this weapon and sell it to the highest bidder?"

"I am certain of it," said Annika.

"How?" said Corvalis.

Annika sighed. "Because she is my younger sister."

Caina blinked in surprise.

"You see," said Annika, "my sister and I were born in the Empire, in Varia Province. When the Istarish slavers raided the coasts, she and I were taken captive and sold to a cruel magus living in Cyrica Urbana. Eventually, the Ghost circle helped us escape, and I hoped to make my way back home. But Mihaela...Mihaela had manifested the power. She had talent for sorcery, and wished to learn. But we hated the Magisterium, the College of Alchemists of Istarinmul does not accept women, and the occultists of Anshan kill any women with arcane talent. So we made the long journey to Catekharon, and we have remained ever since."

"You and your sister are estranged," said Caina. "Why?"

Annika sighed. "My face. It reminds her that we were once slaves. Her pride has grown with her power. She does not like to be reminded that she was once a slave. We have not spoken in years."

"A cruel story," said Caina. "I am sorry."

Annika laughed. "Do not mourn for me, Ghost. I was born in a peasant village, and grew up a slave." She waved her cane at the walls of the shop. "Let not my humble shop fool you. I have more money and influence than you think." She smiled. "In Catekharon, only the Scholae would dare to cross Annika the Szald."

"I can believe that," said Corvalis.

"Thank you for your help," said Caina. "The embassy is staying at the Tower of Study. If you learn anything, can you send word at once? Ask for Anna Callenius...and say you have found the silver candle-sticks I wished to purchase."

"It shall be done," said Annika. "And a warning, Ghost."

"What is it?" said Caina.

"Beware," said Annika. "My sister has grown ruthless. And this business with the weapon...it is very strange. The Scholae ignores the outside world. For the Scholae to invite embassies, to offer to sell an artifact of their sciences to a foreign prince...it makes no sense. It has never happened in my lifetime, or in the lifetime of anyone I have ever known. Something dangerous is happening."

"I know," said Caina. "And I intend to find out what it is. Thank you, Annika."

She left without another word, Corvalis following.

If Zalandris or Mihaela had indeed made a weapon of terrible power, Caina would see it dropped into one of the rivers of molten steel.

～

THAT NIGHT CAINA sat alone on a wooden balcony, looking at the glow of molten metal rising from the city. Halfdan, Corvalis, and Irene had gone to attend Lord Titus, but Caina had stayed behind to rest. The constant aura of overwhelming sorcery had given her a splitting headache, so bad that white light flashed whenever she closed her eyes.

The Imperial Guard cohort had been housed in a barracks of the Redhelms, Catekharon's gray-armored soldiers. Lord Titus and his guests had been given fine rooms in one of the strange wooden palaces upon the stone terraces. Caina had never seen anything quite like the palace. The exterior walls had been built of thick wood, but the interior walls had been fashioned of thin wood and paper. The rooms had no doors, only panels of wood and paper that slid aside at a touch. Colorful glass lanterns hung from the rafters, glowing with a sorcerous light.

Caina rubbed her temples.

Gods, but her head hurt. The aura of sorcery was much, much stronger upon the island, and she felt something of awesome power within the Tower of Study. Caina supposed it was the greater fire elemental that the Masked Ones had bound into their service. That explained both the rivers of molten steel and why the city had never fallen. When summoned, elemental spirits either inhabited a human host or constructed a body out an appropriate substance. With the greater fire elemental, the Masked Ones could summon an army of lesser fire elementals...and the lesser spirits would manifest within the molten steel.

An army fashioned of molten metal, burning its way through foes of flesh and blood, was a terrible thought.

And if the Masked Ones possessed such power, why would they need any additional weapons?

She heard the rasp of a footstep against the hallway's polished floorboards.

"Mistress?" said a soft voice.

Caina stood, her hand going to one of the throwing knives hidden in her sleeve.

A man of about twenty stood in the doorway, clad in the orange tunic of a slave, a tray in his hands. A steaming kettle and a pair of clay cups rested on the tray. The slave looked Anshani, with dark hair and eyes and olive-colored skin.

"Yes?" said Caina, making herself relax.

"Your honored father Master Basil has sent me to you, mistress," said the slave. "He said you did not feel well, and bade me to bring you this."

Caina smiled. "Tea?"

"No, mistress," said the slave. "It is called coffee, a drink of Anshan. May I pour it for you?"

"Very well," said Caina, watching the slave.

Something about him seemed off.

Most the slaves she had met had taken great care to never show their emotions around their masters, lest they earn punishment. Yet this man seemed distressed, almost grieved, his eyes red-rimmed. For a moment Caina wondered if he was an assassin, but he looked too nervous.

"If you sit, mistress, I will serve you," said the slave.

"I will stand, thank you," said Caina.

The man blinked in surprise. Caina wondered how often he heard someone thank him. He poured a dark, steaming liquid into the cup and handed it to her. "Please, mistress, drink. Your father will be pleased."

Caina frowned, sniffed the coffee, and took a sip.

"That's..." She thought it over. "That's not bad."

The slave smiled. "I am glad, mistress."

"What is your name?" said Caina.

Again the slave looked startled. "Ah...Shaizid, mistress. I am owned by the learned Zalandris, a Sage of the Scholae, the blessings of the Living Flame be upon him."

Caina took another sip of coffee. "This smells like death, but it tastes better than it should."

All the emotion drained out of Shaizid's face.

"What?" said Caina, looking around, half-expecting to see a lurking assassin. "What is it?"

"Forgive me, mistress," said Shaizid, "but I must return to my duties."

The slave all but fled from the room.

Caina gave the coffee a dubious look. Had it been poisoned? But if the Masked Ones wanted to kill anyone in the embassy, they would kill Lord Titus, not the younger daughter of a merchant. And even if the Masked Ones had figured out that the Ghosts had infiltrated the embassy, they would start by killing Halfdan.

She looked at the glow of the molten metal and shook her head. If the Masked Ones wanted her dead, they wouldn't need anything so mundane as poison.

At least the coffee helped her headache.

~

THAT NIGHT CAINA dreamed again of the empty plain of gray mist.

The Moroaica awaited her, her eyes black and cold, a faint smile on her red lips.

"What is it now?" said Caina. "Why have you brought me here?"

The Moroaica shrugged. "I know not. You brought me here."

"I did nothing of the sort," said Caina.

"Whether you did consciously or not," said Jadriga, "your will summoned me." Her smile took a mocking edge. "Tonight you did not have that assassin to share your bed and work you to exhaustion."

Caina said nothing. She knew that Jadriga could see through her eyes and hear through her ears. The thought that Jadriga had seen everything Caina had shared with Corvalis was not something she wanted to contemplate.

"I suspect," said the Moroaica, "that your thoughts were upon sorcery as you slept...and so your will reached for me. For I know more about sorcery than any other living being."

"The Masked Ones might know more," said Caina.

Jadriga laughed. "The Scholae are fools, little more than relics of Maat. They are mere shadows of the power once wielded by the necromancers of the Kingdom of the Rising Sun." She tilted her head to the side, considering. "But useful fools nonetheless."

"Why?" said Caina. "Is this weapon your work?"

"Mine?" said the Moroaica. "I have had no hand in the creation of their miserable little weapon. But they will aid me nonetheless. Soon, child of the Ghosts, soon you will see my great work come to pass... and you will see this corrupt and vile world remade in a new form."

She gestured, and Caina sank into a black and dreamless sleep.

7

SORCERERS

The next afternoon Caina realized the rivers of molten steel gave the Masked Ones an important advantage.

They had no shortage of hot water for baths.

Her room featured an enormous stone tub, large enough for two people. Caina had not taken a proper bath since leaving Cyrioch, and she scrubbed the away accumulated grime and sweat with vigor. After that, she drew a second bath, closed her eyes, and leaned against the side of the tub, enjoying the warmth that soaked into her limbs.

It almost made her forget her headache.

She considered inviting Corvalis to join her, but regretfully decided against it. The orange-clad slaves of the Scholae were every-where, and no matter how unworldly Annika thought the Masked Ones, Caina was sure at least some of the slaves spied for their masters. A mercenary guard slipping into the room of his employer's daughter might be beneath the notice of the Masked Ones...or it might not.

And Caina had no doubt the Masked Ones' spells could pry secrets from the minds of their victims with ease.

After her bath, she dried off before the mirror in her bedchamber

and dressed herself. When she had masqueraded as Countess Mari-
anna Nereide, she had the help of servants to dress. Anna Callenius
had no such luxury, but fortunately the garb of a merchant's
daughter was less elaborate than that of a noblewoman. Over her
shift she donned a blue dress with black trim upon the sleeves and
hem, its neckline just high enough to remain within the bounds of
propriety. Around her waist went a belt of black leather, holding a
single sheathed dagger. She arranged her hair in an elaborate crown,
pinned it in place, and donned silver earrings with sapphires and a
silver chain around her throat.

Beneath her sleeves she hid sheathed throwing daggers, and
concealed a pair of slender daggers in the sides of her high-heeled
boots.

After she finished, Caina examined herself in the mirror. She saw
no trace of a Ghost nightfighter, or of the Balarigar, or a caravan
guard, or any of the other myriad disguises she had used. Instead she
saw the pretty young daughter of a prosperous merchant, dressed to
draw the eye of a powerful and wealthy husband.

She looked a great deal like her mother.

Caina shuddered. Her mother had often worn blue to match her
eyes, just as Caina did.

She put aside the thought and left her room, walking to join the
others on the terrace outside the palace. The molten metal illumi-
nated the city in the distance, the waters of the lake rippling in the
moonlight. Halfdan and Corvalis stood at the edge of the terrace,
while Claudia awaited nearby, clad in a high-collared green gown,
jewels sparkling in her ears and golden hair.

"Ah, daughter," said Halfdan. "You look lovely. Surely I shall have
two wealthy men for sons-in-law by the end of the year."

Corvalis bowed over her hand and kissed it, a gesture which,
Caina noted with amusement, let him look right down the front of
her dress. "Yes. My master is indeed a fortunate man."

Claudia sniffed. "I would like to think I have more to offer than
mere beauty."

Caina could not decide if that was an insult or not.

"Oh, indeed," said Halfdan. "A clever daughter is a jewel beyond price. As a jeweler, I ought to know. Now, come. Let us see what kind of weapon the Masked Ones would sell to the highest bidder."

AT THE INVITATION of the Scholae, the various ambassadors and their entourages gathered in the Hall of Assembly, on the ground level of the massive Tower of Study. Lord Titus strode inside, flanked by six of his bodyguards and six of the Imperial Guards. Halfdan followed him, stern and sober in his merchant's robe, and Caina, Claudia, and Corvalis walked after. Lord Titus wore an expression of Imperial dignity, suitable for a lord of high Nighmarian birth.

But even Titus Iconias's stern expression dissolved into astonishment when he saw the Hall of Assembly.

Caina could not blame him.

The Hall was huge, easily the size of the Praetorian Basilica in Malarae, its walls and floor and ceiling covered in gleaming white stone. A river of molten steel flowed down the center of the hall, divided by three bridges, and Caina felt the presence of the potent warding spells that kept the heat from cooking everyone in the room. The far end of the hall opened into a vast cylindrical chamber of white stone, and Caina saw a round pool of molten steel shimmering there, covering fully half the floor.

A dozen different streams of glowing metal came from the pool and flowed into different directions, no doubt towards the aqueducts heading for the city itself.

"Gods," whispered Claudia. "The amount of sorcerous power it takes to maintain that...the entire Magisterium combined could not manage it."

Caina believed her. Her skin crawled and tingled, so sharply that it sometimes felt as if she walked into a wind of needles.

"That is interesting," said Halfdan, "but at the moment, I more interested in who has respond to the gracious invitation of the Scholae."

Caina followed his gaze. A group of Anshani nobles waited near one of the bridges, clad in fine silks and gleaming armor. A large man stood at their head, his hand resting upon the hilt of his scimitar, his face cold and cruel beneath a graying beard. Caina thought the Anshani khadjar looked familiar.

Then it clicked.

"That's Nadirah's father, isn't it?" said Caina, remembering the renegade Anshani occultist lurking in the slums of Cyrioch. "Arsakan, the Shahenshah's brother."

"Gods, you're right," said Corvalis. "I see the resemblance now."

"If the Shahenshah sent his favorite brother," said Halfdan, "then he indeed takes this seriously."

"They all did," said Corvalis. "I see embassies from the Kyracians, the Istarish, Alqaarin, the other free cities..."

"Come," said Halfdan, glancing to the side. Lord Titus stood speaking with one of the Sages. "The foreign princes will have brought their own merchants and spies. It would be unseemly, of course, for us to approach men of lordly rank. But everyone expects merchants to gossip and seek advantage...and, perhaps, to gain some information?"

"And that," said Caina, "is how we shall discover the intentions of the other embassies?"

"Did I not say," said Halfdan, "that a clever daughter is worth more than jewels?"

He strode into the crowds, Caina and the others following.

KYLON LOOKED through the Hall of Assembly, trying to keep his arcane senses under control.

It was difficult.

Power, incredible power, radiated from the pool of molten metal in the round chamber. Kylon knew how in desperation the last Archon of Old Kyrace had broken the binding upon the greater fire elemental beneath the city, destroying both Old Kyrace and the invading Imperial army.

And most of the island upon which Old Kyrace had stood.

"Gods of the brine," whispered Cimon. He stood with Alcios of House Kallias, and both men gazed with consternation at the river of molten metal. "Could these Sages have truly harnessed the power of a greater fire elemental?"

"Let us hope so," said Kylon. "Else the city will explode."

Both men gave him an alarmed look, and he stifled a grim laugh.

"No," said Kylon, "it's not the Masked Ones who are the danger here. If they wanted to conquer the world with their sorcery, they would have done so already. No, it's whoever purchases this damnable weapon. That is the true danger. We must ensure that New Kyre obtains the weapon, my lords."

Both Cimon and Alcios nodded, yet the words felt empty upon Kylon's lips. The Masked Ones' weapon, whatever it was, was too powerful for mortal hands to wield. Kylon had seen the cost of seeking such power.

He remembered Andromache dying upon the floor of Scorikhon's tomb.

"Come," said Kylon. "I suppose it is only polite to greet our fellow ambassadors."

He started across the floor, making for one of the bridges over the molten steel. An honor guard of six ashtairoi accompanied them, their cuirasses and helms polished to mirror brightness. Kylon extended his arcane senses as much as he dared, at least enough to sense the emotions of the men and women around him.

For mortal men were but water...and Kylon's peculiar talents let him sense it.

Tension, fear, and anger washed over his senses. The various ambassadors maintained airs of polite interest, but Kylon detected their fears. He also felt the vast power gathered in the Masked Ones, and the arcane strength of some of the ambassadors.

Sorcerers of power had gathered at the Scholae's invitation.

His eyes wandered over the embassy from the Empire of Nighmar. Would it come to blows between the Imperials and the Kyracians? Kylon had inflicted a grievous defeat upon the Imperial fleet, and doubtless whatever lord commanded the embassy would recognize Kylon. And if the Kyracian and Imperial embassies fought, the Masked Ones would expel them from the city.

Perhaps that would be for the best. At the least, it would keep the weapon from falling into the hands of the Empire.

He decided to greet the Anshani embassy first. Anshan sold a great deal of grain to New Kyre, and in exchange, the Kyracian fleets did not harass Anshan's merchant shipping. If the Shahenshah decided to push away New Kyre, it would be disastrous.

Kylon spotted the Anshani ambassador, a tall, stern man in scale armor with a gray beard, took a step towards him...and stopped.

Something familiar brushed against his arcane senses.

"Lord thalarchon?" said Alcios.

"A moment," said Kylon.

The emotional presence against his senses felt like a sheet of ice covering a pit of lava. Iron self-control and discipline, a mind cold and cunning like a blade of ice. Yet a heart that burned with fury.

"Her," said Kylon.

The Ghost was here.

~

"Master Basil," murmured Claudia, her voice urgent. "That man? I think he is an Anshani occultist."

"How do you know?" said Corvalis.

"Look at his shadow," said Caina. "Or, rather, his shadows."

The gaunt man in the elaborate black Anshani robe was seven feet tall, towering even over Arsakan and his anjars. A long gray beard hung to his belt, and his black eyes glittered like disks of stone. Every man and woman in the Hall had a shadow thrown by the molten river's glow.

The man in the black robe had three of them. They rotated him slowly, like dogs circling around their master. The other Anshani, even Arsakan, kept well away from the shadows. If Caina concentrated, she felt the cold, dark sorcery crackling around the man.

"Gods," said Corvalis. "Just like Nadirah."

"That," said Halfdan, "is not any occultist. That is Yaramzod the Black himself, brother of Arsakan and the Shahenshah, and the most powerful sorcerer in Anshan."

"I see why Marzhod was so frightened of him," said Caina. There was not a hint of mercy or compassion in Yaramzod's face, only cold contempt and arrogance.

"Some of the most powerful sorcerers in the world have come at the Scholae's invitation," said Halfdan. "You see there, with the Istarish emir? That is Callatas, a master alchemist of Istarinmul's College of Alchemists. He is at least two hundred years old."

Callatas was short, his hair hidden beneath an elaborate turban, his white robes crisp and brilliant and glittering with jewels. And like Yaramzod, she saw no trace of mercy or kindness in that proud face. Around the alchemist and the emir stood hulking men in black plate armor, their helms wrought in the likeness of grinning skulls. A pale blue glow came from the eyes of their helmets. They were the Immortals, the elite bodyguards of the Padishah and his favorites, and alchemical elixirs enhanced their strength and speed...but also induced homicidal fury and a sadistic delight in pain.

She remembered fighting the Immortals in the streets of Marsis. For a moment the entire dreadful battle flashed before her eyes. The running and the fighting, the screams of dying men and terrified women. Sicarion's mocking laugh. Andromache's lightning ripping from the sky, the freezing mist dancing around Kylon's sword as he hunted her...

Even as the memories flickered through her mind, she saw the Kyracian embassy walking towards Lord Titus.

And she saw the man leading the Kyracian embassy.

Her expression remained calm, but every muscle in her body tensed, and her hands twitched towards the throwing knives in her sleeves. Halfdan and Claudia, distracted by the embassies, did not notice, but Corvalis did.

"What is it?" he whispered.

Kylon of House Kardamnos was speaking with Lord Titus.

KYLON SKETCHED a short bow before Titus Iconias. The stout Nighmarian lord watched him with a cold expression, as did his Imperial Guards.

"I am Kylon, High Seat of House Kardamnos," said Kylon, "lord thalarchon of the seventh fleet, and Lord Ambassador of the Archons and the Assembly to the Scholae of Catekharon."

Titus gave the exact same shallow bow, like a man saluting his opponent before a duel. "And I am Titus, Lord of House Iconias, twice Lord Governor of Caeria Majoria, three times Lord Governor of Mardonia Inferior, twice Lord Commander of the Ninth Legion, and the Emperor's Lord Ambassador to the Scholae of Catekharon."

"You do me honor," said Kylon, his eyes scanning Titus's entourage.

Where was the Ghost hiding?

"As do you," said Titus. "We did not expect the Assembly to send the Shipbreaker himself."

"Some have named me such," said Kylon. He saw Titus's own bodyguards and the black-armored Imperial Guards in their plumed helmets. Behind them stood a middle-aged man in merchant's robe, a pair of young women in rich gowns, and a lean man in chain mail. A Nighmarian merchant, his daughters, and their guard, Kylon surmised.

No sign of the Ghost.

"And why should they not name you such?" said Titus. "For you have certainly broken a great many of my Emperor's ships. And my Emperor does not forget such losses."

"Nor should he," said Kylon. "Many brave men died."

His eyes fell upon the younger of the two women. She was short and slender, clad in a black-trimmed blue gown with a plunging neckline, jewels glinting in her ears and at her throat. She looked like a pretty, empty-headed woman with no more ambition than catching a powerful husband. Certainly nothing like the Ghost he had seen in Marsis.

But he felt the woman's icy emotions.

"And many more men died," said Titus, "when your city and the Padishah of Istarinmul betrayed our treaties and attacked Marsis. Many men, and many women and children, as well."

"Yes," said Kylon, still looking at the merchant's black-haired daughter. "I was there. The plan was my sister's, for both she and Rezir Shahan sought to seize Marsis in one bold stroke. Yet they failed and are dead. And now the rest of us are left to fight the war they began."

"You sound almost as if you disapprove," said Titus, glancing over his shoulder to see what Kylon was staring at. A brief smirk crossed his face. No doubt he thought Kylon infatuated.

"May I be blunt, my lord?" said Kylon, not waiting for a reply. "This war benefits neither of us."

Alcios scowled and cleared his throat.

"A curious thing to say," said Titus, "given that you have won most of the victories."

Kylon shrugged. "To what avail? The Empire is vast. We cannot conquer it. And New Kyre is far from the Empire, and your fleets cannot reach us. We bleed each other to little gain."

For a moment Titus appeared surprised. "I had not expected to hear that, Kylon of House Kardamnos. You speak more wisdom than I expected. Perhaps I shall have glad tidings to bring back to my Emperor." He scowled. "Unless the weapon of the Masked Ones destroys us all."

"Yes," said Kylon. "That."

The black-haired woman looked at him.

It was her. She looked nothing like the exhausted, sweaty, bloody, black-clad figure he had seen in Marsis. But he recognized those cold blue eyes.

She was the Ghost.

"If you will forgive me, my lord," said Kylon, "may I speak to one of your followers? The merchant and I have had dealings in the past."

"What?" said Titus. "Yes, of course."

"My lord High Seat, my lord stormdancer," said Kylon, "please keep Lord Titus company while I am gone."

They blinked at him in astonishment, but nodded.

Kylon stepped before the merchant, who made a deep bow. The Ghost watched him without expression, and the lean man in chain mail glared at him.

"My lord High Seat," said the merchant, "you do me honor. I am Basil Callenius, a master merchant of the Imperial Collegium of jewelers. Once peace returns to our two nations, I would be most honored to offer you my wares." He gestured at the women. "These are my daughters, Irene and Anna."

"Thank you," said Kylon. Undoubtedly the merchant was a Ghost himself. "I wish to speak with your daughter Anna for a moment." He hesitated. "She...knew my late sister."

Basil looked at the Ghost.

"Of course, Father," she said, her expression calm. "It would be my honor."

"Please," said Kylon. "Walk with me."

CAINA SAID nothing as she walked with Kylon along the far wall of the Hall of Assembly. Some of the other ambassadors shot them amused looks. No doubt they thought Kylon infatuated or seeking an easy romantic conquest.

She knew better.

He looked different. It had been only a year since the attack on Marsis, but Kylon looked older, his expression grimmer.

Would he try to kill her for what had happened to Andromache?

"Did you find him?" said Kylon at last in Kyracian.

"Who?" said Caina in the same language.

"The boy," said Kylon. "The son of your friend." She saw his sword hand curl into a fist. "The boy you defeated my sister and slew Rezir Shahan to save."

"I did," said Caina. "He lives with his mother and father in Malarae now, and is apprenticed in his father's foundry." She paused for a moment. "His father is the Champion of Marsis."

Kylon's response was half-laugh, half-sigh. "Indeed? The gods have peculiar humor. You defeated Andromache and slew Rezir to save the boy, and I assume his father slew Kleistheon to save his son. Had that boy and his father been elsewhere, Marsis would have fallen."

"Perhaps," said Caina. "Yet I didn't defeat Andromache. She defeated herself."

"I know," said Kylon. They stopped, the glow from the metal throwing harsh shadows over his face. "I could not blame you. Or myself. Taking vengeance upon either of us would have been pointless." He took a deep breath. "Andromache...made her own decisions. And those decisions led her to ruin."

"So instead," said Caina, "you decided to take vengeance upon the Empire."

"By destroying the fleets?" said Kylon. "Andromache started the war, but it has outlived her. Your Empire would destroy New Kyre if it could, Ghost. You know that as well as I do. So even though Andromache started the war for nothing, I will fight to defend my city from destruction."

"That is why you are here, isn't it?" said Caina. "To obtain the weapon for New Kyre."

Kylon scowled. "If I must. And that is the same reason you are here."

"No," said Caina. "I will destroy the weapon, if I can."

"Rather than give it to your Emperor?" said Kylon. "If it is as powerful as the Masked Ones claim, the Emperor could use it to destroy all of his enemies."

"Andromache thought the power in the Tomb of Scorikhon would her destroy all of her enemies," said Caina, "and you saw how that ended."

Kylon said nothing for a moment, and Caina shot a glance over his shoulder. She saw Halfdan speaking with some Istarish merchants as Yaramzod and Callatas conversed, but Corvalis was watching her. Probably ready to aid her if Kylon attacked.

She appreciated the gesture, but Kylon could cut down both her and Corvalis in a matter of seconds.

"Perhaps you are right," said Kylon. "It would be better if the weapon was destroyed. But you and I will be the only ones to think that. Certainly the others will do what is necessary to claim it." He took a deep breath. "I cannot allow the Empire to have the weapon. Not for any reason. Because if the Empire takes it, New Kyre will be destroyed."

"If," said Caina, "the weapon truly exists."

Kylon titled his head to the side. "You think it does not?"

"The Masked Ones must have something," said Caina. "Else why summon us here? But if they have such a powerful weapon, why sell it? Why not keep it?"

"I do not know," said Kylon. "I will think on what you have said, Ghost."

He walked back to the other Kyracians. Caina watched him for a moment, and then returned to Halfdan and the others.

"Who was that?" said Corvalis.

"Kylon Shipbreaker," said Halfdan.

Corvalis's eyes got a little wider. "You know him?"

Caina nodded. "We tried to kill each other in Marsis." She looked at Halfdan. "We might be able to convince him to help destroy the weapon."

Claudia frowned. "A Kyracian stormdancer?"

"He has seen firsthand what too much arcane power can do to a woman," said Caina.

She expected Claudia to take offense at that, but Claudia had stopped paying attention. She stared at the entrance to the Hall of Assembly, all the blood draining from her face. Caina turned, her hands twitching towards her weapons.

Men in black robes with red sashes strode through the door,

flanked by soldiers in ornate black armor. Their breastplates bore the sigil of an opened book with a lidless eye resting upon the pages.

The sigil of the Imperial Magisterium.

"The magi?" said Corvalis. "What are they doing here?"

That made no sense. The Empire had already sent an embassy with Lord Titus. But the Magisterium considered itself the rightful ruler of the Empire. And if the Magisterium could get its hands on the weapon of the Masked Ones, Caina had no doubt the First Magus would use it to seize control of the Empire.

"Oh, gods," said Claudia. "Father is here."

Corvalis said nothing, but Caina saw the muscles around his eyes tighten.

A fat man in a black robe walked in the midst of the magi, a purple sash around his waist. Even from a distance, Caina saw the family resemblance. The man had the same green eyes and blond hair as Corvalis and Claudia. And he had the same arrogant, cruel expression as Callatas and Yaramzod.

The same utter certainty of his own arcane might.

For the first time Caina looked at Decius Aberon, the First Magus of the Imperial Magisterium.

"Irene, Cormark," said Halfdan. "We've made a mistake. We should have expected the Magisterium to send its own embassy. Get back to our rooms, now, and stay there until I send for you. If the First Magus sees you, we're..."

The doors to the Hall of Assembly boomed shut, a half-dozen Redhelms standing before the exit.

"My lords and ladies!" said a dry voice, amplified through a spell. "All our guests have arrived, and the doors to the Hall have been sealed! We can now deliberate in privacy...and show you the weapon that will remake the world forever."

8

A DEMONSTRATION

C aina turned, as did everyone else in the Hall.

A Masked One in a white linen robe stood atop one of the bridges over the river of steel, face hidden behind an ornate jade mask. Unlike the other Masked Ones, the Sage wore a golden collar wrought in the shape of falcon's wings around his neck. Near him stood a half-dozen other Sages, silvery rods in hand.

Caina saw Khaltep Irzaris standing at the foot of the bridge, watching the Masked Ones.

"I bid you welcome," said the Masked One with the golden collar, "in the name of the Sages of the Scholae of Catekharon. I am Zalandris, the Speaker of the Scholae, and it is my task to treat without outsiders. By custom, those who attain the degree of Sage do not remove their masks in public. But since this is not the custom in your lands, I will accommodate your mores."

His tone was patronizing. Like a stern teacher condescending to supervise a game among his students. He drew aside his mask, revealing a thin, lined face with a wispy white beard. He looked like a kindly grandfather, and his expression lacked the hardened cruelty Caina had seen in the First Magus and Yaramzod and the others.

Decius Aberon stepped forward, gazing at the unmasked Sage with hard eyes.

"You might be wondering," said Zalandris, "why we have invited you here. The Scholae has only rarely interfered in the affairs of the outside world. We have promised you a weapon of sorcery, a weapon so potent that its wielder shall dominate the world."

Silence answered him, the lords and sorcerers glancing at each other.

"Perhaps you thought this a trick or some sort of game," said Zalandris. "I assure you it is not. The weapon is very real. But we do not sell it for motives of crass profit or mere political power. Rather, we sell it to you for a higher purpose. This weapon will end all war forever."

Caina blinked in surprise.

"This weapon is so terrible," said Zalandris, "so potent, that it will put an end to all war. No more will men lift swords and spears against each other. Fear of this weapon will ensure that peace reigns over the world."

Caina stared at the Sage, incredulous. She had considered theory after theory to explain why the Masked Ones would create such a weapon and then sell it. A ploy to conquer the world? A trick to kill the most powerful sorcerers of neighboring lands?

She had never seriously considered that the Masked Ones were naive.

"These are bold claims, I know," said Zalandris, "but you shall see the truth of them with your own eyes. Come this way, please."

He left the bridge and strode deeper into the Tower of Study, and the various ambassadors and sorcerers followed him.

~

ZALANDRIS LED them to the balcony of a smaller hall. No molten rivers of steel flowed through this hall, and dozens of sorcerous lanterns hung suspended on chains from the ceiling. Looking over the balcony's ornate stone railing, Caina saw dozens men in ragged clothing standing forty feet below. All of them carried weapons and shields, and looked at each other with wary expressions.

At the other end of the hall stood a peculiar metal statue.

The thing was twenty feet tall and had been crafted in the shape of a warrior clad head-to-toe in plate armor. Red plate armor, in fact, which explained who had purchased Irzaris's shipments of red Nhabati iron. Hundreds of Maatish hieroglyphs adorned the statue. The thing must have weighed tons, and Caina wondered if the floor had been reinforced to support the weight.

She felt a potent aura of sorcerous power around the statue.

Zalandris strode to the railing, and a silence fell over the ambassadors. The ragged men looked up, fear on their faces.

"Gods," whispered Caina.

"What is it?" said Corvalis. The First Magus and his party stood twenty yards further down the balcony. As far as Caina could tell, neither the First Magus nor any of the magi had noticed Corvalis and Claudia.

"He's going to use the weapon on them," said Caina. "This is...this is a demonstration."

"My lords and ladies!" said Zalandris. "Look below you. The Redhelms arrested these forty-seven men for capital crimes. Some for murder, some for kidnapping free citizens to unlawfully sell as slaves, some for rape. In Catekharon, men guilty of these crimes go to the gallows. However, a new world is at hand, a world free of war and battle. Therefore, as Speaker of the Scholae, I have decreed that these men shall have a chance to live. They will face our new weapon, and if they can overcome it, I shall set them free. "

"A gladiatorial contest?" said the First Magus. His voice was resonant, commanding, and filled with scorn. "You had us travel all this way to watch a damn gladiatorial contest?"

"Aye!" shouted one of the ragged criminals. "Hope you enjoy the show, you fat bastard! Come down here and I'll..."

Decius Aberon's expression did not change as he flicked a single finger, and Caina felt a surge of sorcerous power. The criminal's throat exploded in a spray of blood beneath a blast of psychokinetic force, and the ragged man collapsed to the white stone floor.

"Does anyone else," said the First Magus, "have any other amusing comments? I so enjoy witticisms."

None of the other criminals spoke.

"First Magus," said Zalandris, "please refrain from killing the prisoners. This will reduce the efficacy of the demonstration."

"My apologies, my lord Speaker," said Decius with a florid bow. "Please continue."

"The demonstration," said Zalandris, sweeping his rod over the railing, "will now begin."

The criminals tensed, and the ambassadors craned their necks.

Nothing happened.

"This," said Yaramzod the Black, his voice like the rasp of dead leaves on a tomb floor, "is an utter waste of time."

And as the echo of his words died away, the hieroglyphs upon the crimson statue flared with white light.

A spike of arcane power shot through Caina, so fierce that it made her dizzy, and she had to grab Corvalis's arm to keep from falling over.

And then the metal statue moved.

It took one step forward, and then another, the stone floor ringing with the impact. The hieroglyphs at its joints flared brighter, and the masked helm of its face swiveled back and forth, examining the prisoners. Caina stared in astonishment. The thing was enormous. It couldn't possibly move under its own power.

Yet it did.

"Kill it!" screamed one of the prisoners. "Kill the damned thing and we go free!"

The men charged with yells, weapons raised, and began striking. Metal clanged as they rained blows with their maces and swords upon the statue's armor. Yet they did no damage to it. She supposed if they hammered enough, they could eventually pry away some of the armor, but...

"A walking statue?" said Decius with a laugh. "Such a wonder, my lord Speaker. Perhaps you can show us a wind-up monkey next? Do..."

The statue moved.

And it moved far faster than anything that large should be able to move.

A steel fist crashed into one of the men. The man's head, shoulders, and most of his chest exploded into a red mist, and what was left of the criminal fell in a bloody heap to the ground. The statue's armored foot came down and smashed another man to a gory heap.

For a moment the criminals frozen in stunned silence.

And then the killing began in earnest.

The steel statue moved through the criminals in a whirlwind, killing with every step. Its fists turned men to bloody pulp, its armored boots smashing skulls and ribs. Some of the men screamed and flung themselves at the statue, striking at its cuirass and helmet. But the statue simply reached up and crushed the criminals one by one, like a child squeezing ripe fruit. Others fled and tried to hide beneath the balcony, or fell to their knees and pleaded for mercy.

It did no good. One by one, the animated statue hunted down the men.

The stench of blood and ruptured bowels filled the air.

Caina watched the carnage with horrified fascination. She was no stranger to violence, yet she had never seen such brutal killing, had never witnessed a weapon that could rip men to bloody pulp. Not even the strongest warrior could fight such a thing. Even a powerful magus could do little against several tons of animated steel.

She saw Decius Aberon gazing at the spectacle, seeming amused and intrigued. The other ambassadors were fascinated, and Caina saw a few of them casting the spell to sense the presence of sorcery, no doubt hoping to probe the spells binding the moving statue. Kylon watched the bloodletting without expression, his hand resting on the hilt of his sword.

Caina heard a retching noise, and saw that Claudia had ducked into the corner to throw up.

The metal statue caught the last criminal by the leg and lifted the screaming man, letting him dangle over the floor. It gripped his other leg and yanked.

The resultant mess fell in a wet heap to the floor.

Stunned silence fell over the hall.

Zalandris clapped his hands once. Hidden doors opened in the hall below, and dozens of orange-clad slaves hurried out to clean up the mess.

The statue's faceless helm rotated to stare at him.

"As you can see," said Zalandris, "the glypharmor is most potent. These were violent men, accustomed to fighting. Yet they perished in a matter of moments. Weapons of wood and steel cannot harm the glypharmor, and only the most exceedingly potent sorcery can even begin to damage it. An entire Imperial Legion could not stand against it."

The slaves labored to clean up the gore, using some sort of powder to soak up the blood.

"So," said Yaramzod in his dry voice. His shadows twitched and whispered around him, and the other sorcerers and ambassadors gave him a wide berth. "What manner of creature is this? A spirit bound within steel? Even the most inept occultist could conjure up a spirit and bind it within a simulacra."

"Or a summoned elemental?" said the older stormdancer standing next to Kylon. "In ancient times, the stormsingers of Old Kyrace possessed the skill to call up elementals and bind them within material bodies."

"Skill," said the First Magus with a smirk, "that New Kyre has lost."

Yaramzod let out a hissing laugh, his shadows rotating around him. "A skill that your own Magisterium has not yet regained, First Magus."

"I fear you are both incorrect," said Zalandris. He lifted his voice. "Mihaela!"

The red statue shivered, the white light in the hieroglyphs fading away. Caina heard a series of loud clicks, and the statue's head rolled back, its cuirass splitting apart and swinging open like a door.

Suddenly she understood. The weapon was not a statue. It was not an elemental spirit bound within material form.

It was a suit of armor.

A woman climbed down from the armor and dropped to the floor, ignoring both the slaves and the blood. She was a tall, lean Szaldic woman of about thirty-five, and wore a peculiar costume of black boots, trousers, and a black leather vest that left her arms bare. Tattoos marked her muscular arms, and her black hair hung in ragged strands to her shoulders. Cool blue eyes swept over the sorcerers and the ambassadors.

She showed not a hint of emotion, especially given that she had just killed almost fifty men.

"Master?" said the woman, her Szaldic accent thick.

"This is Mihaela," said Zalandris, "the most able of my Seekers. The glypharmor was her design. I was dubious, but her success has surpassed my wildest expectations. And in the glypharmor, we have an instrument that will end war for all time."

"You do, Master," said Mihaela. "A warrior wearing a suit of glypharmor is impervious to almost all material weapons, can move with the speed of a racing horse, and has the strength of a hundred men. One warrior wearing this armor can destroy an army."

"An impressive achievement, girl," said the First Magus. "The spells upon your toy are indeed potent. Yet even the most potent spell can be unraveled."

Mihaela gave an indifferent shrug. "True, First Magus. A group of sorcerers of sufficient power, working in concert, can unravel the spells upon the glypharmor. But these spells are most difficult to dispel. Any sorcerer attempting to unbind a suit of glypharmor would soon find himself torn to pieces by the others."

"Others?" said Decius. "What others?"

Mihaela grinned. "Why, the other warriors in suits of glypharmor. For we of the Scholae can make as many of them as we wish. You have seen what one suit of glypharmor can do. Imagine ten. Or a hundred. Or perhaps an entire army?" She grinned. "So. Which one of you gets to conquer the world..."

"Mihaela," said Zalandris, voice calm. "It is the role of the Speaker to stand for the Scholae. Not for a mere Seeker."

"Forgive me, Master," said Mihaela.

But Caina saw the flash of hatred in her blue eyes.

"You have seen the demonstration, my lords," said Zalandris. "Let us now return to the Hall of Assembly. Refreshments have been prepared, and we can talk in comfort. And we shall...how do the merchants say it? Ah, yes. We shall let the bidding begin."

9

HAGGLING

"That," said Halfdan, "was rather cleverer than I expected."

"It is utterly impossible," said Claudia.

Caina had no answer for that. She had seen sorcery do strange and terrible things...but she had never seen something like the glypharmor.

They had returned to the Hall of Assembly. Slaves had set up tables and chairs, and now circulated among the nobles and sorcerers with trays of food and drink. Yet few seemed to have any appetite.

The First Magus, Caina noted, ate heartily.

She looked at Claudia and Corvalis. Halfdan had led them to a table in the corner, behind Lord Titus's bodyguards, and so far the First Magus had not noticed his estranged children. But if he looked too closely...

"That kind of sorcery should not be possible," said Claudia, her arms folded across her stomach. The carnage in the smaller hall had shaken her. "There are limits to the amount of sorcerous force a material object can contain. The kind of power it would take to move that much metal that quickly...gods, it should have blasted half the Tower of Study to ruin. It's impossible."

"Impossible or not," said Corvalis, "we saw it with our own eyes.

Here, have some wine." He plucked a glass from a passing slave. "It will help settle your stomach."

Claudia took the glass with a murmur of thanks, and Caina looked at the far end of the Hall and into the round chamber.

The suit of glypharmor stood at the edge of the molten pool, the sullen glow reflecting off its polished plates. Mihaela waited at the foot of the armor, looking over the ambassadors with a cold expression. Khaltep Irzaris stood at her side, speaking. From time to time Mihaela's lips twitched in amusement, but her expression did not change.

"It is," said Caina, "a very clever trick."

"But what's the trick?" said Claudia, shaking her head. "The Scholae promised a weapon, and it's as powerful as they claim."

"Because," said Caina, still watching Mihaela and Irzaris, "a hundred of those things could conquer the world, but I'd wager every denarius in the Empire that the Sages know how to disable them. And they're selling the glypharmor itself, not the secrets of how to construct it. That armor is tough, but I doubt it's invincible. Some idiot could drop his suit into a lake, or a clever foe could bury it in a landslide. Which means that whatever nation buys the glypharmor will need to buy more...and they'll become completely dependent upon the Scholae for their power."

"A nice little trap," said Corvalis.

His hand found hers beneath the table, and Caina gave it a squeeze.

"Well reasoned, daughter," said Halfdan. "But what do we do about it?"

"That," said Caina, "is a much harder question."

"We could just kill Mihaela," said Corvalis, "if she's the only one who knows how to make the things."

"Corvalis!" said Claudia.

"His name is Cormark," said Halfdan.

Claudia gave an impatient nod. "Yes, yes, our disguise. Which should remind you that you are not an assassin any longer!"

"No," said Corvalis, "but the skills haven't left me. And you saw how she butchered her way through those prisoners. If someone like our father buys the glypharmor, the same thing will happen across the world."

"It may be too late," said Caina. "Mihaela couldn't have built that suit entirely by herself. Zalandris and some of the other Sages most likely know how to do it. And she may have kept records."

"Or her knowledge might fall into the wrong hands," said Corvalis. "You know how a man like the First Magus thinks, Basil. He might decide to kidnap Mihaela and torture her into revealing her secrets."

"That would be a bold risk," said Halfdan, "given how the Scholae would respond to an attack."

Corvalis gestured at the glypharmor. "A tremendous risk...but an equally tremendous payoff."

"If the knowledge of how to create glypharmor spreads," said Caina, "the world will rip itself apart in a war."

"I agree," said Halfdan. "So. This leaves us with two options. We either try to destroy the glypharmor and all knowledge of its creation here. Or, we make sure that the Emperor obtains the glypharmor... and then we destroy it."

Claudia blinked. "You will not take it back to your Emperor?"

"No," said Halfdan. "I have seen war, daughter. It is already terrible enough without the use of glypharmor."

Caina nodded. "A worthy task."

"But a daunting one," said Corvalis. "And we are short on time. For all we know one of the embassies will buy the armor tonight."

"No," said Halfdan. "They won't. I suspect the Masked Ones like to do things in a leisurely fashion. Comes from living for centuries, I suppose. And Lord Titus told me what they have planned. Zalandris will meet with each of the embassies individually and hear their offers. After that, he will announce each bid and give the embassies a chance to make counter-offers. Only then will the Scholae decide who receives the armor."

"Quite the elaborate little game," said Caina.

"But what do the Masked Ones even want?" said Corvalis. "They already have the sorcerous power to rule the world. What more do they want? Cities? Lands? Slaves? Riches?"

"An end to war," said Caina.

The others looked at her.

"You heard what Zalandris said," said Caina. "He thinks the glypharmor is so powerful that kings and lords will not dare to use it, that mere fear of the weapons will keep men from launching wars."

"I assumed that was just rhetoric," said Corvalis.

"No," said Caina. "I think he truly believes it. He's a fool. A learned, powerful fool...but a fool nonetheless. He truly believes the glypharmor will bring an end to war." She looked at Halfdan. "That is how you can get Lord Titus to buy the glypharmor, if it comes to that. Have him claim that the Emperor will put an end to war if he obtains the glypharmor."

"Do you really think," said Corvalis, "that the Masked Ones are such fools?"

"I do," said Caina. "They never leave their city, and they spend all their time with their spells and books. For all their power, they have no idea how men truly act. If the glypharmor leaves Catekharon, it will spark a war unlike anything seen in history. But the Masked Ones are foolish enough to think it will bring peace."

Claudia sniffed. "Is not bringing peace a noble goal?"

"Aye," said Caina, "and it's also a noble goal to feed the poor and hungry. But if I try to feed them with rocks and stones, that makes me a fool. A well-intentioned fool, but a fool nonetheless."

Claudia said nothing.

"Very well," said Halfdan. "I shall speak with Lord Titus. Hopefully your insights will give him an edge over the other ambassadors."

"I doubt," said Corvalis, "that it would occur to my father to frame his offer in terms of peace."

"That is my hope as well," said Halfdan, rising to his feet. "You two stay here, and try to slip away soon as Zalandris opens the doors. If the First Magus sees you, he will realize that you are Ghosts, and that would be disastrous."

"I think," said Caina, "that I shall speak with Kylon."

"The stormdancer?" said Claudia with a frown. "Why? He is a foreign sorcerer. No doubt he would run amok with the glypharmor if given the chance."

"I don't think so," said Caina. "He has seen what too much power in the wrong hands can do."

"Very well," said Halfdan.

Caina gave Corvalis's hand one last squeeze and stood, her eyes sweeping the embassies. One of the slaves caught her eyes. Shaizid, the young man who had brought her coffee. He stood staring at Mihaela with mixed fear and longing on his face.

Gods, she hoped the poor fool wasn't in love with the Seeker.

Shaizid saw her staring, flinched, and hurried back to his work.

Caina felt her eyes drawn to the towering suit of glypharmor. Something about it...fascinated her. Not that it was a weapon of death unlike she had ever seen, an engine of killing. No, she felt...drawn to it, almost compelled towards it.

It reminded her of that strange attraction she had felt to Maglarion's great bloodcrystal, the huge crystal he had created from her blood.

The thought chilled her.

The strange attraction was likely a result of the spells Mihaela had bound upon the armor.

Caina put aside the thought and went in search of Kylon.

"Gods of storm and brine," said Alcios, yet again.

Kylon could not blame him.

They sat at one of the tables, flanked by the ashtairoi guards. Kylon stared unseeing at a glass of wine in his hand. Alcios ignored his food, too stunned to eat. Only Cimon, with the instincts of a veteran soldier, ate the food.

Perhaps he was the only sensible man in the room.

"Think of what the Assembly could do with a hundred warriors arrayed in glypharmor," said Alcios, his eyes bright. "We could at last smash the Legions of the Empire in open battle. We could tear down the walls of Marsis and claim it for our own. Gods of storm and brine! We could even assault Malarae and claim the Imperial Citadel itself! Our ancestors warred with the Empire for centuries, and we could do what Old Kyrace never did! We could throw down the Empire itself, and..."

"No," said Kylon, voice quiet.

The mood of the Hall of Assembly washed over his arcane senses. He felt a great deal of fear and anxiety. But there was also a tremendous amount of raw excitement. Of anticipation. Lust, almost. Every man here had seen what the glypharmor could do...and every man now dreamed of using that raw power to destroy his enemies.

The glypharmor was a slab of raw meat thrown into waters churning with sharks.

The resultant carnage would not be pretty.

"No?" said Alcios, astonished. Contempt flooded his emotional sense. "My lord thalarchon, why not? Why should we not claim this weapon? For if the Empire takes the glypharmor, they shall use it to break down the walls of New Kyre and smash the Pyramid of the Storm to rubble."

"Because," said Kylon, "we are the fish, and the Sages offer poisoned bait upon a steel hook."

"I do not understand," said Alcios.

"The Scholae offers to sell the glypharmor," said Kylon, "but will they sell the secrets of its making? No. If we take the glypharmor and use it to conquer our enemies, we will become dependent upon it. And that, in turn, means that we shall become the slaves of the Scholae. How will we repair the glypharmor if it is damaged or lost in combat? What price will the Scholae demand for new suits of glypharmor?"

Alcios's frown deepened, and Kylon sensed a thread of doubt in the older man's emotional aura.

"It seems clear," said Cimon around a bite of cheese, "that whatever happens, we must keep the Empire from claiming the glypharmor."

Alcios scowled. "How can you eat at a time like this?"

"You have spent more time upon campaign than I, my lord High Seat," said Cimon, unfazed. "A soldier must eat when he can." He took a drink of wine. "Especially when the battle seems close at hand."

"Do you think it will come to violence?" said Alcios.

"Unquestionably," said Kylon. "It would not surprise me if someone tries to kidnap Mihaela, or steal..."

He blinked.

The Ghost stood some distance away, staring at him.

"Pardon, my lords," said Kylon, rising.

"What?" said Alcios. "Her again? My lord thalarchon, this is hardly the time for a seduction."

"It is not," said Kylon, "but it is precisely the time to learn what I can about the Empire's intentions."

He walked away without another word.

The blue-eyed Ghost waited as he approached. Her emotional aura, that peculiar mixture of icy cunning and burning rage, washed over him. "Lord Kylon."

"Anna Callenius," said Kylon, "though I assume that is not your real name."

"It is not," said the Ghost.

On impulse he offered his arm, and she took it. Physical contact would give him a better handle on her emotions. But she would know that.

Which meant she wanted him to know that she was telling the truth.

They walked into the empty space of the Hall, alongside the river of molten steel.

"Tell me," said the Ghost, once they were out of earshot of the others, "what did you think of Zalandris's demonstration?"

"It reminded me of Andromache," said Kylon.

The Ghost turned her cold eyes towards the hulking suit of crimson armor. "Andromache was shorter."

"But she said many of the same things," said Kylon. "She claimed the power in the Tomb of Scorikhon would bring victory and security to House Kardamnos and New Kyre. Now my men say the same thing about the glypharmor. Yet the power in Scorikhon's tomb was a trap."

"And you think," said the Ghost, "the same thing of the glypharmor?"

"Perhaps," said Kylon. "Any nation using the glypharmor would become dependent upon it, just as we of New Kyre are dependent upon our fleets for both our security and our prosperity."

"Yet the Kyracians," said the Ghost, "can build their own ships. You cannot build your own glypharmor."

"As you say," said Kylon. "So you see my fear. If New Kyre buys the glypharmor, we would become the slaves of the Catekhari." He shook his head. "But I cannot permit the Empire to take the armor. For I know your Emperor would use the glypharmor to smash the walls of New Kyre and subdue the Kyracian people."

"Or the Magisterium, for that matter," said the Ghost. "If Decius Aberon claims the armor, he will first use it to claim the Empire, and then to conquer the Empire's enemies." She paused, looking up at him. "Would it not have been better if the Tomb of Scorikhon had never been opened? Perhaps it would be best if the glypharmor never saw the light of day."

"You mean it should be destroyed," said Kylon, glancing at Mihaela, "and all knowledge of its creation eradicated."

"My lord stormdancer has a gift for stating matters clearly," said the Ghost.

Kylon sighed. "Spare me the flowery speech. I have no use for it."

"But you have gotten better at it," said the Ghost.

"I am now the High Seat of House Kardamnos and a thalarchon of New Kyre," said Kylon. "I've had no choice. Very well, Ghost. Go back to your masters and tell them that if we have the opportunity to destroy the armor and the knowledge of its creation, you shall have my full aid." He slipped his arm from hers and looked her in the eye. "But understand this. If the choice is between letting the Empire or New Kyre claim the armor...then I will do my utmost to claim it, regardless of the consequences."

She regarded him without expression. When they had fought in Marsis, he had thought she would look quite attractive, cleansed of blood and sweat and clad in proper women's attire, and he had not been wrong. But he knew hers was a perilous beauty. The coldness in her emotional sense never wavered, and if she thought it necessary, she would kill him without hesitation.

Just as she had almost slain him in Marsis.

"Very well," said the Ghost. "I know you will do what you think is right, whatever the cost to yourself."

"I will defend my city," said Kylon.

She almost smiled. "Sometimes what you think is right and the best way to defend your people are two different things."

The Ghost bowed and left without another word.

CAINA WALKED AWAY, her boots clicking against the gleaming stone floor.

Kylon's reaction did not surprise her. His first loyalty was to New Kyre. But he could still see reason, and if she could find a way to destroy the glypharmor, he would aid her. Now if Halfdan could get the aid of another embassy...

A sudden tingle washed over her skin, so sharp that she gasped.

Sorcery. Powerful, potent sorcery, strong enough to overwhelm even the mighty aura of the Tower of Study.

Caina turned, and saw that she had wandered only ten yards from the glypharmor.

The red statue filled her eyes, drawing her like an iron nail to a lodestone...

"Ah," said a man's voice. "Anna Callenius. So good to see you again. Who knew that we would meet again here?"

Caina blinked, and saw Khaltep Irzaris standing at the foot of the armor, a smile on his lean face. Mihaela stood next to him, arms folded over her chest.

"Who is this, Irzaris?" said Mihaela, scowling.

"Oh, simply an acquaintance chance-met upon the road," said Irzaris. He stepped forward, bowed, and planted a kiss upon Caina's hand. Then he straightened up and guided her towards the glypharmor. The tingling grew worse as they drew closer, and Caina saw hundreds of hieroglyphs crawling up and down the arms and legs of the armor and covering its cuirass in an intricate design.

"Impressive, is it not?" said Irzaris. "I suppose you had no idea that my red iron would be used to create something so...magnificent?"

"Irzaris," said Mihaela, "we do not have time for this. If you want to find some empty-headed merchant's whelp to warm your bed, do so later. I require a great deal of..."

"Do not fret," said Irzaris. "You shall have the materials you require. And this is a night of triumph, is it not?"

Mihaela scoffed with disdain. Caina saw an opportunity in that. If Mihaela thought her a fool, then perhaps the Seeker might reveal some useful information.

"It is...very large," said Caina.

"Large," said Mihaela. "Yes. How very profound. Do you have any other useful insights?"

Caina opened her mouth to answer...but found her eyes drawn to the glypharmor.

Suddenly she wanted to touch it.

Mihaela gave an ugly laugh. "I think she is scared of it, Irzaris. And why should she not? What does the little girl of a fat merchant know about power?"

"I think," said Caina. "I think that it is making me dizzy."

"Perhaps you've had too much wine," said Irzaris with a smile. "I can find you a place to lie down."

Mihaela snorted. "Subtle."

"I should rejoin my father," said Caina. "Thank you, but..."

A stabbing bolt of pain shot through her head.

The hieroglyphs upon the armor flickered with white light.

"What the devil?" said Irzaris, stepping away from Caina in alarm. "It's activating!"

Mihaela looked more intrigued than worried. "It appears to be reacting to her."

"That's impossible," said Irzaris. "She has no arcane talent."

Caina didn't.

But the Moroaica did.

The hieroglyphics upon the armor flared, the room spun around Caina, and everything went black.

10

OLD BLOOD

Caina fell through an eternity of swirling gray mist.

Confused, broken thoughts danced through her mind. She could not remember how she had gotten here. She remembered a hulking suit of crimson armor, remembered pain stabbing through her head...

Blood. There had been so much blood.

Had the blood been her own? Had she died?

The mists vanished.

Caina stood again in her father's library, looking at her mother's corpse, blood pooling across the floor. Then in Maglarion's lair, screaming as the necromancer cut into her and extracted her blood for his spells...

No. She did not want to remember that. She was tired of death, tired of sorrow. She did not want to remember it any longer.

She concentrated and forced the memories away.

Again gray mist swirled, and a different set of recollections came to her.

Laughing with Theodosia in the Grand Imperial Opera.

The tears in Ark's eyes as he saw Tanya for the first time in five years.

Carrying Nicolai back to his father after the Kyracians and the Istarish had been defeated.

Lying with Corvalis in her arms, her moans tearing from her throat...

A shiver went through the gray mists, and white light devoured the world.

~

WHEN IT CLEARED, Caina found herself standing underneath a brilliant desert sun.

She stood on a street of gleaming stone, whitewashed houses rising overhead. In the distance she saw splendid temples and palaces of built of white stone, shining like jewels in the sunlight. Hieroglyphs covered the sides of the temples, and gold sheathed many of the stone columns.

Suddenly Caina knew that she stood in ancient Maat, in the capital city of the Kingdom of the Rising Sun during the height of its splendor. But how? She had never been there ...

All at once she realized this was not a dream but a memory.

But not one that belonged to her.

A scream rang out, and Caina turned.

She saw a group of soldiers standing before one of the houses. The soldiers wore bronze chain mail and helms, carrying spears with bronze heads. A man in a stark white robe stood in their midst, a frown of impatience upon his face and a golden torque around his neck. His head had been shaved, even his eyebrows, and black makeup lined his eyes.

Caina realized he was one of the mighty necromancer-priests of ancient Maat.

But how did she know that?

The soldiers wrestled two people from the house. One was a middle-aged man with the ink-stained fingers and slumped posture of a professional scribe. The second was a beautiful girl of fifteen or sixteen with dark eyes and black hair.

Both the scribe and the girl were terrified.

"Rhames," pleaded the scribe, "no, don't do this, please, please..."

He spoke Maatish, but somehow Caina understood him.

"Silence," said Rhames. "I'll never understand why you wallowed in this folly. Your daughter's beauty has captured the eye of the Great Pharaoh himself. She will share his tomb as one of his consorts, and shall receive eternal life at his side as one of the Undying." He gave an irritated shake of his head. "You ought to be honored. Instead you hide like a cringing barbarian."

"You'll murder her," said the scribe, "in the name of your false gods and that cruel tyrant you call a Pharaoh..."

"Blasphemy!" said Rhames. "I will not tolerate this!" He pointed at one of the soldiers. "Carry out the sentence."

The soldiers went into action. Two of them seized the scribe and forced him to his knees. The girl ran to him with a cry, but the other men caught her. Another soldier drew a bronze axe and lifted it over his head.

The axe came down.

A crimson jet splattered across the white street.

"Father!" screamed the girl, struggling against the soldiers. "Father!" Her cries dissolved into wordless howls of grief and rage.

"I do not understand why you weep," said Rhames. "You have shall be one of the Great Pharaoh's consorts in the next life. You will become one of the Undying, and you shall never grow old or ugly." He shook his head. "But women have never been rational. Bring her. We must begin the transformation at once."

The soldiers dragged the screaming girl away, and Caina saw her eyes.

They were the Moroaica's eyes.

∾

THE VISION DISSOLVED, and Caina found herself back in the plain of gray mist.

The Moroaica stood nearby, clad in her red robe. She was always calm, always collected, and always spoke to Caina with distant amusement.

But not now.

Her hands clenched and unclenched, her shoulders shaking with fury. Tears even glinted in her eyes and trickled down her pale face.

"You should not," hissed Jadriga, "have seen that."

"Then why," said Caina, "did you show it to me?"

"My power is trapped within you," said Jadriga, "and it reacted rather...strongly to the necromancy in the glypharmor. I lost control for a moment, and showed you more than I intended."

Part of Caina's mind noted that necromancy had been used in the making of the glypharmor. The rest of her mind regarded the Moroaica with stunned fascination.

"Your father," said Caina at last. "They killed him in front of you."

"I told you," said Jadriga, "that we were more alike than you might wish. That I was once like you, long ago."

"I thought," said Caina, "that you were only trying to sway me. To corrupt me into something like yourself."

"I was," said Jadriga. "But why use a lie when the truth would be just as effective? I understand you, Caina Amalas, child of the Ghosts. You are what you are because your father was murdered in front of you...just as I am what I am because my father was murdered in front of me." Her red lips tightened into a hard line for a moment. "And because of the consequences of that murder."

Caina hesitated. She had seen the children Jadriga had kept captive in the black vaults below Black Angel Tower, had watched as Jadriga almost unleashed the demons from their prison. Maglarion, Sicarion, Ranarius, and Andromache had been Jadriga's disciples, and Caina had seen the horror and death they had unleashed.

Her own father had died at Maglarion's hand, and the necromancer had almost destroyed Malarae. The Moroaica was a monster, an author of death and misery.

Yet Jadriga's father had been murdered in front of her, just as Caina's had.

If Jadriga had become such a monster, could Caina do the same? If she had the ability to wield sorcery, would she have become someone like Andromache or Agria Palaegus?

Jadriga closed her eyes and took a deep breath.

She had just seen her father die again, and Caina knew what the felt like.

She lived with the memory every day.

"I'm...I'm sorry," said Caina at last. She raised a hesitant hand and touched Jadriga on the shoulder.

The Moroaica whirled, her face a mask of fury.

"Do not touch me!" she said. "Do not ever touch me!" Caina stepped back in sudden alarm. "We are more alike than you know, child of the Ghosts. You slew Maglarion in vengeance for your father. But I made them pay. They say the Kingdom of the Rising Sun perished in its own dark sorcery? I unleashed that sorcery! I threw down their empire and ground it into the dust. I sealed the Great Pharaohs in their tombs and left them to scream for eternity in darkness and madness. I set Rhames's spirit to burn, and cast it upon the desert winds for all time. I repaid the Great Pharaohs a thousand times over for what they did to me!" Her black eyes blazed. "But still it is not enough! Slay one tyrant and a dozen more take his place. The world is broken, Ghost, a prison of rot and decay that spawns monsters. The gods did this to us. They created this torture chamber of a world and left us to suffer in it! They will pay, Ghost! I will make them pay! I will see the gods themselves suffer as we have suffered, and repay them for all the agony their broken world ever wrought!"

Her voice rose to a scream of fury, and the mists howled around them like a storm. Caina lost her footing and fell into nothingness, the gray mist swallowing her whole.

~

AN ARGUMENT FILLED HER EARS.

"The girl was always light-headed," said Halfdan. "I fear the carnage has quite overloaded her nerves." His voice carried a hint of reproach. "Had I know that we would see such…violence, certainly I would not have exposed her delicate sensibilities to it."

Mihaela's laugh was mocking. "Pah, she faints at the sight of a little blood? It is just as well she was never a slave. She would not have lasted a week."

"Mihaela," said Zalandris. "That is quite enough."

"Do not deny," said the First Magus, "that she reacted to some flaw within the armor. This weapon of yours is no good if it poses a threat to any potential wielders."

"My design is perfect," said Mihaela, "and…"

Caina's eyes opened.

She lay upon the floor, the sullen red glow of molten metal painting the stone ceiling overhead. As she feared, a ring of people stood around her.

It seemed that she had made a scene.

"Ah," said Mihaela with a sneer. "See? She has awakened. No harm done."

"Daughter," said Halfdan, kneeling beside her. "Are you all right?"

"I…I think so," said Caina.

Halfdan helped her to stand.

Caina shot a quick look around the ring of faces. Some of them looked at her with amusement, but most with wariness. That was not good. If they held her in suspicion, it would make it that much harder to destroy the means of creating the glypharmor.

She could think of only one way to dissuade them.

Caina took a deep breath and started to cry. Theodosia had taught her how to cry on cue, and it proven useful. Contempt flashed over the faces of the ambassadors and sorcerers, while others simply looked embarrassed.

"I'm…I'm so sorry, Father," said Caina, trying to catch her breath. "I don't…I don't know what happened. I was looking at the armor, and I got so dizzy, and then…"

She sobbed again and buried her face in his chest.

"Ah, well," said Halfdan, patting her on the shoulder. "No harm done. I suppose you're just tired."

"Gods," said Mihaela. "All this fuss over a crying girl?" She laughed. "Perhaps Irzaris has gotten her with child and thrown her moods into chaos."

"What?" said Irzaris. "I did nothing of the sort. My conduct toward Master Basil's daughters has been nothing but honorable."

"I'm sorry to have...made such a scene," said Caina. "I...I just do not feel well."

"Master Basil," said Zalandris, "I suggest you take your kinfolk and retainers back to your rooms. Today's business is concluded, and I will not listen to any offers until tomorrow."

"Thank you, my lord Sage," said Halfdan, bowing to the Masked One. "Come along, daughter. Let's fetch Irene and Cormark and get you to bed. You can tell us all about what happened."

Caina nodded and Halfdan put his arm around her shoulders and steered her away from the crowd. He would want to know what she had learned, and...

"Wait."

Halfdan stopped. That voice sounded almost familiar...

A Masked One stepped free from the crowd. Like the others, a jade mask covered his features, and he carried a rod of silvery metal in his left hand. Unlike the others, his right leg twitched and jerked as he walked, and he seemed in dire need of a cane.

Caina felt a twinge of alarm.

"Talekhris," said Zalandris. "What is it?"

"The girl may have been injured by the glypharmor's sorcerous aura," said Talekhris. "If she is sensitive to the presence of sorcery, the powers within the armor might have done her injury."

"That is a very remote possibility," said Zalandris, raising a hand to forestall Mihaela's protest.

"Nevertheless," said Talekhris. "She is a guest of the Scholae, and I would have no harm befall her."

"Very well," said Zalandris. "If the girl consents to it."

"Your face," said Caina. "I want to see your face."

"So be it," said Talekhris, lifting his jade mask.

Caina stared into the face of the Masked One she and Corvalis had killed in Cyrioch.

11

THE WATCHER

"No," said Caina. "No, Father, I don't want to go with him. He frightens me."

But her mind spun furiously beneath the show of fear. How was Talekhris still alive? His mask and rod had disappeared from the Inn of the Defender, but Marzhod had dumped his corpse into Cyrioch's harbor. Had Marzhod betrayed them?

Or had Talekhris come back to life?

Decius Aberon let out a nasty laugh. "Your daughter frightens easily, Master Basil."

"I fear," said Halfdan, "that she inherited her mother's sensitivities."

Caina certainly hoped not.

"I can see why she would fear me," said Talekhris. He was the same man they had seen in Cyrioch, Caina was sure of it, with the same blue eyes, the same limp, the same graying brown hair. "But I swear, Master Basil, that I will return your daughter unharmed to you. I will swear it on the names of whatever gods you wish, and offer whatever you want as surety."

Caina blinked. Talekhris wanted to talk to her. He needed to know something that she did. Or, he thought she knew something he needed to know.

Either way, Caina could use that.

"If...if you think it best, my lord Sage," said Caina, looking up at Halfdan. "If you will allow it, Father."

"If it pleases you," said Halfdan.

"Yes," said Caina. "I think it will."

For Talekhris certainly knew things that she needed to know. How he had survived Corvalis's sword through his chest, for one. And perhaps he knew how Mihaela had built the glypharmor, and why the Moroaica had claimed necromancy had been used to create the armor. The Scholae forbade the practice of necromancy, which meant if Mihaela had somehow used necromantic spells to create the glypharmor, Caina had a chance of convincing the Masked Ones themselves to destroy the weapon.

"Very well," said Talekhris, beckoning. "Please come with me. We will be gone but a moment, Master Basil."

The Masked One led Caina from the Hall of Assembly.

CAINA FOLLOWED Talekhris up a narrow flight of spiraling stairs. The Sage moved slowly, grunting in pain with every step.

"That would go faster," said Caina, "with a cane."

"So it would," said Talekhris, not looking back. "But life is pain. It must be endured."

"Like a sword blade through the chest?" said Caina.

He looked back at her, and she could not tell if he was angry or amused. "Yes. Precisely like that. Like the sword blade you rammed into my heart."

He kept climbing, wincing with every step.

At last the stairs ended, and they came to another grand hall, similar to the one where Zalandris and Mihaela had held their ghastly little demonstration. Stone pedestals stood here and there, and objects rested upon the pedestals, swords and shields and cups and daggers and bowls. In the center of the room a long staff of gray metal rested upon a coffin-sized plinth. Fingers of crimson flame danced around the staff, only to harden into glittering ice crystals a few moments later, and then to melt into flickering sparks of blue-white lightning.

Caina's skin crawled with the presence of potent sorcery.

"What is this place?" said Caina.

"The Chamber of Relics," said Talekhris. "It is something of a museum. Here we house the most powerful artifacts wrought by the Scholae, objects too dangerous to ever see the light of day." He pointed at a silver dagger upon a stone plinth, the blade sheathed in an ornate scabbard of silver and black. "That is the Stormbrand, capable of controlling the air with more power than the assembled stormsingers of the Kyracian people. That sphere will extinguish every fire within a ten mile radius, and transform the stolen heat into a weapon..."

Caina had left her ghostsilver dagger in her room. Ghostsilver was proof against sorcery, and perhaps she could use it to destroy these objects.

Or perhaps their sorcery was too strong for even ghostsilver.

"And that," said Talekhris, pointing at the strange staff as the lightning morphed back into flames, "is the Staff of the Elements."

"What does that do?" said Caina. "Light fires?"

"Among other things," said Talekhris. "It grants control over the primal elements, and it can awaken a greater elemental from its hibernation."

Caina blinked. "This thing can actually awaken a hibernating elemental?"

"In an instant," said Talekhris, "though it would not be under the command of the Staff's wielder."

"Gods," said Caina, remembering how long it had taken Ranarius to find a spell capable of awakening a greater elemental. "You could destroy the world with that staff. What the hell is wrong with you?"

"I'm sorry?" said Talekhris.

"The Scholae," said Caina. "The Masked Ones claim to pursue knowledge for its own sake. But first you made that staff, and then the glypharmor! Do you seek for ways to destroy the world simply for your own amusement?"

Talekhris looked away. "Once I would have dismissed you as ignorant. Now...now I do not know." He took a deep breath. "But we are not here to discuss the failings of the Scholae."

"No, we're not," said Caina. "And I know why you brought me here."

"Why is that?"

"You want to know," said Caina, "if I am the Moroaica or not."

He stared at her in silence for a moment, his fingers tight around the metallic rod. Caina had seen him use it in Cyrioch, but she suspected Talekhris had only employed a small portion of its powers.

"Are you?" said Talekhris.

"You tell me," said Caina.

He scowled. "This is not a game."

"It is," said Caina. "Your own Speaker is playing a game right now, even if he doesn't realize it. Gathering together the most powerful and ambitious men in the world and throwing that weapon into their midst? There will be fighting before this is over. You might as well drop a dozen gladiators into a pit and offer to give the last one standing his freedom."

"You surprise me," said Talekhris. "You are neither the weeping child I saw in the hall nor the happy woman I saw walking with her lover in Cyrica Urbana. Who is truly beneath those masks, I wonder?"

"A Masked One accusing another of wearing a mask?" said Caina. She did not like his implication that she had been wearing a mask with Corvalis. "How poetical. But we did not come here for a debate, did we? Tell me why you think I am the Moroaica, and why you tried to kill me for it."

"The mask of a Sage," said Talekhris, "grants many powers. One of them is the ability to see into the shadows of the netherworld."

"As the Anshani occultists do," said Caina.

"They possess the second sight," said Talekhris, "but the mask bestows it to a far greater degree. With it, I beheld the Moroaica's power within you." He frowned. "And yet...and yet her aura has not subsumed yours, as it did with the others."

"Others?" said Caina.

"I have fought the Moroaica in nine of her incarnations," said Talekhris, "and slain her five times. At least those I can remember." He shook his head. "Every time, she had dominated her host. Yet...I see two souls within you. I do not understand."

Neither did Caina. Talekhris claimed to have fought Jadriga nine times. She knew the Masked Ones lived for centuries, yet if Caina's dream had been accurate, Jadriga had been born in Maat. And Maat had been destroyed over two thousand years ago.

Just how old was Talekhris?

"Nor do I understand," said Caina, "why you are standing here now. I saw a sword go through your heart, and I know your corpse was dumped into the Cyrican Sea."

"I was," said Talekhris. "It was most inconvenient."

"So how are you still alive?" said Caina.

"A bargain, then," said Talekhris. The rod rested in loose fingers at his side, like a master swordsman readying his weapon for a strike. "You tell me if you are truly the Moroaica...and I shall tell you how I survived."

"Very well," said Caina. "I slew the Moroaica in Marsis, and her spirit entered my body. But she is unable to control me. I was... scarred by sorcery when I was a child. Because of that damage, she occupies my body, but she cannot control me."

"Truly?" said Talekhris. "But...yes, I see. That makes a great deal of sense. Yes." He frowned in chagrin. "So if I had slain you in Cyrica Urbana..."

"Then you would have freed the Moroaica to claim another host," said Caina. "You didn't think that through, did you?"

"Apparently not," said Talekhris.

"Now," said Caina. "You will tell me. Why are you still alive?"

"The Moroaica," said Talekhris.

"You are one of her disciples?" said Caina, wondering if Talekhris was a creature like Sicarion. Perhaps Talekhris had helped himself to a new heart from a hapless victim.

"In fact," said Talekhris, "she was mine."

"You taught her?" said Caina.

"It was," the lines of his face tightened in a frown, "nine hundred years ago. Or perhaps eight. I cannot recall. She claimed to be one of the Szaldic solmonari, come to study from the Sages of the Scholae. I took her as a Seeker. But soon I realized her knowledge far exceeded my own, and she possessed a profound mastery of ancient Maat's necromantic sciences." He shook his head. "But she fooled me long enough to learn many of the Scholae's secrets. Eventually I discovered her deception and we fought. I thought I had driven her off...but she had taken all the knowledge she needed."

"Nine hundred years ago?" said Caina. "Can the Sages truly live so long?"

"We cannot," said Talekhris. "Twenty years after she fled, I found the Moroaica in Anshan, and slew her in a duel. But she returned soon after in a new body. Again I hunted her down and slew her...and again she returned in a new body. I realized she would outlive me by moving from body to body, and would do terrible harm with the knowledge she had stolen from the Scholae."

"So you ensured," said Caina, "that you would live as long as she did."

She wondered if Talekhris was a necromancer, and her hands wanted to reach for her throwing knives.

He shook his head. "You think me a necromancer? I would not use her own methods to pursue her. But there was another way. An artifact of elemental power, tied to the earth itself. When I am slain, it forces my spirit back into my flesh...and I live again."

"Immortality, then," said Caina.

"Of a sort," said Talekhris.

"But there is a price," said Caina, "isn't there?"

"What do you mean?" said Talekhris.

"You might be...returned to your body again and again," said Caina, "but your injuries are not always healed." She pointed at his right leg. "Else I wouldn't have been able to defeat a Sage of the Scholae by throwing a frying pan at him."

"A frying pan?" said Talekhris.

"And I would wager it has damaged your memory, too," said Caina. "You met the Moroaica eight or nine hundred years ago? I think you would remember that. I suspect with every death you lose a little more of your memory."

"Why do you think that?" said Talekhris.

"Because," said Caina. "You said I drove a sword through your heart. I didn't. I only distracted you by hitting your bad leg with a frying pan. I think you would remember that."

Talekhris said nothing for a moment, and Caina stared at him.

"You," said Talekhris, "are rather clever for a merchant's daughter."

"I think you have figured out what I really am by now," said Caina.

"A Ghost," said Talekhris. "Sometimes your order has aided me, throughout the centuries, though I doubt you remember." He sighed. "And I do not remember. You are correct about the memory loss. The mortal mind...the mortal mind was not designed to handle the strain of such a long life. I say I have slain the Moroaica five times, but those are only the times I remember. It could be more. I have tried keeping records...but sometimes she finds and destroys them." His voice grew quiet. "I was married, long ago. Yet I cannot remember my wife's name. I cannot even remember her face, Ghost."

"How many times have you died?" said Caina.

"More than I can remember," said Talekhris. "The Moroaica has slain me. Her disciples have slain me at her bidding." He shook his head. "Her pet assassin has slain me, twice, merely for the amusement of it."

"Assassin?" said Caina. "You mean Sicarion? Short man covered in scars?"

"Is that what he calls himself now?" said Talekhris. "Yes. He was once an initiate of the Magisterium during the Fourth Empire. The Magisterium expelled him because he enjoyed killing too much even by the standards of the Fourth Empire. The Moroaica took him as a disciple, and he has killed at her bidding ever since."

"Not any more," said Caina. "He's dead. Ranarius killed him in Cyrioch."

"Good," said Talekhris. "The Moroaica has caused great harm over the centuries. Her disciples, however, lack her intelligence and self-control, and are often worse."

"Do you have a plan for defeating her?" said Caina. "Some way to finally stop her?"

"Not yet," said Talekhris. "I have tried to break the necromantic spells upon her spirit. I have tried to imprison her spirit, to keep it from inhabiting yet another body. Time and time again I have failed. I have wandered long in the horrid ruins of ancient Maat, seeking the secrets of their necromancy. For I do not understand how she moves from flesh to flesh, and until I do, I cannot stop her."

"So you're not going to kill me?" said Caina.

"Attacking you was a mistake," said Talekhris, "and I apologize for it. Indeed, I wish you long life. How old are you? Twenty-one?" Caina nodded. "Then I pray you live to one hundred and twenty-one, Anna Callenius. As long as you live, I have a respite. I can seek some way of defeating the Moroaica without fear that she is doing harm elsewhere."

Caina nodded. Here was the lever she could use to gain Talekhris's aid.

She hoped.

"You could help me," said Caina, "to live a long life."

"How?" said Talekhris. "By keeping you a prisoner at the Tower of Study? The Scholae would not approve."

"Do you think," said Caina, "that the Scholae approves of the glypharmor? Of Zalandris offering it for sale?"

"Opinion among the Sages," said Talekhris, "is...divided."

"And what about you?" said Caina. "Do you approve?"

Talekhris looked away, gazing at the frost crackling around the Staff of the Elements.

"No," he said. "I know what Zalandris thinks. He believes the glypharmor is a weapon so powerful that men will abandon war in fear of it. In this, I believe, he is a fool. He has not left Catekharon for three hundred years, and has forgotten the world outside the walls."

"But you have not," said Caina.

"No," said Talekhris. "I have traveled from the barbarian lands north of the Empire to the dusty ruins of Maat. Nations and kings come and go, but the hearts of men do not change." He tapped his chest. "In the heart of every man waits a lust for power. Like a sac of poison. The temptation of too much power ruptures the sac and floods the mind and soul with corruption...and the glypharmor is more power than any one man should possess."

"Then help me to stop it," said Caina.

"To claim the armor for your Emperor?" said Talekhris. "Do you believe he was the wisdom to wield such might?"

"No man has the wisdom to wield such might," said Caina. "I would see the glypharmor destroyed and the knowledge of its creation lost."

"Truly?" said Talekhris. "I am surprised. Most Ghosts would jump at the chance to seize power for their Emperor."

"I know better," said Caina. "You have been honest with me, so I shall be honest with you. I hate sorcery. It is a vile, abominable thing, and it brings nothing but suffering and death. If I could kill every last sorcerer in the world, every magus, every occultist, I would do it."

Belatedly she thought of Claudia.

"Such candor is rare," said Talekhris. "But it is unseemly for one Sage to oppose another."

"Even if," said Caina, "necromancy was used to create the glypharmor?"

Talekhris's blue eyes narrowed.

"Impossible," said Talekhris. "I felt no aura of necromancy around the armor, nor did I see it through my mask. Zalandris would never countenance such a thing. The Scholae has few rules, but it enforces them zealously. Necromancy is strictly banned."

"The Moroaica," said Caina, "told me there is necromancy in the glypharmor. That's why I collapsed in the Hall of Assembly. Her power reacted to the necromantic force within the armor."

Talekhris frowned. "She speaks to you?"

"Sometimes, in my dreams," said Caina, wondering if it had been a mistake to share that.

"If Mihaela used necromancy to create the glypharmor," said Talekhris, "the Moroaica would recognize it." He shook his head, rolling the metallic rod in his fingers. "I would not put it past Mihaela to do such a thing. She is...determined."

"The same could be said of you," said Caina, "given that you have chased the Moroaica across the centuries."

"True," said Talekhris. "But Mihaela, I think, is the mind behind the glypharmor. She used Zalandris's lessons to create it...but she created it, not him. And she convinced him to offer it for sale to the world."

"It seems strange for a woman like Mihaela," said Caina, "to create such a weapon in order to promote peace and harmony among nations. She must have some other motive."

"Precisely," said Talekhris. "Your logic rings true. If you can find proof that necromancy was used in the creation of the glypharmor, then I will help you to destroy it."

"Thank you," said Caina. "One more question."

Talekhris nodded.

"You can see the Moroaica's spirit within me," said Caina. "Why can't the other Masked Ones?"

"Because I have altered the spells upon my mask to seek her," said Talekhris. "And because I am a curiosity among the Sages. They think me a doddering madman, forever pursuing a phantasm that does not exist. Zalandris understands my mission, but few others do." He tapped a finger against the side of his rod. "But be wary. If any of the Sages learn that the Moroaica inhabits your flesh, they may well overreact and kill you on the spot."

Caina nodded, chilled, and went to find Halfdan and the others. Questions and fears chased each other through her mind. But one question burned at the forefront of her thoughts.

Jadriga had recognized the necromancy Mihaela had used to create the glypharmor.

Did that mean Mihaela was another disciple of the Moroaica?

12

THE FIRST MAGUS

"You let her go off alone?" said Corvalis, keeping the anger out of his tone.

He stood with Basil and Claudia in the corner of the Hall of Assembly, keeping a wary eye on the lords and sorcerers. The furor from Caina's collapse had died down. The Redhelms had reopened the doors to the Hall of Assembly, and the ambassadors started heading for their quarters.

Corvalis wanted to slip away with Claudia before their father saw them.

But as long as Caina remained with Talekhris, they could not.

Corvalis had rammed his sword through Talekhris's heart. How was the man even still alive? Did that mean the Masked One was a necromancer?

And would he try to kill Caina?

"Anna," said Basil, voice low, "can take care of herself."

"That Masked One tried to kill her in Cyrioch," said Corvalis. "Perhaps this is his chance to do it properly."

"Perhaps," said Basil, "but if he wanted to kill her, there would be better ways to accomplish it than by walking off with her in front of a crowd of witnesses. No, from what you said, he was...intrigued by

Anna. This is his chance to learn more about her. And she, in turn, has the opportunity to learn more about him. Why he tried to kill her, for one. And perhaps she can glean some useful information about the glypharmor."

Corvalis gave a reluctant nod. He had killed men with swords, with daggers, with his bare hands. Yet he had never seen anything like the glypharmor. One man with a suit of glypharmor could destroy an army with ease. If the glypharmor left Catekharon, it would change the world, and not for the better.

Claudia shook her head. "The Masked One is probably more in danger from her than the other way around. Her hatred of sorcerers is irrational."

"No, it's quite rational," said Basil.

"I hardly think so," said Claudia. "Her hatred of sorcery clouds every decision. It..."

"The hatred would only be irrational if she didn't have a reason for it," said Basil. "She has a very good reason for it. So her hatred is perfectly rational."

"Such an eloquent syllogism," said Claudia. "Hopefully it will not occur to Anna, lest she cuts Talekhris's throat."

"He won't try to kill her," said Basil. "She won't try to kill him, either. Information is sometimes more valuable than a life. She will learn some things that we need to know...and then we shall decide how to act."

"But suppose she cannot control herself," said Claudia. "Suppose..."

"She will," said Corvalis. "I have seen her masquerade as a caravan guard, a Sarbian mercenary, an opera singer's maid, and a merchant's daughter. Every time the impersonation was perfect. I would not have known it was her."

Yet that thought made him uneasy. He had seen how easily she moved from one persona to another. Did she regard him as a passing amusement? Or, perhaps, as a useful tool? He remembered a slave of the Kindred who he thought had loved him, but...

No. He could not think like that.

"She is a good actress," said Claudia. "What of it? That means..."

"That means," said Corvalis, "she has the self-control to keep herself in check. She'll..."

"Shut up," said Basil, his tone hard. "We have to go now."

Corvalis turned his head.

A jolt of alarm went through him.

"Go," he said. "I'll come back later for..."

"Too late," said Basil, straightening up.

"What is it?" said Claudia, and her eyes grew wide.

Decius Aberon strolled towards them, a wide smile on his ruddy face. Corvalis had not seen his father for years, not since Claudia had convinced him to flee the Kindred. The First Magus had not changed. His green eyes still glittered with cold arrogance, and his plump face was hard with contempt and pride.

"Oh, gods," whispered Claudia. "He'll kill us"

"The Sages won't allow it," said Basil. "He won't start a fight here and risk losing his chance at the glypharmor."

"No," said Corvalis. His heart sped up at the memory of a thousand punishments, a thousand petty cruelties. "He won't bother to kill us himself. He'll hire assassins to make it look like an accident."

"That's not funny," said Claudia.

"I wasn't joking," said Corvalis.

Then his father stood before them. Decius's cold eyes swept over them, glittering like a Sage's jade mask. Corvalis suddenly felt like he was twelve years old again, enduring his father's disappointment that he had no arcane talent.

And then his father had sold him to the Kindred for years of torment.

"Well, well," said Decius. "Basil Callenius of the Imperial Collegium of jewelers. It has been far too long."

Basil made a polite bow. "First Magus. You do me honor. Do you require jewelry? I can make a brooch wrought in the shape of the Magisterium's sigil. I think it would go nicely with your ceremonial robes."

"It would," said Decius. "And such a generous offer. But, alas, I think your other employer might take offense."

"My other employer, First Magus?" said Basil. "I am a merchant, and naturally I wish to have as many customers as possible."

"But your chief customer," said Decius, "is doddering old Alexius Naerius."

"I believe you are referring to His Imperial Majesty," said Basil, "the Emperor of Nighmar."

"A man who has no business ruling," said Decius. "The Empire is in a state of chaos, Master Basil. The disorderly and slovenly commoners do not show proper respect to the nobles. The nobles and magistrates waste their time scheming and plotting rather than contributing to the greater glory of the Empire."

"How positively dreadful," said Basil. "I assume, of course, that the magi would make for better rulers."

"Indeed they would," said Decius. "With the strong hand of the magi overseeing the Empire, we would enter a new golden age."

His eyes turned towards Corvalis and Claudia.

"And children," he said, "would no longer be so disrespectful of their parents."

Claudia tensed, and Corvalis put his hand on her shoulder.

"Nothing to say?" said Decius. "No matter." He turned his attention back to Basil. "Are you aware of your two new hirelings' sordid history? They have quite the dark past."

"It was my understanding," said Basil, "that they were your bastard children. I suppose that is a sordid enough past for any man or woman."

Decius laughed. "Basil, Basil. Insulting the First Magus of the Magisterium is hardly the path to a long and profitable career. Did you know that Claudia betrayed me, forsook her oaths to the Magisterium, and fled the Empire? And did you know that Corvalis here was once an assassin of the Kindred? I thought that all brothers and sisters of the Kindred had the death sentence upon them."

"A man can change," said Basil.

"He cannot," said Decius, lip curling with contempt. "Corvalis was broken and remade into a weapon. He was once my weapon, and then my foolish daughter convinced him to betray me. Now he is your weapon. He cannot even speak for himself."

"I can speak," said Corvalis, "just fine."

Decius's smirk was indulgent. "A dog can be taught to bark on command, but still has nothing useful to say."

"I am not," said Corvalis, "your dog."

"You were my dog," said Decius. "Now you are the Ghosts' dog. That is the only difference. You are still who I molded you to be, Corvalis."

"A killer," said Corvalis, his free hand tightening into a fist.

"A killer," agreed Decius. "You ought to thank me, really."

"For what?" snarled Corvalis. "Selling me to the Kindred? All the people you had me kill? All the blood on my hands? I should thank you for that?"

"For every bit of it," said Decius. "I made you exceptional, Corvalis. You're not particularly intelligent, and you have no arcane talent. The Kindred took you and made you into a killer without peer. Without them, you would be another useless bastard child of a nobleman, a wastrel squandering his life with wine and prostitutes. Rather than a man who will help build the new order."

"Truly," said Basil, "he was fortunate to have such a wise and prudent father."

"Mockery, Basil?" said Decius. "Let me share one of Corvalis's lessons with you. You know the Kindred reward successful assassins with gold and wine and comely slaves to warm their bed. Young Corvalis grew rather taken with one of his bed slaves. Attached, even." He smiled. "A folly. So I hired the slave to kill him in his bed. If she succeeded, I would free her."

Corvalis said nothing. He did not want to remember this.

"She surprised him and almost killed him...but he was faster and killed her first," said Decius. "The Elder of Artifel told me that he wept like a child."

"Corvalis," whispered Claudia, looking at him with wide eyes.

He had never told her about that.

"You were right about one thing, Father," said Corvalis. "I do owe you. I owe you so much. And by all the gods, I will repay it."

"You won't," said Decius. "A dog might wish to bite his master's hand...but the master is still the master."

"You are a monster," said Claudia, her voice tight. "I thought...I thought being a magus would be a wonderful thing. That we would serve the people of the Empire, that we would protect and defend them. Instead we are tyrants, and you would make us into crueler tyrants yet."

"I would," said Decius. "The common mass of men are nothing more than dumb animals, more interested in rutting and their next meal than higher matters. Those of us with arcane talent have a duty and a right to govern mankind. An Empire ruled by the Magisterium will be a better Empire, and will lead the way to a better world."

"You would bring back slavery to the entire Empire," said Claudia.

"And I would be right to do so," said Decius. "For the great mass of men is fit for nothing but the collar. It is for their own good, Claudia. As you will learn, once you return to us."

"What do you mean?" said Claudia.

"Ranarius turned you to stone with that pet elemental of his," said Decius. "But he failed, and paid the price for his failure. You have been chastised enough, I think. Return to the Magisterium, and all shall be forgiven. Great days lie ahead of us, and you can be a partner in the new order to come."

Claudia said nothing, and for an awful moment Corvalis wondered if she would accept the First Magus's offer. She had loved their father until Corvalis's return had shown her the awful truth of what the Magisterium really was.

"No," said Claudia. "No, Father. I have seen you for what you really are. I will not help you torture and murder innocents in pursuit of your own power, and will not help you enslave the Empire."

Decius smiled, but Corvalis saw the rage in his eyes.

"Pity," said the First Magus. "But there is one thing you don't understand. You belong to me. You both belong to me. And I will make you suffer for your betrayal. You'll scream, Claudia, and you'll beg for mercy. You'll wish you were one of the slaves toiling in the fields of Cyrica before I'm done with you." The green eyes shifted to Corvalis. "And you, my wayward dog...why, a dog must be beaten for disobedience, no? You loved that pretty little slave of yours. A weakling like you will fall for another woman sooner or later. And when you do, I'll take her from you and make her suffer for your disobedience."

An image of Caina at the First Magus's mercy flashed through Corvalis's mind. He knew what kind of tortures Decius Aberon enjoyed inflicting upon his prisoners.

"Decius," said Basil, still pleasant, but this time his voice carried an edge, "while this show of bluster is amusing, it has grown tiresome."

"Indeed?" said Decius. "You doubt my ability to carry out my promises?"

"Not at all," said Basil. "But if you do, I suspect Zalandris will be disinclined to sell you the glypharmor. The honored Sage has the idea that the wielder of the glypharmor will bring peace to the world...and I doubt he will choose a man who murdered his own son and daughter."

"Perhaps not," said the First Magus. He turned his head. "Torius!"

Corvalis knew that name.

One of the battle magi strode over, the black plate armor clanking. The man was about thirty-five, with a hard, lean face and harsh green eyes. His blond hair and beard had been cut to stubble, and a sneer spread over his lips as he looked them over.

"Well, Father," said Torius. "It seems your favored pet and wayward dog have returned. Shall I kill them?"

Corvalis watched his older half-brother. Torius was a strong magus and the oldest of Decius Aberon's bastard children. He had served as the First Magus's strong right hand for years, dispatching Decius's enemies and enforcing the will of the Magisterium.

And he was at least as cruel as Decius. As a child Corvalis had suffered his attentions more than once.

"Torius," said Corvalis. "Somehow you get uglier every time we meet."

Torius laughed. "Little Corvalis. Skulk back into the shadows where assassins belong. Or would you rather face me in open combat?" His armored hand fell to the hilt of his sword. "I would enjoy that. Let us see if the miserable tricks of the Kindred allow you to stand against a battle magus of the Magisterium."

"Now, now," said Decius. "Our hosts would take it amiss if we spilled blood in their Hall. This is merely a friendly conversation." His smile did not touch the green ice of his eyes. "Until we meet again."

Decius turned his back and strolled away. Torius smirked, and then rejoined his father.

They stood in silence.

"Well," said Basil at last. "That was certainly pleasant."

"Then you have a twisted understanding of pleasure," said Corvalis. "We may as well wait for Anna now."

After some time Caina returned to the Hall, her blue skirts whispering against the white stone of the floor. Her expression was calm as ever, but Corvalis knew her well enough by now to see the hints of strain around her mouth and eyes.

"You are feeling better, daughter?" said Basil. "The Sage found no damage from your...episode?"

"Yes, I'm fine," said Caina, looking back and forth between them. "Did I miss something?"

LATER THAT NIGHT Corvalis leaned upon the railing of his room's balcony, looking at the reflection of the glowing steel upon the smooth waters of the crater lake.

He thought of his father's threats.

He thought of Claudia's hesitation when the First Magus had asked if she wished to return.

And he remembered the slave woman who had tried to kill him. He had thought Nairia had loved him, but he had been a fool.

Was he a fool now?

He heard the faint whisper as his door slid open and reached for his sword hilt.

But it was Caina. She wore only a robe, her hair down and her makeup scrubbed away.

"What did Basil say?" said Corvalis.

"Tomorrow we're going to speak with Annika," said Caina. "All of us. She has contacts throughout the city. If Mihaela used necromancy to create the glypharmor, she might have built the armor at a location outside the Tower of Study, away from the Sages' notice. One of Irzaris's warehouses, maybe. Annika might know where to find it."

Corvalis nodded. "You should go back to your room and get some sleep. Tomorrow will be a long day."

She blinked, and it was as if a mask fell away. She looked younger, somehow, and tired, so very tired.

Corvalis held out a hand, and she crossed to him and rested her head against his chest.

"I have nightmares, sometimes," she said, her voice little more than a whisper. "Such terrible nightmares."

"As do I," said Corvalis.

"I don't want to sleep alone tonight," Caina said. "Let the slaves gossip. I don't care."

Corvalis nodded. "It would make sense for your masquerade. A merchant's daughter would seek the arms of her illicit lover after episode trying day."

Strengthening her disguise. Was she wearing a disguise with him, even now? Would she one day try to cut his throat, as Nairia had done?

She slumped against him a little more.

"I don't want to sleep alone," she whispered. "Please."

Corvalis nodded and led her to bed.

13

A WEEPING SLAVE

The next morning, Caina dressed for the desert.

She pulled on a robe of sand-colored cloth and a heavy turban. Around her waist went a belt of worn leather holding a dagger and a sheathed scimitar. She kept her hair concealed beneath the turban, and shaded her jaw and cheeks with makeup to create the illusion of stubble. Caina was too pale and too short to look properly Sarbian. But few enough Sarbians ever came to Catekharon, and her disguise would fool casual observers.

Especially in the midst of Saddiq's men.

"Gods," said Corvalis, adjusting his own robe. "How do the Sarbians fight in these? Don't they trip over the hems?"

"They're divided front and back," said Caina. "But they prefer to fight on horseback. Shoot their enemies full of arrows, ride away, and then hit them again a few hours later. It works. Both the Empire and Anshan have lost armies in the Sarbian deserts. Ready?"

Corvalis nodded, and followed her into the hallway. Halfdan and Claudia awaited them there, both clad in Sarbian robes. Halfdan, as always, melded into his disguise, while Claudia seemed anxious and ill at ease.

"You look," said Halfdan, "positively disreputable. Like you'd cut my purse and my throat and dump my corpse into the lake."

"Don't be absurd," said Corvalis. "You see how still those waters are? I dump you in the lake, everyone in the city and the Tower of Study will see it. Much more sensible to dump you in the aqueduct. All the molten metal would burn away the evidence."

Caina laughed.

"That's not funny," said Claudia. There were dark circles under her bloodshot eyes. The encounter with her father had done little to help her get a good night's sleep. "I'm sure our father and Torius will do that to us, if they get the chance."

"Let us laugh while we can," said Halfdan. "Matters will become grim soon enough. In the meantime, we shall find Saddiq and carry out that tyrant Master Basil's errands."

THE AMBASSADORS, AND THE AMBASSADORS' guests, had been lodged in the various palaces ringing the Tower of Study, but the Masked Ones had housed the ambassadors' various guards in a Redhelm barracks near the causeway to the city proper. Caina was surprised there hadn't been a riot. Saddiq and six of his men waited outside the barracks, and straightened up at Halfdan's approach.

"Aye?" said Saddiq.

"Master Basil has given us instructions," said Halfdan in Cyrican with a Sarbian accent. "We are to go into the city and purchase supplies. Some cloth, some silk from the Anshani factors. And some silver candlesticks. Apparently the master's daughters have taken a shine to them."

"Indeed," said Saddiq. "One must be attentive to the whims of one's womenfolk."

He grinned at Caina, and she grinned back.

"Come," said Saddiq. "The sooner we return, the sooner the master will be pleased."

"WE'LL STOP HERE," said Halfdan as Annika's pawnshop came into sight. "We will meet you back at the Tower of Study."

"As you say," said Saddiq. "We shall make haste. I do not like this half-empty city. Why would anyone want to live near this coven of unnatural sorcerers?"

Caina understood.

Saddiq and his men went about their errands, while Caina, Corvalis, and Claudia followed Halfdan into the pawnshop. The interior remained as gloomy and dusty as Caina remembered. This time Annika sat upon a stool, her cane propped against the counter, making notes in a ledger. She wore a green Anshani-style robe, and would have looked pretty if not for the scar marring the left side of her face.

"Well," Annika said, looking up. "Sarbians from the great desert of the north. One sees many strange things living in the City of the Artificers, but Sarbians are rare indeed. How may I serve you?"

Halfdan pulled off his turban. "Annika. You are looking well."

Annika blinked and set aside the ledger. "Marcus Antali?" That was another of Halfdan's aliases. "Ah, you clever scoundrel! I never thought to see you again."

She heaved to her feet, grabbed her cane, and to Caina's surprise, hobbled across the room and gave Halfdan a hug.

"It seems you have come to some prosperity," said Halfdan.

Annika snorted. "Of a sort. Still, it is good to be a big fish in a small pond, no?" Her smile faded. "I thought this business with the Scholae was already serious when Anna and Cormark came to visit." She shot a glance at Caina and Corvalis. "But for you to come in person from the Empire...the Emperor takes this very seriously, does he not?"

"As he should," said Halfdan. "Mihaela demonstrated her weapon last night."

"I heard," said Annika. "My friends among the slaves of the Tower told me. A terrible weapon, a suit of living armor that rends men like a child crushing insects." She shook her head. "How could Mihaela create such an evil thing? Does she not see the wicked uses to which it will be put?"

"Perhaps she does," said Caina, remembering Mihaela's sour expression, "and she rejoices in it."

"Perhaps," said Annika. "Mihaela...carries a great deal of rage."

"Understandably," said Halfdan.

Annika shook her head. "As do I. But we all carry scars. Yet that does not give us the right to inflict scars upon others in retribution."

"Wisely said," said Halfdan.

"Bah!" said Annika, but she smiled. "Wise is simply a polite way of calling a woman old. I should beat you with my cane." She sighed. "But you shall have whatever aid you require, if it is in my power. My sister and I owe you our lives and our freedom. I remember, even if Mihaela does not."

Caina should not have been surprised to learn that Halfdan had been the one to arrange their freedom. The man seemingly had friends and associates everywhere.

"Thank you," said Halfdan. "We will need your help."

"The Emperor wants Mihaela's armor?" said Annika.

"No," said Halfdan. "We want to destroy both the armor and the knowledge of its creation."

Annika stiffened. "Then you will kill Mihaela?"

"I would prefer," said Halfdan, "that she may be made to see reason."

That was an evasion.

"But that may not be necessary," said Halfdan. "I don't know how Mihaela created the glypharmor, but I am certain of one thing. She used necromancy to forge it."

"Necromancy?" said Annika. "The Scholae forbids its use within the city. And surely one of the Sages would have sensed its presence. The Sages prefer to ignore the outside world, but they are strict about this. Any necromancers found within the walls of Catekharon are slain at once."

"Nevertheless, I am certain," said Halfdan. "And therein lies our opportunity. If we can prove that the glypharmor is a product of necromantic science, the Sages will turn against Mihaela and destroy the glypharmor. Then no one will obtain the armor, and the problem will be solved."

"But do we truly know for certain," said Claudia, "that Mihaela used necromancy to create the glypharmor?"

"We do," said Halfdan.

"We do not," said Claudia, looking at Caina. "We only have her word for it."

"That is enough for me," said Halfdan.

"It shouldn't be," said Claudia. "That room was filled with sorcerers, and none of them said anything about sensing necromantic power in the armor. The Sages have wielded sorcery for centuries. Surely they would have sensed something."

"You think I am lying?" said Caina.

"I think you believe yourself to be telling the truth," said Claudia. She looked at Halfdan. "But you know how much she hates sorcery. Maybe she is seeing things where there is nothing to see."

"Then," said Caina, keeping her temper under a tight grip, "what else would you suggest? That we approach Mihaela and ask her nicely?"

"Yes," said Claudia. "You're so quick to assume that she used necromancy, that there must be a dark secret behind the glypharmor. Perhaps Mihaela is simply a genius."

"She was always clever," said Annika.

"Maybe she discovered something, some application of arcane science that never occurred to the old men of the Scholae," said Claudia. "Rather than fearing her, we should recruit her. Think of how her skills and knowledge could aid the Ghosts."

"That is a poor idea," said Caina. "You saw what she did with the glypharmor. Even if she did not create it with necromancy, then she still used her power to forge a terrible weapon. The Ghosts would be no more trustworthy with that weapon than anyone else."

"You speak," said Claudia, "as if sorcery is some sort of corrupting power that ruins everyone who wields it."

"It is," said Caina.

"That is irrational."

Caina felt her temper start to slip. "I have seen little enough evidence otherwise."

"What about me?" said Claudia. "I was a magus." Annika's eyes got a little wider. "Do you think I will become a monster? Are you going to cut me down where I stand?"

"We will have to wait and see, won't we?" said Caina.

Corvalis looked at her, eyes narrowed, and Caina felt a pang of guilt. Claudia was Corvalis's sister, and Caina had all but threatened to kill her. But if Claudia went too far, if she betrayed the Ghosts, if she started using necromancy, then Caina would kill her without hesitation.

The thought chilled her.

And Corvalis would never forgive her.

That thought made her feel even worse.

"This discussion is pointless," said Halfdan. "We cannot act until we know more. And the first thing we need to know is how Mihaela created the glypharmor."

"It seems our best approach," said Corvalis, looking away from Caina, "is to find out where Mihaela created it."

Annika shrugged. "She has rooms in the Tower of Study. Many of the more favored Seekers do. But they are warded and guarded."

"There might be a better way," said Caina.

They all looked at her.

"Mihaela made the glypharmor out of red steel from Nhabatan," said Caina, "and we know who is bringing that steel into the city."

"Who?" said Annika.

"A Catekhari merchant named Khaltep Irzaris," said Caina.

Annika laughed. "Irzaris? Irzaris is working with Mihaela?"

"You know him?" said Halfdan.

"Better than I would like," said Annika. "The man is a scoundrel, and will deal in anything that turns a profit. He has contacts with every bandit gang and shady mercenary company in the free cities. From time to time he hires them to attack caravans, seize the merchandise, and sell the merchants and their guards to the Istarish slavers' brotherhood. He has an opulent mansion on the other side of the lake, and warehouses full of merchandise." She snorted. "Villainy pays, it seems."

"Until the payment comes due," said Halfdan. "Irzaris is friendly with Mihaela. They spent a great deal of time talking last night."

"And perhaps," said Annika, "he is behind the raids."

"Raids? What raids?" said Halfdan.

"In the last several months," said Annika, "there have been a number of attacks on villages and caravans west of the city. Bold attacks, too, and no witnesses ever left behind. The Redhelms haven't been able to find the raiders. But none of Irzaris's interests were ever touched."

"He wouldn't be the first merchant to hire men to kill his competitors," said Corvalis.

"Aye," said Caina, "but why bother, if he's selling the red steel to Mihaela?"

Halfdan shrugged. "Irzaris would hardly be the first man to allow greed to scramble his wits. However Mihaela creates the glypharmor, it seems Irzaris is the weakest link in the chain. I think we will have a look around his warehouses."

"If you do, be careful," said Annika. "Irzaris is a scoundrel, but he's not a fool. He keeps his warehouses well-guarded."

"Fortunately," said Halfdan with a smile, "we are not fools, either." He bowed and planted a kiss upon Annika's hand, who laughed. "It is good to see you again, Annika. I am pleased you have prospered."

"Yes," said Annika, waving a hand at the shelves, "my kingdom of dust and old pans."

"Or you have your wealth hidden," said Halfdan.

Annika smiled. "It's as if some clever man once taught me that ostentatious wealth draws unwelcome attention. And that secrets and friends are often far more valuable than any amount of gold."

"A wise woman," said Halfdan. He looked at the others. "Come along. We have a burglary to plan."

He led the way from the shop, and Claudia refused to look at Caina as they left.

THAT AFTERNOON, Caina lay down on her bed, trying to rest.

While still disguised as Saddiq's men, they had taken a trip around the curve of the lake and located Irzaris's warehouse. The ugly, squat building of brick and clay tiles sat at the western end of the city. Armed guards kept watch at the door, but Caina noted that the guards paid no attention to the warehouse's roof. If Irzaris was as cheap as most merchants, he would have built skylights into his warehouse's roof rather than bother with the expense of lamp oil or enspelled glass globes.

Those skylights made for a convenient access point.

Tonight Caina and Corvalis would break into the warehouse and look for additional information.

Corvalis and Claudia had gone off together, talking. Caina closed her eyes, resting her head against the pillow, and tried to sleep. Tonight would prove difficult, and she needed her rest.

Instead her mind returned to Corvalis and Claudia.

What was she going to do about them?

Caina had worked with men and women she disliked before, with men and women who had hated her and held her in contempt. None of it had troubled her. She had even worked with sorcerers before. Rekan, a traitorous magus of the Magisterium, had taught her to guard her thoughts from sorcerous intrusion.

But Caina hated sorcery.

And she had not been sharing a bed with Rekan's brother.

Caina sighed and rubbed the heels of her hands over her face. Claudia was right. Caina loathed sorcery, hated it more than anything. It had taken her father and her ability to bear children. And she had never met a sorcerer whom she liked or trusted.

But maybe Corvalis was right. Maybe Claudia was different.

Caina got to her feet, scowling. Corvalis said nothing, but she could see how much her dislike for Claudia bothered him. How could she blame him? Claudia was his sister. He had loved her so much that he had dared terrible risks to save her. Claudia had been his only family, the only person he loved for years.

What could Caina offer against that?

Perhaps it would be better if she broke it off with Corvalis.

To her surprise, she felt her eyes sting at the thought.

She stalked to the balcony, looking at the lake. This was all new to her. She had never been close to a man before, not like this, and she didn't know what to do. She wished she could talk to Theodosia about it.

At the very least, Caina could be more civil to Claudia.

No matter how much she detested sorcery.

She heard footsteps at the doorway and turned. A young man in an orange slave's tunic stood there, his hands brushing at his sides in a fit of nervousness.

"Shaizid," said Caina. "I need nothing at the moment, thank you."

"Mistress," said Shaizid. "You look...you look very sad."

Caina stared at him.

"Forgive me," said Shaizid, flinching as if she had struck him. "I meant...I meant no disrespect mistress, no disrespect..."

"Do not worry about it," said Caina. "I was thinking. Remembering the past. And sometimes the past is...quite sad."

"Yes," said Shaizid. "It is, mistress."

Something clicked inside Caina's mind.

"What did Mihaela do to you?" she said.

"I...I don't understand," said Shaizid. "Please..."

"I've seen the way you look at her," said Caina. "And I've heard you crying. Mihaela promised you something, didn't she? Something you want very badly. But she hasn't delivered it, and you're too afraid to approach her."

"I must go, mistress," said Shaizid, turning. "Please..."

"Shaizid," said Caina.

The slave froze, his thin limbs trembling.

"I might be able to help you," said Caina.

And perhaps, the cold part of her mind realized, she could learn something useful from him.

Shaizid stood motionless for a long time.

"My sister," said Shaizid at last.

"What was her name?" said Caina.

"Ardasha," said Shaizid. "After great Ardashir the Golden, one of the mightiest Shahenshahs of our homeland. We were sold to the Scholae very young, but quickly rose in the Sages' favor." He managed a smile. "No one can prepare coffee as well as Ardasha and I...and the Sages drink a great deal of coffee."

"I can imagine," said Caina.

"Then Ardasha manifested the power," said Shaizid. "A sorcerous talent. Strange things happened around her...she could read minds, or call objects to her hand just by thinking about it. So the Seeker Mihaela accepted her as a student."

"Wait," said Caina. "The Seekers can take students of their own?"

"Yes," said Shaizid. "The Seekers may do whatever they wish, so long as they obey their Sages and follow the rules of the Scholae. Ardasha was freed, and Mihaela took her as a student. She said...she said that once she became a Seeker in her turn, she would buy me and set me free..."

"What happened instead?" said Caina.

"I don't know," said Shaizid. "Ardasha disappeared months ago. Mihaela refuses to speak to me, and has the seneschal beats me whenever I ask. I cannot approach the Sages to ask them. A slave cannot speak to a Sage. No one will talk to me, and I do not know what happened to Ardasha!" He sobbed, once, and rubbed his hand across his eyes. "Mistress, forgive me, this..."

"No," said Caina, and she touched his shoulder. "No. I am...only a merchant's daughter. A merchant's younger daughter. But I swear to you, I will find out what happened to Ardasha, if I can."

"Thank you," said Shaizid. "Thank you, mistress." He shivered. "I must...I must return to my duties."

He left without another word.

14

HALF-BROTHERS

Caina and Corvalis left the Tower of Study before nightfall disguised as caravan guards. Corvalis wore his usual clothing, a leather jerkin over chain mail, worn boots and trousers, sword and dagger at his belt. Caina wore a leather jerkin studded with steel rivets, daggers hidden in her boots and throwing knives strapped to her forearms. She had raked her black hair to fall in greasy curtains over her face and pulled up the cowl of her ragged brown cloak. She looked like any other dusty caravan guard, albeit one shorter than most.

She also carried a leather satchel, its strap over her chest, extra tools riding inside the bag.

"We'll watch the place for an hour or so," said Corvalis. "Long enough for dark to fall and for the guards to get bored. Then we'll circle around back, scale the wall, and go through the skylights."

"A good plan," said Caina.

Corvalis grinned. "I thought you might like it. Gods know you've probably broken into more places than I have."

"I have no recollection of that, of course," said Caina.

Corvalis snorted, and they walked in silence for a while, circling along the lake.

"How is Claudia?" Caina asked at last.

Corvalis sighed. "She can't make up her mind about you. You saved her life, our lives...and you hate her."

"I don't hate her," said Caina.

Corvalis looked at her.

Caina shook her head. "At least...not her directly. I hate sorcery. And she is a sorceress."

"I understand why you hate sorcery," said Corvalis. "I've seen your scars. You haven't told me how you got them, but I can guess."

Caina did not answer.

"Claudia is not like the others," said Corvalis. "Not like the First Magus or the occultists."

No, thought Caina. Corvalis did not love the other sorcerers.

"She thinks the glypharmor is a good idea," said Caina.

"She doesn't," said Corvalis. "You saw what happened. She was so sickened she threw up at the demonstration."

"Then why doesn't she think necromancy was used to create the armor?"

"I think," said Corvalis, "she sees something of herself in Mihaela. A woman trying to use her sorcery to change the world for the better. Misguided, maybe...but trying to change the world nonetheless."

"Gods," said Caina, "I hope not."

"Would you really kill her?" said Corvalis.

"Who? Mihaela?" said Caina.

"No," said Corvalis. "Claudia."

"She's your sister, Corvalis," said Caina. "I'm not going to hurt her."

"But if she does something you don't like," said Corvalis. "If she goes over the line."

Caina opened her mouth, and then closed it.

"Gods," said Corvalis, looking away. "You would, wouldn't you?"

"What you would do?" demanded Caina. "If she started wielding necromancy? Or started working for a slavers' band? Or is she decided the First Magus was right after all and returned to the Magisterium? Would you go along with her?"

"Of course not," said Corvalis. "I'd try to talk her out of it, make her see sense."

"But if she refused?" said Caina. "What then?"

"I..." Corvalis shook his head. "This is not the time to discuss this. We have a task. We can talk about it later."

"Very well," said Caina, and they lapsed into silence.

The shadows lengthened as they walked, and soon they came to the western side of Catekharon. Abandoned warehouses lined the streets, a wasteland of crumbling brick and cracked clay tiles. Some of the warehouses had guards, and four men in chain mail stood before the double doors to Irzaris's warehouse, watching the streets with wary eyes.

They stared at Caina and Corvalis as they passed, and Caina started telling Corvalis a joke in Caerish, putting a drunken stagger into her walk, while Corvalis laughed.

"Well?" said Corvalis once they rounded a corner, out of sight of the guards.

"The northern wall of Irzaris's warehouse," said Caina. "I doubt the guards make an effort to circle the building. Once the sun goes down, we'll climb up to the roof and go through the skylights."

Corvalis nodded, and they circled around Irzaris's warehouse, making sure to stay out of sight of the guards. In a nearby alley stood a stack of abandoned crates, and they slipped behind the pile. Silence hung over the alley, and as the sun disappeared beneath the city's western walls the clouds overhead glowed, reflecting the sullen light from the canals of molten steel.

"Makes it easier to see, at least," said Corvalis.

"The Scholae installed enspelled lamps on the main streets," said Caina, reaching into her satchel, "but not back here. Just as well."

She pulled out a long black cloak.

The cloak was a wondrous thing, black as shadow and light as air. Only the Ghosts knew the secrets of making shadow-cloaks, of infusing shadows within silk. The cloak allowed Caina to hide in the shadows much more effectively while letting her move with far greater stealth. It also shielded her thoughts from mind-altering spells, and made her almost undetectable through sorcery. Caina pulled on a mask and hung the cloak over her shoulders, pulling up the cowl to shadow her face.

"I would like one of those," said Corvalis. "I can think of a few times when it would have been useful."

"Like right now," said Caina, speaking in the disguised, rasping voice she used while wearing the cloak. Anyone who saw her would not see Basil Callenius's spoiled daughter. Instead they would see a hooded shadow speaking in a grating rasp.

"You'll have to teach me how you do that," said Corvalis.

"Later," said Caina. "This way."

They hurried through the narrow alleys and soon reached the back wall of Irzaris's warehouse. Caina reached into her satchel and drew a coil of thin, tough rope, one end tied around a collapsible steel grapnel. She opened the grapnel and threw it, and felt it catch on the metal gutter twenty feet above.

She gave the rope a tug, made sure it was solid...and then stopped.

"What is it?" whispered Corvalis.

"Sorcery," said Caina. "Nearby."

She had grown used to the constant overpowering aura of sorcery surrounding the Tower of Study and the canals of molten metal, ignoring the damned headaches as best she could. But now she felt the presence of weaker sorcery from within the warehouse.

"Wards?" said Corvalis.

"Maybe," said Caina, closing her eyes and trying to concentrate on the unpleasant sensations. "I...don't recognize it. If it is a ward, it's a weak one."

"Then perhaps we've found Mihaela's hidden workshop," said Corvalis.

"Perhaps," said Caina.

"I'll go up first," said Corvalis. He hauled himself up hand over hand, moving with admirable silence, and crouched on the edge of the roof. After a moment he nodded, and Caina hurried up the rope. She gripped the edge of the gutter and started to pull herself up...

The air rippled.

A dozen men stepped out of nothingness, moving to surround Corvalis in a semi-circle. Eleven of the men looked like common mercenaries, clad in chain mail and leather, swords in their hands. The twelfth man wore elaborate black plate armor and carried a black sword. He grinned at Corvalis, his pale green eyes glinting in the sullen glow from the clouds overhead.

Torius Aberon.

"You know," said Torius, pointing his sword. "I had my doubts about this little plan. I didn't think anyone would be clever enough to trace the trail back to the warehouse. But the Ghosts are like cockroaches. You turn up everywhere." He smiled. "And like cockroaches, you must be stamped out."

"Torius," said Corvalis, drawing his weapons. Caina took a deep breath, reaching for a throwing knife...

"Though I am surprised," said Torius, "that you were stupid enough to come here alone."

Caina froze. Why didn't Torius see her? Then her brain caught up to her surprise. It was night, and she was wearing her shadow-cloak. Torius couldn't see her, and the cloak would shield her from any sensing spells.

That gave her a chance to act.

One chance.

Because if she did not think of something clever, both she and Corvalis were going to die.

"How did you appear like that?" said Corvalis. "A nice trick. I could have sworn the rooftop was empty."

"A Seeker shared a useful spell with me," said Torius, still grinning. "The arcane science of illusions. The Magisterium has neglected it, which seems unwise."

Good. Corvalis was playing for information.

Caina slipped one of the throwing knives from her belt.

"I suppose," said Corvalis, "this elaborate ambush is Father's doing?"

"Father," said Torius, "hates you, Corvalis. You know how he feels about disloyalty. But this has nothing to do with you. You just had the poor luck to blunder into my trap. I was hoping to snare one of the stormdancers, or perhaps an Anshani occultist." He laughed. "You saw how those fools drooled over the glypharmor. Any one of them would rip the world apart to get their hands on just one suit. It made sense that at least one of the ambassadors would try to figure out how the armor was created." He waved his sword at Corvalis. "Which is why we are having this conversation."

Caina pulled the rope up behind her, the knife clenched in her fingers.

"And what," said Corvalis, "would Father do with a captive storm-dancer or occultist?" He smirked. "Assuming a magus of your feeble skills could even capture one."

"That," said Torius, "is not your concern. It's a pity you hate Father too much to join us, Corvalis. Your skills would prove quite useful in the next few days."

"Oh?" said Corvalis. "So why don't you invite me to join you?"

Torius laughed. "Invite a Ghost spy into our midst? Yes, that would go well. The truth is...I find you contemptible, Corvalis. Contemptible and weak. I heard how you wept when your precious little Nairia tried to kill you. I cannot abide weakness. A pity you haven't found some other woman. I would enjoy killing her in front of you first."

Torius had inherited his father's charm.

"And Father will reward me for killing you," said Torius. He glanced at his mercenaries. "Kill him. Make sure to leave the head intact. The First Magus will want it for a trophy."

The mercenaries moved, Corvalis lifted his sword and dagger, and Caina sprang into motion.

She surged to her feet, threw back her arm, and flung the throwing knife with all her strength behind it, her arm snapping like a whip. The weapon hurtled handle-over-blade from her hand.

Torius's armor reached high enough to cover his throat, so she aimed for his right eye instead.

But her aim was off, and Caina's knife clipped the right side of his jaw. Torius doubled over with a shout of surprised pain, hand shooting to his face, while the mercenaries hesitated in sudden alarm.

"Run!" shouted Caina, hand dipping into her satchel.

She yanked out a small glass vial. When they had destroyed the Haven of the Kindred in Cyrioch, Caina had found the formula for the elixir within the vial among the Elder's records.

She only hoped she had prepared it correctly.

Corvalis saw the vial and sprinted towards her.

Caina flung the vial against the rough clay tiles of the roof, and the glass shattered. There was a brilliant white flash, and a plume of smoke erupted from the roof. She heard confused shouts as the mercenaries stumbled in the smoke.

The distraction would not last long, but hopefully long enough for Caina and Corvalis to get away.

Corvalis reached her side, and she grabbed the rope and shoved it into his hands. Corvalis gave a sharp nod, and Caina wrapped her arms around his chest.

And then they jumped off the roof. Caina hoped she had guessed the length of the rope properly.

She had, and they came to a jerking halt two feet above the alley, swinging on the rope. Caina pushed away from Corvalis and landed, and Corvalis did the same, knees flexing to absorb the impact.

They sprinted down the alley.

"Kill them!" roared Torius, his voice booming over the rooftops. "Find them and kill them both!" But by the time the mercenaries climbed down from the roof, both Caina and Corvalis would be long gone. They raced into the street, the four guards at the warehouse's door gaping at them...

A black blur shot overhead and landed a dozen yards away with a clang of steel.

Torius glared at them, blood dripping from the gash on his jaw.

Like the other magi, the battle magi unleashed blasts of psychokinetic force, using their very thoughts as weapons. Unlike the other magi, the battle magi trained using bursts of psychokinetic power to enhance the strength of their arms and legs, making them stronger and faster than ordinary men.

And capable of superhuman feats, like leaping from a warehouse rooftop in full armor.

"The other way!" said Caina.

"Stop them!" roared Torius, pointing at the warehouse guards. "A hundred gold coins to the man who brings me their heads!"

The warehouse guards sprinted into the street, blocking the other direction. Caina heard shouting from inside Irzaris's warehouse as the men atop the roof hastened for the doors.

"Damned Ghosts and your damned tricks," growled Torius, lifting his sword. Caina backed away, looking back and forth. Torius blocked one end of the street, the guards the other. "Smoke bombs and knives." She saw a narrow door in the warehouse to her left, splintered and worn. No doubt it was the slaves' entrance. "Let's see if your tricks can stop this."

Caina felt a surge of power as Torius gathered strength for a spell, and the doors to Irzaris's warehouse swung open, the mercenaries spilling into the street.

"Corvalis!" said Caina. "Left!"

Corvalis flung himself against the narrow door with all of his strength. Caina wondered if it would hold, if she and Corvalis were about to die...

But the door was old, and it ripped free of its hinges. Corvalis darted through the door, and Caina raced after him. And as she did, she heard a roaring noise, felt a rushing wind, and a black blur hurtled past her.

Torius, running in a sorcery-enhanced charge. But his sorcery allowed him to run so quickly that he could not change directions easily once he started moving. He thundered past the doorway, and then Caina ran after Corvalis. The warehouse's interior was deserted, a thick layer of dust covering the planks of the floor. The double doors on the far wall stood ajar, leading to another street.

"There!" said Caina. "Go!"

They ran for the double doors and jumped through them as the mercenaries stormed into the warehouse.

"Where?" said Corvalis. "The main streets?" Redhelms patrolled the main streets of Catekharon, and they would respond to any fighting. Caina doubted Torius would be willing to cut down the Scholae's soldiers in order to kill Corvalis.

But the battle magus was fast, and Caina didn't know if they could reach the main streets before Torius killed them.

A memory surfaced, a workshop she had seen on the way to Irzaris's warehouse...

"Follow me!" said Caina, and she ran to the right. They left the abandoned warehouse behind, and came to a street lined with workshops. She saw a potter's shop, a blacksmith, a store selling goblets, and...

There. Just as she remembered. A carpenter's workshop.

She risked a glance over her shoulder, and saw a dark blur atop the abandoned warehouse as Torius jumped from it.

"In there!" said Caina, pointing at the workshop.

Corvalis nodded and put his boot to the door. One, two, three kicks later and the door splintered, and he shoved aside the wreckage and hurried inside. The room looked little different than any other carpenter's workshop Caina had seen. She saw racks of tools, stacks of lumber, and shelves and chairs in various states of completion.

And a layer of sawdust covering everything.

"Through the back door," said Caina, "right now."

She reached into her satchel, fingers closing around another vial.

Corvalis raced across the workshop, threw aside the bar, and opened the back door. Beyond Caina saw another narrow alley. Corvalis stepped outside, and Caina followed.

Then she stopped, turned, and stared back into the workshop.

"Get clear of the door," said Caina.

"What..." started Corvalis.

"Do it!" said Caina.

A moment later Torius Aberon appeared at the front door, kicking aside the remains of the door. He saw Caina and stepped forward with a grin, his sword coming up, her skin crawling as she felt him summon power...

In one motion she threw the glass vial into the shop and flung herself to the side. She heard the shattering glass, glimpsed the white flash from the corner of her eye...

And then a wall of hot air exploded from the shop's back door and slammed Caina against the far wall. A sheet of flame erupted from the door, and Corvalis grabbed her shoulders and dragged her away. Caina got to her feet and stumbled into him, her ears ringing.

"What did you do?" said Corvalis, shouting over the roar of the flames.

"That story you told me," said Caina. "In Cyrioch, while we were hunting Mhadun."

Corvalis gave her a puzzled look.

"About the master assassin who spent weeks stuffing sawdust into a crawlspace and blew up his victim," said Caina. She gripped his arm and caught her balance. "I'm just...I'm just glad it actually worked..."

Corvalis laughed. "Gods, you're clever."

Caina grinned behind her mask. "Let's get out of here before the Redhelms notice the..."

A hulking shape wreathed in blue light burst from the back door of the burning workshop.

It was Torius. A shimmering shell of blue light surrounded him, a ward to keep the flames from touching his flesh.

"Guess I'm not that clever," Caina said.

Torius lunged at them, and Caina sidestepped, yanking a dagger from her belt. Corvalis parried Torius's first blow, striking back as the blue glow faded from the black armor. Torius growled and dodged, but a hair too slow, and Corvalis's sword struck home.

Yet the blade rebounded from the battle magus's black plate armor.

Caina flung a knife, aiming for Torius's face, and the black sword came up. The knife bounced from the blade with a clang and clattered the ground. Corvalis struck again, but the older man jumped back, Corvalis's strike clanging off his shoulder plates.

Caina drew another knife. Corvalis would need a heavier weapon to get through Torius's black steel plate. Yet Torius himself was not moving with his earlier superhuman speed. The ward against flame must have drained his powers. If Caina could knock him off his feet, Corvalis could land a killing blow.

Torius raised his free hand to cast a spell, but Corvalis was faster. He attacked with a quick series of swings, disrupting Torius's concentration and driving the battle magus back. Caina threw another knife, and Torius jerked his head to the side, the blade spinning past his ear.

"Damn you!" he roared, lifting his sword.

For a moment a hint of fear flickered across his expression.

He drew back his free hand, and Caina felt the surge of arcane force.

"Corvalis!" she said. "A spell..."

Torius thrust his hand, and invisible force erupted from his armored fingers and slammed into Caina. The blast knocked her back a half-dozen steps and sent her sprawling to the ground, and she saw Corvalis fall with a grunt.

"This isn't finished," snarled Torius, his jaw dripping with blood and sweat. Caina staggered back to her feet, ready to meet his attack, but Torius turned and ran with spell-enhanced speed. He reached the end of the alley, jumped over a workshop with a stupendous leap, and vanished from sight.

Why had he fled?

She crossed to Corvalis and offered a hand, and he climbed back to his feet.

"It seems," said Corvalis, "that we scared him off."

A flicker of motion caught Caina's eye.

"I don't think," she said, turning, "that we were the ones who scared him off."

A man dropped from the rooftops and landed in the alley. He had dark hair and brown eyes, and wore gray leather armor, a blue-green cloak hanging from his shoulders. In his right hand he carried a sword of Kyracian design, the blade swirling with freezing mist. Caina felt the faint touch of his arcane senses.

It was Kylon.

15

RED STEEL

Kylon looked at the two Ghosts. He did not think they would attack him, but caution rarely went amiss.

And he had not thought two Ghosts could face a battle magus of the Imperial Magisterium and survive.

"Well," said the taller of the two Ghosts, a man with close-cropped blond hair and pale green eyes. "Are we going to fight?" His emotions brushed against Kylon's senses, fear and anger overlaid with iron discipline and self-control.

The smaller Ghost, the one in the shadow-cloak, said nothing. Kylon's arcane senses could not penetrate that cloak, but he had a good idea of who was inside it anyway.

"You're one of Decius Aberon's sons," said Kylon, "aren't you?"

"Aye," said the green-eyed man. "Are you here to kill us?"

"No," said Kylon.

"Then why are you here?" said the man, lifting his sword.

"Corvalis," said the shorter Ghost, and Kylon recognized the voice. The Ghost drew back her cowl and pulled off her mask, and Kylon found himself staring at the face of the woman who called herself Anna Callenius. "If he wanted us dead, he could have let Torius kill us."

Without the cowl of the shadow-cloak, he could sense her emotions, and she knew that. Which meant that whatever the Ghost told him next, she wanted him to know that she was telling the truth.

Or she was an even better actress than he had guessed.

"So I take it," said Corvalis Aberon, "that you're not here to kill us?"

"No," said Kylon. "Though I am curious why you were fighting Torius Aberon."

"To kill him, of course," said Corvalis.

"You weren't going about it very well," said Kylon. He looked at the Ghost. "Though when I saw the building catch fire, I should have known you would be near."

Her lip twitched. "I only set fire to that warehouse in Marsis twice."

"His ward against the fire depleted his strength," said Kylon, pointing at the burning workshop. "If he had not fled, I would have killed him."

"And now you will kill us, I assume?" said Corvalis.

"No," said Kylon. He released some of his power. The freezing white mist around his sword blade vanished, and he slid the weapon into its scabbard. "The time has come for us to work together."

The Ghost said nothing, but he felt the ripple in her emotional sense.

"Oh?" said Corvalis. "Work together to do what? Claim the armor for New Kyre?"

"To destroy it utterly," said Kylon.

The Ghost's blue eyes narrowed. "You said you would prefer to destroy the armor, but you would claim it for New Kyre if you saw no other course."

"I have reconsidered," said Kylon. "The glypharmor will destroy whoever purchases it."

"Were you not paying attention during Mihaela's demonstration?" said Corvalis.

"I saw everything that you did," said Kylon. "But consider. If the Assembly of New Kyre claims the glypharmor, every other nation will turn against us. The glypharmor is too powerful for our foes to do otherwise. The Empire, Istarinmul, Anshan, and the free cities will put aside their traditional enmity to destroy us, lest we use the glypharmor to dominate the world. And the same would happen to your Empire if Lord Titus claims the glypharmor."

Kylon's city could not survive such a war. New Kyre was powerful, but fragile. It was only one city, dependent upon trade for its wealth and food. A war over the glypharmor would destroy trade and slowly squeeze the Kyracian people to death.

A touch of dark humor went through the Ghost's emotions. "Then perhaps we ought to let the First Magus claim the armor so the nations will unite and destroy the Magisterium. The world would surely be improved for it."

"Perhaps," said Kylon, "but half the world would be destroyed in such a war."

"Very well," said the Ghost. "We will hear you out. I suggest we discuss this well away from here. Sooner or later this fire is going to draw unwelcome attention."

Corvalis stared at him with open suspicion. Kylon did not care. He suspected Corvalis would do whatever the Ghost told him to do.

"Very well," said Kylon. "This way."

The Ghost took a moment to tuck away the shadow-cloak and pull up the cowl of her rough brown cloak, giving her the look of a caravan guard. Kylon was amazed the transformation. The figure standing before him bore no resemblance to the lovely young woman he had seen in the Hall of Assembly, or to the shadow-cloaked figure that had sown such terror among the Istarish soldiers in Marsis.

"Let's go," said the Ghost.

Kylon led them away from the burning workshop.

※

"WHAT IS THIS PLACE?" said the Ghost.

Kylon had taken her and Corvalis to a public house near

Catekharon's eastern gate. Dozens of low tables were scattered around the common room, and men, mostly Anshani and Istarish, sat on cushions around the tables, speaking in low voices and sipping from clay cups. Colorful Anshani tapestries hung from the brick walls, and slaves in orange hurried back and forth.

"It is called a coffee house," said Kylon. "An Anshani custom. Both merchants and nobles gather in these places and drink coffee as they discuss business."

He seated himself on a cushion, and the two Ghosts followed suit. A slave hurried over, and presented them with three cups of coffee.

"Interesting," said the Ghost. "A pity there are no such places in Malarae. I suspect much business is conducted of the sort the Ghosts wish to hear."

"I suppose," said Corvalis, "that you will stand out in a place like this."

"Less than you might think," said Kylon, taking a sip. He had never drank coffee growing up, but after becoming a stormdancer he had helped capture a pirate ship with a cargo of Anshani coffee beans and developed a taste for it. "Anyone who sees us will assume that I am a Kyracian merchant, and that you are merely my guards."

"The best lies," said the Ghost, "are told with the truth. If we pretend to be here to discuss business...then let us discuss business." Her icy blue eyes examined him. "You said you had decided to destroy the armor. How did you find us?"

"Purely by accident," said Kylon. "During Mihaela's demonstration, I saw her speaking with a Catekhari merchant named Khaltep Irzaris. Irzaris has an unsavory reputation in New Kyre, and I thought it odd that he would be friendly with a Seeker of the Scholae. Therefore I decided to investigate further."

A flicker of surprise went through the Ghost's emotions. "Your instincts were correct. Irzaris is supplying the red Nhabati steel Mihaela used to create the armor. One of his caravans traveled with Lord Titus's embassy."

Kylon nodded. "I hoped by tracing the source of Mihaela's

supplies, I could find her workshop, and learn how she created the glypharmor."

"In hopes of making it for yourself?" said Corvalis.

Kylon shook his head. "In hope of destroying it. You have no reason to trust or believe me. But I spoke the truth when I said I wanted that armor destroyed."

He remembered Andromache dying on the floor of that tomb. He had seen what happened when men reached for power beyond their grasp.

"In any event," said Kylon, "I learned the location of Irzaris's warehouse, and was making my way there when I saw the fire. I noticed several bands of mercenaries searching the streets, and saw you confronting Torius. I assume he set a trap for you?"

"Aye," said the Ghost, "but not us specifically. It seems that Torius, too, thought someone might investigate Irzaris's warehouse." Her brow furrowed. "But why lay a trap there? Why not break into the warehouse himself? Surely the First Magus must want to make glypharmor himself. Why..."

"Wait," said Corvalis, his green eyes narrowing, his emotional sense flooding with suspicion.

"What is it?" said the Ghost.

"You know Torius Aberon, stormdancer?" said Corvalis.

Kylon nodded, intrigued. He had assumed Corvalis was a simple fighter, but it seemed he had some level of cunning.

"I didn't see you speak with him at the Hall of Assembly," said Corvalis, "and the Magisterium considers the sorcerers of New Kyre to be dangerous barbarians. He wouldn't have socialized with you unless he had a good reason."

"You're right," said Kylon. "I have met him before."

The Ghost looked at Corvalis, and to Kylon's utter astonishment, he sensed warmth in her emotional aura, something different than the usual molten hatred that shimmered beneath her icy mind.

The Ghost and Corvalis were in love.

And to his even greater astonishment, he felt a mild pang of jealousy. But only a mild one. The Ghost was lovely, albeit when wearing proper women's clothing, and her mind was sharper than a razor. But she was dangerous. Her hatred of the magi drove her on, like oil poured onto a fire, and sooner or later it would lead her to destruction.

Along with anyone close to her.

For a moment Kylon felt pity for Corvalis Aberon, but he pushed it aside. The safety of New Kyre was Kylon's concern, not the fate of one Ghost and her lover.

"When did you meet Torius?" said the Ghost.

"When he came to New Kyre several months ago," said Kylon. "Torius has been sailing on a regular basis for one of the free cities south of New Kyre. In retrospect, it is clear he has been visiting Catekharon on behalf of his father."

"Why did he come to New Kyre?" said the Ghost.

"Because," said Kylon, "he was sailing on a merchant trader from Malarae. Normally we would have stopped and destroyed his ship, since our nations are at war. But Torius negotiated a pact in the First Magus's name for safe passage to the free cities."

"He did?" said the Ghost, her expression darkening. "And what did the Assembly receive in exchange?"

"Information about the Imperial fleet," said Kylon.

"Then Decius Aberon," said the Ghost, "has betrayed the Empire in pursuit of his own agenda."

Corvalis shrugged. "You're surprised? The Magisterium has always regarded itself as the rightful government of the Empire. And my father will do whatever he wants, if he can get away with it."

"He'll regret this," said the Ghost. "So the First Magus sent Torius in secret to Catekharon before the Scholae issued its invitations." She gazed into her coffee. "Either he already knew about the glypharmor..."

"Or he knows something about its creation," said Corvalis. "Or he assisted Mihaela with funds and supplies. He's done that sort of thing before. From time to time he will support a magus's secret research in hopes of gaining a useful weapon. Remember Ranarius and the Defender?"

"Who is Ranarius?" said Kylon, puzzled.

"He was the preceptor of the Cyrioch chapter of the magi," said the Ghost, "and one of the Moroaica's disciples." Kylon scowled. "But he's dead. It seems that both Irzaris and Torius might know part of the process to construct glypharmor."

"But if they do," said Kylon, "why did the First Magus come at all? Why not simply have Torius bring him the knowledge?"

"Because," said Corvalis, "my father is a serpent. Torius must only know part of it. If Mihaela gave him the entire...spell, or design, or whatever, the First Magus would kill her to make sure the knowledge did not spread to his foes."

"Then the First Magus is here," said the Ghost, "for a negotiation of his own. The others are haggling to buy completed glypharmor, but the First Magus is negotiating in secret for the knowledge of creating the armor."

"What could he possibly offer Mihaela and Zalandris?" said Kylon.

Corvalis shrugged. "Zalandris probably knows nothing of this. Maybe Mihaela wants money, or power, or legitimacy. If she joined the Magisterium, my father would likely make her one of the high magi, and she would have more power than all but a few men in the Empire."

"There is power enough in Catekharon," said Kylon.

"Sorcerous power," said the Ghost, "not political power. And what is the point of sorcerous power if not to amass political power?"

Kylon disagreed, but he knew not to press the point with her. "Then we must discover what Torius and Irzaris know."

"We'll have a devil of a time getting anything out of Torius," said Corvalis. "He's not stupid, and he almost finished us tonight. He'll be on his guard now."

"Irzaris, then," said the Ghost. "He'll be well-guarded, but a merchant's guards are an easier target than a battle magus."

"What do you propose?" said Kylon.

Her emotional aura grew icier. "We abduct him and make him talk."

"Your...friends will have to arrange that," said Kylon. "I cannot do it. I have a guard of ashtairoi, but if I assault Irzaris, the Scholae will expel the Kyracian embassy from the city. You will need to do it in secret."

Her smile was chilly. "We've had some experience with that."

"I suspect so," said Kylon, taking another sip of coffee.

"We shall find out more," said the Ghost, "and I will make contact once we do."

Kylon nodded. He did not trust the Empire, and he certainly did not trust the Emperor's Ghosts. But in a peculiar sort of way, he did trust her. Or, more precisely, he trusted her hatred of sorcery. If there was a way to destroy the glypharmor, she would do it heedless of the cost.

"Very good," said Kylon, rising. "I will await your message."

"Kylon," said the Ghost.

Her tone made him sit back down.

"There is one other thing," she said. "Somehow Mihaela used necromancy to create the glypharmor."

"We think," added Corvalis, and Kylon sensed a ripple of annoyance in the Ghost's aura.

But he hardly noticed. Necromancy was a crime in New Kyre, its practitioners executed. And Andromache had wielded it, using the Moroaica's secret spells to make herself the most powerful Kyracian stormsinger in centuries. With that power, she had become one of the city's nine Archons.

And that power led her to destruction.

"Necromancy," repeated Kylon, and he remembered what the Ghost had said about Ranarius. "Then... Mihaela is a disciple of the Moroaica? Like my sister?"

Corvalis blinked in surprise, and Kylon rebuked himself. No one save for Kylon and the Ghost knew the truth. Still, Andromache was already dead. If the rumor spread of necromancy, it would seem like only one more calumny heaped upon a defeated Archon.

"I don't know," said the Ghost, frowning. "She might be. Or maybe a student of one of her disciples. But it hardly matters. One of the Sages has been trying to kill the Moroaica for centuries."

"Unsuccessfully, it seems," said Kylon.

The Ghost nodded. "But the Scholae refuses to have anything to do with necromancy. A legacy of their history in Maat. If we can prove that Mihaela used necromancy to create the glypharmor..."

"Then the Scholae will kill her for us," said Kylon.

Again the Ghost nodded.

"But we are not yet sure it is necromantic," said Corvalis.

Again that ripple of annoyance went through the Ghost's emotions.

"It makes sense," said Kylon. "Those hieroglyphs upon the armor are Maatish, and necromancers ruled the Kingdom of the Rising Sun. Old Kyrace warred against them for centuries."

"And if the First Magus gets his hands on the glypharmor," said the Ghost, "you might have to face a new form of Maatish necromancy."

"Then it is better than no one wield the glypharmor at all," said Kylon, rising once more. "I will await word from you. If you have need of my aid, call upon me."

He left the coffee house, thinking. He had no doubt that the Ghost could do what she claimed. But he would not leave the fate of New Kyre entirely in her hands.

He would destroy the knowledge of the glypharmor, whatever the cost.

CAINA FINISHED HER COFFEE. Corvalis noticed that she had developed quite a taste for it since arriving at Catekharon. He preferred wine, though he had to admit that coffee kept the wits sharp.

They left the coffee house and walked back to the Tower of Study, the canals of burning steel filling the night sky with an eerie glow.

"Do you trust him?" said Corvalis.

"Kylon?" said Caina. "Of course not."

"For a man you do not trust," said Corvalis, "you told him a great deal."

"I don't have to trust him," said Caina. "I have something better than trust. I understand him. He is a man who will do what he sees as the right thing, even if he does not like it. And he is wise enough to see the danger of the glypharmor. So I trust him to help us destroy it."

"Even though he is a sorcerer," said Corvalis.

"Aye," said Caina.

"But you hate sorcerers," said Corvalis.

Her expression turned blank. "Sorcery is hardly my favorite thing."

Corvalis took a deep breath. "So you trust Kylon of House Kardamnos to act as you wish...but you do not trust Claudia."

"We shouldn't talk about this here," said Caina.

Corvalis gestured at the deserted street around them. "No one is around to hear us."

"No," said Caina at last, voice quiet. "No, I don't trust her."

"Why not?" said Corvalis. "Because she can use sorcery? The stormdancer can use sorcery."

"Because I understand her," said Caina.

"What?" said Corvalis, forcing down the anger. "How can you possibly understand her? Have you known her all your life?"

"You haven't known her all your life," said Caina. "You were separated for years. And during those years she became a magus."

"So?" said Corvalis. "How is that any different than a stormdancer?"

"She thinks like a member of the Magisterium," said Caina. "Kylon thinks like a stormdancer, which means he will do whatever is necessary to defend New Kyre. Claudia thinks like a magus."

"She doesn't think like the other magi," said Corvalis. "She wants to use her sorcery to help people."

"That is the problem," said Caina.

"That she wants to help people?" said Corvalis. "Would you prefer her to act like Ranarius, ready to destroy half the Empire to make herself stronger?"

"No," said Caina.

"Then what's wrong with using her sorcery to help people?" said Corvalis.

"Because she believes it gives her the right to rule over people," said Caina.

Corvalis opened his mouth to argue, and found that he did not have an answer.

"She wants to use her powers to help," said Caina. "I believe that, I truly do. But she thinks the power gives her the right to help. Even if the people she is helping do not seek her aid. Even if they do not want her help. That is not very different than ruling over people. Your father would say he is acting for the good of the Empire..."

Corvalis glared at her. "Claudia is nothing like my father!"

"She is," said Caina, not flinching away from him, "whether you like it or not. I'd wager Decius Aberon says he acts for the good of the Empire, doesn't he? That the Empire would be better served with the magi ruling, rather than the Emperor and the Imperial Curia. That the commoners and nobles would be happier if they heeded their sorcerous betters. I would wager your father even believes that himself. But that's not what he's really doing, is it? He's increasing his own power and authority, all in the name of the good of the Empire. What he did to you, selling you to the Kindred...he did it because he claims to use his powers to help people."

"She is not like my father," said Corvalis, his hands curling into fists.

"Not yet," said Caina, "but that's how it will start. She'll want to use her power to help people. Then she'll help them whether they want it or not. After that, she'll use her power to force them to act as she thinks they should, all for their own good. And then she'll need more power to help more people, and she'll be no different than any other magus."

"She left the Magisterium," said Corvalis.

"But she still acts like a magus," said Caina. "She's not convinced the glypharmor is a bad idea. And she's always ruled you."

Corvalis laughed. "What are you talking about? She spent over a year imprisoned as a statue. Hardly a way to rule over me."

"You only left the Kindred," said Caina, "because of her. She decided to leave the Magisterium because of what you showed her, and she convinced you to go along with her. And when she joined the Ghosts, you came with her. I doubt she's ever questioned that you will do whatever she wants, because she has sorcery and you..."

"Enough!" said Corvalis. "She was the only one who cared about me for my entire life! I doubt you would understand. Your entire family was slain, and..."

He regretted the words as soon as they came out of his mouth, and he stopped himself. But it was too late. Caina's eyes widened, and for an instant he saw the pain flash across her face.

Then her expression returned to the cool, distant mask.

"You're right," she said. "I don't understand. We should return to the Tower of Study. Master Basil will want to know what we've learned..."

"I should not," said Corvalis, "have said that."

Caina stopped, looked back at him, and closed her eyes.

"No," she said, voice soft. "You shouldn't have." She looked at him. "But...perhaps I have been too critical of her. Maybe...maybe not every sorcerer would turn into a power-mad tyrant at the first opportunity." He heard the doubt in her voice. "Perhaps it would have been better if she stayed with Theodosia. I suspect...I suspect working undercover is not Claudia's strength."

"Gods, no," said Corvalis. "She would have hated the fun we just had."

"Fun?" said Caina.

Corvalis shrugged. "How often do you get to burn down a building?"

She lifted an eyebrow. "More often than you might think." She took a deep breath. "I do think it is noble. How much you risked to save her."

"Thank you," said Corvalis. "I know you have your reasons to hate sorcery as much as you do. Gods know I'm not fond of it either. But Claudia is not a monster. Nor will she become one. I swear it."

"If you say so," said Caina, "then I will trust you on it."

"Because you understand me?" said Corvalis.

"Yes," said Caina, "but because I do trust you."

They walked back to the Tower of Study together.

16

SUBTERFUGES

The embassies gathered for dinner in the Hall of Assembly as guests of the Scholae.

This time, the Catekhari served their guests in a peculiar fashion. Rather than offer tables and chairs, slaves circulated through the crowds, bearing trays of wine and coffee. Caina helped herself to coffee, while Halfdan took a flute of wine. Other slaves followed, carrying trays of unusual foods. Fish crusted with bread crumbs, popular in New Kyre. Goat meat fried on skewers, a favorite of the Anshani nobility. Dates crusted with sugar from Istarinmul, and bread fried in olive oil from Malarae.

"A peculiar custom," said Corvalis, popping a sugared date into his mouth.

"I read that it was Maatish in origin," said Claudia, again wearing a green gown of elaborate design. Caina wondered how much Halfdan spent on clothes to maintain their various disguises "The pharaohs held dinners like this, serving foods from the various lands conquered by the Kingdom of the Rising Sun."

"To display their dominance?" said Caina.

Claudia blinked. Perhaps she had expected Caina to lecture her. "Ah...yes. The foods were brought as tribute to the pharaoh."

"Or perhaps he simply liked dates," said Corvalis, eating another.

"Unlikely," said Claudia. "The Kingdom of the Rising Sun never reached north of what is now southern Anshan, and..."

Caina listened to Claudia's history lesson with one ear and looked at the guests. The various embassies stood in small, defensive knots, the lords and sorcerers staying close to their various retainers. She saw Yaramzod the Black speaking in a low voice to the Arsakan, saw Kylon talking with another stormdancer. Only the merchants circulated freely. Which had been the entire point of inviting merchants along with the ambassadors.

That, and turning a profit.

Khaltep Irzaris approached, clad in a fine tunic of spotless white linen.

"Master Basil," said Irzaris with a polite bow. "I trust business has gone well?"

"Indeed it has, Master Khaltep," said Halfdan with a bow of equal depth. "It seems there are a great many jewelers in Catekharon with a need for raw gemstones."

"Yes," said Irzaris. "They make a fine profit selling the Sages cut gems for their enspelled artifacts...and you, in turn, can make a fine profit by supplying them with uncut stones."

"And you, I suppose," said Halfdan, "have made a profit of your own. With your red steel used in the production of such a...prominent artifact."

He looked across the Hall to the central chamber where Mihaela had stood with her suit of glypharmor. There was no trace of her now. Caina supposed she was busy producing more of the damned things.

"I have," said Irzaris. "The greatest profit of my career, Master Basil." He sighed and took a sip of wine. "All these years traveling from one end of the world to another, selling baubles only for a few coppers of profit, and all this time, I never realized the secret."

"What secret is that?" said Halfdan with a laugh. "I am not adverse to profit myself."

"Power," said Irzaris. "Find those who will one day have power, and supply their needs. You see, it is rather difficult to acquire power without the proper materials, and I can supply the proper materials."

"I would not have expected," said Halfdan, "a Seeker to possess power."

"Mihaela?" said Irzaris. "Not yet, my friend, not yet...but she will."

"It sounds like you are quite besotted," said Halfdan.

Irzaris snorted. "Mihaela? No, she is wed to her work. But she is set to rise high...and she will remember her loyal friends. And when that happens, I will be one of the most prominent men in the free cities, perhaps in the world." He smiled at Claudia, bowed over her hand, and planted a kiss upon her fingers. "Though, alas, wealth and power are hollow if a man has to enjoy them alone."

Claudia attempted to smile, though it looked more like a cringe. "You are...very flattering, sir."

"And very direct," said Caina, and Claudia shot her a grateful a look.

Irzaris gave her a condescending smile. "Fortune favors the bold, my dear."

"Though I do wonder," said Caina, "why a woman would wish to marry a man who made such dreadful weapons."

Irzaris grinned. "Money, of course. Men crave beauty...but women desire security, do they not? Safety and security and comfort, and a strong man can provide all three."

"You speak truly, Master Khaltep," said Halfdan. "I can see some profitable business between us. Why don't we...ah, daughter." He put a hand on Caina's shoulder. "There's a slave with some more bread. Why don't you bring him over here?"

She followed his eye and saw Shaizid hurrying across the Hall.

"Of course, Father," said Caina.

She gathered her skirts in her hands, crossed the Hall of the Assembly, went over the bridge crossing the flow of molten steel, and approached Shaizid.

The slave straightened up as she approached. "Ah...mistress. Yes. May this slave serve you?" He looked at his feet. "My...my question of you, mistress. Did you..."

"Shaizid," said Caina, "I need your help. And, no, I have not yet found Ardasha. But if you help me now, I might get closer to finding an answer."

"What would you have of this slave, mistress?" said Shaizid. He met her gaze, briefly, and then looked at his feet again.

"Do you know the Sage Talekhris?" she said.

"Yes, mistress," said Shaizid. "He is reclusive, even for a Sage. Often he is gone from the Tower of Study for long periods of time."

"Take me to his rooms," said Caina.

Shaizid flinched. "Mistress...it is not allowed for a slave to approach a Sage."

"You won't be approaching a Sage," said Caina. "You'll be merely taking me to his rooms so I can approach him."

Shaizid hesitated.

"If he asks," said Caina, "I will tell him that I found his rooms on my own. He will never know that you were involved. And if I speak with him, perhaps I can learn what happened to Ardasha."

That made up Shaizid's mind. "This way, mistress."

He led her from the Hall of Assembly and up a long, narrow flight of spiraling stairs. Shaizid turned a corner, and Caina found herself on a balcony encircling the cylindrical chamber at the heart of the Tower, the pool of molten steel glowing far below. Wooden doors lined the balcony, each carved with elaborate Maatish hieroglyphs.

"Where are we?" said Caina.

"Near the top of the Tower," said Shaizid. "Some of the Sages keep their quarters here." He swallowed. "A slave...a slave should not be here. I must go, mistress."

"Thank you," said Caina. "If I learn anything, I will let you know. Which door belongs to Talekhris?"

Shaizid pointed, bowed to her, and fled back to the stairs. Caina crossed to the door, surprised at how easy this had been. For all their power, the Masked Ones seemed indifferent to their security. Perhaps they did not expect...

She stopped a foot from the door, a crawling tingle passing over her skin.

Powerful wards waited upon the door, wards that would burn her to ashes should she touch the wood.

She suspected that knocking upon the door was out of the question.

Caina reached for her belt. A sheathed dagger with a curved blade waited there, and it looked like the sort of ornamental weapon a wealthy woman might carry. She drew the dagger, the silvery blade gleaming. The weapon had been fashioned from ghostsilver, a rare metal that was harder and lighter than steel.

It was also proof against sorcery.

Caina took a deep breath, rested the tip of the dagger upon Talekhris's door, and raked it across one of the hieroglyphs. The dagger's hilt grew hot, painfully hot, beneath her fingers, and the blade flashed with a white glow. The door shuddered in its frame, and Caina hoped it would not explode into a rain of splinters...

The door jerked open, and Talekhris stood there, his silvery rod leveled at her face.

"Anna Callenius," he said. He scowled at the door. "You ruined several of my wards."

"I would have knocked," said Caina, "but I suspect the door would have exploded."

"Not quite," said Talekhris, frowning at the groove she had carved into the wood. "But the results would have been...equally deleterious. If you wished to speak with me, why did you not send a message?"

"Because," said Caina, "I need to speak to you without anyone overhearing. Sending a message would rather defeat the point."

"Very well," said Talekhris. "Enter."

Caina followed the Sage into his rooms.

The chamber beyond looked like a bizarre mixture of a workshop, a library, and a museum. Wooden shelves sagged beneath the weight of books and scrolls in a variety of languages. Glass display cases held daggers, bowls, rings, and amulets, and Caina felt the sorcerous power within them. A variety of tools, glass jars, and peculiar metal instruments stood on long wooden tables, and metal shavings and sawdust gritted beneath her boots.

Talekhris had been chasing the Moroaica for centuries...and in all that time, Caina doubted his rooms had been cleaned even once.

"What do you wish of me?" said Talekhris.

"Assistance," said Caina.

"Elaborate," said Talekhris, his eyes distant. "Have you found proof that Mihaela used necromancy to create the glypharmor?"

"Not yet," said Caina, "but I know where to find it. Mihaela built the glypharmor with red steel from Nhabatan. She bought that steel from Khaltep Irzaris, a merchant of this city. So our plan is to get Irzaris and force him to talk."

"How?" said Talekhris.

"By kidnapping him from his mansion and...persuading him," said Caina.

"That is a bold plan," said Talekhris. "He will be well-guarded."

Caina shrugged. "It is our only option. Taking him in the Tower of Study would earn the ire of the Scholae. Attack him in the street, and we might draw the attention of the Redhelms. Kidnapping him from his mansion is the best option."

"And what is it that you need from me?" said Talekhris.

"Any Sage can command the Redhelms?" said Caina. "Is that correct?"

"It is," said Talekhris. "Few bother. Zalandris usually oversees the Redhelms, since it is the Speaker's role to deal with the outside world."

"Then," said Caina, "I need you to order the Redhelms to stay away from Irzaris's mansion tomorrow night. No matter what happens, no matter what reports they receive, they need to stay away from Irzaris's house."

"And you think," said Talekhris, "that Khaltep Irzaris will have proof Mihaela used necromancy to forge the glypharmor?"

"No," said Caina. "At least, he won't have all the information we need. He's...one more link in the chain. And if we follow that chain long enough, we'll find what we seek."

"A sound plan," said Talekhris. "Very well. I shall speak with the

commander of the Redhelms, and bid him to ignore anything...
unusual happening at the house of Khaltep Irzaris."

"Thank you," said Caina. "One other question. Apparently
Mihaela took a slave named Ardasha as a student."

"I recall that," said Talekhris. He closed his eyes for a moment, as
if thinking. "Yes. It was a few months before I left Catekharon to...to
find you, as it happens."

"Do you know what happened to her?" said Caina.

Talekhris shrugged. "I fear not. I take no Seekers of my own, and
pay little attention to their doings. She was here when I left...and I
assume she is now gone?"

"Apparently Mihaela promised her freedom," said Caina, "but
Ardasha has not been seen for months. Her brother is desperate to
find her."

"I will make inquiries," said Talekhris. "Though I suspect
Ardasha learned just enough spells to suit her and then fled. Such
things have happened before when a slave becomes a student of a
Seeker."

"Her brother seems certain," said Caina.

A smile flickered over Talekhris's face. "I am sure he does. Love
often blinds us to truths we find...unpalatable."

Caina thought of Corvalis and Claudia.

"And a question for you, Ghost," said Talekhris.

"I will answer it," said Caina, "if I can."

He picked up a cane from a table and leaned upon it. "The
Moroaica. Since we last spoke, has she...appeared in your dreams
at all?"

"No," said Caina.

"And you do not see her in the waking world?" said
Talekhris. "Like a vision or a hallucination that only you
can see?"

"No," said Caina.

Talekhris sighed. "Has she ever arranged to have you killed? She
has many disciples, and if she can appear in your dreams, she can
also communicate to them through their dreams. Surely she must

know that if you are slain, she is free to claim a body that she can control."

"No," said Caina. "Sicarion wanted to kill me to free her, but she forbade him from doing it."

"Why?" said Talekhris, half to himself. "Why not kill you?"

Caina hesitated. "She...thinks she can recruit me, given enough time. That once I understand her grand design, that I will aid her willingly, even enthusiastically."

"Would you?" said Talekhris.

"Of course not," said Caina. "I have seen the carnage and the horror she has wrought. And I doubt she has any grand design. Only a desire for power and the destruction of her enemies."

Yet Caina was no longer so sure, not after the vision she had seen of Jadriga as a girl. Perhaps Jadriga was wandering through the centuries taking revenge on anyone who reminded her of the men who had slain her father. But perhaps she did have some greater plan, some vision to reshape the world.

But what?

Talekhris grunted. "That is only a half-truth. She never does anything for a single reason. Always there is a larger goal. But what? Why would she want to come to Catekharon wearing your body?"

"Do you think she arranged all this?" said Caina. "The glypharmor and Zalandris's invitation? She couldn't have possibly known I would come to Catekharon."

Yet she did not believe her own words. Coincidences were only the signs of an underlying pattern she could not yet see.

"I am unsure," said Talekhris. "Perhaps she simply wishes to recruit you. If she fails, the decades of your life are only a short time to one who has lived millennia." He gazed at a table, eyes distant. "And yet...I wish you long life and health, Ghost. For the longer you live, the longer the Moroaica is trapped."

"You can help guarantee my health and long life," said Caina, "by making sure the Redhelms stay away from Irzaris's mansion tomorrow night."

She left without another word.

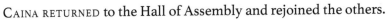

CAINA RETURNED to the Hall of Assembly and rejoined the others.

"Ah, daughter," said Halfdan. "Did you find the slave with the bread?"

"No, Father," said Caina. "I fear he quite eluded me."

"Pity," said Halfdan. "Well, we shall eat soon enough. Master Khaltep has generously invited me to dinner at his mansion tomorrow evening to discuss matters of business. I may bring one companion with me, and since I am a grim widower, I suppose one of my lovely daughters shall have to accompany me."

"Master Khaltep," said Corvalis, standing at Halfdan's side, "strongly hinted that he would very much like Claudia to see his collection of Anshani tapestries."

Claudia sniffed. "I do not enjoy the thought of enduring that... that preening huckster's ungracious attentions." She sighed and squared her shoulders. "Still, Father, if it will assist your...business efforts, I suppose I can survive one evening."

"Thank you, daughter," said Halfdan with grave dignity, though Caina saw the amused twinkle in his eye.

"I am affronted," said Caina, hiding her smile. "One daughter, and not two? Am I so fat and ugly that I failed to catch his eye?"

"At least you wouldn't have to endure his attempts at wit," said Claudia. "I suppose you can take consolation from that."

"And," said Corvalis, "from other places."

He winked, and Caina did her very best not to laugh.

17

GRINNING SCARS

That night Caina stood in her shift in Claudia's room.

"Please," she mumbled around the pins in her teeth, "hold still. I don't want to draw blood."

Claudia sighed and shifted on her stool. "I dislike the idea of being dangled as...as bait. I might as well dress up like an Istarish harem girl and parade myself in front of him."

Caina, who had done that once, said, "It would be better if you stayed fully dressed." She plucked a pin from her teeth and adjusted Claudia's hair. "There. That's better."

Claudia peered in the mirror. "It...does look better, doesn't it?" She raised a tentative hand to her hair. "I never thought of wearing it that way, I admit."

Claudia knew virtually nothing about cosmetics, and had planned to wear the same gown from last night to Irzaris's mansion. She had grown up as an initiate of the Magisterium, and had spent her time studying the use and history of sorcery. Details such as the use of cosmetics and the finer points of dressing had eluded her education.

So Caina had volunteered.

"How do you know all this?" said Claudia as Caina finished her hair. "I thought you would know about knives and daggers and poisons, not...well, not this sort of thing."

"Who says I can't know both?" said Caina. "Theodosia taught me when I was younger. The Ghosts are spies, Claudia, and we are most effective when we do not draw attention to ourselves. And that means knowing how to dress appropriately, whether at a noble's ball or at a dockside tavern."

"That makes sense," said Claudia. "Still, I do not like using myself as bait. I am a magus of the Magisterium, not..."

"You're not," said Caina, her voice sharper than she intended. "Not any longer." She forced her tone back to calm. "You're a Ghost now, and that means doing what is necessary."

Claudia swallowed. "As you say. Well, let's get on with it."

Caina helped Claudia into her gown, a pale green dress that left her shoulders and a portion of her chest bare.

"Isn't that," said Claudia, "rather, ah, low in the front?"

"That's the point," said Caina, reaching for the cosmetics. "You're going to distract him while Corvalis and I do other things. And to distract him, you need to look distracting."

"I cannot comprehend how the man can be attracted to me," said Claudia, "when I so obviously despise him."

"I suspect he does not care what you think of him," said Caina.

She arranged Claudia's jewelry and applied the cosmetics as Theodosia had taught her, reddening Claudia's lips and cheeks, lining her green eyes with the faintest hint of black. When she finished, Caina stepped back to admire her handiwork. Claudia was a beautiful woman, and with the addition of a proper gown and makeup, she looked almost radiant.

"Yes," said Caina, "I think you'll distract Irzaris."

"I do look nice, don't I?" said Claudia, peering into the mirror. "Thank you."

Caina inclined her head. "Just don't let Irzaris get you alone."

"Oh, gods, no," said Claudia. "I doubt Basil will let it happen." She rolled her eyes. "I've never looked this good...and I have to waste it on someone like Irzaris. His Anshani tapestries, indeed! I've never heard such a clumsy euphemism."

Caina laughed, and Claudia looked at her with surprise. Then she, too, laughed.

"I admit," said Caina, "I've never heard anyone call it an Anshani tapestry."

"Not that I would know," said Claudia. She gestured at herself. "Or how to seduce a man, for that matter." Her face got a touch redder behind the makeup. "I've never, well..."

Caina nodded. "I understand."

"Um," said Claudia. "You and Corvalis. Have you..."

Caina could not decide whether to laugh or take offense at the question.

"We have," said Caina.

"Oh," said Claudia. "If you get with child, will you leave the Ghosts?"

"I can't," said Caina, feeling the familiar sadness. She hesitated, and then decided to tell Claudia the truth. "You may have noticed I... do not care for the magi very much. When I was a child, they murdered my father and left me unable to bear a child."

"Oh!" Claudia's hands flew to her mouth. "Oh, I had no idea. I'm sorry." She hesitated, and then touched Caina's shoulder. "I suppose...I thought...well, I am sorry. I see why you don't like me very much."

"I think," said Caina, "I viewed you through the lens of my past experiences, not yours. I should not have done that."

"Well, I am glad to have met you," said Claudia. "And not just because you saved my life. You...make Corvalis happy. He's never been happy for...if he's told you anything about his past, you know why."

Caina nodded. "He makes me happy, too." She took a deep breath. "We'd best get moving. We have a lot of work to do."

Claudia nodded, and Caina went to get dressed.

∿

AN HOUR later Caina stood with Corvalis in the shadows and looked at the mansion of Khaltep Irzaris.

The mansion stood in Catekharon's richer western district, away from the gates and the noise of the main streets, surrounded by the homes of other wealthy merchants. Irzaris might have been born Catekhari, but he had built his mansion in the Anshani style. It stood four floors high, faced in gleaming white stone, its façade an arcade of slender columns with delicate columns. According to Annika, the house followed the design of most Anshani mansions and had been built around a central courtyard with a garden and a fountain.

"It seems," muttered Corvalis, "that selling red iron to a Seeker pays quite well." He wore chain mail and leather, a heavy shield slung over his back, sword and dagger ready at his belt.

"Aye," said Caina. Like Corvalis, she wore leather and chain mail, though the unaccustomed weight of the mail made her shoulders ache. Still, the others wore mail, and it would look odd if she did not. "And gods know into what other pies he has thrust his sticky fingers."

"But," said Annika, "we shall find out tonight." The Szaldic woman leaned upon her cane, draped in a heavy cloak.

Caina stood with Corvalis, Annika, Saddiq, and a dozen of Saddiq's men in the alley across the street from Irzaris's mansion, hidden in the shadows. Saddiq's men had shed their desert robes and wore chain mail and leather, weapons bristling from their belts and harnesses. Without their robes, they looked like any other group of hardened mercenaries.

Which mean no one would blame the Sarbians or Basil Callenius for what happened next...which in turn meant no one would even begin to suspect the Ghosts.

"I hope," said Corvalis, "that your slave knows what he is doing."

"He is not my slave," said Annika with a smile, "he is Master Khaltep's slave. And he also happens to be my friend. Friendships are important, Master Cormark. Because he is my friend, I know that he works in Irzaris's kitchens...and that he is not terribly fond of his master. He will be more than willing to do what I ask, in exchange for Basil arranging his freedom. And speaking of Basil, here he comes."

A pair of sedan chairs carried by eight burly slaves strode into sight, flanked by four of Saddiq's mercenaries still clad in their distinctive robes and turbans. The bearers squatted, and Halfdan and Claudia descended from the sedan chairs. Halfdan offered Claudia his arm, and they walked to the doors. A pair of slaves pulled them open, and Caina saw Irzaris stride out to greet his guests.

And then they vanished inside.

"Now we wait," said Annika.

"How long?" said Corvalis.

"Perhaps an hour," said Annika. "My friends in Irzaris's house tell me the cook feeds the guards after the master sits down for dinner."

Caina nodded. She saw several guards, two of them standing at the doors, and two more patrolling the mansion's flat roof. No doubt others awaited within. Irzaris did not seem the sort of man to take chances with his personal security.

After an hour or so, a thin man in a slave's tunic emerged from the mansion. He offered some bread and a skin of wine to the guards, who began to eat.

And a few moments later, the guards toppled over.

"Did you kill them?" said Saddiq, blinking in surprise.

"Of course not," said Annika. "That would defeat the purpose of keeping this quiet, no? If we need to make Irzaris disappear...the guards will awaken and find their master missing. Whereas if they wake up and find their master lying a pool of blood, they will create more of a fuss than we want."

"Though it would be ideal," said Caina, "if they find their master safe and sound, after he's told us everything we wish to know without making trouble."

Corvalis nodded. "Now?"

"Wait," said Caina, staring at the mansion's roof. After a moment she saw the silhouettes of the guards topple. "Now. Don't kill anyone unless it's necessary."

She tugged a black mask in place over her face, a tight hood that only left her eyes visible. Corvalis and Saddiq did the same, as did the other men.

"Well," said Annika with a laugh. "Don't you look like the perfect collection of thugs? I fear I shall be robbed."

"You won't," said Caina. "Keep your shop ready. We might need a place to take Irzaris." Annika nodded. "Let's go. Corvalis, do the talking."

"As you say," said Corvalis, taking the lead. Caina followed, as did Saddiq and the other Sarbians. Corvalis threw open the doors and strode into the interior hall of Irzaris's mansion, weapons ready. A glittering mosaic covered the floor, and elaborate Anshani tapestries hung from the walls. Apparently they had not been a euphemism after all.

They hurried into the dining hall. An elaborate chandelier hung overhead, studded with dozens of glowing, enspelled crystals. Beneath the chandelier stood a low table, and Halfdan, Claudia, and Irzaris sat on cushions in Anshani style. Irzaris shot to his feet, eyes wide. Halfdan's mouth fell open in shock, while Claudia shrieked and lifted her hands to her throat.

They played their parts well. Theodosia would have been proud.

"What is the meaning of this?" thundered Irzaris. "How dare you invade my home! Guards! Kill them! Guards! Guards..."

His voice trailed off as no guards appeared. Annika's friends had done their work well.

"I assure you," said Halfdan, his voice quavering, "that I am worth more alive than dead, and that both my daughter and I, if we are left unharmed, will fetch a fine ransom from the Imperial Collegium of Jewelers..."

"Shut up, old man," said Corvalis in growling Anshani. "We're not here for you."

"And you are here for me, hmm?" said Irzaris, his tone dripping contempt. "Do you have any idea who I am? I have the favor of the Scholae itself! Run while you still can, and..."

Corvalis punched him. Irzaris fell backwards across the table, sending both food and wine splattering everywhere. Caina had never seen a man look so astonished.

"Come along," said Corvalis, "while you still have some teeth left."

He seized Irzaris's collar, hauled him to his feet, and dragged the merchant along. Caina followed, sword in hand. Corvalis pushed open a door and strode into the room beyond, still dragging Irzaris. The room looked like a study, a desk in one corner and shelves of curios lining the walls. A half-open door next to the desk led to the mansion's central courtyard.

Corvalis dumped Irzaris on the floor and rested the tip of his sword against the merchant's throat.

"And now," said Corvalis, "you are going to tell us everything."

Irzaris scowled and spat some blood upon the floor. "Everything about what?"

"How Mihaela creates the glypharmor," said Corvalis.

Irzaris burst out laughing. "Oh, this is rich! Who hired you, hmm? Arsakan and his decrepit brother Yaramzod, I suppose, since you're speaking Anshani. Or was it perhaps..."

Corvalis gave the merchant a gentle tap with his sword point. "That doesn't answer the question."

"You're wasting your time," said Irzaris. "I am just a merchant. I know nothing of sorcery, and I have no idea how Mihaela..."

"He's lying," growled Caina in Anshani, making sure to keep her voice disguised. Trying to sound like a normal man was harder than the rasping voice she used while wearing her shadow-cloak.

"No," said Irzaris, "I am not. I..."

"Do not trifle with us," said Caina. "We know you are closer to Mihaela than you claim. We know you have supplied her with counsel, in addition to red Nhabati iron." She took a calculated guess. "And we know that you orchestrated those attacks outside Catekharon."

Irzaris blinked in surprise. "How did you know...no, I don't know what you're talking about."

"A merchant paying mercenaries on the sly to attack his rivals is nothing new," said Caina. "But the attacks had a second point, didn't they? Mihaela used them to frighten Zalandris into supporting her work. She brought a little war to his doorstep, and convinced him that her glypharmor could end all war."

Irzaris said nothing.

Caina nodded to Corvalis.

Corvalis kicked Irzaris in the gut. As the merchant doubled over, wheezing for breath, Corvalis stooped, seized Irzaris's right hand, and broke his little finger.

Irzaris's shriek of pain echoed off the ceiling.

"Please," said Caina, leaning closer as Irzaris clutched his wounded hand, "tell us what you know. How does Mihaela create the glypharmor?"

"You're dead," spat Irzaris.

"I do not think," said Caina, "you are in any position to make threats. Tell us how Mihaela makes the glypharmor while you can still feed yourself..."

"You don't understand," said Irzaris. "That's not a threat. That's a promise. You don't know who you're threatening."

"A merchant?" said Caina.

"Mihaela," said Irzaris. "I know what you think. She's just a Seeker. Zalandris is the mind behind her skill. But you're wrong. The glypharmor is her work, and Zalandris is a feeble old puppet. Who sent you, hmm? The First Magus? Callatas? It doesn't matter. They'll be dead, all of them, once Mihaela finishes her work." He laughed. "And you'll be dead, too, once..."

Caina felt a surge of arcane power, distinct against the tingling aura that hung over the entire city.

Someone was casting a spell nearby.

"Sorcerer!" said Caina, taking a sideways step. "It..."

The door to the courtyard exploded, shards raining across the floor. Irzaris sat up and grinned.

"Aid me!" he shouted. "I told them nothing! Kill them all, and..."

A cloaked and hooded man stepped through the door and lifted a hand. A bar of darkness wreathed in green flame burst from his fingers and slammed into Irzaris's chest. Irzaris collapsed to the floor with a scream, the ghostly green flames dancing over his limbs. He twitched like a landed fish, screamed once more, and then went motionless.

Caina lifted her weapons, as did Corvalis. She could not see under the cloaked man's hood, but she saw that he wore leather armor, a sheathed sword on his left hip and a dagger on his right.

Something about the shape of the dagger's handle tugged at her memory.

"Well," said the cloaked man, his voice rusty, "he always did like to talk too much." He spat a laugh. "An unpleasant quality in a man."

Caina knew that voice at once.

"No," she said. "You're dead. I saw you die."

"Ah," said the cloaked man. "Mistress. So good to see you again." He drew back his hood.

His bald head and hairless face were hideously scarred, and almost looked as if they had been stitched together out of pieces of old leather. His left eye was green, while the right was a sulfurous yellow-orange. Even from a distance, his stench filled Caina's nostrils, a hideous mixture of rotting meat and clotting blood.

"Sicarion," said Caina. "I saw you die."

"I beg to differ," said Sicarion. "You saw Ranarius throw me out of the Palace of Splendors with his spell. The landing hurt, but it didn't kill me. Though I did have to replace one of my kidneys and both of my legs." He grinned. "I would kill him for it, but I suppose you did it for me. Destroyed by his pet elemental? Appropriate. When he still served the mistress, I warned him that his pets would turn on him."

Caina had seen Sicarion use his twisted necromancy before. With his spells, he harvested limbs and organs from living victims and grafted them onto his own flesh. It had transformed him into a grotesque, scarred monster...but it had also allowed him to live for centuries and survive multiple mortal wounds.

"That's where Mihaela learned the necromancy for the glypharmor," said Caina. "You taught her."

"She is such a clever girl, mistress," murmured Sicarion. "Give her a coin, and she'll turn it into three. But tonight has been delightful. I've wanted to kill Irzaris ever since I met him." His mismatched eyes shifted to Corvalis. "And I've wanted to kill you for years."

"Try," said Corvalis, pointing his sword and dagger at the scarred assassin.

Sicarion began casting a spell as Caina and Corvalis both dashed forward, weapons raised. Sicarion flung out a hand, and Corvalis ducked, trying to dodge whatever sorcery Sicarion unleashed.

But at the last minute Sicarion pointed at Caina.

A blast of invisible force struck Caina across the chest and stomach, and the spell picked her up and flung her into the wall. One of the shelves cracked, curios spilling around Caina, plates and daggers and statuettes falling to the floor. The breath erupted from her lungs in an explosive gasp, and she fell atop the broken shelf. The spell had not been enough to kill her. But it had been enough to stun her, and Sicarion drove at Corvalis with fury. In his right hand he wielded a sword, and in his left an ugly dagger with a serrated edge. Caina had seen him use that weapon to carve limbs from his victims and graft them onto his own body.

And he would do the same to Corvalis.

Caina heaved herself to her feet as Corvalis backed into the hallway, his blades ringing against Sicarion's weapons. Caina raced after them, yanked a throwing knife from her belt, and flung it with all her strength. It struck Sicarion in the shoulder, cutting his cloak, but bounced away. He must have been wearing mail beneath his leather armor.

Corvalis backed into the dining hall. Halfdan and Claudia shot to their feet, and Saddiq and his men gripped their weapons. Corvalis retreated, and Sicarion stepped to the left. Caina hurried after him, hoping to stab him in the back, but Sicarion slid along the wall.

He let out a low laugh.

"Is that your lovely sister, Aberon?" said Sicarion. "So you freed her from the stone after all. Such a pretty face. Perhaps I'll slice it off and keep it as a souvenir."

"What sort of devil are you?" said Claudia, her voice tight.

"You must be Sicarion," said Halfdan.

"My fame proceeds me," said Sicarion with a mocking little bow.

"You can't fight all of us," said Halfdan. "I suggest you surrender."

"You are correct," said Sicarion. "I cannot fight all of you. But why should I bother? You'll be dead in a few days anyway..."

He flung out his hands, and Caina felt the spike of arcane power. Invisible force erupted in all directions, knocking her to the floor and toppling Saddiq and his men like toys. Halfdan fell against the dining cushions, while Claudia managed to keep her feet, her hands raised in a warding spell. Corvalis fell to one knee, and Caina glimpsed a flare of white light as the Ulkaari tattoos shielded him from the worst of the spell.

But it was not enough. Sicarion whirled and fled through the mansion's doors.

~'

"I THOUGHT YOU SAID," said Halfdan, "that he was dead."

Caina, Corvalis, and Claudia sat the table in Halfdan's sitting room. They had searched the streets and alleys around Irzaris's mansion, hoping to catch Sicarion, but the scarred assassin had vanished without a trace.

But he would be back. Caina was sure of it.

"I did think he was dead," said Caina. "Ranarius threw him from the top of the Stone. I didn't think anyone could survive a fall from that height." She shuddered. "I wonder how many people he had to kill to...repair himself."

"What sort of creature is he?" said Claudia.

"A necromancer," said Caina. "His spells let him take body parts from other people and attach them to his own flesh. Cut off his hand, and he'll merely steal one from someone else."

"We fought once, in Artifel," said Corvalis. "After Ranarius turned you to stone. I foiled him from killing someone, and he's promised to kill me ever since."

Halfdan poured himself some wine from a carafe on the sideboard. "I think we know how Mihaela learned the necromancy she used in the glypharmor."

Claudia frowned. "This Sicarion taught her?"

"It seems likely," said Caina, thinking. The Moroaica had not appeared to Caina since the incident with the glypharmor. Was the glypharmor one of her plots? Though Jadriga had warned Caina of danger in the past...

No. She had warned Caina about Ranarius, and Ranarius had rebelled against her. If Jadriga wanted Mihaela's plan, whatever it was, to succeed, she would not warn Caina.

"Then it's possible," said Corvalis, "that the First Magus knows more than we thought. Sicarion has done errands for him in the past."

Claudia's frown deepened. "Surely not even Father would associate with...with such a creature."

"He's a magus," said Caina. "There is nothing a magus would not do..." She caught herself and started over. "Decius Aberon is the sort of man who would murder his own children if it brought him greater power. You know that better than I do."

"What about Irzaris?" said Corvalis. "We left his mansion a mess. And it's no secret that you visited him for dinner."

"We will do nothing," said Halfdan. "When his guards and slaves awake, they will find Irzaris dead in his study without a mark on him, thanks to Sicarion's spell. Both Claudia and I will say that Irzaris made inappropriate advances on her, and we were so offended that we left."

"That's true enough," muttered Claudia.

"His death will be a mystery," said Halfdan, "but no one will be too interested in solving it. There's too much at stake. All the ambassadors will assume that one of the other ambassadors murdered Irzaris to find the secret of the glypharmor's creation."

"Which will increase the pressure on Mihaela," said Caina, "if she thinks someone is coming after her."

"And men under pressure," said Halfdan, "make mistakes. Women, too, for that matter. If Mihaela is frightened, she might do something rash...and then we have our chance. In the meantime, I suggest we get some sleep. It has been a long day, and tomorrow promises to be longer."

THAT NIGHT CORVALIS slept in Caina's bed. She suspected the various ambassadors and embassies were too consumed with their own problems to take note that a merchant's daughter was sharing a bed with her father's guard.

Besides, it was the sort of thing a wealthy merchant's daughter might do.

And she was surprised to learn that nothing fired the passions like a brush with death.

After they finished, after Corvalis had fallen asleep, Caina focused, thinking about the Moroaica. She intended to hunt down the Moroaica in her dreams, to force Jadriga to answer questions.

But no dreams came, and Caina sank into a dreamless sleep.

18

AN INVITATION

"**G**o into the city," said Halfdan, "disguised as my daughter, and visit Annika's shop. Take Corvalis and Saddiq with you. Word must have leaked out of Irzaris's death, and I want to know what the rumors say."

Caina nodded, dressed herself in a simple gown appropriate for travel, and left the palace, Corvalis at her side. They walked along the stone terrace, the crater lake stretching alongside them, the smooth waters reflecting the aqueducts of molten steel overhead.

"A pity," said Corvalis, "that Barimaz isn't here. One of his sausage rolls would ..."

Caina reached the top of the stairs to the causeway and froze.

Mihaela stood at the bottom of the stairs, gazing up at her.

Caina had expected Mihaela to do something unexpected...but not quite this.

The Seeker wore her usual boots, trousers, and black leather vest, her blue eyes cold and hard in her lean face. She climbed the stairs, and Caina saw the heavy muscles shifting in the woman's arms. As she drew closer, Caina felt the tingle of sorcery. Mihaela wore an odd variety of earrings, rings, and bracelets, and Caina was sure every last one of them carried protective spells.

She reached the top of the terrace, frowning at Caina like a scholar scrutinizing a rare manuscript.

Caina bowed. "Seeker."

"I remember you," said Mihaela, her Anshani thick with a Szaldic accent. "The merchant's daughter, the one who kept flirting with Irzaris. As I recall, the sight of blood was too much for you."

Did Mihaela know that Caina was a Ghost? Had Sicarion told her?

Best to maintain her masquerade.

"I am sorry if I spoiled your demonstration, Seeker," said Caina. "All that blood was too much for me..."

"You do not appear to have a single thought," said Mihaela, "in that pretty little head." She smiled. "How hard you must work to maintain that impression. Are you a sorceress?"

Caina blinked. "I'm sorry?"

Did Mihaela know that Caina carried the Moroaica's spirit? Sicarion knew, and if he had told her...

"Are you," said Mihaela, speaking slowly, "a sorceress? Do you have a knowledge of the arcane sciences? Can you wield your thoughts as a weapon? Do you practice the sciences of pyromancy, oneiromancy, necromancy, or wield the elements themselves as a weapon?"

"No," said Caina. "I am just a simple woman, I fear."

Mihaela gripped a ring on the middle finger of her left hand. Caina felt a tingle, and realized Mihaela was using the ring to cast a spell. She reached for a knife, but Mihaela released the ring.

"Not a sorceress," said Mihaela. "I thought as much." She looked at Corvalis. "And are you?"

"A sorceress?" said Corvalis. "Surely the stubble should give it away."

"Do not display impertinence with me," said Mihaela. "Do you have arcane ability or do you not?"

Corvalis shrugged. "I just kill people who need killing."

"A fine sentiment," said Mihaela. "Come along. I will speak with your master."

She walked away without a backwards glance. Corvalis looked at Caina, and she shrugged. Best to see how this played out. Caina followed Mihaela, Corvalis at her side, and the Seeker entered the palace proper. She slid aside the paper door to the guest suite. Halfdan still sat at the table with Claudia, eating breakfast.

Claudia's eyes grew wide.

"Seeker," said Halfdan, rising with a bow. "You do me honor. Have you come to peruse my wares? I have many fine jewels in my inventory, and..."

"Do," said Mihaela, "be silent."

Halfdan shrugged and stopped talking. Mihaela paced back and forth, scowling, her heavy boots clicking against the gleaming floorboards. She walked to the window, gazed at the lake for a moment.

"This used to be a volcano," she said, "the prison of a greater fire elemental. The Scholae built the Tower of Study here to tap the elemental's power." She waved a hand at one of the aqueducts crossing the lake. "All that molten metal is part of the spell keeping the thing bound. But the Sages can't give up the power now, even if they wanted to, because the fire elemental would consume them."

"So to paraphrase the old Szaldic proverb," said Halfdan, "they have a wolf by the ears, and cannot let it go."

"Precisely," said Mihaela. "Though the Anshani and the Istarish say a lion, not a wolf." She turned from the window, scowling. "Let us lay aside all games and speak plainly."

"Nothing," said Halfdan, "would delight me more."

"I doubt that, Basil Callenius," said Mihaela. "I know that is not your name. I know that you are a Ghost, probably a high-ranking one, and that these," she waved a hand at Caina and the others, "are your spies."

"That," said Halfdan, "is an interesting supposition. Who, I wonder, put such ideas into your head?"

Mihaela smirked. "Did Sicarion tell me, you mean?"

Caina's hand twitched towards the hilt of a knife.

"Sicarion?" said Halfdan.

Mihaela sighed. "Are you incapable of anything but riddling talk,

Basil Callenius? Fine. I know that Khaltep Irzaris was found dead in his mansion this morning without a mark on him, though there were signs of struggle. I have seen Sicarion use a spell that kills in such a fashion, a bar of shadow wrapped in green fire."

"And you know Sicarion?" said Halfdan.

"Yes," said Mihaela. "He has tried to kill me thrice."

"I can relate," said Caina.

"Can you?" said Mihaela with a scoff. "I know why Basil brought you. A pretty-faced girl to seduce the merchants and the lords and part them from their secrets. Irzaris was practically ready to fall into bed with you. Be silent when your betters are speaking."

Corvalis scowled, but Caina remained silent, thinking. Irzaris had been trying to seduce Claudia, not Caina. Which meant that Mihaela had misjudged both him and Caina. And if she continued to underestimate Caina, that could prove useful in the future.

"As you say," mumbled Caina, making her voice sulky.

"Better," said Mihaela.

"Why would Sicarion want to kill you?" said Halfdan.

Mihaela shrugged. "Perhaps I offended him in some way."

"My lady Seeker," said Halfdan, "you wish to speak without games and riddling talk? Very well. Since you have entered my rooms, you have spoken of philosophy, history, and made the egregious accusation that I am a spy for the Emperor of Nighmar. Yet for all your words, I notice you have still failed to come to the point."

Mihaela smirked. "Good. I prefer direct words. Very well. I have a wolf by the ears, to use your proverb, and I think you can help me to release it without having my throat ripped out."

"The glypharmor," said Halfdan. "That is your wolf."

Mihaela scowled. "Precisely." She paced back to the table. "Do not listen to Zalandris's fine-sounding words about peace and brotherhood. I created the glypharmor for the same reason I joined the Scholae. Wealth and power."

"Enough wealth and power to keep you from becoming a slave again?" said Halfdan.

"Bah," said Mihaela. "You have been talking to Annika, haven't you? My sister is a wretched fool. The Ghosts would have had us squander our lives luring fat noblemen into bed to steal their secrets." She shot a look at Caina. "But I had higher things in mind."

"Such as wealth and power," said Halfdan, "but the glypharmor has drawn the attention of those with too much power."

"You know the Bostaji?" said Mihaela.

"The personal assassins of the Shahenshah of Anshan," said Halfdan.

"Twice they have tried to kidnap me at the command of Yaramzod the Black," said Mihaela. "Once I was almost waylaid by the Immortals, no doubt sent by Callatas and that fat emir, I forget his name. And then that scarred devil Sicarion..."

"He, too, tried to abduct you?" said Halfdan.

"He tried to kill me," said Mihaela, "and he has come close." She flexed her fingers. "I am not without power. Even a Seeker of the Scholae is a match for sorcerers of other lands. I have wounded him in our fights. Yet every time he comes back healed, if more scarred. I am sure he killed Irzaris in order to get at me." She paced back and forth again. "So, yes, Basil Callenius, I have got the wolf by the ears, and if I let go, he'll devour me. I have no wish to spend the rest of my days as a slave of the First Magus or Yaramzod the Black. But the glypharmor, and the knowledge of its creation, is the only thing of value that I possess." She thumped her chest. "I am the only one who knows the complete spell. Not Zalandris, not any of the other Sages. Only me."

"Let us have more blunt speaking," said Halfdan. "You want to let go of the wolf before it devours you...and to do that, you are coming to the Ghosts for protection?"

Mihaela nodded.

"And what do you offer in exchange?" said Halfdan.

"The glypharmor suits I have already completed," said Mihaela, "and the knowledge of how to create more."

"You'll give them to the Ghosts?" said Halfdan.

"No." Mihaela smirked and pointed at Claudia. "But I might give them to her."

Claudia blinked.

"Me?" she said at last. "Why me?"

"Because," said Mihaela, "you are a magus."

"I...I most certainly am not!" said Claudia. She was a terrible liar. It was a quality that would have been admirable under other circumstances. "I am...I am the eldest daughter of Basil Callenius, and came with him to Catekharon to find a wealthy husband..."

"Do all Ghosts," said Mihaela, "like so poorly?" She glanced at Caina. "The weak-stomached child and the incompetent liar. Does the Empire rest upon such pillars?" She turned back to Claudia. "I can tell you are a magus, and a strong one. Enough magi have visited Catekharon that I know the aura of a magus when I feel it."

Magi such as Torius Aberon, Caina wondered?

"Why me?" said Claudia.

"Because you are a magus," said Mihaela, "and you understand the responsibility of power."

"A curious thing to say," said Claudia, "given that you tried to use your power for wealth and aggrandizement."

"I spent my childhood as a slave," said Mihaela. "I desired security and freedom, not the good of mankind. Yet even I know what it is to bear power. Sorcery presents its own set of peculiar temptations. I could twist the minds of those around me and make them into my own personal slaves, just as I was once enslaved...but such folly would quickly draw the attention of those with the power to destroy me. So any wielder of arcane science must know a measure of restraint." She leveled a finger at Claudia. "Any sorcerer can understand that, even a tyrant like Yaramzod or the First Magus. But the Ghosts are the only ones who will neither kill me nor enslave me. And you are the only sorceress I know among the Ghosts."

"Very well," said Claudia. "So you will give the glypharmor to me, personally?"

"I said I will consider it," said Mihaela. "I wish you to join me for dinner, tonight, and we shall discuss it further."

"We shall be honored," said Halfdan with a bow, "to attend."

Mihaela scowled. "Not you. Just her."

"Alone?" said Claudia.

"You will be perfectly safe," said Mihaela.

"I am afraid," said Halfdan, "that I cannot allow her to go alone."

Mihaela laughed. "She is in no danger from me, Basil Callenius. I cannot decide to give her the glypharmor if she is dead, no?"

"Nor will you be able to give her the glypharmor," said Halfdan, "if Yaramzod or Sicarion come for you and Irene is accidentally slain in the fighting."

"That is so," said Mihaela. "Very well, you may take one other with you."

Claudia looked from Caina to Corvalis and back again.

"Anna," said Claudia. "I want Anna to come with me?"

"Her?" Mihaela laughed. "The seducer? A poor choice. My tastes run to men."

"And I insist," said Halfdan, "that Cormark accompany them both. A master merchant certainly should not allow his daughters to go unescorted."

Mihaela's eyes narrowed, and then she shrugged. "If you wish. Your little masquerade is no concern of mine."

"And before you go," said Halfdan, "two questions."

Mihaela sighed. "If you must."

"I must," said Halfdan. "First, we suspect necromancy was used in the creation of the glypharmor. Was it?"

"Necromancy?" said Mihaela. "You are jesting, yes?" She laughed. "No, I did not use necromancy. The Sages kill any Seeker they catch wielding it. And necromancy is a crude and...inelegant science. It is beneath me."

"Thank you," said Halfdan. "There is one other point. Some months ago you took a slave named Ardasha as a student. What became of her?"

"Sicarion killed her," said Mihaela.

Caina felt a chill.

"The first time he attacked me," said Mihaela. "He cast a spell...and, well, Ardasha simply got in the way. I fear she was dead before she hit the floor. Now. Do you have any other questions about dead slaves, or shall we attend to more important business?"

"Thank you for your candor," said Halfdan.

Mihaela shook a finger at Claudia. "Come to my rooms by the first bell of the evening. The slaves will know the way. Do not be late."

She left without another word.

"I don't believe," said Caina, "a single thing that she said."

"Oh, certainly some of it was true," said Halfdan. "Sicarion might have tried to kill her. I suspect she began as his student, and fled to the Scholae when her relationship with him turned sour."

"Surely Annika would have known," said Claudia, "had her sister been apprenticed to such a creature."

"Sometimes there are secrets," said Halfdan, "even between sisters."

"What should I do," said Claudia, "if she does give me the armor and the secrets of its making?" She hesitated. "Should I use them?"

Caina frowned. There was an odd light in Claudia's eyes.

"Absolutely not," said Halfdan. "I doubt she has any intention of giving you the armor or the spells to create it. And even if she does, using the glypharmor might be dangerous. The sorcery could have damaging effects upon your mind or body."

"If she doesn't intend to give her the armor," said Corvalis, "then what is the point of this? Why bother with the dinner?"

"She needs something," said Caina. "Whatever her purpose for creating the glypharmor, I doubt it is as simple as selling it for fortune and glory. She has something else in mind. But she can't get it on her own. Which means...which means it must be something you can do, Claudia."

"Me?" said Claudia. "I am quite out of my element in this business. What could I possibly do?"

"I do not know," said Halfdan, "but I intend to find out, if you think you can go through with this. Mihaela may intend you harm."

Claudia took a deep breath and glanced at Caina. "I can do it. I suppose if you can go blade to blade with the likes of Sicarion, I can sit down to a pleasant dinner with a dangerous woman."

Yet the strange, fascinated light did not leave her eyes.

"Glad to hear it," said Halfdan. "Perhaps tonight we shall finally have some answers.

THAT AFTERNOON CAINA NAPPED, hoping to conserve her strength for the dinner with Mihaela.

And this time, the Moroaica came to her dreams.

Again Caina stood on the strange plain of gray fog, the mists billowing around her. The Moroaica waited a short distance away, clad in her crimson gown, her black hair hanging wet and loose around her shoulders, her black eyes pits into nothingness.

They stared at each other.

"Better," said Jadriga at last. "It grows harder to resist your summons, child. A pity you have no arcane talent. You would have made a formidable sorceress."

"Don't insult me," said Caina. "What is Sicarion doing in Catekharon?"

Jadriga shrugged. "Killing people, I imagine. He enjoys it."

"Why did you send him here?" said Caina.

Again the Moroaica shrugged. "Who says I sent him here?"

Caina took a step closer. "Answer the question."

Jadriga's red lips moved into a smile. "Child, child. You can summon me in your dreams...but you cannot compel me. You are not strong enough for that. No more than I am strong enough to force you to submit to my will."

Caina could not force Jadriga to answer any questions. But Caina's mind was her weapon, not her strength. If she wanted any useful information out of the Moroaica, she would have to use her wits to get it.

"Mihaela," said Caina, "reminds me of you."

"Does she?" said Jadriga. "I doubt that. Nor does she remind me of you. She has known pain as a child, as we did...but both you and I responded in the same way. We sought to change the world. She merely wishes to become strong. She was tyrannized as a child...and now she seeks to become the tyrant."

"Then she is not," said Caina, "one of your disciples?"

"Ah," said the Moroaica. "Clever. No, she is not one of my disciples. I have never met her."

"Then has Sicarion met her?" said Caina.

Jadriga smiled again. "Knowledge has a price, child. I will answer your question...but, in turn, you must answer one of mine."

"Very well," said Caina. "Did Sicarion meet with Mihaela?"

"Probably," said Jadriga. "I do not know for certain. When I am not there to control him, Sicarion tends to pursue his own amusements. Nor am I aware of his every action. So he most likely met with Mihaela. But I cannot say for certain."

"Then you are certain necromancy was used to create the glypharmor?" said Caina.

"That is another question," said the Moroaica. "If you want the answer, you must answer one of mine."

Caina sighed. "Fine. What do you want to know?"

"Do you love Corvalis?"

Caina blinked. Of all the things Jadriga could have asked, she had not expected that. "What?"

"It is a simple question," said Jadriga.

"Yes," said Caina. "I do."

"Why?" said Jadriga.

"I wouldn't expect you to understand," said Caina.

"You mistake me," said Jadriga. "You have seen my past. I understand love. I loved my own father...just as you loved yours. So. Why do you love Corvalis Aberon?"

"That," said Caina, "is a second question."

The Moroaica nodded.

"Because he is brave," said Caina. "Because he has suffered so much, endured so much, and it hasn't ruined him. Because he is strong enough to defy his father, the Kindred, and the entire Magisterium because he knew it was the right thing to do." She swallowed, forced herself to calm. "Because...he knows what it is like to be alone, too."

"He will turn on you, in the end," said Jadriga.

"Because he is one of your disciples?" said Caina. "A treacherous scoundrel?"

"That is a question," said Jadriga. "And, no, he is not one of my disciples. He will turn on you because he loves his sister more than he loves you, and his sister hates you. Not as much as she will, but it is beginning."

"He's known Claudia longer," said Caina.

"He will choose her," said Jadriga, "over you."

"He might not," said Caina, trying to keep the anger out of her voice. "And why are you telling me this? So I am as lonely and miserable as you?"

"Because it is the nature of the world," said Jadriga, "to torment us. To break us and inflict pain upon us. One day Corvalis Aberon will abandon you. Or, given the nature of your life, you will see him die in agony in front of you. You think that loving him will make you happy. But it will not. Instead it will only add to your pain."

"Everyone dies," said Caina. "Even you. And you now owe me two questions."

"One question," said Jadriga. "You asked if Corvalis was my disciple or not."

"That was a rhetorical question," said Caina.

"And a rhetorical question," said Jadriga, "is nonetheless still a question."

"For the gods' sake," said Caina. "The Moroaica, sorceress of legend and terror, dickers like a fishwife at the Great Market of Marsis."

Jadriga laughed, and for an instant she sounded almost young.

"One question, then," said Caina. "How do you know that Mihaela used necromancy to craft the glypharmor?"

"Because I can see through your eyes," said Jadriga, "and I saw the hieroglyphs upon the glypharmor."

"You can read them?" said Caina. She pointed at the Moroaica.

"And that is part of my original question. Elaborate upon your answer."

"And I dicker like a fishwife?" said Jadriga. "The hieroglyphs upon the armor are a spell of Maatish necromancy. The necromancer-priests of Maat used to embalm the pharaohs, the nobles, and the high priests using salts and chemicals to preserve their bodies, but they also sequestered the heart in a separate stone jar. The spell was used to bind the spirits of the embalmed men to the jars containing their hearts, thereby allowing the spirit to return to its embalmed corpse and live forever in its tomb."

"After a fashion," said Caina.

"Indeed," said Jadriga. Her dark eyes flashed. "I underwent the process myself. I do not recommend it."

"So that's how you move from body to body," said Caina. "Your heart is hidden in a stone jar buried in Maat somewhere, and that allows you to claim new bodies."

"Ah," said Jadriga, "but that is a question. And I have no more questions I wish to ask you."

She waved a hand, and the dream ended.

19

REMAKE THE WORLD

That night, Caina, Corvalis, and Claudia followed a slave through the corridors of the Tower of Study.

The Sages kept their rooms at the Tower's top, but the Seekers' quarters occupied the Tower's base, not far from the hall where Mihaela had demonstrated the glypharmor. The slave led them through a long, wide hallway with a tall ceiling. A stream of molten metal ran down the center of the hall, the air above it rippling, and Caina felt the power of the wards that kept most of the heat at bay.

"I wonder why," said Corvalis, "the Sages felt the need to run a stream of molten steel through the hallway. Trip on your way to the privies in the middle of the night, and you're burned to ashes, and all because you had too much wine before bed." He wore his usual chain mail and leather, weapons ready at his belt, and Caina could tell he expected trouble.

"If Mihaela told us the truth," said Claudia, "this molten metal is part of the spell that holds the greater fire elemental bound. Most likely the molten metal came first, and the Sages built the Tower around it."

They had passed hundreds of doors, and yet the slave kept walking. There were only a few hundred Sages, and perhaps twice that many Seekers. Yet the Tower of Study was large enough to hold thousands. Perhaps by turning away from the outside world, the Scholae had cut themselves off to gradually wither away and die.

That was just as well. The world, Caina thought, would be a better place without the Masked Ones and their knowledge.

"Here, mistress," said the slave. "The Seeker Mihaela resides here. Shall I knock?"

"Please," said Claudia.

The slave bowed, knocked at the door, and then departed without another word.

The door swung open, and Mihaela stepped into the hall. "You have arrived? Good. We can get on with things." She turned. "Come inside."

The room beyond was austere. A long wooden table ran its length, plates and food laid out. A bookcase held a few volumes and scrolls. There was no artwork, no decorations of any kind. Caina supposed Mihaela had her workshop hidden somewhere else. Within the city, perhaps, or in some forgotten corner of the Tower's corridors.

"Seat yourselves," said Mihaela, dropping into the chair at the end of the table, "and eat." She smirked. "I have no patience with courtly manners. I suppose you must find that shocking, but I care about results, not intentions."

"Not at all," said Claudia, seating herself with considerably more grace. "I can understand that."

"Then," said Mihaela, "we may be of use to each other after all."

The food was Szaldic. Roast pork and potatoes, with glasses of the bitter black beer the Szalds preferred over wine or ale. Mihaela and Corvalis ate with vigor, while Claudia only picked at her food.

"Tell me," said Mihaela around a mouthful of potatoes. "How did you and the First Magus become estranged?"

"He's a vicious tyrant who treats his children as disposable tools," said Corvalis.

"I knew that," said Mihaela. "When I was slave, I was owned by a magus of Cyrioch. But I wasn't talking to you, assassin, but to your sister. Why did you leave the Magisterium?"

Claudia hesitated, staring at her beer for a moment, and then began to speak.

"When I was a child," she said, "I was afraid of my father...but he was not cruel to me. I thought he was stern, but kindly." She sighed. "Later I realized he only found me useful because of my arcane talent. I was raised to be a magus of the Magisterium, and that was what I wanted to be. I wanted to use my sorcery to help people, to better them."

Caina kept the frown from her face.

"But my brother," said Claudia, "had no arcane talent, and so my father sold him to the Kindred." She looked at Corvalis. "I thought that he had joined them by choice, to learn to fight the enemies of the Empire and the Magisterium. But we met again as adults. He told me what the Kindred had done to him, what my father had made him do..."

"And so your eyes were opened," said Mihaela. "You saw the Magisterium for what it was."

"I planned to leave with Cormark," said Claudia. "To find someplace I could use my spells for good. But our father found out. One of the high magi commanded a lesser earth elemental, and my father ordered him to turn me to stone as a punishment."

"Truly?" said Mihaela. "I am impressed. I doubted anyone in the Magisterium could manage to bind an elemental."

"My brother escaped the assassins my father sent after him," said Claudia, "stole the statue that I had become, and pursued the high magus who had turned me to stone. With some help," she glanced at Caina, "the high magus was defeated, and I was restored."

"And so you joined the Ghosts," said Mihaela, gesturing with her fork.

Claudia nodded.

"It is," said Mihaela, "an interesting story. Now I shall tell you mine." She smirked at Caina. "But it is grisly in places. It might be too much for your delicate ears."

Caina feigned a shudder. "I shall manage, thank you."

"We shall see," said Mihaela. "Well, if you have spoken to Annika, you probably know some of it. We were from the Szaldic provinces of the Empire, and slavers kidnapped us as children. Eventually we were sold to a cruel magus in Cyrioch. He knew I had the talent, and began training me to use as a weapon. Eventually Annika made contact with the Ghosts, and they slew the magus and we escaped. But I wished to learn more of the arcane sciences, so we came to Catekharon." She scowled. "Annika grew jealous of my power, and now skulks in her junk shop. Yet I stayed here. Zalandris took me as a Seeker and taught me many things. But it was never enough. I needed more power. Enough power to make sure no one would ever enslave me again."

"And so you created the glypharmor," said Claudia.

"Yes," said Mihaela, scowling.

"The Ghosts can help you," said Claudia, leaning closer. "My father or the others will enslave you, if they get their hands on you. But the Ghosts can give you freedom and safety, if you tell me the secret of creating the glypharmor."

Mihaela laughed. "And then you shall cut my throat and dump my body in the molten metal, no?"

"Of course not!" said Claudia. "I am sincere."

"I am sure you are," said Mihaela. "Yes, I think you truly are. Unusual. Let me ask you a question, Irene Callenius. Let us say I gave you a choice. You could lay down your arcane power and be free of it forever. Or you could keep it, and do as you pleased with it. What would you say?"

"I would keep it, of course," said Claudia. "I could do so much good with it."

This time Caina did not manage to stop her frown, but neither Mihaela nor Claudia noticed.

"Good," said Mihaela. "Very good. I have decided that you can help me after all."

"Then you'll tell us how to make the glypharmor?" said Claudia.

"Not yet," said Mihaela, getting to her feet. "But I will tell you another secret." She grinned. "You think I am a fool."

Something about that smile unsettled Caina.

"I never said that," said Claudia.

"Oh, no, no," said Mihaela. "A merchant's daughter is far too polite to say such things. But you were thinking it." She jerked her head at Caina, ragged locks of black hair sliding over her hard face. "Even the seductress was thinking it. Oh, poor Mihaela created a weapon so powerful she cannot control it, she'll get enslaved by those dreadful sorcerers and magi." She laughed, long and loud. "But do you know my secret?"

Caina started to reach for one of the knives hidden in her sleeves.

"I made the glypharmor," said Mihaela. "I know the spells that bind it, inside and out." Her mocking smile widened. "And I know how to control those spells."

Claudia blinks. "That means...that means..."

"That means," said Caina, "that Mihaela can control anyone wearing a suit of glypharmor."

"Cleverer than I expected from you," said Mihaela. "You are correct. Anyone wearing glypharmor has free will...until I decide that he does not. No one wearing glypharmor can attack me. And whenever I choose, I can turn any man wearing glypharmor into my puppet." She snapped her fingers. "Just like that."

"Gods," said Claudia. "That's...brilliant."

Caina could not argue. Mihaela had been playing both the Sages and the ambassadors as fools. Whoever purchased the glypharmor would think they had claimed an invincible army...but they would only be putting a slave's collar around their necks.

"I thought so," said Mihaela.

"So...you've changed your mind, then?" said Claudia. "You want to abandon your plan and seek refuge with the Ghosts?"

"No," said Mihaela. "We're going to do something grander, Irene Callenius, you and I. We are going to change the world. Because I am going to tell you how to control the glypharmor. You, and you alone."

Claudia blinked, stunned...and Caina saw that odd light come into her eyes again.

"Me?" said Claudia. "Why?"

"Because," said Mihaela. "You have vision that both the Ghosts and the other sorcerers lack. You see how we can make the world better."

"We will have to speak to Basil first," said Caina, but the other women ignored her.

Even Corvalis ignored her, his eyes fixed on Claudia.

"This is what we'll do," said Mihaela, her voice urgent. "You will go to each of the embassies, and tell them that the Sages have agreed to sell them three suits of glypharmor, no more and no less. I will summon the Sages to the Hall of Assembly, and you will bring the embassies. We will then explain that the Scholae has decided to give them each three suits in order to maintain balance and prevent war among the nations. Of course, the most powerful men from each embassy will want to try the armor at once...the First Magus, Yaramzod the Black, Callatas, all the others. They'll put on the suits..."

"And when they do," said Claudia, "you'll control them."

"I shall," said Mihaela.

"That's monstrous," said Caina.

Mihaela laughed. "This from the woman who fainted at the sight of a little blood?"

"That was more than a little blood," said Caina. "And you're planning to take the most powerful sorcerers in the world and turn them into your slaves."

"That is exactly what I plan to do," said Mihaela. "Do you think that monstrous? You should not." She looked at Claudia. "You have seen firsthand the crimes of your father. And I assure you the other sorcerers have committed darker atrocities. By putting them under our control, we would be doing the world a favor."

Claudia said nothing. Corvalis looked back and forth between her and Caina.

"You would overthrow one set of tyrants," said Caina, "and replace them with yourself."

Mihaela snorted. "Now you simply parrot the words of your circlemaster. If I wanted to hear a song and see a dance, I would pay you for the privilege." She looked back at Claudia. "We have the right to do this. Don't you see? Our sorcery gives us the right. Can you imagine what we could do if we forced the most powerful sorcerers in the world to bend to our will? We could bring the war between the Empire and Istarinmul and New Kyre to an end. We could force the Magisterium and the College of Alchemists and the Anshani occultists to use their powers for the greater good, rather than their own selfish ends." Her voice grew more urgent. "We could change the world in a way no one has ever dared!"

And to Caina's alarm, Claudia nodded.

"What you say makes a great deal of sense," said Claudia.

"What guarantee," said Caina, "do you have that Mihaela will be any better than your father?"

"The best guarantee of all," said Mihaela. "Power. I will share the control of the glypharmor with Irene. We shall serve as checks upon each other. If attempt something excessively dangerous, Irene will stop me...and if she becomes mad with power, I will stop her."

"And if you both agree to do something evil," said Caina, "then there is no one to stop you."

"We will do nothing evil," said Mihaela with scorn. "The First Magus and Yaramzod the Black and all their cronies, they are the evil ones. Surely you know that just as well as I do." She smirked. "But, let us be candid. This is beyond your comprehension, no? You are not a sorceress, and so have no conception of the responsibility that comes with the power. The obligation to create a better world."

"I understand that obligation," said Claudia, voice soft. "I understand it very well."

"Irene," said Caina, "you cannot..."

"My name," said Claudia, rising to her feet, "is Claudia Aberon."

"Damn it," said Caina, standing as well. "Do you not understand the purpose of a disguise? You are a Ghost..."

"I am a Ghost," said Claudia, "but I was a magus, and I am still a sorceress. Mihaela is right. I have a duty to use my power to make a better world. And this opportunity is astounding." Claudia took a deep breath. "I could make a better Magisterium, one devoted to the people of the Empire. We could force an end to the war, force all nations to live in harmony. Why should we not do this? You hate the magi more than anyone I have ever met. I thought you would see the wisdom in this."

"You don't have the right to do this!" said Caina. She had hoped to maintain her disguise in front of Mihaela, but if Claudia was going to do something so foolish... "Even if Mihaela isn't lying to you, you don't have the right to do this. You would appoint yourself tyrant over the whole world." She paused. "It is exactly the sort of thing your father would do."

Caina expected Claudia to react with anger, but she only shook her head.

"Mihaela is right," said Claudia. "You do not have arcane power. You don't understand the obligations that imposes. I have to do this... and I have the right to do this."

"Oh, I understand just fine," said Caina, gripping the edge of the table. "You think your power gives you the right. Your sorcery lets you force people to do as you wish. You're no better than a thug forcing a weaker man to hand over his coins. At least the thug doesn't have the temerity to claim he's doing it for the victim's own good." Her anger flared. "If I had known you would do something as stupid as this, then I would have left you imprisoned in the stone."

She saw Corvalis's hand curl into a fist.

Claudia only smiled, a patronizing, calm smile. "Your hatred of sorcery is clouding your judgment, Anna. Once this is done, I think you will understand."

"No," said Caina. "You are not doing this."

Mihaela laughed. "You have grown tiresome. Go run to your circlemaster and report what we have done. He will be unable to stop us. Just as you will."

"Cormark," said Caina.

Corvalis hesitated.

"Damn it, Cormark," said Caina.

"A moment, sister," said Corvalis.

He followed Caina into the hall.

"We have to go to Basil, now," Caina said, as soon as the door closed behind them. "Claudia doesn't know the risks she is taking. I know Mihaela used necromancy to create the glypharmor. At worst, Claudia is walking into a trap, and at best, Mihaela is going to use her as a tool and kill her later. We have..."

"She might be right," said Corvalis.

Caina blinked in surprise. "You cannot be serious."

"I am," said Corvalis. "Mihaela makes sense. If she has truly built a way to control the glypharmor into her spells, then we have a chance to cripple the Magisterium. To make my father pay for what he has done."

"Mihaela is lying," said Caina.

"Claudia is willing to take the risk," said Corvalis. "And I trust her judgment."

"More than mine?" said Caina.

"In this, yes," said Corvalis, voice quiet.

Caina blinked. That...had hurt more than she thought.

"She is right about this," said Corvalis. He would not meet her eyes. "You do hate sorcery, enough that...enough that you will not take an opportunity when it opens before you. If we can do this, it will be the greatest victory the Ghosts have ever won."

"It will be the greatest mistake the Ghosts have ever made," said Caina. "Putting that much power in Mihaela's will be a disaster."

"Claudia will keep her in check," said Corvalis.

"And Claudia will be just as bad," said Caina.

"Why?" said Corvalis, his eyes narrowing.

"Because no one can be trusted with that kind of power," said Caina. "Damn it, Corvalis, she's turning herself into a slaver. She's enslaving evil men, true, but she's still turning them into slaves."

Corvalis shook his head. "What has she done to make you distrust her so?"

"I wouldn't trust myself with that kind of power," said Caina, "let alone Claudia."

His eyes narrowed. "Why not? What has she ever done against the Ghosts? She convinced me to leave the Magisterium and seek a better life. She joined the Ghosts, and she has done everything that you and Basil asked. Yet you have never stopped thinking that she's some sort of devil in training!"

"She's a magus!" said Caina. She realized that she was shouting, but there was no one else around to hear. "She's doing everything your father would do if he had the chance, and you're so wrapped around her little finger that you're too damned blind to see it!"

"And you hate her too much," said Corvalis, "to realize this is the Ghosts' best chance to crush the Magisterium. All because you can't get over your grudge against sorcery."

A tremor of anger went through Caina, and she forced herself to stay still.

"I am going to Basil," said Caina, "and he will stop this."

"Basil isn't blinded by hate," said Corvalis, "and he'll agree with us."

Caina stalked away without another word.

20

ALL IN ONE PLACE

C aina hurried through the Tower's halls, her heels clicking against the floor. She supposed she should have felt sad, should have felt betrayed.

Instead, she only felt fury.

Gods, she had been such a fool.

She should have known better. A magus of the Magisterium would not change. And she should have known that Corvalis would do whatever Claudia told him. No matter what Claudia did, no matter what mad folly she pursued, Corvalis would follow her.

Corvalis...

"Gods damn it all," whispered Caina. "I should have known."

Her eyes stung. She wiped the back of her hand across them and kept walking.

She had to find Halfdan and warn him. Between Saddiq's tribesmen and whatever mercenaries Annika found, they could gather enough men to stop Mihaela. But that would mean violence inside the Tower of Study, and the Scholae would respond...

Later. She could plan later. And the decision rested with Halfdan.

She returned to the Hall of Assembly. The Hall was deserted, the glow from the river of molten steel painting the walls with sullen light. Caina looked into the cylindrical chamber at the Tower's heart and saw a dark shape outline against the glow of the metal.

Kylon stood there, gazing into the pool.

Caina strode towards him. If Mihaela and Claudia really were planning to give away the glypharmor, Kylon had to be warned.

Perhaps he could help stop them.

She did not bother masking her footfalls. With his water sorcery, she had no chance of sneaking up on him without her shadow-cloak.

Kylon turned as she approached, a lean shadow against the glowing metal. "Ghost."

"Lord High Seat," said Caina.

"Is it not peculiar," said Kylon, "how close we can stand to the metal? I have seen the foundries in New Kyre. The smiths must layer themselves in heavy leather, lest the heat of the steel burn them."

"The wards keep the heat at bay," said Caina. "If not for the Masked Ones' sorcery, this entire place would melt. Little loss as that would be."

"You are distressed," said Kylon.

"I've come to warn you," said Caina. "Do not attempt to wield a suit of glypharmor, or allow anyone in your embassy to do so. Mihaela can control anyone wielding the glypharmor."

Kylon let out a long breath. "Ah. That explains much. Then this was a trick, was it not? A ploy to lure the most powerful sorcerers in the world here and take control of them? Like gathering your foes in once place to kill them all at once."

"It gets worse," said Caina. "Mihaela has apparently convinced Zalandris to give three suits of glypharmor to each embassy. He thinks the weapons are so powerful that no one will dare use them, that this will ensure peace between the nations."

"Then he is an even bigger fool than I thought," Kylon said with a sigh. "Those suits of armor will either trigger the bloodiest war in history, or Mihaela will use them to enslave half the world ..."

He blinked, frowning.

"All in one place," he murmured.

"What is it?" said Caina.

"This is a trap, obviously," said Kylon. "But Mihaela runs a steep risk by giving the glypharmor to all of the embassies. The more ambassadors that are involved, the more likely it is one of them will realize the danger. It would be easier to take over the ambassadors from the Empire and Anshan. So why invite all the embassies?"

Caina frowned. "To enslave them, of course."

"All at once? Mihaela seems too methodical to make such a gamble," said Kylon. "I assume the embassies will gather in the Hall of Assembly," he glanced over his shoulder, "to receive the glypharmor."

Caina nodded. "Along with the entire Scholae."

"This isn't about the glypharmor," said Kylon. "Or, at least, the glypharmor is only a lure. Mihaela wants to gather the embassies and all the Sages in one place."

"Why?" said Caina.

"I know not," said Kylon, "but I doubt her intentions are good."

"How can you be sure?" said Caina.

"Because it is what I would have done," said Kylon. "Because it is what I have done. How do you think we destroyed your Emperor's western fleet? We struck dozens of targets along the coast south of Marsis, and caused so much havoc that eventually the western fleet gathered to confront us."

"And then you broke the fleet," said Caina.

It made a disturbing amount of sense. Caina had no doubt Mihaela's motives for giving away the glypharmor were sinister. But why? What was her ultimate goal, if not to enslave the most powerful sorcerers in the world?

Caina didn't know, but she had to find out.

"I have to find Basil," said Caina. "He needs to know about this."

Kylon frowned. "Where is your...sister? And your bodyguard?"

"Mihaela has convinced my sister," said Caina, "that she is acting for the greater good. And my...bodyguard has gone with her."

"I see," said Kylon. He could sense her emotions, she knew. She wondered what he made of the tangle of anger and pain that swirled through her mind. "Go. I will warn the men of my embassy to stay away from the glypharmor, and I will also warn the other ambassadors. Most likely they will not believe a word I say. But if I can spread enough doubt, perhaps that will keep them from touching the armor." He looked towards the doors. "Perhaps between us we can find a way to stop whatever madness Mihaela has planned."

Caina nodded and headed for the doors. Once she was outside, she gripped her skirts and broke into a run. She had to warn Halfdan, and they had to take action at once. Mihaela would act soon.

She reached Halfdan's rooms and looked around. The sitting room was dark, the fireplace cold. Caina turned, intending to head for the barracks and warn Saddiq, and a piece of paper lying on the table caught her eye.

It was a note, and she recognized Halfdan's small, tight handwriting.

"Damn it," muttered Caina, reading the note.

Halfdan had taken Saddiq and his men and gone into the city. Annika's friends had spotted Torius Aberon moving through Catekharon, hiring every mercenary and caravan guard he could find. She feared that he planned to seize Mihaela and claim the glypharmor for the Magisterium, perhaps this very night. Halfdan and Saddiq had gone to investigate.

"Damn it," said Caina again, sliding the note into the fireplace. She struck a spark against the kindling and watched the paper burn, her mind racing.

There were too many moving pieces to this puzzle. Mihaela and the glypharmor. The spell of enslavement built into the glypharmor. Whatever secret pact Mihaela had made with the First Magus and the Magisterium, and whatever arrangement Sicarion had with Mihaela.

Something was going to happen tonight, and Caina did not know what. Was it her fault? Had she been so distracted by Corvalis that she had lost her wits, had failed to notice what was happening right under her nose?

Perhaps when he had come to her room in the Inn of the Defender and kissed her, she should have pushed him away. She...

A greasy tingle went over her skin.

Someone was casting a spell nearby, and it had the feel of necromancy.

She dropped to a crouch, yanking the curved ghostsilver dagger from her belt. Again she felt the icy tingle. Caina closed her eyes and concentrated. It felt as if the spell was coming from outside.

She left the sitting room, darted into her bedroom, retrieved her shadow-cloak, threw it over her shoulders, and went outside. Caina ducked into the shadows on the broad stone terrace outside the palace, looking left and right. Darkness hung over the Tower of Study, pale lights shining in its high windows, the aqueducts of molten steel throwing their crimson light into the sky.

Caina saw a shadow moving beneath one of the aqueducts. She glimpsed a mottled face in the cowl of a heavy cloak, the skin scarred and slashed.

Her breath hissed through her teeth.

Sicarion.

It was just as well she had donned her shadow-cloak. Without it, he could sense the presence of the Moroaica within Caina. She watched as he moved slowly, carefully, towards the Tower of Study. Had he come here to kill Mihaela? Or had he come to aid her?

Either way, if Caina followed him and remained unseen, perhaps she could find the details of Mihaela's plan.

Caina hurried back into her room. She stripped off her dress and threw it aside, and retrieved different clothes from the false bottom of a trunk. She dressed in black boots, black trousers, and a black jacket lined with thin steel plates to deflect knives. A belt went around her waist, holding knives, a coil of rope, lockpicks, and other useful tools. Black gloves went over her hands, and a black mask concealed her face. Last of all she pulled on her shadow cloak, hooked the ghost-silver dagger in its scabbard to her belt, and slid a pair of daggers into hidden sheaths in her boots.

She left the palace and spotted Sicarion, still making his slow, careful way towards the Tower.

Caina glided from shadow to shadow, following him.

21

BLOOD AND STEEL

S icarion moved from shadow to shadow like a wolf stalking its prey, and if Caina had not already known he was there, she never would have found him.

The aura of necromantic sorcery he radiated made it easier to find him.

Caina followed him from shadow to shadow. From time to time he glanced around, and when he did, Caina remained perfectly still, letting her cloak blend with the shadows. Sicarion's mismatched eyes swept over her, but he never saw her.

Or, at least, he pretended that he did not, and was leading her into a trap.

If Sicarion was leading her into a trap, she had no choice but to walk into it. This was her best chance of finding out Mihaela's plan.

And she was sure Sicarion had not seen her.

Mostly sure.

Sicarion paused before the gates to the Hall of Assembly, outlined in the glow of the molten metal. He cast a spell, muttering under his breath, and his form flickered and wavered. Caina recognized the spell. It was a simple incantation of psychic sorcery, designed to keep anyone from noticing his presence. It would not fool the Sages, but it would work on the slaves.

But if Caina kept her cowl up, the spell would not affect her.

She followed Sicarion through the Hall of Assembly, around the pool of molten metal at the Tower's heart, and into the Seekers' quarters. She slipped her hand around her ghostsilver dagger. There was absolutely no place to hide in the hall corridor, and the sullen glow of the molten metal left no shadows for her cloak. Yet Sicarion's pace picked up, and he did not look over his shoulder. No doubt he thought himself safe. Caina half-expected him to enter Mihaela's rooms, but he strode past the door. She felt a surge of excitement. If Sicarion wasn't going to Mihaela's rooms, then he was going to Mihaela's hidden workshop.

And perhaps Caina could at last find out how Mihaela had created the glypharmor.

Sicarion strode deeper into the Seekers' quarters. This part of the Tower was unused and deserted, and a faint layer of dust covered the floor. At last Sicarion stopped before a door, and Caina pressed herself into a nearby doorway, hoping it was deep enough to keep him from noticing her.

Sicarion took one look around, then cast a spell at the door. Caina felt a pulse of sorcery, and the door swung open. Sicarion strode through it, and the door shut behind him with a thump.

Caina hurried forward and examined the door. A series of sigils and runes covered the planks, and she felt the waiting power. A warding spell, she thought, cast to grant access only to certain people. She concentrated, and behind the door she felt the presence of...

Nothing.

Absolutely nothing.

Which was peculiar. Every other inch of the Tower radiated sorcery. Practically every inch of Catekharon, for that matter. Yet from behind that door she felt...nothing at all.

The room beyond had been shielded with a ward designed to block any divinatory spells. Which meant that whatever Mihaela did in that room, she didn't want the Sages to know about it. Though perhaps Mihaela needn't have bothered. If the other Sages were anything like Zalandris, Mihaela could set fire to the Tower of Study and the Masked Ones would never notice.

Caina examined the sigils. They were not Maatish hieroglyphs, and she recognized several of the sigils from the warding spells favored by the magi. If she opened the door, the resultant release of power would rip her to shreds.

Unless she damaged the wards first.

"Should have inscribed them on steel, Mihaela," muttered Caina, lifting her ghostsilver dagger.

She scratched at the sigils with the dagger, sending wooden shavings to the floor. Sweat trickled down her face and back, but her hands remained steady. She had done this before, but it was always risky...

One of the sigils pulsed with blue light, charring the wood, and Caina took an alarmed step back.

But the light did not spread.

Caina sighed in relief and went back to work, defacing the sigils one by one. After a few moments, the entire door pulsed with blue light, the sigils turning to smoking char. The ward collapsed, and Caina felt the power drain away.

She took a deep breath and opened the door quietly.

The room beyond reminded her of Talekhris's workshop. Heavy worktables supported a peculiar array of equipment and glass bottles, though Mihaela had more metalworking tools than Talekhris. Wooden bookshelves held scrolls, and Caina saw that most of the scrolls were written in Maatish hieroglyphs. Maglarion had killed Caina's father just to claim one Maatish scroll, and with that scroll he had almost destroyed Malarae. She shuddered to think what he might have done to claim Mihaela's library.

The air smelled like spilled blood and burnt meat.

The stench was coming from a door on the far side of the workroom.

Caina crossed to the door and listened for a moment. She heard nothing but silence, and she felt no wards upon the door. Another deep breath, and she stepped through the door.

The next room was a large hall, similar to the one where Mihaela had slaughtered the criminals. The sullen glow of molten metal came from a door on the other side of the hall, and in its light Caina saw a dozen steel coffins lying scattered across the floor.

The smallest was the size of a small child, while the largest was at least twelve feet long. Maatish hieroglyphs covered the coffins. Had Mihaela been robbing Maatish tombs? But from what Caina understood, the ancient Maatish had buried their dead in coffins and sarcophagi of gold and stone. Not steel, and steel coffins would have rusted away centuries ago.

Mihaela had made these things. But why?

The smell of burned flesh came from the caskets.

Caina peered inside the nearest coffin. A heap of something like charcoal lay inside the gleaming coffin, and after a moment she realized that it was burned bone. Dozens of grooves had been carved into the inside of the coffin, like channels designed to drain away blood, and more hieroglyphs marked the grooves. A faint, jagged aura of sorcery surrounded the thing. It had once been the locus of powerful spells, but the spells had collapsed, leaving only a steel coffin and a burned skeleton.

Why go to the trouble of making the damned things? If Mihaela had wanted to burn someone alive, the gods knew there were easier ways to go about it, and...

Her breath hissed through her teeth.

No. These weren't coffins.

They were molds.

She remembered her visit to Ark's foundry in Malarae, watching as his workers poured molten metal into molds to create swords and armor for the Imperial Legions. Mihaela had made these coffins as molds for the glypharmor. These must have been early attempts, failed experiments before she settled upon a final design.

But if they were molds...why did each of the coffins hold a pile of burned bones?

A distant scream reached Caina's ears.

She whirled, ghostsilver dagger in hand, but saw no movement. Again the scream rang out, coming from the glowing doorway on the far side of the hall. Caina hurried forward, boots making no sound against the floor, and peered through the doorway.

The presence of powerful sorcery washed over her, jabbing at her skin like icy needles.

The hall beyond was as large as the Hall of Assembly itself, and a thick stream of molten metal ran through the center of the floor. The air felt like a blast furnace, and Caina wondered if the wards around the liquid metal had weakened. Dozens of suits of black, gleaming glypharmor stood scattered around the hall, looming like statues. Boxes and crates and barrels lay in heaps, and Caina saw worktables laden with tools and books. The scream rang out again, followed by a terrified sob.

Caina crept forward. Fortunately, the suits of glypharmor and the discarded crates provided plenty of cover. She slid around a table and came to a halt. A suit of red glypharmor stood here, motionless as the others. All the other suits were black, but this one was red.

It was the one Mihaela had worn during her demonstration.

Again Caina felt that curious attraction to the armor, its aura of power buzzing inside of her head. She stepped forward, hesitant, and reached out a single hand to touch the red steel.

A vision flashed through her head, a string of disjointed images. A screaming girl dragged by armored men, a flash of molten steel, and horrible burning as invisible chains closed around her arms and legs...

Caina jerked her hand away, the vision fading.

Best not to touch the armor.

She crept across the room, sweat dripping down her face and between her shoulders. She passed several of the black suits of glypharmor, and while she sensed their aura of power, she felt none of that peculiar attraction. Once she touched the black steel and nothing happened.

For some reason, only the red suit drew her.

Caina shook her head, moved closer to the molten steel, and heard a voice.

Mihaela's voice.

Caina ducked behind a crate and peered around its edges.

The first thing she saw was the mold. An enormous steel coffin, twenty feet high, stood upright at the edge of the molten canal. It was more elaborate than the others, every inch covered in an intricate maze of Maatish hieroglyphs. Its lid stood open, and inside Caina saw more grooves, along with a net of chains.

Chains that looked designed to hold someone in place.

Boots clicked against the stone, and Mihaela strode into sight, stopping beneath the massive steel mold. She carried the silvery rod of a Sage in her right hand. Two mercenaries stood on either side of her, and with a start Caina recognized them.

They had been with Torius Aberon at Irzaris's warehouse.

"So," said Mihaela. "Scarred one. So good of you to return at last."

Sicarion walked into sight from the other side of the mold. The mercenaries tensed, their hands going to their swords, but Mihaela only looked amused.

"What were you doing?" said Mihaela. "Skulking about and trying to steal my secrets?"

"I was merely admiring your craftsmanship, Seeker," said Sicarion. "Your work has improved greatly since we first met."

"It has," said Mihaela. "Zalandris has proven willing to share his secrets in the glorious cause of peace, the senile old fool. And the few spells you shared have proven to be of occasional use."

"Such thunderous praise," said Sicarion. Caina forced herself to remain motionless as his mismatched eyes passed over her hiding place. "You have abandoned the Nhabati iron in your design."

"Not entirely," said Mihaela. "The red steel would take the spells," she waved her rod at the red glypharmor, "but there were...irritating complications. So I added steel taken from the canals." She pointed at the stream of molten steel. "The resultant alloy proved most receptive to the binding spells."

"Good," said Sicarion. "It's just as well the pharaohs of Maat never had your metallurgic skill. Else they still might reign in the south."

"Spare me the lectures upon history," said Mihaela. "The pharaohs lie in the dust of the past, and the future belongs to us."

"Very well," said Sicarion, looking at the upright coffin. "This is the Forge's final design, then?"

"Yes," said Mihaela. "It eliminated the defects found in the previous versions, and draws molten metal and power directly from the spell binding the fire elemental." She gestured, and Caina saw metal pipes running from the coffin to the molten canal. "With the increased efficiency, we can make hundreds of suits of glypharmor a day."

"Impressive," said Sicarion.

"We are ready to begin the first step," said Mihaela. "I persuaded Zalandris to give glypharmor to each of the embassies, and I duped one of the Ghosts into summoning the ambassadors for me. Once they gather, I will have the Forge moved to the central chamber off the Hall of Assembly...and the first step will begin."

"One of the Ghosts?" said Sicarion, surprised. "Truly? Which one?"

"One of the women," said Mihaela. "Decius Aberon's bastard daughter. Not the other one, the one who calls herself Anna Callenius. Which surprised me. I thought Anna would be the greater fool."

"Do not underestimate her," said Sicarion. "She is most dangerous."

"Yes," said Mihaela. "I live in dread of a merchant's pampered daughter."

"You should," said Sicarion. "You are ready?"

"We are," said Mihaela. "Though we will have one final demonstration."

Sicarion sighed. "Torius insisted?"

"He did," said a man's voice, and Torius Aberon came into sight, still clad in his black armor. "This is a bold plan, Mihaela...but a warrior only commits himself when he is sure of victory."

Mihaela smirked at him. "The greatest rewards go to the boldest. But if you insist upon one more demonstration...well, an additional suit of glypharmor would not go amiss." She beckoned. "Bring him."

Two more mercenaries came into sight, dragging a fat man in the black robe and purple sash of a master magus between them. The magus's face gleamed with sweat, and his eyes darted back and forth. Caina recognized him from the First Magus's embassy.

"Marcus," said Torius with a smile. "You're looking well."

"Torius!" spat Marcus. "What is this? Have you lost your mind? I've always supported your father! You..."

Torius backhanded him with an armored fist, and blood flew from Marcus's mouth.

"My father," said Torius, "doesn't know about this. Not yet, anyway." He grinned. "I look forward to the expression on his face when we feed him into the Forge. Maybe he'll look as surprised as you do right now."

"What?" said Marcus. "What are you doing to me?"

"This," said Torius, "is going to hurt a lot."

"Prepare him," said Mihaela.

The mercenaries ripped away Marcus's robe and underclothes, leaving him naked. The magus tried to fight back, but Caina sensed Torius's constraining spell, and without his sorcery Marcus was no match for the mercenaries. They shoved him into the massive steel mold, wrapped him in the harness, and pulled on the chains. The chains lifted Marcus, holding him suspended in the center of the mold.

"Torius!" shrieked Marcus. "What do you want? I'll give you anything. I'll do anything! Anything!"

"I want," said Torius with a smile, "you to die in agony."

He gripped the coffin's lid and heaved, and it swung shut with a tremendous clang, drowning out Marcus's shriek.

"You said the pharaohs of Maat used this spell to bind their souls to their hearts," said Mihaela, lifting her rod. "They were fools. Else they would have bound their souls to something like this."

She muttered a spell, and Caina felt the icy tingle of necromantic sorcery. White fire flared in the hieroglyphs covering the coffin, and a ripple went through the molten metal. The Forge shuddered, and Mihaela made a sweeping motion with the rod.

The power in the air redoubled.

"Torius!" Caina could hear Marcus's faint scream through the thick steel. "Please! Damn you, Torius! Help me! Help..."

Mihaela gestured, and the Forge's sigils flared with white light as the pipes sucked up molten metal from the canal.

Torius's screams dissolved into a hideous hissing crackle, and the stench of burning meat flooded Caina's nose. Fingers of white lightning crackled up and down the Forge, the hieroglyphs glowing brighter, the stone floor vibrating. The power radiating from the Forge grew sharper, so potent that it caused Caina physical pain. She gripped the edge of the crate to keep her balance and shielded her eyes from the Forge's light.

The glow faded, and the sharp pain against Caina's skin vanished.

"An impressive light show," said Torius. "Did it work?"

Mihaela sneered. "Of course it worked." She lifted her rod and pointed. "Come forth!"

The Forge's steel door swung open, and a black suit of glypharmor stepped out. The hieroglyphics upon the plates of its arms and legs and cuirass pulsed with white light, reflecting in the dark steel.

"I trust," said Mihaela, "that removes any doubts?"

"Quite," said Torius, gazing at the glypharmor.

"Remarkable," murmured Sicarion. "You can control it remotely?"

"In a limited fashion," said Mihaela. "Simple commands only. Not well enough for combat. For anything more than straightforward movement, it needs a wielder. Stop!"

The glypharmor halted, the light in the hieroglyphs dimming.

"A pity you can't control them remotely during combat," said

Sicarion. "An army of invincible automatons would kill quite a lot of people."

"I can disable them," said Mihaela, "in case either of you decides to get clever and betray me."

Torius laughed. "Betray you, my dear Mihaela? When your genius has brought us these weapons? We shall have to split the world between us...but a third of the world is still enough for any man." He grinned, his green eyes glinting in the glow from the canal. "And the expression on my father's face when we chain him into the Forge...ah, that alone will almost be payment enough."

"Enough to give up a third of the world?" said Mihaela.

"I said 'almost'."

"If this latest demonstration satisfies your doubts," said Mihaela, "then we will begin. Have your men take the Forge to the central chamber. Claudia Aberon should have gathered the embassies by now. Once I retrieve the Stormbrand from the Chamber of Relics, the work can proceed."

"As you say," said Torius. He waved a hand at the new-made suit of glypharmor. "Can you get Marcus out of the way first?"

"Move," said Mihaela, pointing her rod. "Ten paces forward, and then remain motionless."

The glypharmor clanked forward, and Caina eased back from the crate.

She had everything she needed. Mihaela had murdered Marcus in that ghastly Forge, and somehow his death had created the glypharmor. It was plainly necromancy. Caina could go to Talekhris and warn him, and once the Scholae knew that Mihaela had used necromancy, they would stop her...

The glypharmor halted, and as it did, its boot struck an empty barrel. The sheer force and power of its stride sent the barrel tumbling into the air, and it slammed into the crate in front of Caina. The crate hit Caina's side, and she lost her balance and fell to the stone floor.

She rolled to one knee, and saw Mihaela, Torius, and Sicarion staring at her in astonishment.

"What the devil?" said Torius.

Sicarion began to laugh.

"A Ghost!" said Mihaela, pointing her rod. "What are you idiots waiting for? Kill him! Kill him now!"

A dozen mercenaries charged towards Caina, even as Mihaela, Torius, and Sicarion all began casting spells.

22

STOP TALKING AND KILL HER

C aina rolled to her feet, ghostsilver dagger in hand, and sprinted for the door. She heard the shouts of the mercenaries, and her skin crawled with the presence of arcane power as Mihaela and the others cast spells. Caina darted around a crate and ducked between the legs of a suit of black glypharmor, but the mercenaries still closed. She was fast, but too many obstacles stood between her and the door ...

The tingling against her skin grew sharper, and Caina dodged behind a suit of glypharmor.

An instant later a blast of invisible force brushed her and sent her spinning across the ground. The glypharmor clanged like a bell, a vibration going through the steel, and for a moment Caina feared it would fall upon her and crush her.

But the glypharmor was far too heavy for a single spell to move.

Caina staggered to her feet as the first mercenary lunged at her. She dodged his sword thrust, free hand dipping to her belt. A throwing knife glimmered in her fingers, and she stabbed at the mercenary with all her strength. He brought up his blade to block, the knife spinning to the floor, but that gave Caina the opening she needed to lunge with her ghostsilver dagger. The blade tore open his throat, and the man fell.

Three more mercenaries came at her, and Caina ran. The men fanned out, trying to drive her towards one of the suits of glypharmor. Caina darted to the left, so close that one of the mercenaries' swords brushed her shoulder. A large crate stood before her, big enough to hold a grown man, and Caina jumped. She seized the edge of the crate, heaved herself up, and rolled over the far side. She landed in a crouch, her legs buckling to absorb the impact, and sprinted.

By the time the mercenaries got around the crate, she was twenty yards away. The doorway loomed closer, and beyond Caina saw the glint of the steel coffins. Just a little farther, and she could get back into the main hallways of the Tower of Study and warn Zalandris or Talekhris.

A black blur shot overhead and landed between Caina and the doorway with a clang.

Torius Aberon leveled his dark sword and grinned.

"I remember you," he said. "The Ghost following my idiot half-brother. Well, you'll..."

Caina flung a throwing knife at his face, and Torius blocked with his sword. The knife clattered away, and Caina reached into her belt for another.

But Torius surged forward with a spell, his sorcery driving his legs with superhuman speed. Caina dodged, but not fast enough. Torius's sword missed her, but his armored shoulder struck her arm, and she went sprawling to the ground. She hit the floor with a bone-rattling thump, and scrambled back to her feet. Torius was fast, but she knew firsthand that a sorcerer using a spell to enhance his speed could not change direction quickly. If she could get to the doorway before ...

A blur of motion in the corner of her eye caught her attention, and Caina saw a barrel hurtling towards her. She ducked, and the barrel shot over her head and bounced off the floor. Caina straightened up and saw a crate leap into the air and fall towards her. She dodged, and caught a glimpse of Mihaela striding towards her, flicks of her enspelled rod sending debris shooting into the air.

"Kill that Ghost!" said Mihaela. "Must I do everything myself? If he gets away it will mean our heads! Kill him!"

She swung the rod, and a pair of barrels shot towards Caina. Caina ducked under the first barrel and dodged around the second as Torius spun to face her. She felt the surge of arcane power as he hurtled forward, his armor a black blur.

Caina rolled between the legs of a suit of glypharmor as Torius charged. The battle magus shot past the glypharmor, and Caina scrambled to her feet. She had a clear path to the door, and...

An empty crate slammed into her back. The impact drove her to the ground, the breath exploding from her lungs.

The mercenaries closed around her.

Caina sprang to her feet, snatched a throwing knife from her sleeve, killed one of the men with a quick throw, and then killed a second with a slash of her ghostsilver dagger. But there were too many mercenaries. Four men grabbed her arms and twisted, ripping the bloody dagger from her hands. Two of the men drew back their swords, and Caina braced herself for the killing blow...

"Wait!" Mihaela strode closer. "Take off his mask first."

"Why?" said Torius with a scowl. "Just kill him and have done with it."

"I want to see if Claudia was clever enough to betray me," said Mihaela. "I thought the girl was a fool...but perhaps she fooled me. Take off his mask, now."

One of the mercenaries pulled back Caina's cowl and yanked off her mask.

She had the satisfaction of seeing the shock on Mihaela's and Torius's faces.

"Her?" said Mihaela. "The merchant's daughter? Surely this is some trick!"

Torius snorted. "Aye, but we were the ones tricked. I thought her my half-brother's toy." He shook his head. "Instead she is a Ghost nightfighter, and left three of my men dead upon the floor."

"I should have listened to Sicarion," said Mihaela. She looked around with an irritated scowl. "And where is Sicarion?"

"I don't know," said Torius. "He ran off during the chase."

Mihaela shrugged. "No matter. He'll be back soon enough." She pointed the metallic rod at Caina's chest. "Anything useful to say before I kill you?"

"You should flee now," said Caina, "while you still can."

Mihaela snorted. "Since you so clearly have command of the situation."

"I don't," said Caina, "but the Sages will. I damaged your wards. They would have sensed the necromancy you used to murder Marcus and create that...that thing." She jerked her head at the suit of glypharmor. "If you run now, perhaps you'll get out of Catekharon before they find you."

"The Sages," said Mihaela, "the mighty, learned Sages, would not bestir themselves if the city burned down around their ears." She frowned. "And the Forge does not use a great deal of necromantic force, since the victims' own arcane talent provides the bulk of the power."

Caina blinked...and the puzzle made sense.

Horrifying sense.

"That's it, isn't it?" said Caina. "That's what this is all about."

Mihaela's frown deepened. "All about what?"

"That Forge of yours," said Caina. "It creates glypharmor, but it uses the victim's soul to power the armor. Except it only works with sorcerers. There must not be enough arcane force in the soul of someone without the talent."

"The soul acts as a channel," murmured Mihaela. "And a sorcerer's soul draws substantially more power than the soul of someone without sorcerous skill. The Forge binds the victim's soul to the armor, which then acts as a channel to power the glypharmor." She smiled. "I would feed you to the Forge, if you had any talent. I understand the process is...quite painful."

"That's monstrous," said Caina. "You've condemned them to eternal imprisonment and torment to fuel your own power."

"Gladly," said Mihaela. "They would do the same to me, if they had the power."

"That's why you convinced Zalandris to send out the invitations," said Caina. "So you could lure the most powerful sorcerers in the world here, murder them, and transform them into glypharmor."

"You are as clever as Sicarion thought," said Mihaela. "Did you see those preening fools? Yaramzod the Black and Master Callatas and Torius's fat pig of a father all think they'll take my glypharmor and make themselves the masters of the world. Instead they're going to die screaming in my Forge, their souls enslaved to my armor for all time. The Sages, too, the pompous old fools. I will put their talents to better use than they ever managed."

"And then what?" said Caina. "You'll conquer the world?"

"Exactly," said Mihaela. "Torius and Sicarion have gathered reliable men, and I shall equip them with the glypharmor. First we will subdue the free cities and forge them together in an empire of our own. We shall smash the walls of New Kyre and shatter its fleets in the harbor. Anshan, Istarinmul, the Empire...all the world shall be ours."

"Ours?" said Caina, looking at Torius. "Or yours?"

"Do not be absurd," said Mihaela. "I created the glypharmor, yes, but I cannot use it alone. I need an army. One woman cannot rule the world alone. We shall..."

"Mihaela," said Torius, "far be it from me to point out the obvious, but I suggest you stop talking and kill the damned Ghost already."

"She might know something useful," said Mihaela.

"Or," said Torius, "she is convincing you to tell her the entire plan, which she will use against you if she escapes."

Mihaela's eyes narrowed. "I see. Very clever."

"Kill her now," said Torius.

"Excellent idea," said Mihaela, pointing the silvery rod.

Caina jerked against the mercenaries, but they were too strong, and she could not move. White light flared around the tip of Mihaela's rod, and Caina's skin crawled beneath the presence of arcane force ...

Then she felt a massive spike of power.

A blast of invisible force struck Mihaela and flung her across the room. She slammed into the legs of a suit of glypharmor and hit the ground, the rod rolling away from her fingers.

"What?" roared Torius, beginning a spell.

A voice like thunder boomed through the hall. "No one move!"

Caina turned her head, and a wave of relief shot through her.

Talekhris limped through the doorway, his silver rod crackling with power in his right hand.

"Not another step!" said Torius. "Surrender or..."

Talekhris flicked the rod, and a psychokinetic burst drove Torius to the floor. Mihaela scrambled to her feet, her eyes narrowed.

"Don't bother," said Talekhris, stopping next to the mercenaries. Their hands dug into Caina's arms, and she saw the terror on their faces. "You have no spell that can threaten me."

"Sage," said Mihaela, "I am working upon a task for the Speaker, and Zalandris will not be pleased if..."

"Stop lying," said Talekhris. "I was certain you used necromancy in the creation of the glypharmor, but I had no way of proving it." He glanced at Caina. "I was not clever enough to discover your secrets, but I suspected this Ghost would be. Therefore I kept a careful eye upon her, and followed her here." He pointed at the Forge. "Powering the armor with the soul of a spellcaster? Clever. Clever, and monstrous. But it ends now."

"This isn't over," said Mihaela. Torius tried to rise, but Talekhris gestured, and another blast of force knocked the battle magus down.

"You're wrong," said Talekhris. "I have not spent centuries battling the Moroaica only for a foolish Seeker to build a necromantic horror within the Tower of Study itself. Both you, Mihaela, and you, Torius Aberon, will surrender yourselves to my custody. Your mercenaries may depart, so long as they never return to Catekharon."

Torius got to his feet. "You're confident, old man."

"These are my terms," said Talekhris. "Surrender now, or I will kill you both."

Mihaela smirked.

"Very well," she said, spreading her arms. "I surrender. Come and take me."

Talekhris nodded. "Good. Put down the rod and..."

He jerked, his words ending in a strangled gasp.

A foot of bloody steel blade erupted from his chest, a crimson stain spreading across the white linen of his robe. A dark shape stood behind him, a scarred hand resting upon the Sage's shoulder.

"How many centuries have you pursued my mistress?" said Sicarion, twisting the sword. "I've lost count. All those centuries, all those battles...and after all this time, you're still not very good at this."

Talekhris groaned, and Sicarion ripped his serrated dagger across the Sage's throat. Sicarion kicked him off the sword blade, and the Sage staggered forward a step and collapsed, lying in a spreading pool of his own blood.

He did not move.

Caina stared at the corpse.

She had gambled, and she had lost. Mihaela would murder both the ambassadors and the Sages, and use their deaths to fuel her armor and launch the bloodiest war in the history of man.

And Caina was about to die.

"Sicarion," said Torius with a laugh. "You have a gift for good timing."

"And where were you hiding?" said Mihaela.

"When the Ghost arrived," said Sicarion, "I expected she might have damaged the wards during her entry." He prodded Talekhris's corpse with the toe of his boot. "It turns out I was right."

"Just as well," said Torius. "Dump his body into the metal."

"Don't bother," said Sicarion. "He has pursued my mistress for centuries, even though I've killed him over and over again. He'll wake up in a few days, and then you can feed him into the Forge." He laughed. "A fitting end."

"Pursuing your mistress?" said Mihaela. "I thought you said your mistress was dead."

"She is," said Sicarion. "Presently."

"Enough," said Torius. "Mihaela, kill the Ghost and we'll begin." He looked at Sicarion. "Unless you have a use for her?"

Sicarion grinned at Caina. Jadriga had ordered him not to kill her.

But Caina realized the Moroaica had said nothing about others.

"She's too dangerous to leave alive," said Sicarion. "Kill her immediately."

Caina looked at Mihaela just as the silver rod glowed, a harsh white light filling her vision.

When it cleared she found herself lying on the floor, a burning pain devouring her chest.

Part of her mind realized that her heart had stopped.

Images flashed before her eyes. Her father. Halfdan. Theodosia. Corvalis.

Gods, gods, she wished she could have seen Corvalis one last...

Nothingness swallowed her.

23

CORRUPTED AIR

"Thank you, Corvalis," said Claudia. "I know that we are doing the right thing."

Corvalis managed a distracted nod.

He stood with Claudia on one of the bridges over the river of molten metal in the Hall of Assembly. They had spent the last hour bringing word of Mihaela's offer to the various embassies and ambassadors. Some had reacted with pleasure, others with contempt, and a few with alarm.

But every last one of them had shown interest, and Corvalis had no doubt they would come.

Even his father.

Decius Aberon had sneered and blustered, amused that Zalandris and Mihaela would send a renegade assassin and a former sister of the Magisterium to deliver their messages. But he would come, nonetheless.

Already Corvalis saw the magi entering through the doors to the Hall, his father in their midst.

No sign of Torius, though. The battle magus was likely doing an errand for the First Magus. But the rest of the embassies had gathered, eager to receive the suits of glypharmor that Zalandris had promised.

And they would walk right into Mihaela's trap.

Assuming, of course, Mihaela had told the truth.

Corvalis trusted Claudia's judgment. He always had, especially after his training with the Kindred. He did not have much of a conscience left, not after what the Kindred had done to him and made him do, but Claudia knew the proper course of action.

Unless Caina had been right.

Corvalis had seen the pain in her eyes when he had refused to help her. It had not been there long. Just an instant, and then her cold mask closed over it.

He did not have much of a conscience left...but what he had now stung him.

But it would be worth it. Once his father and the other magi put on the suits of glypharmor, Claudia and Mihaela could control them. Then they could cripple the Magisterium forever. Surely Caina would see that was worth it.

Unless she was right.

He gripped the stone railing and bowed his head, thinking. He trusted Claudia's judgment ...but Caina was cleverer than anyone he had ever met. She thought it was a trick, though she had not been able to provide a better explanation than Mihaela's.

"Brother," said Claudia, touching his arm. "She will forgive you. Once we bring our father to heel and force the nations to peace. Then she will understand." She sighed. "I wish we could have convinced her. But she hates me too much to see reason. If I said the sky was blue, Anna would go outside to see for herself...and then decide that the sky had changed color due to a sorcerous plot."

Claudia was not entirely wrong. But Corvalis was not certain that she was right, either. Mihaela might indeed plan to enslave the leaders of the sorcerers, but Corvalis was sure she was holding something back. Maybe not anything that would harm the Ghosts or the Empire, but something nonetheless.

"Perhaps you are right," said Corvalis.

Claudia smiled. "I know I am. Anna will understand. You'll see."

Corvalis hoped so. Watching her walk away from Mihaela's rooms had hurt more than he had expected.

He had no longer thought he was capable of feeling that much pain.

Mihaela and Zalandris entered the Hall of Assembly, followed by dozens of Sages in their jade masks, and Corvalis forced aside his fears. He had to stay focused.

Because he strongly suspected matters were about to become violent.

To his surprise, he saw Torius walking alongside Mihaela, clad in his black armor, his sword waiting at his hip. There was an excited edge to his half-brother's expression that Corvalis did not like. Mihaela herself carried a silvery object in her right hand, and Corvalis thought she had a Sage's rod. But as she drew closer, he saw that she instead carried an ornate dagger in a sheath of silver and black.

Something about that dagger tugged Corvalis's memory, something that Caina had told him...

"What is Torius doing with her?" said Corvalis.

Claudia shrugged. "Mihaela said she had solicited the First Magus's aid to draw him here."

Corvalis looked at his father. "Then shouldn't Torius be with our father to deflect suspicion?"

In fact, Decius Aberon was looking at Torius with a scowl. Clearly he had not expected to see Torius with Mihaela.

"I don't know," said Claudia. "It won't matter once our father climbs into his suit of glypharmor."

Corvalis started to answer, and then Zalandris's voice echoed through the Hall.

"Honored guests of the Scholae!" said Zalandris, his golden collar glinting in the metal's dull red glow. "Thank you for coming."

"This summons," said the First Magus, "is most unusual."

"Indeed," said the khadjar Arsakan, folding his thick arms over his chest. "We have spent a week negotiating with you, offering you wealth and lands and estates. And now we find you offering glypharmor to every one of us!"

Corvalis saw a stir on the other end of Hall. Kylon of House Kardamnos walked past the embassies, wearing his gray leather armor. None of his men were with him, and he had discarded his gray-green cloak.

He was expecting trouble.

"You are correct, my lord khadjar," said Zalandris. "The Seeker Mihaela has shown me the correct path. Often the young who can see paths invisible to the weary minds of their elders. I thought that the glypharmor, wielded in the hands of one monarch, would guarantee peace. But Mihaela persuaded me that the power of the glypharmor would be too much of a temptation for any man to wield. I allowed Mihaela's work to proceed because I thought it would bring peace between nations, but the glypharmor is too powerful. Only by giving glypharmor to each nation and order of sorcerers, to each king and college of arcane sciences, can we guarantee peace..."

"You," said Kylon, his voice ringing off the ceiling, "are a fool."

Zalandris blinked, and a stunned silence fell over the Hall.

Corvalis had never seen a man look so astonished. He supposed very few men insulted a Sage of the Scholae to his face.

"I beg your pardon?" said Zalandris, drawing himself up."

"Are you deaf as well as blind?" said Kylon, stopping a dozen yards from the Speaker. Mihaela glared at the stormdancer, while Torius rested his hand on the hilt of his sword. "I said you are a fool."

"What is he doing?" hissed Claudia. "He'll ruin everything!"

Corvalis stared hard at the stormdancer. Caina had trusted his judgment.

"Threats?" said Zalandris. "How amusing. Is that what this is, my lord thalarchon? I am a fool for not giving New Kyre the glypharmor? And if I don't, you'll bring destruction upon the Scholae? Threaten the Scholae, and you will see the meaning of destruction for yourself, Kylon of House Kardamnos."

"I do not threaten," said Kylon. "I merely state the truth." He pointed at Mihaela. "You have allowed your Seeker to use the resources of the Scholae for her own aggrandizement."

"You lie, Kyracian," said Mihaela. "Like anyone who studies under the Scholae, I work to advance our understanding of the arcane sciences."

"But the Lord Speaker is not the only fool in this chamber," said Kylon, looking around. "I am surrounded by them."

"Speak for yourself, stormdancer," said the First Magus. "Since your wretched little city-state launched a war against the might of the Nigh-marian Empire, any reasonable man would question your wisdom."

"I call you a fool," said Kylon, "because you are so willing to lay your heads upon the block based upon Mihaela's honeyed words."

"Are you the blind man, Kylon Shipbreaker?" said Yaramzod the Black, his shadows slithering around him. "We have seen the glypharmor's might. Do you call that a trick?"

"It is not a trick," said Kylon, "but a trap. Mihaela has laid a snare upon the spells binding the glypharmor. She can enslave any man wearing the armor." He looked at the gathered ambassadors. "She convinced Zalandris to give three suits of armor to each embassy here. The most powerful men in those embassies, of course, would claim the glypharmor for themselves. And as soon as they donned the armor, they would be trapped."

"How does he know?" whispered Claudia.

Caina must have told him. To his surprise, Corvalis felt relief. Kylon Shipbreaker had a towering reputation, and if he discredited Mihaela in front of the Scholae and the ambassadors, no one could claim the glypharmor.

Had that been Caina's plan all along?

No. The pain in her eyes had been real.

"Lord Kylon," said Zalandris with the air of a man lecturing a pupil, "your fears are groundless. The glypharmor is perfectly safe to wield. It..."

"Have you examined it yourself?" said Kylon.

Mihaela glared at him.

"I am certain..." began Zalandris.

"Have you," repeated Kylon, "examined it yourself?"

"Such a task," said Zalandris, "would be beneath the dignity of a Sage of the Scholae."

"Then you arm your students with potent spells and permit them to run about unsupervised?" said Kylon. "I may have understated the case, my lord Speaker, when I named you a fool."

"Rubbish!" said the First Magus. "This is merely a plot to seize the glypharmor for yourself!"

"It is not," said Kylon. "The embassy of New Kyre will not claim a suit of glypharmor, and we reject the Scholae's treacherous gift. I swear this by the names of the gods of salt and brine, of storm and sea, and I vow that we shall never lay a finger upon the glypharmor." He took a step closer to Zalandris. "For we have no wish to become Mihaela's slaves."

"No, no, no," whispered Claudia, clutching at the bridge's railing. "No! This was our best chance."

Corvalis stared at Kylon. Caina trusted him, but it was plain that Kylon also trusted her. He trusted her so much that he was willing to defy the Scholae to its face, to level these accusations before both the ambassadors and the assembled Sages.

Why hadn't Corvalis trusted Caina that much?

He felt a wave of shame.

A murmur went through the ambassadors, and Corvalis saw the sudden doubt in their expressions. Political games were one thing. But for Kylon to reject the glypharmor so forcefully and irrevocably was something else entirely.

"You've gone mad, my lord thalarchon," said the First Magus, but Corvalis knew his father well enough to see the doubt there. "To reject such power?"

"Perhaps this is a trick of your own," said Yaramzod the Black. "If the armor was truly a tool of enslavement, you would say nothing and let us be ensnared."

"You are my enemies," said Kylon, "but I would not wish such a profound enslavement upon even you. And I would not place such power into the hands of a woman like Mihaela."

That, too, sounded like Caina.

"You seem certain of this," said Zalandris.

"Sage!" said Mihaela. "You listen to the slander of this...this power-seeking lordling?"

But Zalandris ignored her.

"I am certain of it," said Kylon, "because it is true. All men are fools at one time or another, my lord Speaker, but do not continue to be a fool. Do not let her deceive you."

"What do you suggest?" said Zalandris.

"Examine the glypharmor for yourself," said Kylon. "I am sure Mihaela has given you many promises. Put those promises to the test. Command her to show you how the glypharmor is made. You believe the glypharmor will put an end to war and bring peace between nations. If you would wield such power...then you have a responsibility to understand how that power is created."

"The Scholae is devoted to knowledge," said Zalandris. "Your requests seem reasonable."

"You cannot believe him!" said Mihaela.

"I trust you, certainly," said Zalandris, "but it is necessary to put the minds of our guests at ease. I will examine the glypharmor myself, along with your workshop. I have been looking forward to seeing it. Once I have, I..."

"Shut up!" said Mihaela. "Gods, how I have wearied of your incessant droning!"

Again Zalandris looked shocked. "Mihaela?"

"Enough of this farce," said Mihaela, yanking the silver dagger from its patterned sheath.

And suddenly Corvalis remembered the dagger.

Caina had described it to him, using her particular eye for detail, after her strange meeting with Talekhris in the Chamber of Relics. Talekhris had called the weapon the Stormbrand, and said it granted its wielder the power to control the element of air.

"Go," hissed Corvalis, grabbing his sister's arm and steering her from the bridge. "We have to go, now!"

"What are you doing?" said Claudia. "We need..."

"She's going to do something," said Corvalis. "This has been a trap all along. You've ..."

"That is from the Chamber of Relics!" said Zalandris. "You should not have taken it without permission!"

"I would tell you to shut up, old man," said Mihaela, "but I know you will not. So I will just have to do it myself."

Mihaela swept the Stormbrand over her head, and the air around her began to ripple. An instant later Zalandris fell to his knees, eyes wide, face red, and the Sages of the Scholae fell like leaves from the branches of a dead tree. A wave of panic went through the ambassadors, and Kylon drew his sword.

Corvalis had seen Ranarius use that spell in Cyrioch. It corrupted the air around the victim's head, inducing unconsciousness. The Kyracian stormsingers used it to take prisoners alive.

And with the Stormbrand, Mihaela could stun everyone in the hall.

"Run!" shouted Corvalis, giving Claudia a shove.

But she would not move.

"What's happening?" she said. "What is Mihaela doing? Corvalis, we've got to..."

He grabbed her arm and ran for the nearest exit, taking deep breaths as he did so. If he could get enough air into his lungs, he might be able to stay conscious even when the corrupted air reached him. They ran through the Anshani embassy, and Corvalis saw both Yaramzod the Black and Arsakan collapse, Arsakan's armor rattling, Yaramzod's shadows slithering into him like a serpent retracting its tongue.

"Corvalis!" said Claudia, coughing and clawing at her throat. "Corvalis!"

Corvalis opened his mouth to speak...and the corrupted air washed over him, the world around him rippling.

"Down!" he hissed, pushing Claudia to the floor. The corrupted air produced by the spell was lighter than normal air, and rose quickly. If he could press low enough, perhaps the air would pass them over.

Claudia slumped against the floor, eyes closed. Corvalis fought to hold his breath, but at last he had to breathe, and he felt himself grow woozy. The room spun around him, his head swimming.

But he stayed conscious.

After a long moment he got to his feet and looked around.

Hundreds of men and women lay sprawled upon the floor of the Hall of Assembly, lining both sides of the molten river. The assembled Sages of the Scholae lay upon the floor, their white robes making them look almost like lily petals scattered across the stone.

Scores of mercenaries moved through the Hall, some barking orders, while most carried the unconscious guests and Sages into the cylindrical chamber at the Tower's heart. Some sort of strange machine stood at the edge of the round molten pool. It looked like an enormous steel coffin, twenty feet high, its sides, lid, and interior carved with elaborate hieroglyphs. A dozen pipes ran from the coffin's sides and dipped into the molten pool. Mihaela, Torius, and Sicarion stood near the steel coffin, watching as the mercenaries worked.

What the devil were they doing?

Corvalis looked at Claudia. She was alive, but unconscious. He had to get her away from the Hall. He didn't know what Mihaela, Torius, and Sicarion intended for the Scholae and their guests, but it could be nothing good.

"You!"

Corvalis whirled.

A middle-aged mercenary with the grizzled look of a sergeant stalked towards him. "Why are you standing about? We are not paying you for idleness!"

"Sir?" said Corvalis. With his armor and weapons, the sergeant must have mistaken him for another mercenary.

"Devils of the deep! Where do they find you fools?" The sergeant leaned closer, his bloodshot eyes glaring. "Pick up the prisoners.

Carry them to the Forge." He spoke in the overly slow voice men reserved for children and idiots. "Put them in the warding circles. Make sure they're tied up, blindfolded, and gagged. Keep doing that until all the prisoners are secure, or until you get different orders from me."

Corvalis could take the sergeant, he was sure, but there were dozens of men within earshot by now. He could not fight them all. Playing along was his best chance of rescuing Claudia and getting her away from whatever Mihaela had in mind.

"Sir," said Corvalis.

"Get moving," said the sergeant, jerking his head towards a trio of men.

Gods, but he should have listened to Caina.

Corvalis joined the other mercenaries. One of the men grabbed the wrists of a man in the stark robes of an Anshani occultist, and Corvalis gripped the occultist's ankles. Together they carried the unconscious man through the Hall of Assembly and into the Tower's central chamber. A dozen elaborate circles had been painted around the edge of the molten pool, surrounded by intricate glyphs and sigils. Corvalis recognized the design. They were warding circles, designed to neutralize a sorcerer's powers. The Magisterium used them to imprison renegade sorcerers and disobedient magi.

"Down," grunted the mercenary, and they dumped the occultist inside one of the circles. The mercenary worked with practiced efficiency, blindfolding and gagging the occultist and binding his wrists and ankles together behind his back. With his spells dampened by the warding circle and his arms and legs bound, the occultist was helpless.

"Clear!" roared the sergeant Corvalis had seen earlier. "Put your backs into it, dogs, but stand clear of the Forge!"

Corvalis stepped back to watch, making sure not to draw attention to himself. He looked like just another mercenary, but Sicarion, Mihaela, and Torius would all recognize him. And if they saw him, Corvalis doubted he would live for another dozen heartbeats.

Fortunately, the strange machine, the thing the sergeant had called the Forge, held their attention. A trio of mercenaries grabbed one of the unconscious Sages, stripping away the old man's mask and robe. They hung the naked man in a net of chains inside the massive steel coffin, leaving him suspended in its center.

Then they swung the lid shut and Mihaela pointed her rod at the Forge, muttering a spell.

White fire flared in the hieroglyphs covering the coffin, and a ripple went through the molten metal in the pool. The Forge shuddered, and Mihaela made a sweeping motion with the rod. Fingers of white lightning crackled up and down the steel coffin, the hieroglyphs glowing brighter, the stone floor vibrating, a strange howling noise coming from the Forge

Then the glow faded.

"Come forth!" shouted Mihaela.

The steel lid swung open, and a suit of black glypharmor stepped out of the Forge, its hieroglyphs shining with white fire.

"Gods," whispered Corvalis.

"Aye," said the mercenary next to him. "Black witchery. But it pays well."

Somehow Mihaela's sorcery could transform living sorcerers into suits of glypharmor. The invitation, the embassies, all of it – it had all been nothing but a ruse to gather hundreds of powerful sorcerers into the Hall of Assembly.

He had been a fool. Caina had been right to mistrust Mihaela, and certainly right to mistrust Claudia's judgment.

And unless Corvalis acted, Claudia was going to pay for that mistake with her life.

"Come on," mumbled Corvalis. "If we don't keep working the sergeant will have our heads."

"Aye," said the mercenary, turning. "We..."

"You lot!" The sergeant stalked over, pointing at Corvalis. "You and you and you, head to the mistress's workshop. She wants the black chest next to the worktable by the canal. Move!"

Corvalis could not leave Claudia. If he left, by the time he returned Mihaela might have fed her into that ghastly machine. But if he created a commotion, that would draw the attention of Mihaela, Sicarion, and Torius. The Forge held their attention, but if they saw Corvalis...

If they saw Corvalis, he would die, and there would be no one to save Claudia.

"Sir," said Corvalis, and he followed the other two men from the chamber.

24

THE STORMDANCER AND THE ASSASSIN

T he mercenaries strode into the Seekers' quarters, keeping away from the stream of molten metal, and Corvalis followed.

His mind sorted through plan after plan. The long, high corridor was deserted, and Corvalis could overpower the two mercenaries easily enough. Then he could return and escape with Claudia. But what then? Mihaela was building an army of glypharmor, and she would go on a rampage as soon as she was ready. Should he try to find Caina and warn her? Or Basil, perhaps? Basil had allies in the city, and he might have the means to stop Mihaela.

Corvalis gritted his teeth. This disaster was his doing. If he had not listened to Claudia, none of this would have happened.

"What's your problem?" said one of the mercenaries.

"I want a damned drink," said Corvalis.

The man laughed. "You and me both. But once the mistress deals with the sorcerers, all the wealth of the Tower will be ours. You can buy your own damned vineyard then."

They walked through a scarred door and through a hall filled with steel coffins of varying sizes. Corvalis supposed these were earlier versions of Mihaela's Forge. Beyond stood a vast chamber, bisected by another stream of molten metal. Dozens of suits of glypharmor stood scattered around the chamber, along with a random assortment of crates and barrels.

"There," said one of the mercenaries. "The mistress's chest is there."

Corvalis followed the other men to the worktable near the molten canal. As he did, he slipped a dagger from his belt. The other two men stooped over the heavy chest, grunting.

"Help, damn you," snarled one of the men.

"Of course," said Corvalis, driving his dagger into the closest man's neck. The mercenary toppled, blood pouring from his wound. The other man yelled and scrambled for his weapon, but Corvalis was faster. His sword blurred, driving into the mercenary's throat, and the man collapsed to the floor.

Corvalis cleaned his weapons off, dragged the corpses to the canal, and dumped them into the molten metal. The resultant stench was considerable, but hopefully the lack of corpses would confuse any pursuers for a few moments. Corvalis decided to make for the palace where Lord Titus Iconias and his retainers had been housed. He had seen Lord Titus and his bodyguards in the Hall of Assembly, but no sign of Basil or Caina. Maybe Caina had returned to the palace to alert Basil. Corvalis could warn them of Mihaela's true intentions...and perhaps Basil could rouse the cohort of Imperial Guards waiting in the barracks.

If they struck now, they might stop Mihaela before she built her invincible army.

He took a step towards the door and froze.

A glint of silvery metal next to a shattered barrel caught his eye. Corvalis picked it up. It was a curved dagger, the blade carved with flowing characters.

Caina's ghostsilver dagger. She never went anywhere without it.

He saw a motionless form lying next to a crate. Corvalis hurried forward, saw a body clad in all in black, wrapped in a dark shadow-cloak, and...

The blue eyes of Caina Amalas gazed unblinkingly at him.

Unseeing.

She wasn't breathing.

Corvalis dropped to one knee, put his hand upon her neck. She was still warm. But he felt no pulse. He cursed, tugged off one of her leather gloves, felt her left wrist. There was no pulse.

She was dead.

The part of his mind that had been trained by the Kindred noted the details of her corpse. He could not see how she had died. There were no marks upon her, no wounds. One of Mihaela's spells, perhaps. Sorcery had slain Caina's father and left her barren, and now it had taken everything she had left.

The rest of his mind screamed.

Corvalis's breath rasped through his teeth. He looked away, then back at her. Watching her walk away from Mihaela's rooms had hurt.

This hurt...this hurt much worse.

He had only loved two people in his life, his mother and his sister. After his father had executed his mother, there had been only Claudia. When Ranarius had turned her to stone, Corvalis had crossed half the Empire to save her, risking his life again and again to rescue her.

It had never occurred to him that he might love someone else. He had thought he loved Nairia, but that had only been one of his father's cruel jokes. When he first met Caina Amalas, he thought her a cold and efficient killer, a Kindred assassin remade in the image of the Ghosts. Only later had he learned the truth of her.

He had loved her, she had loved him back...and now she was dead because he had not listened to her.

Corvalis bowed his head, his eyes burning. The smoke from the corpses he had dumped into the canal, no doubt.

"I'm sorry," he said at last. "I should have listened to you. Gods damn it all, I should have listened to you. I'm so sorry."

Caina was dead, but Claudia was not. Corvalis would find a way to save her from Mihaela's damned Forge.

And then...and then he supposed he would let Basil kill him.

"I'm sorry," said Corvalis again, kissing her lips. He rose, ghostsilver dagger in hand, and strode for the door. He returned to the corridor and looked around. The hallway remained deserted, and no one had come to hunt for the missing mercenaries yet. Corvalis would break into one of the unused rooms, go out the window, and make his way to the guests' palace. Then Basil could rouse the Imperial Guards, and they could stop Mihaela's mad plan before she burned Claudia to ashes in her Forge.

Claudia. That thought alone kept Corvalis moving, kept him from falling upon his sword.

Caina was dead and it was his fault.

The air in front of him rippled, and Corvalis drew his sword, half-expecting to see Mihaela with the Stormbrand. Instead a man in his middle twenties appeared, his lean body clad in gray leather armor, a sword in his right hand...

Kylon of House Kardamnos.

"Stormdancer," said Corvalis.

"Cormark," said Kylon. He squinted at Corvalis for a moment. "I see you and your sister have realized the truth."

"Aye," said Corvalis. "But Mihaela was telling the truth. The glypharmor was a trap. She...she just didn't say what kind."

"The best lies," said Kylon, "always are mostly true." It sounded like something Caina would say. Perhaps he had heard it from her. "How did you escape the trap in the Hall of Assembly?"

"I recognized the spell," said Corvalis, "and held my breath long enough to keep from falling unconscious. They have Claudia, though."

"Claudia?" said Kylon.

"My sister," said Corvalis. "Irene Callenius."

"Ah," said Kylon. "I assume Mihaela is going to feed her into that necromantic engine of hers? She's making an army of glypharmor."

"Unless we stop her," said Corvalis. "How did you escape, anyway?"

"I, too, recognized the spell," said Kylon, "and warded myself against it. I hoped to kill Mihaela and Torius, but when she used that dagger, hundreds of mercenaries stormed into the Hall, and I could not fight so many on my own. I used a spell of air to escape unnoticed. The Ghost said she was going to Basil Callenius, and that seemed as good a plan as any. If anyone can figure out a way to stop Mihaela, it is her."

"She can't," said Corvalis.

"Only a fool would underestimate her," said Kylon, "as my sister learned, to her sorrow."

As Claudia, too, might learn.

"She's dead," said Corvalis.

"What?" said Kylon.

"I don't know how," said Corvalis. "A spell, I think." He held up her ghostsilver dagger.

"You're telling the truth," said Kylon. "I'm sorry. I know she loved you."

"How did you know that?" said Corvalis. "Did she tell you?"

"The sorcery of water," said Kylon. "For all men are water, in the end. Her aura, Cormark...I have never sensed anyone quite like her. A mind of ice and a heart of rage. At first I didn't think she could love anyone. But she did love you. I am sorry."

Corvalis gave a sharp nod. He didn't want to talk about this with anyone, let alone Kylon. "I am making my way to Basil Callenius. If he can rouse the Imperial Guards from their barracks, we can storm the Hall of Assembly and stop Mihaela before this goes any further."

Kylon nodded. "Lead on."

~

CORVALIS LED Kylon around the stone terrace at the base of the Tower.

Basil Callenius had been busy.

The cohort of the Imperial Guard had formed up alongside the molten river flowing from the Tower's doors, stern in their black armor and helms. Men in desert robes waited at their side, Saddiq at their head, a huge two-handed scimitar in his hand. Basil Callenius stood alongside the Sarbian chieftain, clad in chain mail and leather.

"Lord Kylon!" called Basil in Kyracian.

"Master Basil," said Kylon. "You are a welcome sight."

"My contacts," said Basil, "received word of a disturbance of in the Tower. The Tower has been sealed, and the slaves fled to the city proper. What has happened?"

"The glypharmor was a trap all along," said Kylon. "Mihaela creates it by using the souls of powerful sorcerers. The invitation was merely an excuse to lure hundreds of powerful sorcerers here. Even now she is using some sort of necromantic engine to transform them into suits of glypharmor."

"Claudia's still in there," said Corvalis.

Basil frowned. "And where is Caina?"

"She's dead," said Corvalis. "Mihaela killed her."

Basil said nothing, but his eyes grew hard.

"It was my fault," said Corvalis. "I should have listened to her. I should..."

"Shut up," said Basil. "We have work to do. Fortunately, Lord Titus left instructions that the Guards should obey my commands in an emergency. We are going to storm the Hall, kill Mihaela and her allies, and destroy this necromantic engine of hers."

"She has powerful allies," said Kylon. "Sicarion and Torius Aberon."

Basil scowled. "Torius? The First Magus has such a gift for inspiring loyalty in his children."

"And she is making more suits of the glypharmor," said Corvalis. "Once we attack, some of her men will don the suits."

"We have no choice," said Basil. "We must stop this now. If Mihaela finishes her work, she'll have hundreds of suits of glypharmor and loyal men with which to wield them. She'll launch a war of conquest that will drown half the world in blood. If we do not stop her tonight, we never will."

Kylon nodded. "You have my sword, Master Basil. If you send a runner to my quarters, an additional stormdancer and my men will join us."

"Good," said Basil. "We will need every man. If my contacts are correct, Mihaela has nearly a thousand men in the Tower, and even with your men, Lord Kylon, we have just over seven hundred. We will attack at once. Delay will only strengthen Mihaela."

Basil spoke with the tribune, and the Imperial Guards marched forward. Basil and the Sarbians followed, Corvalis and Kylon walking with them. Guards with axes rushed forward and attacked the doors to the Hall of Assembly.

The doors fell open. Corvalis heard the sudden commotion from within the Hall...and in the distance, saw the flare of white light around Mihaela's sorcerous machine.

Then the Imperial Guards stormed the Hall, and the killing began.

25

SLAVES AND CHAINS

aina drifted through an endless field of gray mist.
She could not remember how she had come here.
From time to time memories flitted across her mind, the mist congealing into scenes.

Her father, sitting broken at his desk.

Maglarion's black lair beneath the hills.

Kalastus laughing as sorcerous fire blazed around him.

Nicolai shrieking for his mother as the Istarish soldiers stormed through Marsis.

Caina herself, lying upon the floor of the Tower of Study.

Dead.

In some ways it was a relief. No more pain, no more fear, no more sorrow.

Perhaps she would see her father again.

But how she wished she could have said farewell to Corvalis.

As the thought crossed her mind, she saw Corvalis kneeling over her, her ghostsilver dagger in his hand.

"I'm sorry," he said, his voice full of pain. "I should have listened to you. Gods damn it all, I should have listened to you. I'm so sorry."

A spasm went through Corvalis, and she saw sorrow on his hard face. She reached for him, but her fingers passed through him as if he were not there.

Then the images dissolved into mist, and the numbness sank deeper into Caina. She felt the mist wrapping her like a blanket as everything faded away...

"This would have been simpler," said a woman's voice, "had Torius just cut off your head."

A woman stood in the swirling gray mist. She wore a gown the color of blood, her dark hair hanging wet and loose around her shoulders, her eyes like black pits into nothingness.

The Moroaica.

Alarm brought some lucidity back to Caina's mind.

"If I'm dead," said Caina, "why are you still here?"

"Because," said Jadriga, "Mihaela is not nearly as clever as she thinks she is. Her Forge is effective, but she has mentally linked herself to it in order to control the glypharmor. Effective, but if the Forge is ever destroyed, she will regret it."

"What does that have to do with me?" said Caina.

"Because Mihaela used a Sage's rod to kill you," said the Moroaica. "And the Sage's rod deals death by severing the victim's soul from the flesh."

"And my flesh," said Caina, "has two souls in it. Yours and mine."

"Correct," said Jadriga. "And Mihaela has just killed me inside of your body. An amusing little coincidence, is it not?"

"Then you're free," said Caina. "Free to claim another body and to start killing people once more."

"I can," said Jadriga, "resume the great work. I would have preferred that you join me. No matter. You cannot stop me."

"I can if I hold you here," said Caina.

"Child of the Ghosts," said the Moroaica, "I have died in your body. You cannot stop me from doing anything."

She flung out her hands, and the gray mist swallowed Caina.

∾

P<small>AIN ERUPTED THROUGH</small> C<small>AINA</small>.

She shrieked, her heels trembling against the hard stone floor. Her heart burned within her chest, thumping against her ribs like the drumbeat of a marching Legion. Caina sucked in a long breath, her eyes swimming into focus. A stone ceiling rose overhead, painted with the sullen red glow of molten metal. A dark shadow loomed over her – a suit of black glypharmor. All around her radiated the tingling, crawling aura of potent sorcery.

She was still in Mihaela's workshop.

After a long moment her heart and her breathing slowed. Caina grabbed at the glypharmor's boot, her fingers digging into the grooves of the hieroglyphs, and sat up.

Mihaela, Sicarion, and Torius were gone. So was Mihaela's Forge. Mihaela most likely moved it to the Hall of Assembly to expedite the transformation process. There was no sign of Talekhris's corpse. Sicarion must have dumped it into the molten metal to slow whatever process allowed the Sage to awaken from death.

Which would explain the faint smell of scorched flesh in the air.

Caina eased herself to her feet, dizziness washing through her. She did not feel at all well, which made sense, given that she had technically died. And worse, the Moroaica had been freed.

And even worse, Mihaela would use the Forge to create an army of glypharmor.

Unless Caina stopped her.

She took a step forward, managed to keep her balance, and then took another.

Though finding a way to stop Mihaela seemed unlikely. Caina was exhausted and alone. Her allies had either been duped by Mihaela or were too far away to help. She didn't even have her ghostsilver dagger ...

In her peculiar dream she had seen Corvalis kneeling over her corpse, pain on his face. He had taken her dagger. And if the vision had been true, that meant he had escaped from Mihaela's trap.

He was still alive. For now.

If Caina could keep him that way.

She turned, trying to ignore the dizziness and the nausea. It was too late to warn Zalandris and the ambassadors. But Mihaela and her mercenaries would be vulnerable while they used the Forge to convert fresh victims into new suits of glypharmor.

Halfdan, Caina decided. Halfdan could draw on Saddiq's mercenaries and additional men from the city. Additionally, she suspected he had some influence over the Imperial Guard cohort that had accompanied Lord Titus from Malarae. If Halfdan could persuade them that Lord Titus was in danger, the Guards would act.

Caina just had to get to Halfdan.

And hope that the Imperial Guards could stop Mihaela before she made too many suits of glypharmor, because one glypharmor-equipped man could wipe out the entire cohort. Half a dozen would be invincible. And a score of them could probably conquer every city for a thousand miles...

There was no time for worry. She had to get moving.

She took a deep breath, gathering her strength...and heard a woman crying.

Caina stopped, hand darting to one of her remaining throwing knives. Her eyes roved over the cluttered workshop. Perhaps Mihaela had kept penned captives here, keeping them chained until she needed them for an experiment.

After a moment Caina realized she could not pinpoint the source of the weeping.

An instant after that, she realized the crying was coming from inside her own head.

She raised her hands to cover her ears. Still the crying echoed inside her own head, a voice full of misery and woe. Was the voice even real? Had Mihaela's spell damaged Caina's mind, leaving her to hear things that weren't there?

"Gods," said Caina. "The last thing I need is to go mad."

The crying stopped with a gasp.

"You can hear me?" said the woman's voice, speaking Anshani. "Please, by the Living Flame, tell me that you can hear me!"

"I can," said Caina, turning in a circle. "Where are you?"

"Here!" said the woman. "I am here! Why can you not see me?"

Caina's eyes fell upon the suit of red glypharmor, the one Mihaela had used to slaughter the criminals. Again she felt the peculiar attraction to the suit. But it was...different, this time, less compelling, less magnetic. Yet it was still there. Some of the attraction had been Jadriga's power responding to the glypharmor, but the Moroaica was gone now.

So why did Caina still feel drawn to the armor?

Flawed. Mihaela had said the designs created using red Nhabati steel had been flawed.

"You," said the woman's voice. "I remember you. I saw you after Mihaela...after Mihaela made me kill all those men."

The armor was talking to her?

The thought was ludicrous. But was it? Mihaela had created it using necromancy, binding the soul of a living sorcerer into the steel. Torius had gloated how Marcus would remaining screaming inside the armor for all eternity. And if Mihaela had said the red armor was flawed, did that mean the soul within retained more power that she had liked?

"You had two souls," said the woman's voice, "one dark, and one scarred. I could see them both. I couldn't see that way when I served in the Hall..."

The realization struck Caina like a physical blow.

"Oh," she said. "You're Ardasha, aren't you?"

Stunned silence answered her.

"You know me?" said the voice at last. "How do you know me?"

"Shaizid," said Caina, limping towards the red glypharmor. "Your brother Shaizid. He asked me to find you."

"Oh, my poor Shaizid," said Ardasha. "I promised my mother I would look after him always, and now I have failed. Oh, Shaizid!"

"Mihaela betrayed you, didn't she?" said Caina. "She murdered you and bound your soul into the armor."

"She promised to teach me," said Ardasha. "She said I would become a Seeker, that I would help her. I thought...I thought if I was a Seeker, I could take care of Shaizid, like I promised my mother."

She groaned. "But she betrayed me. Mihaela strapped me into the Forge, and cast her spells, and...and..."

Her voice dissolved into sobbing.

"I'm sorry," said Caina. "Shaizid is still alive, if it's any comfort. But he might not be for long if Mihaela finishes her work."

"What is she doing?" said Ardasha.

"She lured the most powerful sorcerers in the world here with promises of glypharmor," said Caina. "She's incapacitated both them and the Sages, and she's going to transform them into glypharmor."

"Oh, by the Living Flame," moaned Ardasha. "This is my fault. My fault. If..."

"It's Mihaela's fault," said Caina. "She murdered you."

"Why can you hear me?" said Ardasha. "No one else can. Not even Mihaela. I have screamed and screamed, but you are the first to hear me."

"I think it is because of what happened to me as a child," said Caina. She stopped before the red glypharmor, gazing up at the helm. "I was wounded by a necromancer, and ever since I have been able to feel the presence of sorcery. That's why I can hear you. I think...I'm going to try something..."

She reached out with her bare hand and placed it upon the cold steel of the glypharmor's leg.

An electric jolt shot through Caina. A vision burned before her eyes of an Anshani woman hanging in a net of chains, the links piercing her flesh, blood running down her dark skin. The woman screamed and fought, but the chains held her fast.

And they would hold her fast for all eternity.

Caina stepped back, breathing hard, her head spinning.

"I saw you," said Ardasha, her voice full of wonder. "I saw who you really are. You are the Balarigar. Shaizid and I heard the stories. How the Balarigar freed the slaves in Marsis."

"The Balarigar," said Caina, "is only a story."

"You can free Shaizid," said Ardasha, "and you can stop Mihaela."

"How?" said Caina. "I can't do it by myself. Mihaela and her allies will kill me on sight. I can get help from the Imperial Guards, but just one suit of glypharmor can slaughter them all." Her hands curled into fists. "I might be able to kill Mihaela from a distance with a crossbow. But I can't destroy her damned Forge. Even if I kill her, Sicarion or Torius will keep using the Forge."

"There is a way," said Ardasha, her voice full of terrified hope.

"What?" said Caina.

"Use me," said Ardasha.

"Use you?" said Caina, puzzled. "What does..."

Then she understood.

"No," Caina said. "Absolutely not. The Forge is monstrous, and what Mihaela did to you is monstrous. I will not wield that kind of power."

If she did, she would be no better than Claudia.

"You must," said Ardasha. "You have no chance alone. With my help, you can destroy the Forge and bring Mihaela to account."

"Sorcery is evil," said Caina. "I want to stop it, not use it."

"Mihaela used the sorcery," said Ardasha. "Mihaela did this to me. You will help stop her from doing it to others."

"You were a slave when you came to Catekharon," said Caina. "Mihaela promised you freedom, and instead she enslaved you more profoundly than ever." She shook her head. "If I do this, if I use the glypharmor, I would be no better than her. She made you a slave, and I would do the same in turn."

"You must!" said Ardasha, her voice full of anguish. "Else Shaizid will surely die."

"And using you would be suicide," said Caina. "If I try to attack Mihaela wearing a suit of glypharmor, she'll take control of me."

"She cannot!" said Ardasha. "Not with this glypharmor. The design was flawed. That is why she abandoned using red steel. Her spells of domination did not work. I am still enslaved in the steel... but she cannot control anyone wearing a suit of red glypharmor."

Caina had seen firsthand the brutal power of the red glypharmor. With it, Caina would be all but invincible. She could force her way through Mihaela's mercenaries, smash the Forge to shreds, and kill

Mihaela herself. Neither Torius nor Sicarion would be able to stop her.

But it would mean using sorcery. It would mean using an enslaved soul as a weapon.

"I cannot do this!" whispered Caina.

"Please," said Ardasha. "Mihaela did this to me against my will. But I want you to use me. I give you permission. If you don't...more people will suffer as I have suffered. You can save them."

Caina could use the glypharmor to defeat Mihaela. But Claudia had thought to use the power of the glypharmor for good, and her folly had all but guaranteed Mihaela's victory. What would happen if Caina tried to use the glypharmor?

"Is there no one you want to save?" said Ardasha. "Someone you love as I love Shaizid? Mihaela will wage war against the entire world. If you love anyone, they will perish when she unleashes the glypharmor."

Caina thought of Corvalis, of Halfdan. They would try to stop Mihaela, and Mihaela would kill them both. Kylon and Claudia would be fed to the Forge, enslaved forever as living suits of necromantic armor. Neither of them deserved that. Theodosia and Ark and Tanya and Nicolai lived in Malarae...and if Mihaela was victorious, then one day warriors wearing suits of glypharmor would stalk the streets of the Imperial capital, killing with every stride.

Unless Caina stopped Mihaela first.

"Damn it," she whispered. "How do I get into this thing?"

"Under the bottom edge of the cuirass," said Ardasha. "There is a groove. Rest your hand there, and the armor will open."

Caina ran her fingers along the bottom edge of the cuirass, the potent sorcery within the steel making her skin crawl. Her fingers found the groove, and she felt a flicker in the glypharmor's aura. The cuirass swung open like the doors of a wardrobe, and the helmet rotated back with a metallic groan. The glypharmor's chest was hollow, the steel lined with hundreds of hieroglyphs, and Caina saw a pair of footrests.

She took a deep breath, gripped the edge of the interior compartment, and pulled herself up. Caina caught her balance and stood within the armor, her boots sinking into the footrests.

"Now what?" said Caina.

"There are bars inside the arms," said Ardasha. "Grip them, and the glypharmor will heed your will."

Caina reached into the arms, her fingers curling around the bars, and squeezed. For a moment nothing happened.

Then the cuirass swung shut with a clang, the helmet dropping over Caina's head, darkness and silence swallowing her. She felt as if she had sealed herself in a coffin, and she remembered lying chained atop that metal table in Maglarion's lair, the necromancer standing over her with a glittering dagger.

Then a pulse of sorcery surged through the steel, the hieroglyphs filling the gloom with white light...

...and the glypharmor came alive around Caina.

She felt it wrap around her like a second skin. Suddenly she could see the workshop around her with stunning clarity, hear the hiss of the superheated air over the stream of molten metal. The massive shell of steel felt like a part of her, like a second body around her body of flesh.

A body of steel that felt neither pain nor weakness, a body stronger than blood and bone and muscle.

Much stronger.

"How do I move?" said Caina.

"As if you were walking," said Ardasha. "The armor reads your thoughts, and acts in response to your will."

Caina took a hesitant step forward. She expected the motion to feel cumbersome. Yet she moved as lightly as if she were naked. She took another step, and then another, and it felt no different than strolling along a street in Malarae.

"This is..." said Caina, trying to work moisture into her dry throat, "this is remarkable."

She could not help but admire Mihaela's skill. For all its evil origins, the glypharmor was the work of an unmatched genius.

Neither Maglarion nor Kalastus nor Ranarius had ever made anything like this.

"It is," said Ardasha, voice quiet. "I thought I would help Mihaela make something wonderful. Instead she used me to create a horror. But together we can stop her."

"How much stronger will this make me?" said Caina.

"Much stronger, Balarigar," said Ardasha. "The glypharmor has the strength of a hundred men."

"Let me try something," said Caina.

She came to a stop, turned, and moved in one of the unarmed attacks Akragas had taught her years ago.

Her steel fist slammed into the cuirass of a suit of black glypharmor, striking with enough force to lift the armor a few inches off the ground. It toppled backwards and struck the floor with a deafening clang, the stone tiles of the floor cracking into dust and splinters, a tremor shooting up Caina's steel feet.

She felt her body of flesh blink in surprise. That suit of glypharmor weighed tons, and she had sent it to the ground with a single punch.

"The Hall of Assembly," said Caina. "We have to hurry. Mihaela will have started by now."

She strode towards the door to the Seekers' quarters. The door was far too small to accommodate the glypharmor or the Forge, and Mihaela must have used a different route to move the Forge to the Hall of Assembly.

Caina had no time to search for it.

Steel fists ripped a gaping hole in the stone wall, and she strode through without slowing.

***

"To the foe!" roared the Imperial Guard tribune, pointing with his sword. "Kill every last one of the mercenaries!"

The Imperial Guards bellowed a battle cry and marched forward in lockstep, shields raised, javelins ready. Saddiq and his mercenaries fanned out on the left, scimitars and shields in hand, the men shouting taunts.

Corvalis stayed behind them, sword in his right hand, Caina's ghostsilver dagger in his left. He was an assassin, not a Legionary, and the Imperial Guards had years of experience fighting together as a unit. He would only get in their way. But the Sarbians fought as desert raiders, relying on chaos and disorder, and Corvalis would fight in their midst.

And he could use them as a distraction to hunt down Mihaela.

Basil had asked that of both Corvalis and Kylon. No matter how many men died today, no matter what happened in the Hall of Assembly, Mihaela had to die. She knew how to create the glypharmor.

"Kill them!" Mihaela's voice rang over the Hall. "Kill them all!"

A screaming mob of mercenaries charged the Imperial Guards. The mercenaries kept no formation, and they couldn't have done so, anyway. Hundreds of unconscious men and women, sorcerers and lords and guards both, lay scattered across the Hall's floor. A lot of them were going to die in the next few moments, Corvalis knew, slain by errant blows in the fighting.

Claudia. He had to find Claudia.

"Release!" bellowed a centurion of the Guard.

In one smooth motion, the Guards came to a halt, drew back their arms, and flung their javelins. A rain of steel pelted the charging mercenaries, and dozens of them fell with screams. Corvalis expected the mercenaries to break and run beneath the barrage, but the men kept coming.

Perhaps they feared Mihaela more than they feared the Guards.

The mercenaries crashed into the Guards' line, and steel rang on steel as men fought and shouted and died. Saddiq bellowed a command, whirling his scimitar over his head, and the Sarbians charged into the mercenaries' flank. Corvalis joined the fighting, his sword and dagger dealing death. A mercenary lunged at him, thrusting with a broadsword, and Corvalis blocked with his sword, sidestepped, and opened the man's throat with the ghostsilver dagger.

Another man took his place, and Corvalis cut him down, and then another, and another.

And then he was clear of the melee. Dozens of mercenaries sprinted past him, making for the fighting, but the rest of the Hall was clear of foes. Corvalis spotted Mihaela standing in the round chamber at the Tower's heart, her damned machine perched at the edge of the molten pool. Five suits of black glypharmor stood near the giant steel coffin, no doubt created in the time since Corvalis had left the Hall.

Hopefully Claudia had not been one of them.

Corvalis turned towards the central chamber. If he could get to Mihaela and cut her down, the knowledge of the glypharmor would die with her. And then he could find Claudia and get her away ...

White light flared in the suits of glypharmor. The black armor shuddered, trembling...and then four of the suits started forward, the floor trembling beneath their stride.

Corvalis cursed.

It was over.

If four of Mihaela's mercenaries had gotten into the armor, they would rip apart the Imperial Guards and the Sarbians like wolves among a herd of crippled sheep. Corvalis ran for one of the bridges over the molten river. Mihaela had won, but Corvalis might still have a chance to get Claudia away...

He saw a dark blur in the corner of his eye.

Corvalis threw himself down, and an instant later a black sword tore through the space where his head had been. He rolled back to his feet, sword and dagger before him, and stared into the grinning face of Torius Aberon.

"Brother," said Torius. "I'm very glad you are here. I would have been disappointed if I didn't get to kill you myself."

"You're going to feed Father into Mihaela's damned machine," said Corvalis, backing away. "Turn him into one of those things."

"I thought you would approve. You have no more love for him than I do. A pity you don't have any talent," said Torius, "or else I would do the same to you."

"But if you're going to kill Father," said Corvalis, "then there's no need to curry his favor by killing me."

"Very true," said Torius. "So I'll just kill you because I don't like you." He laughed. "I think I'll make you beg before I kill you, Corvalis."

"Try," said Corvalis.

He had to end this fight, now, with a single blow. Else he stood no chance against Torius's sorcery-enhanced strength and speed.

"Gladly," said Torius, his smile widening as he lifted his sword, and as he did the entrance to the Seekers' quarters exploded in a spray of shattered stone.

WEAPONS OF SORCERY

The door to the Hall of Assembly was not nearly large enough to handle the red glypharmor, but that did not slow Caina in the slightest.

Her body of steel ripped through the wooden door and the surrounding stone wall as if they were thick cloth, broken chunks of stone raining around her. She felt Ardasha's mind against hers, their thoughts merging, felt the dead woman's grief and pain and sorrow.

And her rage, a fury to match Caina's own.

Caina strode into the Hall of Assembly, the ground trembling beneath her steel boots.

A battle filled her sight. The cohort of the Imperial Guard struggled against Mihaela's mercenaries, driving them back with grim efficiency. But that would not matter. Caina saw four suits of glypharmor striding across the Hall, heedless of the unconscious men and women trampled beneath their steel feet. Once the men in glypharmor reached the fighting, the battle was over.

But for a moment, the fighting paused as every man stared at Caina in shock.

She saw Mihaela standing near the Forge in the central chamber, stunned alarm on her face.

"Mihaela!" roared Caina and Ardasha in unison. "This ends now!"

TORIUS GAPED at the red glypharmor, its hieroglyphs ablaze with white fire, and Corvalis had his chance.

He lunged, sword and dagger reaching for Torius's throat.

Torius sensed the danger and jerked aside at the last second. Corvalis's sword clanged off the black cuirass, but Caina's dagger gashed Torius's jaw. His older brother snarled with pain, blood dripping down his neck. Corvalis stabbed again, hoping to land a crippling blow, but Torius's arm snapped up and deflected the thrust.

"You," said Torius, "are going to regret that."

"Mihaela!" roared the red glypharmor, speaking with the voices of two women. "This ends now!"

Corvalis blinked. One of those voices had an Anshani accent. But the other...

Caina? Gods, had Mihaela turned Caina into glypharmor?

The red glypharmor raced across the Hall, making for Mihaela, and Torius struck.

Corvalis managed to block the first blow, dodge the second, and parry the third. He jumped out of Torius's reach, but the battle magus thrust his free hand. Invisible force slammed into Corvalis's chest and threw him back. He struck the railing of one of the stone bridges and clawed at it for balance.

The canal of molten steel yawned beneath him as Torius strode forward.

CAINA SPRINTED FORWARD, Ardasha's fury echoing inside her head.

Mihaela thrust out her silvery rod and cast a spell. Caina felt a vicious spike of power, and Ardasha screamed as Mihaela's will hammered into the glypharmor. The armor slowed, its speed ebbing as Ardasha crumbled beneath Mihaela's psychic assault.

So Caina took over.

She drove the glypharmor forward, the weight of her steel footsteps digging stone chips from the floor. Caina felt the force of Mihaela's will reaching for her mind, but she brushed aside the assault with a snarl. She had contested with Maglarion, with the Moroaica herself.

Mihaela would not stop her.

A stab of fear crossed Mihaela's face, and the mental assault stopped.

"Kill her!" bellowed Mihaela, running towards an unused suit of glypharmor. "Damn you, kill her now!"

The four suits of glypharmor turned, ignoring the raging melee, and raced towards Caina.

∼

KYLON DANCED THROUGH THE BATTLE.

Mercenaries surrounded him, but the sorcery of water let him feel their rage and fear...and when they intended to strike. The sorcery of air lent his arms and legs speed, and he dodged their blows and drove his swings faster than their blocks and parries. And the power of water sheathed his storm-forged blade in freezing mist, and a single cut from his blade turned the blood of his foes to ice.

He cut down another man and sought more enemies. From the corner of his eye he saw Cimon slashing his way through the mercenaries, lightning sparking along his sword. Alcios bellowed commands as he rallied his ashtairoi, his gleaming cuirass spotted with blood. The four suits of glypharmor charged towards the red armor. Kylon wondered who had commandeered it. One of Mihaela's disgruntled allies, perhaps?

No matter. The attack had distracted the men in black glypharmor, which gave the Imperial Guards and the others a chance to beat Mihaela's mercenaries. If Kylon could cut his way to Mihaela, he could end this...

A familiar aura brushed over his sorcerous senses. The aura

brought to mind rotting flesh, clotted blood congealing in the earth, ravens circling over moldering corpses.

He turned and saw a scarred man in a dark cloak.

"Sicarion," spat Kylon, raising his mist-wreathed sword.

"Why, Lord Kylon," said Sicarion in his rusty voice. He held a sword in his right hand and his serrated black dagger in his left. "Or should I say Lord High Seat? Since your sister lies rotting in the darkness beneath Marsis."

"Her death is on your hands," spat Kylon. "You poured lies into her ears, and you led her to her death."

Sicarion gave a lazy shrug. "She shouldn't have been foolish enough to believe me."

"Is that what you did to Mihaela?" said Kylon. "Is all this another errand for your damned Moroaica?"

Sicarion laughed. "How astute, Lord Kylon! Perhaps you are correct. But you will not live to see the end of it."

"No," said Kylon, pointing with his sword, "today you will pay for your treacheries."

He surged forward, the sorcery of air driving him with the speed of an arrow.

Sicarion jumped to meet him, darkness shimmering around him like a cloak.

~

THE BLACK SUITS of glypharmor charged Caina, and Ardasha's panic filled her mind. Ardasha had been a slave and a Seeker's student, not a fighter, and even now the sight of armed men filled her with terror.

But not Caina.

"Be calm," she said, "and do as I say."

Her body of steel, fueled by the power of Ardasha's soul, shifted into one of the unarmed stances Akragas had taught her at the Vineyard. Caina knew how to fight with her hands and feet. But she always preferred to fight with a dagger or a knife, preferred to avoid a direct confrontation with her foes. She was strong and quick, but most men were stronger, and fighting unarmed left her at a grave disadvantage.

But inside the red glypharmor, that was no longer true.

The first suit of black glypharmor came at her, fist drawn back to strike. The armor moved with no elegance, no skill. Caina supposed the mercenary inside it had always fought with sword and shield.

The steel fist shot for her face. Caina dodged, her fingers clamping around the black armor's wrist, and she twisted past. Her foot came up and slammed the black glypharmor in the small of the back, and sent it sprawling to the floor. She wheeled and brought her other foot hammering down, all of Ardasha's power and the weight of the steel behind it.

The red boot crushed the black helmet like a dried husk, and Caina saw blood pooling beneath the glypharmor.

She wheeled as the mercenaries in the other three suits attacked.

~

CORVALIS THREW himself to the side, rolling onto the bridge, and Torius's sword clanged against the stone railing. The battle magus turned, and Corvalis got his own sword up, blocking three swings in quick succession as he backed away. Again Torius raised his armored hand, lips moving in a spell, and Corvalis jumped backwards and landed on the far side of the bridge.

The blast of invisible force clipped his shoulder, and he stumbled and caught his balance as Torius attacked. Steel rang on steel, and only years of experience and training allowed him to block or dodge each of Torius's blows.

But Corvalis could not keep this up. Torius was too fast and too strong, and his battle sorcery gave him an advantage that Corvalis could not match. Sooner or later Corvalis would make a mistake, and the fight would be over.

And there would be no one left to save Claudia.

A tremendous clang filled the Hall, and Corvalis saw the suit of red glypharmor destroy one of the black suits, crushing its helmet beneath an armored boot. Torius's eyes widened, and Corvalis gambled on a strike.

He leaped for his half-brother.

~

A NIMBUS of shadow flared around Sicarion, draining the light and heat from the air.

And as it touched Kylon, he slowed.

The shadowy aura drained away the sorcery of water and air. He stumbled as he caught his balance, and Sicarion lunged, his sword and dagger gleaming with a faint coat of poison. Kylon ducked under the sword and blocked the dagger. Sicarion pursued, thrusting and slashing, and Kylon backed away. He jumped back, out of the reach of the shadowy nimbus...and suddenly the power of air and water returned to him.

Sicarion laughed, spinning his dagger in his left hand. "The mighty Kylon Shipbreaker, eh? Not so mighty without his sorcery."

"Then lay aside your own power," said Kylon, "and face me."

"And why," said Sicarion, "should I possibly do that?"

He charged at Kylon. The shadowy nimbus swallowed him, draining away his arcane strength.

~

THE THREE REMAINING suits of black glypharmor charged at Caina.

"Can this thing jump?" said Caina.

"I...I think so," said Ardasha, and Caina felt the dead woman's terror and exhilaration. "I..."

Caina raced to meet her foes and jumped. Her legs of steel threw her into one of the terrific leaps she had seen Kylon and Torius perform in battle against their foes. She soared over the suits of black armor and landed behind them with a thunderous crash. The entire Hall shuddered, the floor splintering beneath her, and the shock knocked hundreds of men off their feet.

The men in the black glypharmor reeled, and Caina went on the attack. Her foot slammed into the back of a knee, and the glypharmor's leg folded. Caina hammered her fists upon the helm, and it exploded in a spray of twisted black metal and crimson blood. The glypharmor helmets were two inches thick, impervious to almost all weapons, but Ardasha's wrath drove Caina's fists of solid steel.

They struck home like the thunderbolts of the gods.

The glypharmor fell with a clang, and the remaining two suits attacked Caina. She caught a descending fist in her grasp, spun, and twisted, driving her weight past the black armor. The black glypharmor spun as she twisted, forced to turn by her weight and speed, and the sight of the hulking black titan hopping on one foot was so comical Caina almost laughed. She drove the glypharmor into the second suit, and both tangled together, the men inside struggling to pull their armor free from each other.

One fell, and Caina's boot hammered down with deadly force.

The remaining black suit attacked Caina, fists swinging like a drunk in a bar fight. She backed away, dodging and blocking with cool precision. Mihaela had never trained her men how to fight while wearing the suits. The glypharmor offered so much raw power that it hardly mattered. But facing a foe who knew how to fight unarmed, who knew how to make use of the armor's strength, was another matter entirely.

Caina backed away, and at last the black glypharmor overstepped. She seized the armor's wrist, her boot lashing out. Her opponent's leg folded, and the black armor toppled forward.

Right into the canal's molten metal.

Droplets of burning steel splashed everywhere, cooling into beads of hard metal. A hideous scream rose from the black glypharmor, and Caina saw the cuirass and helmet swing open as the mercenary inside tried to escape. That was a mistake. The molten metal rushed into the gap, and the mercenary just had time to shriek before the heat set him aflame and the metal consumed his flesh.

The glypharmor sank, rippling and folding like candle wax.

Caina leaped over the canal and landed on the far side.

"Mihaela!" Her voice boomed out with Ardasha's. "Come and face us!"

She saw Mihaela disappear into the final suit of black glypharmor, the hieroglyphs on its sides flaring with power.

~

TORIUS PARRIED Corvalis's frantic attack, and step by step the battle magus drove him back. Torius's blows came faster and faster, driven by the psychokinetic power of battle sorcery, and Corvalis could barely keep up. Sweat poured down his face, his arms burning with fatigue. He could not hold Torius back much longer...

Then he tripped over the outstretched arm of an unconscious Sage, lost his balance, and fell upon his back.

Torius yelled in triumph and drew back his black sword for the killing strike.

In that instant Corvalis saw the red glypharmor leap into the air and land in a crouch.

The floor heaved and shook from the impact, the molten canal rippling, and dust fell from the ceiling overhead. The Hall of Assembly groaned, and for an instant Corvalis feared the entire Tower of Study would collapse upon them.

And Torius stumbled in the midst of his killing stroke.

Corvalis rolled sideways and the sword missed his shoulder by an inch. The blade clanged off the stone floor with a spray of sparks, and Corvalis saw a splinter fly from the weapon.

Torius was strong, and his sorcery lent his muscles even greater strength.

Too much strength, perhaps, for his sword to endure?

Corvalis sprang back to his feet and backed away as Torius pursued.

Step by step, he let Torius drive him towards the wall.

~

KYLON MET Sicarion's attack without hesitation, the dark aura washing over him.

He laid aside his power and fought with muscle and steel. During the battle of Marsis, the stormdancer Kleistheon had refused to lay down his power when fighting the man who would become the Champion of Marsis. But the Champion, no doubt a student of the Ghost herself, had outwitted Kleistheon and destroyed him with his own sorcery.

Kylon would not make the same mistake.

IIe had practiced with the sword every day since the age of five, and even without sorcery, he knew how to make his blade sing. He blocked Sicarion's thrusts and beat aside his swings. Sicarion's confident sneer melted away, his mismatched eyes narrowing in concentration. Ancient and powerful he might be, but he was an assassin and a necromancer, not a warrior.

Kylon was a warrior.

His sword raked across Sicarion's shoulder, and the assassin stumbled back. Before he could recover Kylon whipped his sword around. Sicarion jerked back at the last moment, but not before Kylon's blade opened a bleeding gash on his forehead.

For the first time a hint of alarm appeared on the grotesque face.

"For Andromache!" roared Kylon as the battle raged around him. He would cut down this vile creature, this devil that had corrupted Andromache and started a war in the Moroaica's name. "For Andromache! For New Kyre!"

Sicarion raised his dagger. The aura of shadow around him shrank, compressing into a single sphere of darkness around the serrated dagger.

And the sorcery of air and water flooded back into Kylon. He lifted his sword, ready to ram it through Sicarion's heart...

Sicarion thrust out his hand, and the sphere of darkness leapt from the dagger's blade and slammed into Kylon's chest.

∽

Caina sprinted across the Hall.

Mihaela charged to meet her, the dark mass of her glypharmor ablaze with white light from the hieroglyphs.

"I killed you!" boomed the Seeker. "I killed you both! Do you think you can stop me? Do..."

"Stop talking," said Caina, and threw a palm strike at Mihaela's helmet. But Mihaela's arms snapped up and deflected the blow, and she stepped into the attack, her steel fists raining a volley of punches upon Caina's cuirass.

Ardasha's scream filled Caina's head, and the hollow shriek of stressed steel thundered in her ears. The cuirass was three inches thick, impervious to sword and arrow and spear and siege engine. But Mihaela's fists were solid blocks of steel, fueled by necromancy and psychokinetic force.

The punches knocked Caina back, the sheer force overwhelming even the glypharmor's power.

"Damned Ghost!" shrieked Mihaela. "Die!"

She shoved, driving Caina towards the molten canal. Caina hammered at Mihaela's helmet again and again, but could not get enough leverage for a proper strike. Step by step Mihaela forced Caina towards the canal...

Caina let her legs collapse beneath her. She fell upon her back, but Mihaela stumbled forward, arms clawing for balance. Caina drove a fist into the back of Mihaela's knee. The strike sent Mihaela tumbling upon her face. Caina rolled to her knees and drove both her fists at the back of Mihaela's cuirass, hoping to crush both it and her. But Mihaela rolled at the last second, her leg swinging, and the edge of her boot caught Caina's helmet.

Caina's head exploded with pain, and even the glancing power of the blow sent her to the floor. Another few inches and the strike would have crushed both her helmet and her skull. Mihaela scrambled to her feet, and Caina did the same.

Mihaela stared at Caina for a moment, and then charged.

~

CORVALIS RACED BACKWARDS, sword and ghostsilver dagger working to fend off Torius's furious assault. His breath rasped through his clenched teeth, and his weapons felt as if they had doubled in weight during the last few moments.

Torius had almost driven him to the wall.

"Pathetic," said Torius. "You are skilled for a Kindred rat, brother, I'll admit that. Any other man would have perished at once." His movements were almost lazy as he beat aside Corvalis's attacks. "But I am a magus of the Magisterium, and you are only a shadow-dwelling rat. And do you know what rats do when you pull away their precious shadows?"

Corvalis's back slammed against the wall, the ghostsilver dagger falling from his numbed fingers.

"They die," said Torius, drawing back his sword.

It blurred forward with superhuman speed.

But Corvalis had anticipated that, and his legs folded the moment the black sword started to move. The blade shot over his head as Corvalis fell to the floor.

Torius drove his sword into a wall of solid stone with all his strength and power.

The blade shattered with a hideous metallic screech, black splinters flying in all directions. Torius screamed and dropped the broken hilt, his armored hands flying up to cover his face.

Corvalis rose, sword gripped in both hands, and hammered the blade upon the crown of Torius's head. He felt bone crack, saw Torius fall to his hands and knees.

Corvalis swung his sword for Torius's neck with all his remaining strength.

His half-brother crumpled into a motionless heap of black armor, his blood pooling upon the floor.

Corvalis let out an exhausted breath, his arms trembling, and scooped up Caina's ghostsilver dagger.

"The Magisterium," he said at last, "should teach their battle magi to wear helms."

Torius, being dead, did not respond.

THE BLAST of shadow slammed into Kylon's chest and threw him back a dozen steps. He landed hard atop the corpse of a slain mercenary, an icy chill washing through him. But this was not the chill of frost and snow. Cold tendrils of necromancy sank into him, sucking away his life and warmth. Veins of shadow crawled over his chest and arms, like black roots sinking into his skin.

"And so ends the mighty exploits of the great Kylon Shipbreaker," said Sicarion. "Pity, really."

He walked closer.

Kylon shuddered. The spell was sucking away his physical strength...but it had not touched his sorcery.

Unfortunately, he did not have the strength to stand.

"You have a good sword arm," said Sicarion. His scarred lips twitched into a grin, his yellow teeth gleaming. "I think I'll take it for my own."

Kylon saw a set of throwing knives resting in the dead mercenary's belt. He remember how the Ghost had used throwing knives in battle with remarkable effectiveness.

Kylon didn't think he could stand...but he thought he could throw a knife.

Sicarion raised his sword.

Kylon snatched a throwing knife and drew on the sorcery of water. White mist swirled around the blade, and he flung the weapon with all the force he could muster. His aim was off, but the power of water drove his arm, and the blade sank to the hilt in Sicarion's stomach.

The scarred assassin stumbled back with a strangled scream, his eyes going wide. No blood came from the wound, and a rime of frost spread over his leather armor. Sicarion ripped the weapon free from his belly with a curse, and cursed again as the fingers of his left hand turned black with frost.

And the icy chill settling into Kylon vanished, the black veins of shadow disappearing.

He surged back to his feet, the sorcery of water filling his limbs with renewed strength. Sicarion twisted aside at the last moment, and Kylon's mist-wreathed blade slashed through his leather armor and tore a gash down his torso, ice spreading over the wound.

Sicarion flung out his good hand, and a bar of shadow stabbed from his fingers. Kylon raised his sword to block it, and he felt Sicarion's cold power strain against the sorcery of water. He stumbled, hands wrapped around his sword hilt as he struggled to hold Sicarion's spell as bay.

Sicarion whirled and fled, vanishing into the chaos as the mercenaries battled the Imperial Guards.

~

CAINA BLOCKED ANOTHER PUNCH, and then another, trying to line up for a blow at Mihaela's helmet.

She realized that she was overmatched.

Caina knew far more about hand-to-hand combat than Mihaela. But Mihaela had created the glypharmor and knew it inside and out.

And that meant she knew the armor's weaknesses.

The glypharmor had protected Caina so far, but she tasted blood in her mouth and her body ached from the battering. Mihaela's blows had left a dozen dents in the crimson steel, and Caina heard an ominous squealing noise every time she moved her arms. She had managed to land a dozen solid blows on Mihaela, but the black glypharmor had not slowed at all.

"It hurts," whispered Ardasha, "it hurts so much."

"We're not finished yet," said Caina, but her words sounded hollow.

Mihaela lunged at her, and Caina dodged away. One of the hieroglyphs on her legs sputtered, and for a moment she stumbled. Caina brought her arms up block the coming attack, but instead Mihaela stepped back, the black glypharmor's stance radiating wariness.

Caina didn't understand. If Mihaela had struck, she could have ended the fight then and there. Why hadn't she pressed her advantage?

Mihaela took a step to the left, and Caina understood.

She was keeping herself between Caina and the Forge. She knew Caina would try to destroy the Forge. If Mihaela blocked the way, she would need only wear down Caina bit by bit.

But the Forge was perched right at the molten pool's edge. The thing was enormous, but if Caina hit it hard enough, perhaps she could knock it into the metal.

"Yes," murmured Ardasha, her voice trembling. "Yes, end it. Let me die. Please let me die at last."

Caina feinted, throwing a palm strike at Mihaela's face, followed by a sweeping kick for her legs. Mihaela jumped back, but the move ment forced her to the left.

And it gave Caina the opening she needed.

She sprinted forward. Mihaela's metal fingers raked at her shoulder plates, but Caina tore free, driven by Ardasha's weakening fury and red glypharmor's colossal mass. She barreled out of the Hall of Assembly and towards the Forge's gleaming steel coffin.

"No!" shouted Mihaela, and Caina heard the thunder of her pursuit.

But she was too slow. Caina leaped, the power of her steel legs throwing her through the air like a catapult stone, and slammed into the Forge with all of Ardasha's strength and the red glypharmor's weight behind her.

The Forge clanged like a tremendous gong, its hieroglyphs pulsing with white fire. Fingers of blue-white lightning erupted from the hieroglyphs, pouring into the red glypharmor. Ardasha screamed in pain, and Caina heard herself screaming with her.

But the Forge began slide backwards into the molten pool. Caina strained against it, pushing with the red glypharmor's arms. Just a little further...

"No!" shouted Mihaela, her footsteps growing closer.

And all at once Caina knew how she could destroy the Forge and defeat Mihaela.

290 of JONATHAN MOELLER

It would only cost her life.

Well. She had died once already today. What was one more time?

Caina whirled, her back against the tottering Forge as Mihaela sprang for her, hands reaching for her helmet.

She reached out, seized Mihaela's shoulders, and pulled the black glypharmor towards her even as Mihaela's steel fingers wrapped around her helmet. Mihaela's own momentum drove her forward, slamming Caina against the Forge.

The Forge toppled backwards into the molten pool, Caina on top of the closed steel coffin, Mihaela pinning her in place.

"Damn you!" shrieked Mihaela, her steel hands closing around Caina's helmet. "Damn you, damn you, damn you!"

The Forge's hieroglyphs sputtered and flared, shooting sparks into the molten steel. Even through the red glypharmor, Caina felt the heat radiating from the liquid metal. Mihaela snarled and tried to pull away, but Caina gripped her shoulders, pinning her in place. This horror ended now. The Forge would burn, Mihaela would burn, and Caina would burn with them, but it was worth it if she could stop Mihaela ...

"No!"

Ardasha's voice rang in Caina's head like a trumpet.

"No! I am dead. I am already dead!" said Ardasha. "But you still live. Go, Balargiar! Look after Shaizid, I beg you." The dead woman's voice grew hard. "I will break Mihaela's precious Forge!"

The red glypharmor's cuirass swung open, the helmet sliding back. The heat exploded over Caina in a torrent, and her awareness of the red glypharmor and Ardasha's presence drained away. Above her she saw the black glypharmor swinging open, saw Mihaela's furious face as she clawed her way free.

"Go!" said Ardasha, her voice fading from the inside of Caina's head.

Caina scrambled to her feet and raced across the rocking steel coffin, the heat searing her face and filling her lungs with pain. Mihaela stumbled after her, snarling and spitting in fury. Caina reached the edge of the Forge and jumped, the molten metal rippling beneath her. For a terrible moment she thought she would plunge into the liquid steel.

But she struck the edge of the pool and rolled across the cracked stone floor, coughing and wheezing from the heat.

Mihaela landed next to her. Caina got to one knee, reaching for her remaining throwing knives, but Mihaela was faster. The rod of a Sage glimmered in her hand, and invisible force slammed into Caina and pinned her against the floor.

"You ruined everything!" howled Mihaela, sweat pouring down her face. "I'm going to make..."

With a hideous metallic scream, the Forge cracked into a dozen fragments. Both the red glypharmor and the black glypharmor melted and warped, twisting into an unrecognizable shapes before they sank into the white-hot steel. Snarling lighting crackled around the shards of the Forge...

Mihaela shuddered, and she started to scream.

A pulse of white light exploded from the Forge's wreckage and ripped through the chamber. The white light shot through Caina, and she felt the tingling pain of powerful sorcery. The light passed through the remaining suits of glypharmor, their hieroglyphs pulsing, and the suits collapsed into piles of broken steel.

Mihaela shrieked as blood poured from her nose and mouth and ears. Jadriga had said that Mihaela had created a psychic link with the Forge.

And if the Forge shattered...would Mihaela's mind shatter too?

Mihaela groaned once, fell upon her back, and did not move again.

Caina tried to stand, and managed it on the fourth try. The battle was almost over. The mercenaries had been slain or driven off, and the Imperial Guard held the Hall of Assembly. Caina gazed down at Mihaela. The Seeker's eyes were glassy, and a thin stream of drool leaked from her open mouth to mingle with the blood.

Evidently linking her mind to the Forge had not been a good idea.

"Caina."

She turned.

Corvalis stood a few yards away, exhausted and bloody. He carried an unconscious Claudia slung over his shoulders, her blond hair trailing down his chest.

"Corvalis," said Caina. She should have been angry, she knew, but she felt only relief, overpowering relief, that he was still alive.

"Gods," Corvalis said. "I'm sorry. I should have listened to you. I should have made Claudia listen to you. I," he blinked several times, a muscle near his eye twitching, "I thought you were dead."

"Not yet," said Caina, and despite everything, she felt herself smile. "Not yet."

The next morning Caina woke up and felt terrible.

She hobbled to the bathtub, her joints aching, her head pounding. Her skin had turned red from the heat of the molten metal, as if from a bad sunburn, and every step hurt. In a week or so she would start peeling like a coat of cheap paint.

Still, it was better than being burned alive.

And better than what Mihaela had done to herself.

The hot water felt glorious against her aching body. For all their folly, at least the Masked Ones knew how to keep their guests in comfort. After, Caina dried off, put on a robe, and limped into the sitting room.

Claudia awaited her there, a tray of food upon the table.

"Caina," Claudia said, voice quiet. "How do you feel?"

Caina frowned. "How do you know my real name?"

Claudia's face grew red. "I'm sorry. I just...I heard Master Basil say it, after I woke up. I'm...I'm sorry if I overstepped."

"No," said Caina. "It's good to pay attention to details. Helps you to avoid mistakes later on."

Claudia could not meet her eyes. "Like trusting a sorceress who wants to kill you and bind your soul into necromantic armor?"

"Something like that," said Caina, "yes."

"I had the slaves bring breakfast," said Claudia, "and coffee."

Caina could smell it. "Thank you. Why don't you sit down?"

She sat, and after a moment's hesitation, Claudia sat as well. Caina helped herself to a cup of coffee, and recognized the smell of Shaizid's work. She gazed into the cup, lost in thought. Shaizid had wept like a child when he had learned of Ardasha's fate. Still, she had seen the fierce pride in his face. Ardasha had helped defeat Mihaela and shatter the Forge.

And Mihaela would never hurt anyone ever again.

"You don't like the coffee?" said Claudia.

Caina blinked, realized that she had forgotten Claudia was there.

"I was thinking," said Caina. "The coffee is wonderful." She took a sip. "A pity they don't have it in Malarae."

Claudia nodded, licked her lips. And as angry as Caina had been with her, she felt a moment's pity. The former magus looked miserable.

"You should probably get it over with," said Caina. "Waiting won't make you feel better."

"I'm sorry!" said Claudia. "I am so sorry. You were right. You didn't even know what Mihaela planned, and you were still right." She blinked, tears in her eyes. "I didn't listen to you, and I got a lot of people killed."

"Most of those people would have died anyway," said Caina. "Mihaela would have acted with or without your help."

"I know," said Claudia, "but she had my help. You were right about me." She wiped a hand across her eyes. "I wanted to use my powers to help people. That's all I wanted to do, the only reason I aided Mihaela. Instead I helped her create a horror...and if you hadn't stopped her, it would have been so much worse. Corvalis would have been killed, Mihaela would have turned me into a suit of glypharmor...and I would have to live with my guilt for all eternity."

"But that didn't happen," said Caina.

"Because of you," said Claudia. "My folly would have destroyed us. The nations would have burned, and millions would have died, and all because of me..."

"Please shut up," said Caina.

Claudia blinked.

"And stop crying," said Caina. "You don't have the complexion for it."

Claudia managed a sniffling laugh. "I don't, do I?"

"And I understand," said Caina, "why you did it."

"Because I am a fool," said Claudia.

"We are all fools," said Caina. "Did Corvalis ever tell you why I hate sorcery so much?"

Claudia hesitated. "Not...in full. He said the magi murdered your father..."

"My mother," said Caina, "was an initiate of the Magisterium, but the high magi expelled her because she wasn't strong enough. So instead she turned to a renegade necromancer. In exchange for his teachings, she sold me to him. When my father found out, she wiped his mind, much like happened to Mihaela. The necromancer took my blood and in the process left me barren."

"Oh," said Claudia in a small voice. "I see why you hate sorcery."

Caina nodded. "And if I could kill them all, I would." She took a deep breath. "If Mihaela had come to me and said she had some weapon, some device that allowed her to kill every single magus in the Empire at once...I would have used it. I would have used it without hesitation. At least you were trying to save lives by forcing peace between the Empire and Istarinmul and New Kyre." Caina shrugged. "So I understand the temptation. But I hate sorcery, so Mihaela's offer was not an enticing one. But for you...you wanted to use your spells to help people, to make their lives better. I can see how resisting Mihaela's offer would have been difficult."

"I believed her," said Claudia. "I thought she wanted to use her sorcery to aid mankind, not to rule over it." She frowned. "But that was what you meant, wasn't it? I wanted to help people, not to rule them. But by enslaving the sorcerers and forcing them to rule as I wish, I would have been using my power to rule over people."

Caina nodded.

"Gods," said Claudia. "That is a hard thing to learn about oneself. That I could be a monster. That I almost made myself into a monster."

"You were right about one thing," said Caina. "You do a have a responsibility to use your power well. Just...not in the way you thought."

"Do you think Basil will have me killed?" said Claudia. "He was...most angry."

"No," said Caina. "I won't kill you, either. Crippling the Magisterium has always been one of the goals of the Ghosts. You just went about it...a little too enthusiastically. But I doubt Basil will use you in the field again. He'll probably set you up with a false identity and consult you when the Ghosts need your knowledge of sorcery."

Claudia shuddered. "Good. I had hoped to prove myself on this trip, but...I suppose I did, didn't I? Just not in the way I wanted. I still wish to be of use to the Ghosts. But, gods, if I can settle in Malarae and never leave again, I think I shall die content. I have seen quite enough of Catekharon."

"As have I," said Caina.

"Thank you," said Claudia. "For...forgiving me. I am not sure I would have the strength to do so in your place."

Caina shrugged. "You're Corvalis's sister. He loves you."

"And you," said Claudia, "love him."

"Yes," said Caina. She could not give him children, but she suspected that did not matter to a man like Corvalis.

"Even though he sided with me against you?" said Claudia.

"He did what he thought was right," said Caina. "I don't think I could respect a man too craven to stand up to me. He loves you, too. You have...something of a prior claim."

Claudia nodded. "Thank you again."

"You can repay me," said Caina, finishing the coffee and getting to her feet, "by helping me get dressed. The ambassadors will be gathering soon, and I'm curious what Zalandris has to say to them."

"Of course," said Claudia. "Though I fear I shall never get the knack of the hairpins you use."

"There's no time like the present."

KYLON OF HOUSE KARDAMNOS stood in the Hall of Assembly, Alcios at this right hand, Cimon at his left, a ring of ashtairoi around him. The other ambassadors stood surrounded by their guards, and Kylon could not blame them, given what had happened in the Hall.

Though their anger was not aimed at each other but at the Speaker of the Scholae.

"The Scholae is grieved that harm has come to guests under our protection," said Zalandris. "Therefore for every man who was slain, we shall pay a dual indemnity, one to his family, and another to his monarch."

"Given the grievous insult you offered the Shahenshah of Anshan," said Arsakan, "you should count yourself fortunate that you do not face the Shahenshah's army."

Kylon snorted at Arsakan's bluster. Zalandris had taken the blame for the disaster, but the Shahenshah's armies had no chance against Catekharon's arcane defenses.

"Indeed," said Zalandris. "Mihaela was a rogue who acted without the permission of the Scholae. Yet she was my Seeker, and the responsibility is mine. Therefore we offer this indemnity, and as further compensation, the lifting of all trade tariffs for your respective nations for the term of twenty-five years."

"That," said the First Magus, "is inadequate."

Decius Aberon stepped away his guards, glaring at Zalandris. Lord Titus's embassy stood some distance away, surrounded by Imperial Guards. Kylon spotted the Ghost standing in the rear with Basil Callenius and Corvalis, her face unreadable as she regarded her lover's father.

"Your idiot student launched an attack upon the Imperial Magisterium," said the First Magus.

"Oh, give it up, Decius," said Lord Titus. "The woman was clearly a renegade. Lives have been lost, yes, but Mihaela would have butchered the Sages alongside the rest of us."

The First Magus sneered. "The lives of your underlings might be worthless, my Lord Titus, but the blood of a magus is worth that a thousand lesser men." He leveled a thick finger at Zalandris. "I demand that you surrender all of Mihaela's research and tools to the custody of the Magisterium..."

"No," said Zalandris. "Mihaela's tools and research were abominations, violations of the Scholae's laws. All her research shall be destroyed, as shall any remaining fragments of the glypharmor and her earlier versions of the Forge."

"Do you think to trifle with the wrath of the Magisterium?" said the First Magus. "Do..."

"Be silent!" thundered Zalandris, and for the first time Kylon saw anger on the ancient Sage's face. "Your own son, Torius Aberon, aided Mihaela in her crimes, and I have no doubt that you conspired with her! I will say this plainly. The wrong is the Scholae's, and we offer recompense for our folly. But Mikaela's vile work will never see the light of day. And should that not be enough for you, should you wish to contest your wrongs by force of arms...then come and attack Catekharon. And you will see that the Scholae does not lack the means to defend itself."

Kylon's sorcerous senses felt the sheer arcane power crackling around the enraged Sage, and the First Magus took a prudent step back.

"I think," said Lord Titus into the silence, "that the Lord Speaker's offer is most acceptable."

The other ambassadors and sorcerers rumbled their assents, and the First Magus stalked to his guards.

"So be it," said Zalandris. "Speak with the seneschals, my lords, and they shall arrange the details of your payments."

He walked from the Hall of Assembly without another word.

"Well," said Alcios, "that was entertaining."

"Indeed," said Kylon. "And we can be certain that the Empire will never use glypharmor against New Kyre."

He turned his head and saw the Ghost standing alone, watching him.

"A moment, my lords," said Kylon, and he walked to join her.

"My lord stormdancer," said the Ghost in a quiet voice. "I am pleased that you survived the fighting."

"As I am," said Kylon. "Though I would have been more pleased if I could have taken Sicarion's head."

"Someday," said the Ghost. "He won't always be able to escape."

"Tell me," said Kylon, remembering his conversation with Corvalis. "Is your name truly Caina?"

A corner of her mouth curled. "You can call me that, if you wish."

"Again you have saved us," said Kylon. "Mihaela would have become as vile as Scorikhon himself, had she succeeded."

The Ghost shrugged. "I had help. The soul bound within that armor, Kylon...she was pleased to revenge herself on Mihaela."

Kylon shook his head. "The Sages should have executed her."

Again she shrugged. "Why bother? Her mind is destroyed. She cannot feed herself, or dress herself, or even wipe the drool from her chin. She'll live for decades like that, trapped inside her own body, just as she trapped her victims within the glypharmor. I think that a fitting punishment."

"You are wise, Ghost," said Kylon. "It is unfortunate that we must be enemies."

"Maybe the Emperor and the Archons can be persuaded to make peace," said the Ghost, "once they learned how Kylon Shipbreaker fought to save the embassies of a dozen nations, including the Empire's, from a horrid enslavement."

"Perhaps," said Kylon. "Until then...this is the Imperial custom, yes?" He bowed over her hand and placed a light kiss upon her fingers. "Until then, may the gods of storm and sea shield you from their wrath, Caina of the Ghosts."

She nodded. "And you, Kylon of House Kardamnos."

Kylon released her hand and walked away. She was indeed a

formidable foe, but someday her luck would run out. Sooner or later, she would push too far, and some enemy would kill her at last.

But Kylon would not be that enemy.

"My lord thalarchon?" said Alcios as he rejoined the ashtairoi.

"It is past time," said Kylon, "that we returned home."

The war with the Empire awaited.

CORVALIS STOOD with Basil and Zalandris as Talekhris walked in a slow circle around Caina.

They stood in Talekhris's workroom in the Tower of Study, the chamber filled with books and scrolls and peculiar oddities. Talekhris himself looked terrible, his blue eyes sunken, his skin grayish, his hands trembling.

Though considering that Sicarion had stabbed him through the heart, he looked excellent.

"Gone," said Talekhris. "She is gone."

Caina frowned. "You're sure?"

"I am," said Talekhris. "The spirit of the Moroaica has departed." He frowned. "And I do not sense her presence."

"Then perhaps she is slain," said Zalandris, putting his hand on Talekhris's shoulder, "and you can rest from your labors at last."

"How long does it take her to claim control of another body?" said Caina.

"Usually the process is instantaneous," said Talekhris. "And certainly there are enough women with arcane talent in the Tower for her to claim one. And yet...and yet I do not feel her presence anywhere."

"Then maybe, lord Sage," said Basil, "she is truly dead."

"No, I think not," said Talekhris. "Perhaps her spirit has fled to somewhere beyond the reach of my senses. I will resume my pursuit. We have dueled each other over the centuries, but one day I will find her and put an end to her crimes."

"Ghost," said Zalandris. "Again I wish to thank you." His weary eyes turned to Basil and Corvalis. "You all fought with valor, but your efforts saved us, Anna Callenius. You stopped Mihaela and destroyed her vile engine of necromancy."

"Perhaps, my lord Speaker," said Caina, "you will take more care when choosing your Seekers in the future."

Corvalis expected the Speaker to take offense, but the Sage only sighed. "I fear you are correct. To be a Sage of the Scholae is to love knowledge for its own sake, to pursue learning without thought of personal advancement. Too many see our knowledge as merely a pathway to power and dominion. So we must remain withdrawn from the world, lest our powers be abused."

"As Mihaela abused them," said Caina.

"An error we shall not repeat," said Zalandris. "The Scholae has paid an indemnity to the others, but we owe you a debt beyond them, for you saved us from a horrid slavery. Ask for anything, and if it is in my power, I shall grant it."

Corvalis wondered what Caina would ask. Wealth? Knowledge? She hated sorcery. Perhaps she would refuse to ask for anything.

"Khaltep Irzaris," said Caina. "I understand he supplied coffee beans to the Scholae?"

Corvalis hadn't been expecting that.

"He did," said Zalandris.

"I ask for every sack of coffee beans in his warehouses," said Caina, "to be shipped to Malarae at your own expense. Additionally, any coins or jewels in his strongbox."

Basil blinked, and then chuckled. "Clever, my dear."

"That is not likely to be a very high sum," said Zalandris.

"It will be enough," said Caina.

"Daughter," said Basil, amused, "are you planning to go into business?"

"In a fashion," said Caina. "One more thing, Lord Speaker. I also ask for the slave Shaizid, sister of Ardasha."

"It shall be as you have say," said Zalandris. "Again you have our thanks, Ghost, and know that you have the gratitude of the Scholae."

Caina bowed to the Sage, and they left without another word.

"I shall speak with Lord Titus," said Basil as they made for the stairs. "He will want to leave on the morrow, I think."

"Good," said Caina. "It is past time we left Catekharon."

"Titus is speaking with the embassy from Alqaarin," said Basil. "I will find you at our guest quarters once we are finished."

He strode off, leaving Corvalis alone on the balcony with Caina. She gazed at the pool of molten metal far below, her eyes distant.

"I knew you were taken with coffee," said Corvalis, "but I think you'll find it hard to drink an entire warehouse of the stuff."

"It's not for me," said Caina. "Though I do intend to drink some of it. But I have a better use in mind."

"Will you tell me what it is?" said Corvalis.

She grinned. "Basil figured it out."

"Basil is smarter than I am," said Corvalis.

"It would ruin the surprise," said Caina, "if I told you."

"Then I won't ask any more of you. I already owe you," said Corvalis, "for keeping Basil from killing me."

She frowned. "Why would he want to kill you?"

"He told me, when we first met," said Corvalis, "that if I ever caused you unnecessary pain, he would have me killed."

"That's sweet of him," said Caina.

Corvalis took a deep breath. "I did cause you unnecessary pain. I am sorry for that."

"I know," said Caina. "It is...well, I have no family, you know that." Corvalis nodded. "But if I did, and if my father was still alive, and he told me to do something I thought foolish...I would believe him. I would trust him. You trust your sister. She just happened to be wrong."

"I think," said Corvalis, "that perhaps I will trust your judgment in the future."

She grinned. "Ah. I knew you were a wise man."

Corvalis shook his head. "This is something I never thought I would understand. Or that it even existed. But I love you, and I cannot tell you how relieved I am that you are still alive."

She smiled, and it was one of the rare smiles that lifted the ice from her eyes. "I love you, too."

CAINA WALKED arm in arm with Corvalis to the palace that housed their rooms.

Shaizid awaited them before the doors.

"Mistress," he said, bowing. "The seneschal has told me. I am your slave now."

"Shaizid," started Caina, but he kept speaking.

"I wish to thank you, mistress," said Shaizid. "You found Ardasha, and you...you freed her." His dark eyes blinked. "I wish...I wish she still lived. But you freed her from the armor."

"Shaizid," said Caina, "as your owner, I free you. Immediately."

Shaizid stared at her.

"I...am free?" he said at last.

"Yes," said Caina.

"But where shall I go?" said Shaizid. "I have no family, no home. What shall I do, mistress? I had thought to serve you, but..."

"You know," said Corvalis, giving Caina a look, "in Anshan, it is customary for freedmen to work for their former masters."

She smiled. He had figured it out after all.

"May I be your freedman, mistress?" said Shaizid.

"I think so," said Caina. "You see, I've come into some money and a supply of coffee beans. I wish to open a coffee house in Malarae, Shaizid, and you shall run it for me."

The possibility had occurred to her during their discussion with Kylon in the coffee house. The Anshani regularly did business in coffee houses, and the foreign merchants visiting Catekharon had taken up the habit. If Shaizid started a coffee house in Malarae, in time merchants and even nobles would gather in the coffee houses to conduct business, as they did in Catekharon.

And if the Ghosts owned the coffee houses, they would learn

many secrets. Secrets the Ghosts could use to keep something like the Forge and the glypharmor from happening again.

"Of...of course, mistress," said Shaizid, blinking. "I have always dreamed of owning my own shop. But...but for you to give me such a kingly gift...why?"

"I promised Ardasha," said Caina, "that I would look after you."

Shaizid's jaw trembled. "Thank you, mistress. In Ardasha's memory, in repayment for your generosity, I swear your coffee house shall prosper."

"Go," said Caina. "Gather your possessions. We shall leave for Malarae tomorrow."

Shaizid bowed and hurried towards the Tower.

"That was generous," said Corvalis.

"Oh, he'll earn it," said Caina. "And the Ghosts need friends in many places, Corvalis. We have many foes."

Mihaela had been defeated, her dream of an empire founded upon the glypharmor crushed...but there were still threats. The war between the Empire and New Kyre and Istarinmul still raged. The First Magus would not cease plotting to seize control of the Empire. Renegade sorcerers and slave traders still preyed upon the commoners.

And the Moroaica was out there somewhere. Caina was sure of it.

"True," said Corvalis, "but we shall face them together."

Her fingers curled around his.

"Yes," said Caina. "Together."

EPILOGUE

After a long time, the woman who called herself Jadriga opened her eyes.

Her vision swam into focus, and she saw that she lay upon a narrow bed in a small room. The blankets felt soft and cool against her bare skin. The only other furnishings were a wardrobe and a mirror, and the heavy iron-banded door had been locked and barred.

She felt the raw might of her sorcery thrumming through her.

Jadriga took a moment to acclimate herself to her new form, enjoying the draw of her breath, the heart pumping beneath her ribs. Wearing flesh had its pains, true, but it also had its pleasures.

She pushed aside the blankets and saw that she was naked. Her legs were long and well-muscled, her belly flat, her forearms and biceps adorned with tattoos of sorcerous sigils. Jadriga rose to her feet and stretched.

Then she walked to the mirror and examined her new body.

Mihaela's blue eyes stared back at her. Jadriga ran a hand through the spiky black hair with annoyance. She had never liked having short hair. The priests of the great pharaoh had made Jadriga shave her head in preparation for the ritual of immortality.

Well, they were dead and she was not.

The hair would grow to a suitable length soon enough.

She examined herself for a moment longer and then nodded in approval. She preferred a younger host, but Mihaela had been fit and strong, and it seemed a shame to let her body go to waste. And her sorcerous talent had been potent, allowing Jadriga to wield her own arcane strength.

Strength that she would put to good use.

Mihaela's mouth tightened in the mirror. The Seeker had suffered grave pain, and in turn she had inflicted grievous suffering upon others. But it was not her fault, not in the end. People were as the world made them. And the world was broken, a torture chamber designed by cruel gods who delighted in suffering.

Jadriga would make them pay. She had made the necromancer-priests and the pharaohs of old Maat pay, had brought the Kingdom of the Rising Sun crashing into the dust.

But that was as nothing compared to what she would do the gods themselves.

It was time to resume the great work.

She clothed herself in a loose gray robe from the wardrobe. More suitable clothing could be located later. The door was locked and barred, but a simple spell opened it, and Jadriga stepped into the corridor.

Two Redhelms gaped at her in astonishment and scrambled for their weapons.

A heartbeat later they lay dead upon the floor.

The woman the Szalds named the Moroaica strode past them without a second glance. She came to one of the balconies ringing the Tower of Study's central chamber, the molten steel glowing far below. The liquid metal was part of the spell binding the great fire elemental, and for a moment Jadriga imagined the destruction that breaking the spell would unleash. Liquid fire fountaining from the earth, the crater lake exploding in a column of ash, Catekharon and the countryside for twenty miles in all directions vanishing in a firestorm.

For all that and more was coming.

A familiar presence brushed her arcane senses, and Jadriga turned.

A hooded shadow walked towards her, mismatched eyes glinting in the depths of his cowl.

"Mistress," said Sicarion with a bow.

"Sicarion," said Jadriga. She paused for a moment, feeling her teeth with her tongue. Speaking with a new mouth was always a strange experience. "You disobeyed me."

"I would never dream of such impudence," said Sicarion.

"Truly?" said Jadriga. "I told you to keep Caina Amalas alive. She would have been most useful to me. Instead you allowed Mihaela to slay her."

She remembered everything she had experienced while in Caina's body. The pain, the fear, the rage. The unyielding determination. And the warmth of her feelings for Corvalis, the sensation as the former assassin kissed her lips...

Jadriga pushed the useless memories aside.

"You mistake me, mistress," said Sicarion. "For Caina had two souls in her body. If we are to be precise, Mihaela killed you, not Caina."

Jadriga laughed. "You argue like a merchant."

"And since we are discussing agreements," purred Sicarion, "you promised that I could kill the world."

"I did," said Jadriga. Sicarion was a mad dog, a vicious killer who lived for the sheer joy of slaying, but he had his uses. "I take it all the Sages and Seekers are below?"

"Dismantling Mihaela's work," said Sicarion. His scarred face twisted into a grin. "All of them are in her workshop. The rest of the Tower of Study is unattended."

"I asked you for a distraction," said Jadriga. "Could you not have worked anything simpler?"

Sicarion shrugged. "You did not specify. And I like killing people."

"Come," said Jadriga.

She strode past him, and Sicarion followed at her right hand.

A short walk took her to the Chamber of Relics and the Scholae's more impressive feats of sorcery. Jadriga ignored them and walked to the center of the room, to where the Staff of the Elements waited upon its plinth. Lightning crackled up and down its length and froze into ice crystals even as Jadriga approached.

"Finally," she murmured, picking up the Staff. The ice crystals transmuted into flames, dancing up her hand and crackling against her wards.

Sicarion laughed. "I wish I could see Talekhris's face when he learns you took it."

"You could peel it off and keep it as a memento," said Jadriga.

She gripped the Staff and lifted it, feeling its might, sorcerous strength to match even her own great power.

It was the first of the relics she needed.

And with those relics, she would remake the world and punish the gods for their cruelty.

THE END

ABOUT THE AUTHOR

Standing over six feet tall, Jonathan Moeller has the piercing blue eyes of a Conan of Cimmeria, the bronze-colored hair a Visigothic warrior-king, and the stern visage of a captain of men, none of which are useful in his career as a computer repairman, alas.

He has written the DEMONSOULED series of sword-and-sorcery novels, and continues to write THE GHOSTS sequence about assassin and spy Caina Amalas, the COMPUTER BEGINNER'S GUIDE series of computer books, and numerous other works.

Visit his website at:

http://www.jonathanmoeller.com